I0659240

CONVERSION THEORY

RICH RESTUCCI

SEVERED PRESS
HOBART TASMANIA

CONVERSION THEORY

ISBN: 978-1-925597-07-3

For those avid readers who enjoy nothing more than an armchair, a great book, and devouring page after page. Much like the creatures in this tome, you will never stop, and you always want more.

In the brain and not the chest.
Headshots are the very best.
Fido

MAJESTIK

A red light flashed near the door.

"Three minutes!" came screaming through our headsets, and I knew it was about to get real. I looked around at the inside of the helicopter, wondering just how stupid I was.

I looked at Kinga, a Marine Corps Forces Special Operations Command jarhead. He was standing and checking the pack of the other MARSOC marine, Remo. Where Kinga is a guy who could kill you from a mile away, Remo is more hands on. Don't get me wrong, Kinga is badass, but Remo used to teach other Marines how to kill. He could use anything as a weapon and could kill with a toothpick. No shit, a toothpick. He was equally as deadly when unarmed.

They both felt me staring at them and looked at me at the same time.

"Are we really doing this?" I asked, pausing in my writing.

"All it takes is all you got." Kinga smirked. "Besides, this is your idea." They both looked at me harder if it were possible.

"Up," said Remo.

I stood and he went over my pack, checking things.

We were about to jump off of a helicopter onto the *Majestik Maersk*, a giant container ship. The last time I had been on this boat, we had gone through a hurricane. I could see the giant vessel out the window. She was adrift and many of the containers had broken loose and were haphazardly tossed askew at weird angles. They created a labyrinth of steel on the massive deck. Many of the huge, colored boxes that I remember from before were nowhere to be seen, having gone overboard during the storm. One was dangerously close to going over now, and hung a full fifteen feet over the edge of the deck. The first bit of weather and it was history.

The *Majestik* looked like skyscraper laying down on the water. It was positively enormous. Oh, yeah, and it was crawling with zombies.

So this is one of my journals, which is basically a zombie story, and if you're reading it, that means I'm dead and you found it someplace, or I've given it to you to read.

My two friends and I are about to embark on a rescue mission to save the collective asses of another group of my friends and some poor folks that were trapped on this death-boat.

But I digress.

The weather was nice as we came in on final approach. *Flat-ass calm* the weatherman on *Atlantis* told us before we left. If you've read my first two journals, then you know that *Atlantis* is a floating asylum (read: oil rig) in the Gulf of Mexico. You also know that I'm going to rescue my big buddy Ship, my girlfriend, and a soldier friend from this boat. Yes, his name is Ship. His parents were mean, I guess.

When I mentioned up above that the deck was crawling, I wasn't shitting you. I could see at least a few hundred of the pus bags as I call them. They had been searching for food before they heard the helo, but now every red, undead eye was on us. The food is me. I'm sure you know this, as we are more than a year into this apocalypse thing, but just in case, you should probably run if you see a dead guy walking. Unless the dead guy is running. Then you should probably know two more things: he's not dead, but still wants to kill you, and you need to run faster than he does.

I know I'm jumping around here. Sorry, I'm scared shitless, and this is the beginning of a new journal.

Remo gave me a clap on the back of my Condor Assault Pack. "You're good."

Remo doesn't talk much. He didn't say a word when he handed me a toothpick. Again, no shit.

The red light turned green with a buzzing sound, and Kinga slid the portal open. The wash from the rotor hit us, and I smelled the sea air again. We were about fifteen feet above the roof of the superstructure on the *Majestik* when Kinga tossed out two black ropes. He and I attached the ropes to a little metal thingy that was attached to my waist. I don't remember what it's called, but when I pull down and back across my waist, it slows my descent during a rappel. Carabiner! It's a carabiner.

I was about to lean out, when the co-pilot held up this journal in front of me. I had left it on the seat. I nodded a thanks, shoved it in my tactical webbing, and zipped down the rope.

I went with Kinga, and Remo followed when we were both down safely. The co-pilot pulled up the ropes and the helo took off. Bastard didn't even wave goodbye. Probably because *he* knew we were already dead, but *we* hadn't figured it out yet.

The rotor wash receded as did the noise of the helicopter. The noise was replaced with the sounds of the dead. There were cries and moans and that rasping hack. It's unnatural, and I longed for the helo to drown them out once more. The bird wasn't coming back though. Our extraction would be by boat, tomorrow night at the earliest. If we were still alive. The boat would wait for 24 hours if no contact was made with us, and after that, we would be written off as dead and left here.

Captain Schumitz of the destroyer *Stockdale* would send another team to die, and would probably keep sending them until he had no one left to send. He had an ulterior motive for us being on this tub; he wanted some data and a key. The key was weird looking and the data concerned experiments on undead. He wanted these things badly, and I couldn't help but believe his higher-ups knew something we didn't.

I hadn't heard the cries of the dead in more than two days. It's not something you get used to, but it's certainly better *not* hearing them.

Remo and Kinga set up a communications system that looked like an upside-down umbrella attached to a stereo. "Pluto, this is Hammer One. How copy, over?"

I strode carefully to the edge of the hatch in the steel roof of the superstructure. I'd used it before.

You really can't imagine how big this ship is until you've been on it. Even from the air, it's huge, but when you're on board, it's like you're in the city walking between big buildings. From this vantage, we were at the highest point of the ship.

I opened the hatch and took a peek in the wheelhouse. Mistake, as the stink that wafted up from there almost knocked me out. I was still gagging when I felt a hand on my shoulder and looked up at Kinga. "Last time you go off by yourself. I'll shoot you next time."

I was twenty feet away from them and didn't think that was *going off by myself*. I decided on discretion, and just nodded.

Remo was there in a moment and passed me a black Sharpie marker. "Don't open any doors unless we're all ready. Draw the inside of the wheelhouse."

I did. I drew the crap out of it right on the white steel of the boat. The wheelhouse was maybe sixty or seventy feet wide, housed at the top of the superstructure. The windows fore and aft looked both out and down, and there was a door (hatch) at the both ends, with a metal stairway descending to the deck stemming from each hatch. Two other doors, these made of wood, led from the back of the wheelhouse to an internal stairway, which in turn led to the interior of the ship.

Kinga pointed to three places, one on each end, and one at the back middle of the drawing.

"Only three ways in?"

"Four if you include this hatch."

Remo used his knife to bang on the side of the steel. We waited a minute and he did it again. We all stared into the hole. There was a ladder down, and we could see some components, but nothing that wanted to eat us. Remo pulled out a mirror on a telescoping stick, extended it, and shoved it in through the hatch.

I raised my eyebrows. "Clear?"

"Negative. Three at least. One standing by the port side hatch, one sitting next to him, and one sitting on the deck halfway across the wheelhouse."

"The wheelhouse was secure the last time I was here. Nothing was getting through the hatches, and the rear doors were locked tight and braced. Why the hell would they leave?"

Kinga used his own mirror and did his own recon. "Do we engage?" I didn't have a mirror, and that shit was going on my list of *must-haves* if I lived through this.

"I can't recon the whole wheelhouse. If there are more sitting down behind the consoles, there could be fifty of them in there."

I shrugged. "So give a yell."

"I would prefer not to compromise our stealth."

"Then what did you bang on the hatch with your knife for?"

He looked at me, then at Kinga, shrugged, and stood. Unpacking a coil of rope, he tied one end to an antenna housing and started toward the front of the wheelhouse. He peered over the edge and I gawked at him.

"What the hell are you doing?"

"Taking a look through the front windows." He tied up, threw the other end of the rope over, and disappeared over the side.

I instantly heard those awful undead cries through the hatch. Remo climbed back up, and Kinga helped him over the edge. "Nope. Only three. Center doors are wide open though."

"So we deactivate the three here," Kinga whispered, "secure the doors as fast as possible and use this as our FOB."

"Uhh… What's an FOB?" The disapproving eye-roll from Kinga made me instantly regret the question. Bastard looked just like Ship would have if I asked him about internet protocols or had said *clip* when I meant *magazine.*

"Forward Operating Base," Remo told me. "It's where we'll store our shit and fall back to if we get into it. We can exfil back through this bulkhead in case of emergency." He rubbed his chin. "I drop down first, take them out with this," he drew his giant knife, "or suppressed fire. You follow and secure the doors." He had indicated Kinga would be the door closer. I was curiously absent from both the clandestine elimination of the undead and the heroic door closing ops. Mine was to be Operation Stay The Hell Up Here And Don't Get In The Way. I could see it coming.

"What about me?" I dared ask.

Remo was still staring at the crude drawing I had made of the wheelhouse. I used to suck at Pictionary. "You're going to stay here and guard our retreat if necessary. Don't let anything get between us and the ladder." I noticed Kinga smirking as he pulled one of three suppressors from a sleeve in his tac-webbing. Prick.

Remo glanced at me staring at Kinga. "Cans on."

I actually knew what that meant. A can was military slang for a suppressor. A suppressor is a silencer for you folks that actually believe in silencers. That shit *isn't* silent, but it's significantly quieter, and it's hard to pinpoint the sound when you hear it.

We all screwed the long tubes to our tactical pistols. We each had three suppressors, and another fact you probably don't know is that they burn out over time. They begin to get louder as you shoot through them, and you have to change them out. They also add weight to the end of the weapon, are a bitch to use in close quarters, and can affect accuracy on a long shot.

I friggin love them. There's something inherently cool about shooting with a suppressor.

Both Remo and Kinga checked the wheelhouse with their little mirrors again. Remo nodded and cat-quietly moved down the ladder. Kinga followed, and I leaned through, scanning. All three zombies were pawing at the front glass on the port side even though one of the windows was broken out starboard-center. Pus bags were still trying to get to the memory of Remo when he dangled out in front of them.

Both of the jarheads crept silently behind the long consoles, and both looked into the open rear doors. There must not have been anything there because Remo kept going, slinking up to the first dead-head. He brought his arm around in a wide arc, perforating the temple of the closest creature. He reversed his hand and stabbed the second one in the same spot. Both dropped. Number three turned, snarled, and before she could take a step had an inch of steel sticking out of the top of her skull. Remo had thrust the blade up under her chin.

Kinga closed the doors and secured them. "Clear."

"Clear," Remo echoed, and checked the port side hatch.

I climbed down the ladder and made sure the starboard hatch was secure. The three of us looked out the windows at the deck. Shit loads of those things meandered through the labyrinth of steel containers. The critters were in varying stages of decomposition, some rotten, and some looking relatively fresh. I was scanning for black camouflage to identify the team sent here before us, but I couldn't see any.

I checked out all the doors once more. The rear doors hadn't been broken down, and honestly, I didn't know if they could be. They were thick wood set in steel frames with top, bottom, and side locking mechanisms. Probably to defeat pirates. The side hatches were comprised of steel, with eight of those little handles used to secure them. They also had locks, and Captain Bob had told me that the windows in those hatches were bullet resistant.

I couldn't help but wonder where Captain Bob had gone to. Why would he leave? His job was to take the *Majestik* and beach it as close to Mexico as he could. It was a suicide mission at the time. This was months ago, before we had a destroyer at our disposal. Now the plan was to evacuate all of the living from this tub and scuttle her. They were going to blow a hole below the waterline and watch her sink.

Some folks had argued that we should clear the ship and use it as a floating hotel, or at least check out the containers. I had argued right back that they were fucking crazy. The ship was crawling with infected, and any of the people who suggested we clear it could feel free to open whatever they wanted on this thing as soon as I was off of it. Nobody volunteered.

"OK," I sighed. "We're secure. What now?"

Kinga put his hands on the console, looking at the innumerable dials, switches, buttons, and lights. "Now we find out where everybody is."

SMALL TALK

What we really needed was implants in people that could be read from a central unit in the *Majestik*'s wheelhouse. Did you see the movie *Aliens*, when the survivors of the initial alien attack are holed up in Operations, and they are looking at electronic blueprints of the facility? They search for the implants and find out that all the humans are in one central location. Exactly how we looked right now, except our prints were paper, nobody had any implants, and we had zombies instead of aliens.

Basically, we were screwed. We could probably search this giant vessel for a week and not find where my friends were hiding. Throw in some infected, and we're here forever.

"I'm going to check the bodies." Both of the boys looked at me like I was crazy. "One of them should have the key that Schumitz wants." I noticed a big body with a black T-shirt covering most of its face. This had been a friend of mine. I actually got a lump in my throat, and felt not a little bit of guilt. I had shot him when he had begun to fade out after being bitten. I got to one knee and touched his hand. The memory of his death was crushing.

The things up here hadn't torn him to pieces, so I could only assume that whatever timeframe it takes for a body to turn unappetizing to the dead had expired prior to them gaining access to the wheelhouse.

I moved to where I remembered the slumped body of Doctor Callus was. She was still there, but stretched out with her hands folded on her chest. Her face was covered with a towel.

I looked at her and immediately felt sad. This woman, however stupid, didn't deserve to die like this. She had forcefully brought hundreds of infected on board this floating sanctuary in order to study them, to find a vaccine or cure or whatever. I hated her for being such an idiot, but looking at her corpse, I started thinking about all the other dead people in the world. They had been people just like me. All dead because of this stupid plague.

But this dumbass had still killed a bunch of people who otherwise would have made it, at least a while longer. I parted her formerly white shirt and saw a chain around her neck. I pulled on the chain and some of her goo came with it. It was nauseating. I jerked the chain and it came free with the same type of key that Schumitz had. It was red, and roundish. A cylinder with pieces cut out of it. Some type of metal.

Why hadn't the first group sent by Schumitz at least taken this key?

I wiped the key on the dead doctor's pants and put it in a small, steel box that Captain Schumitz had given me. The box was attached to a chain exactly like the doctor's, and I put it around my neck.

Remo and Kinga were messing with something when I returned to the consoles. Kinga looked up. "Did she have it?"

"The key? Yeah, but I dunno where the data would be."

"We need to call that in," Kinga informed me. "Where is it?"

I patted my chest. "Safe."

He held out his hand. "I'll take it."

I pulled the whole shebang out of my shirt and handed it to him. He put the chain around his own neck the little box now inside his own shirt. Copycat.

Several dead had made it up the long steel stairway and had begun scratching at the portside hatch window. We all looked and then got back to the task at hand. Kinga began setting up the com-link thing again. I asked him why he didn't just use the *Majestik*'s radio, and he told me it wasn't secure.

Remo shook his head in what could only be disgust and removed his helmet to wipe his forehead. Those looks were usually directed at yours truly for doing something monumentally stupid, but I hadn't done anything dumb for at least ten minutes. At least I didn't think so. Remo picked up a phone and pressed a button. "To the soldiers, sailors, crew, and refugees on board the *Majestic Maersk*: my team is here to remove you from this ship and bring you someplace safe. If you can hear me and are near a phone, please call the wheelhouse." He replaced the receiver, which was on a cord if you can believe it, back in the cradle.

The phone rang in under ten seconds. Remo having kept his hand on it the whole time, picked it up immediately.

"Yes. Yes, we're in the wheelhouse. We have it secured, but we'll need to get to you. Do you have the data Schumitz was looking for? Where are you? How many of you are there? Exfil is a boat coming tomorrow. My team will come for you within the hour. Sit tight."

"WAIT!" I had positively yelled that. Remo gave me a sideways glance. "Ask if Ship, Alvarez, and Donna are with them."

Remo asked and then nodded to me in the affirmative. He passed me the receiver.

"This is Alvarez."

"Are you still ugly?" A large vehicle could have been driven through my smile.

"*Uhh... what? Who is this?*"

My face was in deep shit later, as this particular smile got even bigger and threatened to rip my cheeks apart. "Well, you dumb SOB, you and I came to *Atlantis* together. I met Ship in New Hampshire, I fix stuff, and a crazy CIA guy kidnapped me off of an oil rig. Ugly and *dumb*."

"*You! You bastard! You're alive?*"

"I am, yeah." I could hear him talking to the others with him, but couldn't hear what was being said. There was some crying in the background. It was probably not Ship.

"*Good to hear your voice, buddy! I wish you weren't here though, this is going to get bad. Ship is scribbling furiously, and a certain young lady would like to speak to you.*"

My girl got on the phone. "*Thank you for not being dead.*"

"I do what I can."

"*Where were you? Did they hurt you? How did you get away?*" All of a sudden her tone changed. "*Are you crazy? What the hell are you doing here? You're going to get yourself killed!*" She kept going, and before I could get a word in edgewise, she was telling me that Ship had passed her a message.

There was a pause. "*You're absolutely right.*" She hadn't said that to me. "*Ship says you're an imbecile and should have known better than to attempt a rescue. You're too important to die on this boat. I agree with him! Why are you here?*"

"Well, somebody had to save your dumb asses, and that somebody is me." Remo and Kinga were looking at me. "Uhh... I mean us. We're going to come get you."

"*This horrible ship is crawling with infected. They're everywhere.*" She sighed. "*You should just leave.*"

"OK." I acquiesced shrugging, not that she could see me through the phone. "We're just going to take off. I'll order you a pizza before I go. Oh *darn*. And oh fudge and oh golly and stuff. You have something I need, I can't leave."

"*The hard drives! That's why you're here!*" I heard her snap her fingers. She was always doing that shit, it was unnerving. She also has this nasty habit of screaming "SOCK!" and hitting me across the face with one of her socks. That shit is terrifying, but hilarious at the same time.

"Uh, no. I'm here for you and the other two dumbasses that are with you. I don't give a shit about hard drives. That having been said, who has them?"

Alvarez had the hard drives. They had lost plenty of men getting them though. Of the twelve that had come back to this boat, three were left, but they had picked up another three that had survived for more than a year on this infected tub. I also learned that Captain Bob's body was nowhere to be found when the team had entered the wheelhouse. The rest of the information would have to wait until we got to the survivors, as it was time to get this show on the road.

I was more than a little apprehensive, but it was now or never. Also, if you never saw the movie *Aliens* pre-plague, you're a dumbass.

UPSTAIRS DOWNSTAIRS

Kinga had radioed in to Schumitz on the *Atlantis*, and had left the key secured on the roof of the superstructure. Now if anything happened to us, at least they could get that damn key. So we had that going for us. Our rescue attempt would be in the galley. That's where everybody was holing up.

I had been thinking that the thing to do was what we always did. Set up something that makes a ton of noise as far from us as possible, then move in and do what we want. The problem with that plan was that there was no way to get far away on this boat. The infected were swarming the deck and several were already at the port and starboard hatches to the wheelhouse. We would have to *go quiet* as Remo was fond of saying.

"But what if there are fifty of them right on the other side of this door?" I asked, pointing at the secured heavy doors that led to the bowels of the ship. Wow. Never thought of that until right now. I was about to descend into bowels. Eew. I had already been down there once, and it was bad.

Kinga spat, "Then we're in deep shit. You fall back to the ladder and get out."

"What about you guys?"

"Aww princess, you worried?" Kinga asked checking his rifle. "You're not that pretty."

Remo smirked.

That was unfair. Number one: I *was* worried. These were good men. Number two: I *am* pretty. Classically handsome is the term. "Yeah, I don't want to see you get eaten."

Remo pointed toward the door. He had already listened and had come up with nothing. He unlocked the top and bottom bar-locks and put his paw on the door handle. *On three*, he mouthed. I was nervous as he nodded his head once, twice, and on the third nod threw the door open wide.

Two dead men greeted us. Truly dead. One was slumped to the side on the landing with half his head missing. It was crushed, not shot, which told us a few things. The mostly eaten carcass with what looked like military garb next to him told us other things. The top of this one's head was missing and the smeared spray on the wall communicated to me he had blown his own head off. Bitten or trapped.

The fluorescent overheads and small, sunken wall lights were crusted in gore, bathing the landing and stairs below it in an eerie red-brown light. I peered over the side of the top railing. The stairway was such that each landing blocked my view when I tried to look down, but absolutely no light filtered up from below. I was amazed that the boat still had power after so long without maintenance. Surely they must be low on fuel by now.

Both MARSOC guys panned back and forth with their tactical lights.

"L3's on, lights off," Remo whispered into his mic.

One of the things that Schumitz had provided us was Ground Panoramic Night Vision Goggles. (GPNVG). Desert Coyote in color, the eyepieces actually looked like two sets of binoculars attached by a rail across the top. They were mounted to our helmets, and when they were deployed (swung down to cover our eyes), they made us look like that three-eyed alien from Star Wars, except these things had four eyes. They gave us a wider field of vision than regular NVGs and although bigger, they were lighter on our heads. I flipped the thing down and it turned on automatically. Everything went green.

It was fucking fantastic. I almost giggled. I could see everything. I could read the lettering on Kinga's assault pack. Did I mention it was awesome? 'Cause it was awesome, dipped in awesome with awesome sauce! I took another look down the stairs, but the view was the same. Oh and no way was Schumitz getting these back. Call it hazard pay, but these things were just too cool.

"Me first, then you," Remo pointed at me, "then you, Kinga. Check each door, but don't open it. We go quiet from here on. If we are going to get overwhelmed, or if we get separated, fall back to the stairway and up into the wheelhouse. Exfil to the monkey island if the wheelhouse gets compromised."

Kinga began closing the doors as I wondered WTF a monkey island was. We had left our HK416's on *Atlantis*, and were using MP5SD3's. These were more sub-machine guns than battle rifles, but they were fitted with integrated suppressors.

Kinga leaned toward me when Remo took his first cautious step down the stairs. "The monkey island is the roof of the wheelhouse."

I nodded and began to follow Remo. Our boots made almost no sound as we descended into the darkness. We had been moving down the superstructure for a few minutes when we heard a moan from below and Remo threw up his left hand. We waited, listening, but all we heard was some movement. Nuts clenched, I trailed the MARSOC guy as he moved downward. All the doors inside this tower were locked as we moved down.

We had learned from the crappy, non-electronic blueprints that the galley was in the center of the ship, on deck three. There were six decks, and we were on the landing outside of deck five when we heard the moan again. It was followed by a rasping hack chaser, and they were too close together to be one critter. We had multiple targets in the stairwell. Is it a stairwell on a ship? Nautical terms are beyond me for the most part (I hadn't known what a monkey island was). I will have to ask the boys if we live through this.

We reached deck four and I have to tell you, the green that was my world when looking through these alien eyes was becoming unnerving. I had a great field of vision, and I could see in the pitch black, but the noises of the dead inside this deathtrap were causing me to re-think this operation.

Pitch black. Why was everything pitch black? The power was on, and I can't believe this stairwell wouldn't be lit up like a Christmas tree so the crew wouldn't get killed in here. It didn't make sense, and if something didn't make sense, I should be afraid, and if I'm afraid, I gotta tell the boys.

"Stop," I whispered into my mic. Remo ceased all movements other than to crouch and scan harder if it were possible.

"What?" Kinga whispered. "What is it?"

"Why are all the lights out?"

Kinga stepped forward and crunched on broken glass. I can't believe we hadn't stepped on any before, as all the lights above us must have been broken too except for right outside the wheelhouse. The point is, the broken glass sounded like a shotgun blast in the quiet of our surroundings, and then we heard the moans and cries of the dead echoing all around us.

"Call it!" Kinga whispered into the mic.

"They can't see us, we take them out when they come into... Contact!"

Remo fired once, twice, three times. These weapons were way quieter than our other suppressed weapons, but they still sounded like cannon fire to me. The door to deck five above us opened, and dead poured through. Apparently, the door had only been locked on the stair side. Light also streamed in and I was temporarily blinded. It only lasted a few seconds, but that was a damn long time to be blind when something that wants to eat you is headed in your direction.

Kinga spun and fired, dropping several of the things, and I decided it was time to act. I didn't know how many were coming from below, but there were a shitload coming from above, so I fired at some of them. They probably couldn't see us in the dark, but hey, these are the walking dead, so who knows?

It's difficult to score a headshot with these L3 NVGs on. My first shot took a *Majestik* crewman in the throat, and he didn't give a shit. I adjusted and aimed for his noggin again, but was a bit high and scored a hit on the abdomen of the thing behind him. After my second miss, I was able to compensate, and I dropped the crewman, who promptly collapsed and rolled to the landing below, his brethren falling over him in a heap. The mass looked like a middle-school pig pile. I did not want to play.

I heard Remo call out: "Loading." and I turned one hundred eighty degrees to cover while he switched magazines. He didn't need the cover. He was reloaded so fast I didn't get a chance to pull the trigger, and I turned back to assist Kinga.

"We need to bug!" Kinga said fairly calmly through the mic.

"Can't go down," Remo answered in his steady voice.

I looked at the tangled mound of pus bags that now looked all arms and legs. They were trying to stand but were being pushed and trampled by their hungry cousins. "Not going up!" Perhaps my voice had a twinge of panic to it, but I thought I did well considering. "Way more up than down, Remo! Choose fast!"

"Down then." He sounded like he was asking me to pass the salt at the dinner table. How could he be so calm when we were in such imminent danger? He moved down the stairs one step at a time as he ventilated melons with his 9mm sub-machine gun.

I fired past Kinga's head. "I thought they couldn't see us?"

Kinga dodged a dead hand that snaked out and tried to grab him, then fired into its owner's face. "They can probably hear your constant bitching."

"I've got a path," Remo said, interrupting us both. "Get on my six now."

"Move!" Kinga shouted, and we ran down the stairs after our buddy.

Path? He had a path? There were like, three less infected in our way than there had been up above. Remo used the butt of his MP5 to break the jaw of a dead obese woman, and he pushed through the doors to deck three.

"Nope!" he shouted and began to fire. We pushed through behind him and found out why. The deck three corridor was jam-packed with dead. They were already moving in our direction, and there were at least forty of them in the tight hallway. There was a door to our left. It was a metal hatch actually, and it was locked.

Kinga, brandishing his knife, had already dispatched two of the things with it while simultaneously firing the MP5. He let loose with a kick that bent back a former policeman's leg at the knee. I shot the dead cop in the melon, and spun to face the young man with no lips that had grabbed me and was pulling my face to its maw. I brought my forearm across its forearms and down a bit. The move actually brought the thing's teeth closer to me, but I swung the other way and hit it in the back of the head with my weapon. It wouldn't let go, and I almost went down, but the thing's head snapped left and shit sprayed out of it onto the bulkhead. Thanks, Kinga.

I dropped the lifeless thing, (actually, it let go of me) and continued to select targets. Between the three of us, we were doing well, but not well enough. Kinga was firing behind us up the stairs, Remo was a straight-up Jedi with his knife and sub-machine gun, and I helped when I could.

An emaciated thing slashed Kinga across the face with its skeletal hand and the MARSOC boy took a step back. He also stopped firing and the dead surged forward. They had reached the landing, and four of the horrid things plowed into him, biting. He was still able to get a shot off before he went down, his rifle pinned between him and three hundred pounds of dead people. I have no idea how he did it, but he had his knife in the temple of a guy in a filthy New York Jets jersey and had already shot the bony thing with his pistol, when I reached down to yank off the businessman that was clawing at my buddy's midsection. Guy was heavy, and when I pulled him up, he immediately latched onto my vest and leaned in for a nibble, making that growling sound that some of them make. His head popped before he could reach me, and the shit that flew out of it coated my face.

Gagging and spitting out his gray matter, I shot the two that were on the stairs in front of me, while Kinga grappled with the last one that had grabbed him.

Two. There had only been two in front of me. That didn't compute as there had been more than that a few moments before. Kinga is a hero, but he was tiring, and the thing on him was bigger than he was. He held its face at bay by pushing its throat up, but it was inching closer. I had clicked on empty when I shot the last dead guy, so I let my rifle dangle and pulled my Sig. It was a long draw because of the suppressor, and before I could examine the inner contents of the thing on Kinga, Remo shot it from behind. Except I could hear Remo firing his rifle twenty feet away, and the shot had been louder than it should have been.

I spun and saw a familiar face. "Fast as a snail you are." My buddy Zero smiled and turned to fire into Remo's crowd. "You three numbskulls! In here!" He kept firing and moving as I pulled Kinga up and Remo spun and tactically withdrew. The four of us ran through the now open hatch that had been locked previously. Zero was the last in. He wiped his hand, which also contained a recently fired Desert Eagle .357 Magnum across his forehead.

"What took you assholes so long?"

BOO BOO

We were in a narrow hallway, white walls and a carpet of all things. Light came in via small openings in the ceiling. They were mirrors in tubes to filter in natural light. It was still dark though, but I could see another hatch maybe twenty feet away. Two doors, one on each side of the hall were open, and there was a body slumped at the far end. The cries of the dead and their fists against the steel hatch seemed very close. I guess they were less than an inch away when I think about it.

"Remove your NVGs and I'll turn on the lights," Zero told us. He took his off and we followed suit. The army boy called down the corridor, "Jarek, turn the lights on." The overhead florescent bulbs came to life and Zero studied Kinga and Remo head to toe for a few seconds. "So I'm saving marines again," he sassed and stuck his paw out to Kinga. "Zero." MARSOC introduced themselves, and I threw my arms around this guy and gave him a bear hug. I had always thought Zero was a marine too, but as it happens, he was an army guy.

"Gay." He clapped me on the back. "Gay, alive, and here... What the fuck happened to you?"

"Long story, which I will gladly tell when we get everybody off this tub. What's the plan?"

Zero ejected the polymer mag from his M4, taking a quick look at it before he slammed it back in and yanked the charging handle. "I could use some .556 if anybody thought to bring any. Last suppressor is junk too." He began unscrewing the cylinder from his weapon.

Remo dug in his pack then stepped forward, passing two magazines to Zero. "Schumitz thought you might need these."

"Did he think I might need a fuckin' sandwich too?"

Remo handed him a Power Bar. *Atlantis* had zillions of those things. My favorite was the chocolate peanut butter. Zero tore the package open with his teeth then ripped into the food. "Got separated from the rest of the unit." He grumbled between bites. "Most of them were already dead by the time we made it to the lab. We set up a defensive position at a choke point in the corridor outside the test center. Didn't do shit. The firing inside a steel tube had our ears ringing so loud we couldn't hear the fuckers coming up behind us. I locked the doors and led as many of the dead bastards as I could away. I found Jarek hiding by the engine room." He turned around. "Jarek, come out."

A guy dressed in filthy coveralls stepped out of one of the doors. He wiped his hands on his sides and stuck one out to me. "Jarek Doorshe." Zero smiled because he knew what I was going to say.

"Jerk-douche? Really?"

"Really," he stated. "What is your name?"

Guy had an accent, and I couldn't place it. I stuck my mitt out to shake his hand and introduce us newcomers, but a muffled explosion from the general area of where we had just come from interrupted me.

I looked in several directions. "What was that?"

"That was your buddy, Ship." Zero raised his eyebrows. "He's pretty fuckin' handy. He and a few others are in the galley, but I haven't been able to get to them. These dead fuckers are all through the ship, and I've almost bought it a few times pushing my luck. Now that I have some ammo and some help, we might be able to push through."

Remo rubbed his jaw. "What's the best way to the galley?" He passed another Power Bar to Jarek, then began loading a magazine with some loose rounds.

"Back the way you came," Zero began. "About twenty meters down the passageway, but we aren't going through there and coming out alive. We go this way," he thumbed over his left shoulder indicating the corridor behind him, "shutting the doors I missed on the way. There are a couple places where I know there are some clustered infected, but the five of us should be able to take them."

"Can you draw a map?" Remo produced the same Sharpie he had given me on the monkey island. See? I can remember shit.

Zero took the marker and drew on the bulkhead, pointing with the tip of the pen at key areas as he drew. "This is where we are now. This turn will bring us around the galley to the far side, but it's full of infected. I was able to shut the near hatch, and the far hatch is the galley, so they're trapped in there. This is the ladder to the passageway to the engine room." He crossed off a large area with a big X. "We stay the fuck out of here."

"Why?" I asked maybe a bit too quickly.

"There are a hundred or more dead trapped down there. It's an access passageway to one of the holds. This is where they did their experiments, and where they stored their subjects. Their main lab is down there. The entire hold is crawling with dead fucks. We can go around, but the way is blocked here, and here."

Kinga furrowed his brow. "Blocked by what?"

"This one is where Ship set off one of his IEDs and it bent a hatch closed. We would need tools to get through. Here," he indicated another junction, "there are about twenty infected trapped in a passageway just like this one. We might be able to go through there, but as soon as we flip the hatch handles, all of those pricks will push up against the hatch, and it opens away from us."

Remo put his pack on the floor. All eyes were on him as he pulled out a red-wrapped candy bar from one of the pockets. "This will open it."

I was wondering how a brick of chocolate was going to open a door when Zero disclosed, "Semtex, nice. Where'd you get that Czech shit?"

I had thought he had said *check-shit*, and was totally lost until Remo clarified that *Atlantis* had two pallets of the stuff from the Czech Republic.

"Works great, I've used it before," Zero added and frowned. "I'm a little pissy that nobody thought to give *me* some when I signed up for this fuckin' suicide mish."

Remo and Kinga looked at each other. "*Army*," they both chided at the same time.

Kinga raised an eyebrow and pulled out his own candy bar. "We asked. Looks like it's *you* that needs saving."

Zero smiled, but I was getting antsy. "Pissing match later, let's go get my… our friends." Zero had given me the death eyes when I had said *my*. He was in for a penny just like I was, and had actually been here for a few days, whereas I had just arrived.

All three of them stared at me, and without a word began switching out magazines. I did the same, and reloaded my Sig as well.

Kinga handed Zero an extra radio, the army guy attaching it to himself and installing the earbud. His rifle hung on his single-point sling, the suppressor no longer viable and discarded. He was using a suppressed Sig P226 just like we were, the Desert Eagle in a separate holster on his hip. When we were ready, Zero turned to the new guy. "Jarek, you coming or staying?"

"Coming," he proclaimed, and hefted a fire axe.

"Quiet from now on, just like we did before, okay?" Jarek nodded in understanding.

There were six handles on the hatch. Zero moved five of them into the open position, pausing on the last to look at us. He nodded once, and we tensed. If there were fifty of the things on the other side of this door, we were probably dead. The door opened in, and we would never be able to shut it again. Remember that on the other side of the hatch behind us were a few dozen infected still bashing themselves to pulp trying to get to us.

Zero slowly pulled the handle until the door was no longer sealed. He remained in a crouch as he pulled the door wide. An empty passageway greeted us. No zombies. No smell. No sounds. The fluorescent lights overhead were already on, and we were witness to stains and some of the shit the things leave behind them when they move about, but there were no dead here.

Stepping over the knee-knocker (I still couldn't figure out why some of the doors were doors, and some were hatches. Must have something to do with flooding), Zero scanned the area, then moved forward enough for all of us to step into the corridor. Kinga came last and he secured the door with one handle.

We made it through two corridors, our tactical lights showing that all the doors were closed, before we came upon our first obstacle. It was the closed hatch that Zero had indicated before. There was an orange circle with a line through it and the words DO NOT OPEN with INFECTED underneath was scrawled in that same Day-Glo orange marker.

"This is the hatch with twenty or so of those fuckers trapped in there," whispered Zero into the radio. "We either go through here, or we go down there." Zero took two steps toward a hatch in the floor (I know I write hatch a lot, but that's what they are!) and he pointed down. We peered into the hole. A steel tube-ladder descended into semi-darkness, vague shadows indicating several things were moving about further down the passageway below us. The revealing sounds told us exactly what those sinister forms were. Zero shook his head. "I doubt we would step foot off the ladder before they tore into us."

Remo had taken all of it in quickly. "Agreed. We need to go through there." He indicated the corridor in front of us. "Shut the lights off and use NVGs. Shape charge the hinges, blow them from halfway down this passageway. When they come out, we take them one at a time as they come through the hatch. Jarek holds the rear and opens up the hatches behind us if we need to fall back."

I wrinkled my nose, the stink from the open trapdoor getting to me. "But Remo, we'll be trapped if we have to fall back that far."

"We will, but it will give us time to reload and come up with a plan. Besides, we're already trapped."

I hadn't thought of that. He was right. This damn boat was jam-packed with these rotting shitheads. They were in front, behind, above, and below. We were already stuck here, and I immediately found that even more disconcerting. Thanks, buddy.

"Just one more thing?" Kinga and Zero looked annoyed at me, but Remo seemed interested. "What if we just try opening the door?" I pointed at the white steel. "Why can't we just have a guy forward, he undoes the handles one at a time and slowly, then kicks the door open and runs back to the shooters?"

Remo looked at the other two, and all three of them eye-shrugged at the same time. Zero stuck out his lower lip. "That will take away a few shots as you run back to us, but they'll probably jam the door all trying to get through at the same time. Not a bad plan. And it saves explosives and maybe a concussive blast. Okay, fall back." He looked at me. "Good luck."

I may have mentioned in my journals somewhere, that however badass you, Dear Reader, take me to be, I am not, in fact, MARSOC, a SEAL, a ninja, or Spiderman. I'm a moron sometimes, that's true, and this was one of those times. Of course in my head, one of the *operators* was going to operate on this particular portion of the mission while I sat back as far as possible with my biggest gun, a Bud Light, and some porn. As I had suggested it, however, I would be doing it.

Shit. Didn't they tell me I had to stay back when we were up in the wheelhouse? WTF changed their minds? Imminent evisceration?

As I pondered my stupidity, the guys worked out the plan in detail. I open the door and run like hell, hugging the steel of the right side corridor wall. They would shoot past me if they could, and I would take a standing position and begin firing into the crowd. We would flip down our NVGs, and Jarek would kill the lights, keeping his hand on the light switch. If all went well, we would smoke all the undead and be with Ship and my friends in time for Jell-O shots. If bad shit happened, we flip up our NVGs, everybody yells to Jarek to turn on the lights, and we book it back to the first passage, shutting both doors on the way. Rinse and repeat until we run out of zombies.

I thought Jarek might want to buy his fire axe some dinner and dress it in a skirt he was holding it so tight. "But what about the fast ones?"

"We target them first," Zero told him. "Knees or center mass, just get it on the ground and worry about headshots later." Zero had been looking at Jarek when he said it, but as Jarek didn't have a firearm, the rundown was undoubtedly for my benefit. I wish there was some way of keeping a tally of how many of these things I had killed. I bet it was just as many, or more than Zero.

The crewman had his finger on the light switch, and that made me nervous. "Jarek, don't turn the lights off until we tell you. I don't want to be running back and trying to fumble with my NVGs while these three are shooting past me in the dark." He was wide-eyed and breathing fast, but he pulled his digit off of the switch.

This shit was happening. It had been my idea. Hell, it had been my idea to come save these dumbass friends of mine. Oh, and Ship, when you're reading this later, you don't get to call my intelligence into question unless you do the same for yourself. You're in exactly the same situation I'm in, and we both put ourselves in it. The only difference is, I'm going to pull your fish out of the fire.

My hand had been on the first handle the whole time I had been thinking that all this shit was my fault. I looked back at the other four guys, they had taken up their firing positions. MARSOC on one knee each, Zero standing behind Kinga, unsuppressed rifle raised, and Jarek at the end of the hall. Remo nodded and I flipped the first bar. I listened intently, but could only hear the things on the other side of the steel making the noises they make. I undid three more handles and listened again. Nothing pawing at the hatch that I could tell. I undid number five and put my hand on six. A bit of pee might have eeked its way out of me. I took a big breath, twisted the last handle, and took a step back.

Nothing. They didn't come flooding through as I thought they would have. If this was good or bad, I didn't know. I stepped back up and pushed on the door, but it didn't budge. Another big breath and I turned my gaze on the guys behind me. Kinga appeared bored, and Zero was giving me the *hurry up* look. Remo, as always, was impossible to read.

I grabbed the sides of the hatch, put my boot against it, and pushed for all I was worth with one foot. It opened wide, smacked into one of the things and bounced back at me. The stench that wafted out of that corridor after less than two seconds of open door was almost unbearable. Didn't stop this kid though and I kicked again, the door opening as far as it could and smacking against the bulkhead. The resounding echo of that thump resonated through the hallway and no doubt the entire ship. A shit-ton of red eyes stared at me for a split second, every one of them asking me if I was out of my fucking mind, then they all surged forward. I spun and high-tailed it back down the passageway. The boys started firing, and Zero's rifle sounded like a... a... I don't know something really loud. I got about halfway back when the lights went out. Two steps later, somebody punched me in the side, just above my left hip, and I jerked to the right, slamming into the bulkhead. The firing ceased, but all that meant was that there were dead things intent on a banquet a few feet behind me. Yeah, and I was by far the closest to them.

"Jarek, turn the fucking lights on!" I heard Zero positively scream.

The overheads flared to life, and I dared a quick peek behind me. The dead were about twenty feet away, but when they are that close, it's too close. I got up, my side hurting, and hurried to my place on the line. The bullets whizzed down the tight hallway and the things in front began to hamper the progress of their dead cousins behind when they fell. Somebody yelled something and I saw Kinga reload. I couldn't really hear shit because of Zero's M4.

I shot a kid in the face. I shot a skinny girl with rotting tattoos in the eye. I tried to shoot a freshly killed but severely mauled military guy, but the top of his head popped up before I could squeeze the trigger. I sighted on a guy in green coveralls, but my eyes went out of focus for a second, and before I could reacquire him, he was down. The dead were starting to plug the corridor, and we had killed them all the way back to the hatch. They were still coming, but slower, when I realized my mouth was incredibly dry. I swallowed and tried to sight on another guy in coveralls when the entire ship sort of lurched to the left. Nobody else seemed to be bothered by it, and they kept shooting. I, on the other hand, needed to put my hand on the bulkhead to steady myself. I was also feeling a bit wet. I had not pissed myself! I would never live it down. I touched my side, pain flared there, and I looked at my palm. It was covered in blood, as were my pants and lower tactical vest. The floor hadn't been spared either, and I saw that a large puddle of my red stuff was staining the carpet. The gunshots stopped.

It dawned on me what had happened. "Which one of you fuckers shot me?" I asked, ears ringing. I fell down a deep hole and slumped against the bulkhead.

SHOT. AGAIN

"Pressure! Here, Jarek."

"Syrette?"

"No, we'll need him frosty. It's a through-and-through, but it's bleeding badly. I hope nothing inside got nicked, but we can't go in now anyway. Then there's the fact that I'm not a fuk'n surgeon."

"That is a lot of blood."

"He'll be fine."

"But so much blood…"

"Jarek, are you a medical professional? No? Then let me worry about it for now."

My eyes fluttered open and it was very bright. The overhead fluorescent lighting hurt my eyes. Then I felt some real pain in my side when somebody pushed on my wound. I was on my back on the deck, shirtless with my tactical shit in a pile next to me. Somebody snapped their fingers in front of my face and I focused on them.

"Remo, you shot me."

"You had the poor notion of stepping between the business end of my rifle, and my sighted target."

"It hurts."

"Shit happens. We can't stay here. The weapons fire is sure to bring more of them."

Zero, reloading his Sig, looked down at me. "I closed every door I could without getting bitten when me and Jarek ran through the ship. I couldn't get them all though, so we should be on our toes." He moved off out of my field of vision. "In fact…" He let that statement dangle, and I heard one of the things rasp followed by a single suppressed shot.

"Save ammo," Remo suggested. "Use your knife if it's only one."

"Can you stand?" Kinga asked me.

"Yeah, let me…"

Remo put his hand on my shoulder as I tried to sit up. "Not yet."

"How long was I out?"

Remo wasn't sure. "Two minutes?"

Jarek still had his hands on my side and was pressing down. Remo fished in a small pack he had on his hip. He pulled out a green package and tore it open with his teeth. Pulling out a bandage, he told Jarek to move his hands. The new guy pulled back and a dripping, red piece of some type of cloth came with his mitts. Remo pressed the fresh bandage to my wound, and the Devil himself was unleashed inside me. I actually convulsed the pain was so intense. That little guy that lives in your brain and unleashes the hurt decided his vacation was over, hiatus done. He returned to work, getting on the horse quickly, throwing all the handles, and pressing all the red buttons labeled PAIN. That shit hurt. I bucked and gritted my teeth.

"What... what the *fuck* was that?"

"The entry wound. You ready?"

"Ready for what?"

Remo pulled me forward by the left shoulder, "The quick clot infused bandage will really help the bleeding." He wrapped the bandage around me and pressed it into the exit wound.

I gotta tell you, I'm not a pussy. Really. I've been shot a bunch of times now. I've killed, I don't know, a hundred infected? Maybe more. I've killed bad guys that deserved it, and I don't feel guilty anymore. I went through months of needles in a secret government hospital. I mean, I was in a plane crash a couple days ago, and right now, I was on a huge container vessel, swarming with undead things that wanted to eat me, all because I'm looking to save my friends.

All this having been said, I screamed and some pee came out of me when the jarhead put that shit on my wound. It happened. I didn't want it to happen, it just did. It was an exceptionally manly scream, if such a thing exists, but a scream nonetheless. My upper abdomen and crotch down to my knees was soaked with blood, so nobody saw the piss, but I felt it leave me. I will be embarrassed when somebody reads this, but at the moment of said evacuation, I didn't care, the pain was so extreme. It didn't last long, but it still friggin' hurt. Like, a lot.

I looked at Remo, he looked right back in my teary eyes as he wrapped the bandage around me. When he was done wrapping, he pulled the right side of his T-shirt down and to the right from his collar. There was a circular, indented scar, an obvious bullet wound, probably years old but still evident on his shoulder. "I screamed too."

"So did I," Kinga added, and he had his left bicep flexed. He had the same scar Remo did, but on his arm.

Zero rolled his eyes. "Sissies. Don't get shot and you won't have to scream. Me? I woulda' fuk'n ducked. Get him on his feet, we've got company on the way. A few at least."

My shirt was a hot mess, so I opted to just wear the tactical vest and webbing, but Remo said no. I needed to cover the bandage with some type of cloth or the webbing could rip the bandage open. He wrung out my shirt, and I watched as what used to be inside of me pelted the already soaked carpet in a crimson rain. He helped me put the shirt on, and it was gross. Kinga and Jarek helped me to stand, and Remo carefully put the webbing around me. He shouldered my pack and Kevlar, and I was grateful, but it would interfere with his aim. In point of fact, I had no doubt that this guy would be able to throw an injured hippo over his shoulder with little impact on his aim. He is that badass.

"Contact," Zero whispered into his mic, "three at least, on my twelve. Must have been your girly cries. Fifteen meters." He raised his Sig and let a round go.

Kinga moved forward and took up a firing position next to Zero. They would be shooting through the hatch at whatever was coming.

I was woozy, but still able to make out the *pffft* of the suppressed rounds.

"You alright to stand?" Remo asked.

Jarek took my right arm and put it over his shoulders. "I will help him." We moved toward Kinga and Zero, who had both already stepped over the knee knocker and pressed on.

"Open port on the right," Zero whispered. "Cover." Zero snapped his fingers and waited. Nothing came from the open door, so Zero stepped in front of it, shining his light in. He reached for the doorknob and pulled the door closed. We had closed the gap, and honestly, I was feeling better, although a little cold, which I thought was odd for the summertime. We were in the bowels of a container ship though, and I thought that might be the issue.

A lone creature stepped from another open door out into the corridor and we all froze. It must have heard us closing doors. It was looking away from us, and Zero went into a low crouch, sneaking up to it with his big knife. He switched the knife so it was pointing down in his fist, then jammed it sideways into the thing's temple.

The undead spun and latched on to Zero. I gotta admit, I never saw that coming. The knife was still sticking out of the side of the thing's melon. It surprised us all, including Zero, but he still had the guile to get his forearm up between the thing's teeth and his face. He tried to get his arm under its chin, but it pulled him in and bit down on the meaty top of his arm. He was wearing a long-sleeved tactical shirt, and the dead man apparently didn't get the best purchase because it didn't pull back with a piece of him. To Zero's credit, he gritted his teeth and fought the thing off, not making a sound. Kinga was on the thing before the rest of us could react, popping a neat hole in the side of its dome with his pistol. The exiting round spattered goo all over the bulkhead in a conical pattern and there was a resulting ricochet that scared the shit out of everybody.

Zero reached down to pull his blade from the thing's head. It wouldn't come, so he put his boot on its face and yanked again, the knife coming out with a sucking sound. He wiped it on the dead man's shirt and returned it to its sheath. Even in my weakened condition, I could see the blood on his hand. He noticed too and pushed his sleeve up. He smiled. He actually looked a little smug, "Now that shit just ain't fair. I been runnin' around this damn boat, dodging these assholes," he pointed at the dead man, "for a couple days. I run into Marines, and I'm dead in ten fuk'n seconds."

The wound looked more like a rip than a bite mark. It was semi-circular like all of them are, but this looked pulled instead of bitten. Remo yanked out a gauze pack, but Zero shrugged him off. "Save it."

"You're bleeding," Remo pointed out.

Zero harrumphed, "Yeah, but that bandage won't do much, will it?" He looked at me. "How long do I have?"

"Why does everybody ask me that? I don't know, and I think it varies per person anyway."

Remo held up the bandage. "At worst, this will keep your blood inside you. It isn't bleeding much anyway, so it couldn't hurt."

In the end, Zero acquiesced and Remo patched him up. We all knew he was doomed, and the person who seemed to take it the best was Zero.

"We need to keep moving," he barked, and took point.

I was getting colder, and my bandage was leaking. I could feel the warmth of the blood on my leg and it felt great. Tell me that isn't F'd up? I'm slowly bleeding to death, and my blood makes me feel warm (briefly) when it hits my skin. Jarek was helping me walk, my arm around his shoulders.

Zero opened another hatch, and it was clear for another forty feet. We could hear them on the other side of this hatch. They were beating and pounding and howling and hissing. But not on our hatch, on something else.

"This next area is full of them," Zero told us, wiping his forehead. He already had that rancid cream color to him. He had been bitten less than three minutes ago. "A dozen at least, maybe more. Galley is right on the other side of them. Let's do the same thing we did before, without the lights or shooting of our people." He looked right at Jarek and raised his eyebrows. I heard Jarek swallow hard.

We got into position, Remo and Zero up front, Kinga standing behind them, but I was having trouble focusing and I let the boys know.

"Stay awake," Remo told me. "Don't fire unless they take us down, I don't want you to shoot us."

I flipped him off. "Payback's a bitch."

Remo shrugged out of my Kevlar and handed it to Kinga, who put it to the right of him on the floor. He put my pack to his left and nodded to Zero. The army guy moved forward and popped five of the six handles on the hatch. He looked back at us, nodded, threw the last handle, and pushed the hatch open. It squealed a little, and a shit-ton of red-eyed freaks looked over their shoulders in our direction.

Zero fired three times before he ran back to the line. I was getting really woozy, and leaned against the exterior bulkhead. Zero moved forward as he fired. "Back on the line, Army!" Kinga shouted, but Zero still walked toward the things, shooting. They were dropping like flies, but also like flies, they just kept coming. One tripped over the knee-knocker, and Zero shot it in the back of its melon.

"Out!" I heard Kinga shout and he pulled his pistol. He fired twice before the suppressor burned out and shit got pretty loud.

"Back, fall back," Remo notified casually, and Jarek lifted me off the floor, where I had slumped. He began carry-dragging me back through the hatch behind us. He got me through and we heard a scream. It wasn't the scream of agony and terror that comes from someone being torn apart by a throng of dead people, it was the shriek of a Runner. It fought through the horde, taking a round in the shoulder. I saw the thing take two more rounds as it leapt past its cousins, hitting Zero in the chest and taking him down. It began to shriek and beat at my buddy as both Kinga and Remo ran out of ammo at the same time. Remo pulled his big ass knife and stood, but a blur of motion streaked past him and a fire axe nearly decapitated the Runner. I put my hand on the bulkhead as my support had left me.

28

"Get back!" Jarek yelled, pulling Zero to his feet. He threw the shocked soldier behind him into Remo and Kinga and began hacking at the things in front of him. None of them seemed to give a shit, and they walked right by him. Was I seeing this correctly? Did those fuckers *not* tear into this guy? I was freaked out a bit to say the least. The MARSOC boys dragged Zero through the hatch and began to pull expended magazines. I could see Jarek thrusting with his axe, there was no room to swing with all those pus bags surrounding him. They continued to plod by him and came for us. The last thing I saw before Kinga slammed the door was Jarek pulling some of the things backwards toward himself.

Zero tried to fight Kinga off, "We need to get him!"

"We open that door and we all die!" Kinga yelled back at him.

Zero put his hand on one of the hatch handles anyway, and Remo gently pulled it off. "We can't get to him. He's too far away and we need to reload." Remo shook his head. "He's gone." We fell back to the previous hatch, and everybody began to load their weapons in silence.

Kinga broke the silence, "A dozen huh?"

"I don't know where the others came from. There weren't that many when they chased me out of there. There were fifty at least. Jarek didn't deserve to go out like that."

My mouth was really dry, and I reached for my canteen. I took a swig, and rinsed my mouth. "Yeah, so nobody saw those things walk right by Jarek?"

Zero shook his head. "That's sure as shit what it looked like."

They were halfway done loading their magazines when the first handle on the hatch down the corridor twisted open with a squeak. The second turned and the others began to follow suit. "Holy shit, they're coming through!" Zero yelled.

The boys all slammed their half-loaded mags home and yanked their charging handles, aiming back down the corridor. The last handle spun and the door opened. A disgusting figure, positively coated in gore and indistinguishable on race or gender stepped through and onto the carpet. The only thing that was in any way telling was the axe in its hand.

"Come," it called. "The way is clear."

All four of us looked at each other. Then back at the thing. The thing looked down at itself then back at us. "I am Jarek. I am human, just covered in *them*. Come."

REUNION

Jarek had slain all of the undead. Every one. In one five-minute span, he had killed half as many as I had killed in my entire zombie-slaying career. And he had done it with an axe. Not with a tactical battle rifle, or even a suppressed pistol. With an axe.

That wasn't even the weirdest part. The really crazy thing was that those dead motherfuckers hadn't attacked him. This was a first for me. Since when did these things not want to feast on someone's innards?

Remo, not missing a trick, passed Jarek a white towel. No, I don't know where he got a friggin' towel, that's not important. The important thing was that Jarek wiped his face and anything else he could. Guy was *covered* in zombie shit. Not poop, blood and guts and viscera and brains. Are brains guts? Whatever.

We stepped through the hatch into the next corridor and it looked like an abattoir. All the blood and shit that was on Jarek paled in comparison to the hallway. Each of the noggins of the things on the floor was crushed or caved in. It was gross, and my admiration for this guy went up ten-fold.

"Explain," I heard Zero demand.

"Explain what?" Jarek asked right back, "I do not know why they did not attack me. I am no different than you are." He hefted his axe and smiled. "I did crush all of their heads with this one. You are welcome."

Remo pointed at Jarek's face, "You've got stuff in your beard." Jarek used his now nasty towel to comb his whiskers. Remo turned to Zero. "Is that the door to the Galley?" We all looked at the double doors which had begun to break from the stress of a hundred pounding fists.

"Yeah, that's it." Zero looked at a hatch on the starboard side, "This is how they must have been getting in here." He shut it and turned all six handles. "Fuck 'em. Now we're in business." He knocked on the double doors. "Anybody alive in there? It's Zero and company. We took care of all the infected out here and are just itching to talk to you."

Jarek raised one eyebrow. "We?"

I heard a bunch of shit being moved on the other side of the doors. Heavy stuff sliding and things being tossed aside. The door unlocked with a click, and I was suddenly looking at Alvarez. I smiled despite the pain in my side, and he stepped out, shaking Zero's hand. He noticed the bandage on Zero's arm and looked at him questioningly. "I died," the doomed man quipped. "Good to see you though."

I was leaning on Kinga, and I felt really cold. "When you two are done smooching, can we come inside? It's kind of nasty out here."

Alvarez shifted his gaze to me and sighed. "You blew the pool for me, dickhead." He started toward me, but Zero stopped him.

"Let's get inside the galley. We need to get him looked at, and get Jarek cleaned off."

Alvarez nodded and told us to come in. I didn't make it three steps before I was looking down a long tunnel and darkness claimed me.

When did popular culture decide that zombies wanted brains? When you think about it, it's really the only squishy part of a person that's hard to get to. Your average zombie is all teeth and fingernails, and although I wouldn't call them lazy, they certainly don't go out of their way to take the most difficult path to food, so spending the requisite time to open a noggin for the juicy center isn't at the forefront of their semi-functional minds. How the hell is one of them going to get through your skull using primarily teeth? I don't know about you, but I think that if I tried to bite through somebody's noggin, I would get a mouthful of hair and scalp, and my choppers would just scrape off the cranium. The brain is literally the most difficult organ to acquire. The undead don't give a shit about getting to your brain, they want to take the easy route and go into the abdominal cavity for the important vittles. If a brain is just hanging around, then I'm sure they will swallow it down with limited chewing, but for the most part, the mobile deceased are around specifically because their brains *haven't* been consumed. If the pus bags did eat brains, then this whole apocalypse thing would have been over in a jiffy.

That is what I was thinking, or rather dreaming about, when I felt a searing pain lance through my left side. I didn't want to wake up. I can remember thinking *don't wake up*. Someone was rummaging around inside my body, and it was beginning to hurt. If I could just stay asleep... alas, that was not to be.

My eyes opened and I stared into the fluorescent light above me. This was becoming commonplace and it was beginning to piss me off. Why did they always put me directly under a light?

"I need more light!" a familiar woman's voice proclaimed loudly.

"He's awake!" Alvarez pointed out, and shined a light in my face.

"I really don't want to be. And ouch, that fucking hurts." That had come out of me.

"It's about to get worse there, kiddo." She leaned in and kissed me on the forehead. "Your buddies saved your life with the bandage, but it has to come off."

I heard Jarek ask her: "Are you a medical professional?"

"Who the fuck is this guy, the Swedish Chef?" Damn, that's my girl! "Yeah, I can stitch a bitch, now go clean yourself off in the sink. Nobody else touch him," she thumbed at Jarek, "he's been doused in that shit. Okay, Hon, are you ready? The bandage is going to stick and this is going to hurt like hell. Normally, I wouldn't take this off, but I have to see the wound." She cut the bandage straps with some scissors.

She had called me Hon. Nobody ever called me Hon except my mom. "Do it."

She did it. My girl is not a liar. It really hurt, and I hissed as the bandages came off both sides. It was like ripping off a scab. She poked and prodded and pushed. "Mmmm hmm, yup, yup. I got bad news, lover: you're going to live."

"Doesn't feel like it." I closed my eyes.

"Oh, it's about to get worse." I whipped my eyes open and glared at her. Can you *whip* eyes? I friggin' did. "The reason you're bleeding through the bandage is that at some point prior to it being on you, it got wet. That decreased the efficiency of the hemostatic agent, and the reason it was undoubtedly crispy when it was applied. Fear not, young Padawan, I brought the good shit." She produced a green package from her bag, and I closed my eyes again. "Do you remember how much it hurt when they put the bandage on you?" My eyes shot open for the second time in a minute and I looked at her. Yeah, *shot* is better as a descriptive eye-opening term. "Bite this and don't be a pussy," she grumbled before she stuffed a towel in my mouth and dumped that shit on me.

I already gave you details on how badly it hurt when MARSOC had applied the bandage. This was worse. Way worse. She poured the powder right into the hole in my side, flipped me over, and did the same to the exit wound. As to the shenanigans I pulled when that stuff hit me, I will just write that it was undignified, and leave it at that.

"So then why did he pass out?" I heard Kinga ask.

She sighed. "Shock, adrenaline, and straight-up pain. Getting shot doesn't just hurt, it sends signals to all your systems that there is a problem. Sometimes those systems overreact." I could feel Kinga nodding. "The blood wasn't black or arterial red, and nothing's spurting, so I'm thinking nothing major is damaged." She thought out loud. "What I don't understand is how he got shot when he was wearing body armor."

"We were concerned about bouncers inside a metal ship, so we were using subsonic rounds for our suppressed weapons. The slower round must have skipped off the bottom of the armor plate and gotten him in the side below the plate."

"Bouncers?"

"Ricochets. All metal in here."

"Ah, right. When he wakes up—"

"I'm up," I told her, and moved up on one elbow.

"Whoa there! Lie the fuck back down right now! You sit up when I tell you." I did as instructed. She pulled out a little pen light and shined it in my eyes. Then put her hand on my face. "If you would kindly *stop* getting shot?"

"Believe me, it isn't tops on my to-do list. Shit just keeps happening. Bad luck."

Kinga and Remo were by my side, looking down at me. "Bout time," Kinga griped. "When can he get up? I'm tired of humping his crap." He had my vest over one shoulder.

I smiled and looked at Kinga. "Remo, there's a chink in my armor."

Kinga smiled back and leaned over me. "I'm of Korean descent, you racist douche."

"Well, I *was* in prison."

Zero, Alvarez, and two folks I didn't know showed up in a second too. Alvarez put his hand on my shoulder. "He okay?"

Kinga bowed. "Round-eye fine." He joked in a mock Chinese accent. "He big pussy. He get up soon and carry own shit." He put my vest down and went to look for some food.

I heard thumping on the hatch we had bypassed to get to the galley. "Company already?"

Alvarez looked at the doors. "They never left."

"Okay, everybody back off. You," my girl pointed at me, "sit up slowly. If you crack open my expert dressing, I will put Kwick Klot in your Bud Light." I sat up, and eventually stood. "Arms out." I again did as instructed, and she re-wrapped me with a long bandage.

I looked at Zero, who was talking to Alvarez, Remo, and Kinga. "He's bitten," I told Donna. (My girl.)

"Yeah, I know. I looked at it. It looks like nothing, but nothing is deadly nowadays." She sighed. "He'll never leave this ship, and he knows it."

A shadow fell over me and I smiled. "Speaking of Ships…" I turned to look at him. You guessed it. Stinkeye. Complete with giant arms folded and reproachful eyebrow clench. He passed me a pre-scribbled note. *You escape the clutches of that insane man, cross an infected country to get home, then proceed to get yourself shot on a stupid suicide mission, all because of sentiment.* I looked back at him when I was done reading and he was smiling. He passed me another note. *Thank you.*

He made to suffocate me with one of his ungodly bear-hugs, but my significant other, all five foot three of her, stepped in his way and wagged her finger at him. "And you're supposed to be a genius? What happens when you squeeze him and his pancreas squirts out the hole in his side?" Ship took a step back, visibly frightened. Everybody was looking. "Do you have a spare set of guts on you? No? Then shake hands like men." She stormed off to check on Zero. "All this hugging. Honest to God."

Fully chastised, Ship extended his massive mitt toward me. It was like looking at an infant's hand being held by a pro wrestler. I sighed a sigh of finality and looked up at my buddy. Way, way up.

"It's good to see you, Pal."

He nodded, scribbling. *We have much to discuss. It can wait until we are back at Atlantis. Did you procure the key?*

"I did, yeah. Alvarez has the hard drives?"

He nodded in the affirmative, writing. *We lost several men in obtaining these. It's bad in the hold. They were running experiments on infected down there.*

"Yeah, Zero told me." I stretched a little, testing the limits of my bandages. It hurt, but nothing like before. Remo and Kinga showed up in a few seconds, both looking up at Ship. "Told you he was big." They both looked at me, then back at Ship, Remo sticking his paw out. "Ship, old buddy, this is Remo and Kinga. Without these two, and a few others, I wouldn't be here. They saved my ass countless times."

Kinga shook Ship's hand next. "And he ours. We came to get some communications going between your community on *Atlantis* and ours up in Montana." Ship reached down to the table I had been on, picking up one of the pieces of paper he had passed me earlier. He handed it to Kinga.

Kinga chuckled, passing out some Oreos. "You're welcome. He's rude, dumb, and apparently racist, but he has other... qualities."

Ship put his finger on his nose, and both MARSOC guys laughed.

"Fuck all three of you. You're just jealous because I'm so pretty." Smiles all around. I'm funny. Give me a brick wall and a microphone and I could make a living, or could have if there was a world left.

Remo looked at the rag-tag band of folks in the galley. "Who do I have to fuck to get off this tub? This mission is only half-complete. We need to get this shit back to Schumitz, and I can think of a few hundred cannibals who would prefer we don't make it."

I looked over at the sink. "About that. I have a plan."

THE PLAN

Kinga nodded. "So do I. We shoot the infected in the head as we make our way back to the wheelhouse without getting bitten."

"Right. Good plan. But what if you could make it all the way there, doing just what you said, with no chance of being bitten?"

Everybody followed my gaze toward the sink. "We can't ask him to do that," Remo scoffed shaking his head. "He's a civilian."

"I've got news for everybody: Nobody's a civilian. You hear that?" I pointed to the hatch being beaten on from the other side by rotting, infected fists, "They're civilians. There's only two types anymore, Remo; warriors or undead. You step up now or the species is in the toilet."

"I don't know how this guy," Kinga thumbed at me, "continues to be both elegant and crude at the same time."

Remo was staring at me hard. I didn't like it. "He's right though. We send Jarek back the way we came closing any of the hatches off the main corridor we missed. We bang on this hatch," he indicated the one the infected were futilely smashing themselves against, "Jarek comes in behind them and takes them out one at a time until we're clear all the way back to the wheelhouse."

"I don't like it," Zero protested. Where the hell had he come from? "Who knows if what we saw is what we saw?"

"We *did* see it. They didn't touch him. Then there's the fact that he's still alive." Ship passed me a quickly scrawled message: *Explain.* "I can't, Sasquatch. The dead didn't attack him. He stood in a room with them, smoked them all with an axe, and it was like they didn't give a shit. It doesn't compute." Ship began to scribble furiously, us staring at him for a moment before returning to conversation. "Zero, it's the best way. We know we cleared out everything on the way here. We just need to get rid of the ones in the corridor next to us, be quiet going up the stairs, and we're good. Call the cavalry and shit."

Ship passed me his note. I had no idea how he could scrawl so much so *fast. You assume too much. What empirical evidence is there that the undead will not attack this man? You said you saw him stand among the infected, but there could be dozens of factors involved that we are not yet aware of, any one of which could get him and subsequently us killed if not investigated first. We need to test your hypothesis prior to any excursion.*

My side really hurt. I mean really. I had been shot before, in the head too, and it had hurt but not like this. Some guy popped me in the dome with a wrench a few weeks ago, and I was a mess for a few days. That was worse, but this was close. Of course, I had also been bitten by an infected and gone through a night of hell that would make anybody cry. Yeah, I'm immune to this little apocalypse thing. Probably should have told you up front, but if you've read my other journals, you know by now. Either way, I was holding my side when I finished Ship's note, and he pointed at my wound. I nodded. "I'll be fine." The little fucker that runs all the juices in my body decided that this particular moment was the time to throw the pain switch and I made that pain face. Ship raised his eyebrows and began the stink-eye, but I interrupted him, "How do we test it? My theory I mean?"

He passed me another note. He must have anticipated my question and written this new one as I read the old one. I passed the first note to Remo and took the fresh one. *We'll have to appropriate an infected and see if it wants to attack your friend.*

"You're fuk'n crazy. I'm in." Pain lanced through my side. I hissed a little and Donna was suddenly there next to me with a cup of water.

"Who said you could get up?"

"I did." I gave her the look that told her I was not to be fucked with, so in typical female fashion, she emasculated me in front of everyone.

She pointed at me, "Lie your skinny ass right the fuck back down! You were just shot, idiot, and I don't need you screwing up all I've done to keep you alive. Also," she looked around the room, "someone get him a sandwich! Didn't they feed you in… wherever it was they spirited you off to?" She shook her head. "Assholes." She gently helped me back down and I looked around at the faces of all the douches that had me encircled. Bastards were all smiling that smug smile that says I'm whipped. I can't wait until this little five-foot-nothing waif of a girl goes off on them. She did that storm away thing, and I felt dumb.

"Can't eat lying down," I said to her back and under my breath as she began yanking open stainless steel cabinets.

"Guess we know who wears the penis in this group." Kinga said, complete with smug smile. Douche. "We'll go get your specimen, C'mon, Remo."

Zero shook his head, "I'll do it. I'm dead anyway, so what's the difference?"

Ship shook his head and scribbled something, passing it to Zero. "Huh. I didn't think of that." I held my hand out for the note and Zero passed it to me. *Not necessarily. Statistically, there have to be immunities. Wait until you start getting sick prior to throwing your life away.*

"Still," continued Zero, "how many people do you know of that have been bitten and lived?" Half the room looked at me as Zero continued, "I should be the one who goes."

Kinga shouldered his pack. "The three of us will go." Remo nodded in the affirmative.

"I'm coming too," Alvarez volunteered.

I looked at him like he had three heads. It was tricky because I was on my back and looking up, but I pulled that shit off. "The fuck you are. You're staying here to protect my girl, me, and the Sasquatch." He started to protest but I cut him off, "And I'm not going back to *Atlantis* to tell Kat you got dead because your dumb ass volunteered to go on a dangerous mission after volunteering for a suicide mission." He opened his mouth to say something and I could tell we weren't done. "*AND*, if you say one more word about it, I will tell Kat about this conversation even if you make it back."

He shut his trap fast. Next to Donna, Kat was the one you didn't want to piss off.

The plan was simple: The three military types would go back to that spot where the ladder descended into hell. They would get their collective cowboy on and try to rope one of the infected, dragging it up to them. Easy peasy.

Except *what*? Rope one and pull it up? Were they fucking nuts? I voiced my opinions and was summarily (and quite unkindly) told to shut the F up.

They left and came back fifteen minutes later. All three of them. The only thing missing was the infected, so naturally, we inquired about it, or the lack of it.

Zero shrugged. "They're gone."

"Gone?"

"What, are you a parrot? Yeah, they split and are now in parts unknown." Lynch, the government dick that had kidnapped me, had called me a parrot once. I hadn't liked it then either. "We banged on the ladder and they didn't come. We collectively decided that descending that particular ladder was not mission critical." He must have caught my blank stare. "In other words: fuck that."

"No. Not fuck that." Jarek had finally weighed in. We hadn't told him what was happening because we didn't want to ask him to wade through countless ranks of undead with a fire axe until we knew there was no other way. He'd figured out the plan though. "I will go and see what happens."

Zero put his hand on Jarek's shoulder. "We aren't going to ask you to do this." Except yes we were and everybody knew it.

Jarek smiled. He had to be shitting himself from the fear, but all I could detect was the utter awesome dripping off of this man. "I don't believe you. It is the safest way for everyone to live anyway. I will go and kill them all, then open this door when it is clear." He pointed to the door with the hordes of infected on the other side.

"Jerk Douche!" Everybody looked at me as I sat up again. Donna didn't say anything about my position shift. I threw my feet over the side of the table I had been stretched out on and stuck my paw out to Jarek. "Good luck."

He smiled and shook it. We heard the helicopter on the second hand pump.

MY FAULT

The sounds of the helicopter receded after a couple of minutes. We had been staring at each other in silence, and I jumped a little when someone piped up. It hurt my boo-boo, and I inadvertently let that shit be known.

"We need to contact them to tell them where we are!" cried some husky guy whom I hadn't met yet. He had longish hair, and looked more like a passenger than a ship worker, which didn't make sense.

"Negative," protested Remo immediately. "We don't know anything about them. They could be hostiles."

The heavy dude looked like he was about to cry. "But they have to be better than the alternative!" He pointed at the door being banged on.

"No, they don't." Four of us disagreed at once. Ship was nodding fiercely in agreement with us. "People can be much worse than the undead.

Now the pudgy bastard did start to whine. "But what if they're here to rescue us?"

"They probably are," Kinga told him, trying for a reassuring tone, "but shouldn't we be prudent and check first?"

"This changes nothing," Jarek offered, axe in hand. "We still need to... *oh flookta*... to get away from these things. I will follow the plan and bang on the door when I am done."

I'm sure I'm spelling *oh flookta* wrong, but that's how it sounded. Must mean escape or something like that. I was really starting to like this guy, even though he had gotten me shot. I sort of felt bad that he was about to go off on a zombie killing spree all alone.

"Jarek, this changes *everything*," Zero said. "Now there could be hostiles on board along with the infected. You might be invisible to the infected, but not the guys with guns."

And so began the argument. Banter back and forth about what to do next, how to do it, and who was going to do it. It took a solid two minutes of bickering before I noticed Jarek at the back door. His hand was on the knob (yeah, this was the door we had come through before) and he looked back at me. We exchanged a nod and he slipped out. He hadn't made a sound. I thought nobody had seen, but Remo and Kinga were both looking at me as I switched my glance back to the group. They had seen him go too, as had Alvarez and Ship. I couldn't figure out why Zero didn't catch it until I looked at him.

He was infected. No two ways about it. The corpuscles in his right eye had already begun to rupture, bleeding into the white. I remember it all too well, as I had not only seen it before but lived through it. It didn't hurt at all, and the doctors at Baldy Mountain had told me it was because of a rapid increase in blood pressure in the eyes or some shit like that.

Remo flipped the safety off of his MP5 and Kinga backed up almost imperceptibly. Zero caught that and stopped talking. "What?" he demanded.

Nobody said anything. "What?" he asked again, and Ship passed him a note in dead silence. "Fuck," was all Zero said, dropping the note. "Jarek, take my weapons and…" He looked around for his friend.

I sighed. "He slipped out a minute or two ago."

"Assholes!" He ran to the door, opened it, and disappeared through.

"How long does he have?" Alvarez asked. Everybody was looking at me. Even Hefty Smurf, (the fat dude). Donna had shown up with a Hot Pocket. Pepperoni. Fucking ambrosia. I burned my tongue and didn't give a shit, as I rolled my eyes and shook my head in answer to Alvarez's question.

"Not long," I reckoned through the meat, cheese, and pastry. "A day at the very most." Like I'm an expert. I shook my head again.

"Alright!" Kinga said and pounded his fist on the table. "Let's figure this out. Assuming those two make it to this door." He, like everyone else in the room had done at some point, nodded toward the door with the infected on the other side. "We need to be ready. If there is a hostile fire team aboard this vessel, we should prepare now. They have to come down the stairwell (he had said ladder, but that's what marines say) either way, and it's full of infected. The only other way is to go to the stairwell near the stern, and that's suicide with the deck so crawling with the dead." Remo pulled out his black Sharpie, looked around the room, and began drawing on the table as Kinga continued, "We have to assume they will come through this door, especially if Zero and Jarek clear the corridor." He paused thinking, and looking at Remo's drawing.

A skinny guy, again one of the few I hadn't yet been introduced to, raised his hand. He actually raised his hand. "What?" Kinga demanded.

"There are two other ways down here. They could rappel over the side and use breaching charges to blow the crew door, or they could come through the hold doors. Controls for both are in the wheelhouse, and the crew door, which is twenty feet below the starboard rail, has controls on the interior, but you need a key card. They would still have to get by all those dead folks."

"And who are you?"

"I'm a crewman. I work… worked as Q-MED."

"A medic?" I asked. Kinga rolled his eyes. Prick.

The guy smiled. "No, an unlicensed engineer. Shit rolls downhill, and I'm pretty close to the bottom. Ex-Navy." He stuck his hand out to Remo, who shook it, and then he made the rounds. Firm grip on this guy.

Kinga nodded, "Good intel. They can still only come from these two sets of doors. I would say let's confront them, but this is where the food is, and if we get trapped, I want it to be here."

"We're already trapped," I said, looking at Remo.

"Yeah, but we have food, and these." Kinga tapped his MP5. "The thing I worry about is gas. We only have the three masks."

The conversation moved forward with the military guys pointing here and there and telling people where to go or not to go. They moved some of the shit in the galley around such that they created a killing field while at the same time setting up defenses. It was short work because most of the stuff was bolted down. In just a few short minutes, we heard gunfire outside in the hall, and the radios blared to life, *Shitheads, this is Nobody, come in, Shitheads!* It was Zero. We hadn't set up call signs. We could hear the gunfire over his radio. He didn't wait for a reply, *Jarek is down! I'm hit! A dozen hostiles at least! Falling ba—* Lost that part in auto gunfire, *ETA three minutes!*

"Nobody, Shitheads," Kinga replied, "we read you and backup is on the way." Remo and Kinga began to get ready to leave.

Negative! Nobody will— BOOM! We felt the explosion, it rocked the bulkheads.

"Grenade," Alvarez, Remo, and Kinga all said at the same time.

"You three," Kinga pointed at Alvarez, Ship, and me, "secure this room. Don't open any doors until you hear code word Apple. Anybody tries to get through the door, kill them."

"You can't go!" yelled the whiny guy. "We need you here! We don't have guns!"

Remo nodded at me. "They do."

"We aren't leaving him out there to be shot or ripped apart by those things," added Kinga. "Just get behind the tables and you'll be fine." The guy turned around and literally sprinted headlong into a table. It must have hurt, but to his credit, he just limped around it and went prone in the back.

The gunfire increased, and we heard a couple of rounds hit the hatch. I moved toward the hatch in an attempt to secure it better, but Donna's tiny frame stepped in front of me. Her eyebrows were raised and she looked pissed. I held up my hand in mock supplication, "I need to secure the doors."

"You need to secure your ass to that table or you're going to die."

"If I don't man up, we all die." I put my hands on her shoulders and then did something she totally didn't expect. I leaned down and kissed her on the forehead. Another bullet pinged off the metal bulkhead, and I gently pushed her aside. A shadow fell over me from the rear, and Donna looked up. And up and up. I smiled and turned around, looking up myself. "What is it, big fella?"

He kept the note in the book this time. Just like we used to do. *Good luck getting out of my sight again.* Holy shit. My eyes went all hot. I almost cried. And FU if you think I'm girly. *You* try living through the shit I have and see if you don't get misty when confronted with true friendship. Come to think of it, if you're reading this, you probably have spent some time in a hurt locker. Then you can empathize right? Anyway, I looked back at Ship and he was *not* giving me the stinkeye. I nodded toward the door, and told him my intentions. He nodded and moved off to do stuff.

"What do we do?" Donna asked.

"We fuk'n kill them all. But first, we shore up this door." I heard the sound of metal on metal, and turned to see Ship and Alvarez ripping a door off of one of the walk-in refrigerators. Okay, so they unscrewed the top half and then tore it off, but I'm sure Ship could have shredded through the hull with his teeth if he had wanted. We monkeyed the door so that it blocked the hatch into corridor, then Alvarez screwed it into the wooden floor using the hinges. The top portion was caught on one of the hatch pins, and that shit wasn't moving without serious strength. Or explosives. Shit, I hope they didn't bring any explosives.

What did they want anyway? Why were they here? They had purposely landed on this ridiculous boat, literally covered in plague, but for what? The only thing I could think of was that they wanted the hard drives or the key... Oh shit. I distinctly remember thinking that: *oh shit* at that particular moment. If they were here for the key, then they must have come from *Atlantis*, and that could only mean one thing: we're fucked. All this passed through the microcosm that is my mind quite quickly, and then came the anger. These fuckers had no right. They must have killed people I care about. They had, at the very least, shot Jarek and blown up Zero. They were going to die.

I moved back to the table I had been on and began to check my magazines. Alvarez did the same, and Ship was just finishing up. Two full mags of 9mm with eight rounds in a third magazine. Thirty rounds for my Sig, and a SOG SEAL Pup. My knife was going between somebody's ribs today, and that fucker was not going to be a zombie. That's how mad I was.

Except I was still wicked woozy. I put my hand on the table to steady myself and Ship noticed. That was the least of my worries as Donna was also right there. "You need to—" I cut her off by passing her my handgun.

"Remove the suppressor," I told her. "I think our secret is out."

She took it, immediately checking the magazine. This girl is perfect. Her concern for me was evident. "You should lie down."

I leered at her. "I should be on a beach with you, sipping an umbrella drink. I have the perfect bikini in mind..."

She folded her arms. "You don't have the tits for a bikini." See? Perfect.

Ship and Alvarez both raised their collective eyebrows, looked at each other, and moved away, finding something terribly important to do elsewhere.

I laughed out loud, and it fucking hurt like hell. Zombie apocalypse hero tip number sixteen: Don't laugh when shot unless you need to look cool.

The gunfire outside ceased abruptly. We all looked at each other, and I put my hand to my head, listening intently to the radio I had just shoved in my ear hole. Nothing. Ten minutes later, there was a knock at the back door. "Apple," came over the radio.

Ship, Alvarez, Donna, and I all hunkered down behind some tables and chairs. We aimed our weapons at the sound and covered the door. "Hey, Q-MED. Wanna open the door?"

Without a word, the skinny guy ran over to the door. He glanced back at us and I could tell he was nervous, but he pushed the door open after I nodded at him. Remo and Kinga were there, and they stepped through. "Close it," Remo said. They were both looking at me as they made their way to the table.

My heart was beating a little fast. "Zero and Jarek?"

Kinga shook his head in the negative. "Zero's gone. Jarek is alive, but they have him."

Alvarez sighed in relief. "He's alive at least."

Kinga shook his head again. "He's bitten. Apparently, the fast ones do give a shit about him. One got him on the shoulder."

"Fuck!" I yelled and smashed the table with my fist. It sent tendrils of agony through my side, but I didn't care I was so mad. Pretty sure I had helped kill this guy. "What do these asshats want?"

Remo pulled a laminated piece of paper from his vest and slid it across the table toward me. "You."

WAR AND PEAS

"Not the best picture of you," Donna said. I had to agree. If you've read my other journals, you would know that the dude who grabbed me last year and carted me off to a secret underground facility in Montana had a shitload of these wanted posters made up. He had them tossed out of aircraft all over the place so people would turn me in if they found me. There's a reward. An actual price on my head.

Everybody in the room except for the dude hiding behind the table was staring at me. Even Table-guy was peeking his head out, but he was so scared he didn't know where to look.

"How did they find me?"

Kinga, still staring answered slowly. "They wouldn't say. They did say we have ten minutes to give you up or they're coming for you. They killed Zero, and they believe that killing all of us to get you is acceptable."

"They couldn't have gotten past the *Stockdale* at *Atlantis* though," I breathed. "That boat is designed to kill everything." The *Stockdale* is an Arleigh Burke-class destroyer, with enough armament to take on pretty much anything. It was currently sitting next to our home, *Atlantis*.

"No, I don't see how they could have done that either," agreed Remo. "But that doesn't change the fact that we need to defend ourselves. We can worry about *Atlantis* and the *Stockdale* when we get off this tub."

"You've seen them," I asked, "how do they look? Tough?"

Remo began checking his magazines. "They did not come to play Monopoly." It *would* be that the hilarity drips off of him when we were all about to get dead. "They're fully outfitted." That spoke volumes to me.

"Can we take them?"

Kinga snorted. "Of course. I don't accept that I'm going to die here. Death means I failed and I don't fail. You," he pointed at the skinny engineer guy, "what's your name and what's the best way to the wheelhouse other than up the stairwell?"

"Name's Todd. There isn't a way up to the wheelhouse other than the exterior stairs or the stairs through there. Well… I mean we could go through the hold, up and out through the crew service hatch, and across the deck."

Ship already had a note in his book by the time Todd had finished speaking. The big guy was gracious enough to spin the book around so that we could all see: *NO!*

It was Alvarez's turn to snort. "We would have to face a hundred infected down there, then four hundred more on the deck. Been there, done that. No effing way."

The husky fella, formerly hidden behind the table, and obviously some type of tubby ninja, was suddenly standing next to me, "Leave? You want to leave here?"

Kinga shook his head. "No. I don't want to, but this place is…"

"But you said before that this was the best place to make a stand! There's food!"

"That was before we saw these guys," Remo told him patiently. "They'll get in here eventually."

The dude did something then that was totally unexpected. This is the part of the story where you're thinking that he is some type of antagonist, and says that we should give me to the bad guys, or worse, grabs a gun and threatens us. Nope. "Okay. I'm in," was all he said, but there was plenty of nervous fidgeting and hand wringing.

"We're saved," Kinga said and everybody chuckled. Fat guy too.

Bullets pinged off the hatch and several of us lowered ourselves instinctively. New spears of pain reached into my side when I ducked. The bad guys were killing the infected in the corridor between us and them. Whether they knew we were in the galley was irrelevant. This hatch would bring them right to us.

"We have to go now." Remo looked at all of us intently. "There are more of them than us. They're heavy hitters. They've secured the stairwell and the wheelhouse. We're running low on ammo, and only have three gas masks. They'll come in here and kill us all. They don't know how many fighters we have, or our status. Plus, we have explosives. We can leave some nasty surprises for them along the way."

Kinga nodded. "We exfil back the way we came and catch them as they're going through the corridor crowded with infected."

It was Remo's turn to nod. "Agreed."

"Yeah," I said to sound cool, "good idea."

Both MARSOC looked at me and I felt small.

We grabbed all our shit and moved out into the slaughterhouse that Jarek had created. I was going to shoot somebody for the loss of Jarek. This shit was happening. We made it to the first hatch, moved through it, and kept going. Alvarez closed it behind us.

The second hatch was where Zero had gotten infected. It was also where the ladder to the hold was. I was scared just going in there. When Kinga began to open the third hatch, we were fired upon.

"Fall back!" he screamed, slamming the door closed. "Fuck! Not going this way, there's three at least." Two more rounds mushroomed on the other side of the steel to emphasize his point. A muffled explosion, quite different from the sound of the grenades, sounded from where we had just been.

Alvarez shook his head. "Surrounded."

Remo strode casually over to the ladder and peered down. He shone his light down the hole, shrugged, and started down. Kinga looked at us. "They're on the way, clearing the last corridor. Let's go." He began climbing down as well.

The rest of us were standing at the top of the ladder that descended into the hold, staring down. My side still hurt, but the adrenaline pumping into my body from the knowledge of what we were about to do was winning the battle over substance P.

"Nobody say anything once we're down there," Alvarez told us. "If you talk, we all die." He pointed at the entrance, and turned around to cover us. I moved to the ladder and Ship put his hand on my shoulder. I looked at him and he nodded in the negative. "Sorry, pal, its infected or bullets. Infected win." I started my climb, and soon the eight of us were all at the bottom of the ladder shitting ourselves. Remo moved forward slowly, his NVGs on. He looked perfectly calm. Not everybody had night vision, and although the darkness wasn't absolute, it couldn't have been easy to see. I wouldn't know those troubles, as my NVGs were most certainly on. With them, I could see the remains of something that had been wearing a once white lab coat. It clicked its teeth together at our passing. It couldn't make any other sound as it had no throat at all. It was mostly bones with some gooey shit puddled around it, and it would never move again. It was gross. The signs of the dead were everywhere. Stains of brown, black, and red. Smears on the wall. A bloody handprint. A boot. The typical shit that you would find when the plans of morons trying to study the undead go awry. I had seen it before. Twice.

We were in a wider corridor than above us, with doors and a large open area in front. Our first mobile deceased came out of the darkness from the right, and Remo threw his fist up, then smoked it with his knife. The heavy dude, who's name I never did get, (I'm sure you can see where this is going) didn't stop when the jarhead had thrown up his fist. He just kept walking, staring right at Remo's back. Had this dumbass never seen one single war or cop movie? Ever? Is there a person in the world who doesn't know what it means when the hero military guy in front throws his fist up? I mean, it was dark, but he must have seen the fist. Water under the bridge, because as Remo was removing his giant blade from creature number one's eye, creature number two, which had ninja talents of his own, latched on to Tubby's arm and pulled in for a snack. Ship brought his machete, which looks like a machete, only bigger, down across the dead guy's forearms, severing both of them. The thing stumbled back and moaned at the same time the fat guy screamed like a skinny girl. Dozens of other moans and rasps echoed through the area, and shit got real.

"MOVE!" Kinga whispered very loudly, knowing the jig was up. We all got together in a circle, and began to move forward. A suppressed round came from behind me, then two more. Alvarez was firing into an open door. Remo fired his pistol, also suppressed, forward and I saw a body collapse. I was terrified, but I could see. I remember thinking how scared my half-blind girlfriend and best pal must be when I was grabbed from the side. I brought my arm around fast, whipping the thing laterally, but it didn't let go. Ship's size twenty boot lashed out and kicked the thing in the chest. I saw its ribs go, and all kinds of nasty shit coated my gigantic buddy's foot before he could pull it back. Innards rained down in a foul thick splash. The thing still hadn't let go of me, but I was able to move such that Kinga shot it in the dome and I threw it to the floor. Another one materialized out of the gloom, a young boy, and I shot it in the face. Two more appeared, reaching, and I began to doubt that coming down here was the best course of action.

Everybody except for Todd and Hefty Smurf was firing their weapons, and Todd had come up with a broken broom handle, which he thrust into the eye of a skinny thing in a torn dress. I dared a glance to my left, which was forward of our position, and it was one of those times where I had been blissfully ignorant the second before. A crap-ton of the things were less than thirty feet away, and this didn't account for the other three directions. I smoked the two coming from our right, and I heard Donna yell, "I'm out!" Followed by Alvarez yelling, "Loading!"

We would never make the ladder before these things tore us to pieces, so we had to pick another direction. Kinga chose and he moved forward firing into the crowd. We all focused our fire in that direction, and within seconds, the herd had been thinned enough to get through. I knew what Kinga was thinking, and I had seen this action before, but it hadn't worked out for everybody. We surged headlong into the crowd, shooting, hacking, and stabbing. Part of our problem was we didn't know where we were going, and half our gang couldn't see. One of the things put its hands on my girl, and Ship decapitated it. He took out another with a spectacular backswing that sliced the thing's melon in two from the nose up. It reminded me of a stupid video game I used to play on my buddy's illegal phone in prison, until the top of the creature's dome slid off and fell to the floor.

The fat dude was grappling with an infected behind me when he was tackled by a screamer. Alvarez shot it, but hit it in the shoulder. Remo shot both it and the dead one, the now hysterical guy crying and trying to stand, but slipping in a puddle of viscera. He fell back on his ass in the infected fluids, and was swarmed by four of the things before we could help. His throat was gone before we could fire into them. It looked like we were all going to go out like that. Ship swung his machete, Donna stabbed with her knife, and Todd used his broom like a spear. I shot a mailman, an older woman, a younger guy, missed a guy in scrubs, shot him, and the slide on my SIG stayed back. I fumbled for my last magazine, hitting myself in the boo-boo and yelping. Ship must have thought they had me, because he effortlessly lifted me off of my feet with one hand and pulled me to him. That hurt worse than when I had hit myself. I heard a weapon clatter to the ground, turned to see Remo had dropped his pistol and had that little pump shotgun of his aimed into the crowd. The bass boom of that thing echoed throughout the hold, and I saw two infected drop as he jacked another round. I slammed my last pistol mag home, and fired into the face of something that had gotten close.

Then I grabbed Donna's hand and we all ran, Alvarez selecting targets and firing his M4. That shit was loud too. We made it through the gap, and into the hold proper. We had gone maybe forty feet. "Loading!" I heard Alvarez yell again at the same time I heard several M4s firing. What? What did I just hear?

Kinga yelped and fell forward on one knee, his hand on the floor. I heard a bullet whizz past me, and I spun around. Four dickheads in black camo were back by the ladder shooting at us. I caught one of their tactical lights with my NVGs, and was momentarily blinded. The pricks saved us though, as half of what was left of the crowd behind us made for them. Ship charged me with his machete, swung, and cleaved the thing that was about to bite me from the top of its head to the bottom of its trachea.

There wasn't a lot of time to take in my surroundings, but I could see that the large, open area we were in contained crates of stuff tied down with ratcheting straps and ropes. There were infected weaving their way in between the boxes toward the sound of dinner.

Remo helped Kinga up, and they looked into the dead faces of three infected. I could see that Remo had three magazines in his MOLLE pack, but there was no time to reload. He fired point blank with his little 410 shotgun, and the melon of the dead soldier in front of him ceased to exist. Kinga lashed out with his right boot, and Remo blasted a second dead thing. The third grabbed Kinga and leaned in for a bite. Todd was there with his broomstick, and he caught the creature in the throat. It gave Kinga the one second he needed to back up, bring his MP5 to bear, and blast the thing in the forehead with a suppressed round.

Ship boosted Donna up onto a medium-sized crate, turned to kick the festering crewman that was reaching for him, then the big guy grabbed me. He lifted me up next to Donna, and ran to help Alvarez, who was struggling with something in filthy BDUs. A quick survey of our situation put me in a bad place. There were dozens of undead coming from every direction, and suddenly, I didn't know what to do. For some reason, all I could think of was Lynch. Everything else fled my mind.

The sting of a slap brought me out of my daydreams. "Do something!" Donna screamed and pointed. One of the things was attempting to climb up the cargo net surrounding the crate we were on. I pulled my SOG and thrust it into the eye of the climber. Half a dozen others were reaching for us, their forearms scraping rotting skin onto the edge of the crate. We both had empty pistols, but I had one mag in my MP5, and one mag with fourteen rounds. I looked over at Ship and the three military guys. Alvarez had copied the industrious infected and climbed some cargo netting hanging from the side of a large crate. There were fifteen or so undead just out of arms reach of him. Kinga and ship were inside a Dodge Ram 1500 that was strapped to a giant metal pallet with big steel hooks. Remo and Todd were in the back of the truck. Todd was poking at anything that tried to get too close. Remo had taken up a firing position over the top of the truck cab, and was firing at the guys behind us. They were fighting their own battle, but more had come down the ladder.

We were well and truly fucked. There were too many infected. They were everywhere and still coming. I suddenly got very angry. We could have pulled this shit off if these douche-canoes hadn't shown up and pissed in the punchbowl. I sighted on one that was coming down the ladder and shot him in the back. Hands-down the best shot I had made to date. He fell about four feet, but the fucker got up almost immediately. Body armor. I put a different guy in my sight picture, aiming for his dome, but Donna shrieked and fell off the back of the crate. I looked at her, on her side on the deck. She was moving. I jumped down, helping her up. There were no undead on this side of the crate, but the first one showed its nasty face while I was helping my girl up by her armpits. I got her up and my suppressed 9mm round entered through the thing's left eye. Donna had spun around and was climbing another cargo net, this one quite high. I put my hands on her ass and pushed, hearing sporadic gunfire, screams, and the sounds of the infected. Movement behind me made me spin to face a completely mauled specimen. Half its face was missing, as was the left arm and left side of its throat. The right side of its face belonged to Captain Bob, and that was my undoing.

I blinked, not understanding why Bob would have left the wheelhouse so many weeks or months before. He must have run out of food. The plan was that he was to run this fucking ship of death aground on Mexico's beautiful white-sand beaches, but that had obviously never happened. I was unable to find out what transpired or why nobody from *Atlantis* went to rescue him because, as previously stated, I had been captured and taken to Montana pretty much the moment I had returned from this metal tomb the last time.

The Bob-thing already had one hand and one nub on me before I realized that all those thoughts you just read in the last paragraph had taken the requisite time necessary for Bob to make such a move. I lifted my MP5, and the suppressor hit Bob in the balls, keeping the business end of the weapon safely away from his noggin. Then he did what any self-respecting undead monster would have done during this state of affairs: he bit me.

Now, as you are aware, I had been bitten before. A dead man had been under a truck, I hadn't seen him, and he had chomped down on my calf. It left a semi-circle bite mark through my jeans, and it had broken the skin, undoubtedly infecting me. Before I could hide away and try to die in peace, a duo of heavy éclair-eaters had set upon me on the road, and one of them had taken a scrap of skin off of my collarbone. I had survived both bites. I had gotten tagged again in Tennessee, when one of the things had taken a nibble out of my shoulder. Just a nip, but death to everyone else but me.

Captain Bob, while probably enjoying several hundred *rum* nips over the course of his seafaring career, had simply ceased believing in nipping of any sort during his undeath. I threw my left forearm up to catch him under the chin and force his head back, but to my everlasting shame, I missed. I put my damn arm right in his friggin mouth. He wasted no time in removing a substantial chunk from the underside of my arm. I screamed a high-pitched squeal that was exceptionally undignified when Bob pulled his head back, ripping a big piece of me with it. I watched in horror as he chewed briefly before swallowing.

Sometimes when there's a large wound, the blood doesn't come right away. Sometimes it takes a moment for the veins and arteries and capillaries to realize there has been a WTF moment. Then they catch up and blood floods the area, the pumps returning to normal. This was not one of those times. When the good captain had yanked his head away, my red stuff shot out of me at 867 miles per hour, coating his dead face in thick crimson.

And we had been pals.

I continued to yell, my arm continued to leak, and Bob continued to hold on to me. We grappled for what seemed like three weeks, but in reality was only three seconds. I used one of the techniques I had been taught by Remo, punching my uninjured right arm up under poor Bob's remaining elbow and dropping my left foot back. There was an audible snap as my former friend's arm broke. He didn't consider this an issue, keeping me with his right hand. I brought my right arm up, over, and down, landing my good arm over his newly broken one, and he (grudgingly, if that were possible for these things) released me as I followed through, carrying his face forward and down. I brought my knee up into his face and he went ass-over-teakettle. Before he could do much more, I shot him and the one behind him with my MP5 in their decaying faces. Bye Bob.

"There's more coming!" Donna yelled pointing. She had made it on top of a large box, and was bleeding from her right shoulder. Another of the things came around the corner, and I hastily shot it, then began my climb. I pulled myself up with my right arm, but my left arm weighed an extra twenty pounds. You would think, what with me just losing a few ounces of arm, and a few more of blood, said appendage would be lighter, but no. Lefty didn't want to function properly, and when I finally did get my hand to grip the net, I caught my wound against it and yelled. This was a manly yell, and nothing like the scream that I let loose when the Bob-zombie started to eat me. My lady helped me, and soon we were several feet above the reaching hands, and safely behind a crate of who knows what, that was protecting us from gunfire. With my current luck, said crate was probably housing nitroglycerin.

As previously mentioned, the guys in black camo were getting their own dose of infected, at least two of which were Runners. There were more of the bad guys now though. Several reinforcements had dropped down the ladder. I looked right and saw Remo and Todd doing their best to keep a shrinking number of infected from gaining access to the back of the Dodge. The rear window exploded outward, and Kinga climbed into the back, followed by Ship. I have no idea how he had fit through that window, but he had. Kinga was favoring his right side as he leaned over the cab to fire back at the men in black. Todd was doing quite well with his broomstick, while Ship was cleaving anything that got close with his machete and ventilating craniums with his Glock.

Donna pulled a tube from her pack and squeezed the entire contents into my wound. I gritted my teeth, hissing when she put it in me before I realized the goo didn't hurt at all. A white gauze pad followed by a bandage was next and she began to wrap my arm. It hurt. It hurt worse than my side right now. "I was quite specific about asking you not to get hurt."

"You said shot. I didn't get shot." My eyes went wide, and I brought my hands up to her shoulder. The bandage flew from her hand when I bumped her, and unraveled as it plummeted toward the deck. "Fuckin' idiot!" she yelled in tears. I didn't care as I tore her shirt and looked at what was bleeding. I sighed that wonderful sigh of relief when I finally understood it was only a bullet graze. Funny how getting shot is way better than getting a scratch from an infected. She began pulling up the bandage and I realized that the shooting had stopped. How many rounds had I fired?

There were still meandering dead, but the ones at the truck were down, and the ones at the bad guys were down. As no bullets were flying, I can only assume a ceasefire had been called on both sides.

"Everybody okay?" I heard over the radio.

"Yeah, Remo, we made it. How's Kinga?"

"He took one in the shoulder. He needs the doc."

"Busy!" she yelled as she continued to wrap my arm.

"We heard you yelling," he said. "What happened?"

"Took one on the arm. It isn't bad."

Donna looked at me, then yanked my mic to her face. "It's bad! His basilic vein may been severed. I've bandaged it, but he needs to get home or there could be permanent damage. I need to get him on a table for both injuries, but I think this is worse than the bullet wound."

I pulled the mic back. "What's going on with the douches in black?"

"Seven of the nine have gone back up the ladder, but they lost one. The last one is climbing back up now. I think the dead made them think twice. They'll be back shortly."

I peeked around the corner of my box and saw three dead looking up at me. I shot them one at a time, my arm throbbing. "Remo, is it clear from us to you?"

"Looks to be. You stay there, I'll come get you."

I could hear that growling that some of them do, and I told Remo as much. "I'll be on my toes." I could see him coming, and I tried to cover him, but one of the fuckers surprised us both and latched on to him from the left side. Didn't matter much. This is Remo we're talking about, and he dispatched it quickly. The growler showed up, and I shot it. Easy-peasy. When Remo arrived, he put his back to us to cover us, and Donna and I climbed down.

We threaded our way through the various crates and containers, making it to the truck in short order. Kinga was covering the ladder down the corridor, sixty feet or so away. Remo traded with him, and Donna got to work on the wounded MARSOC's shoulder. His expletives when she dumped that clotting powder on him made me smile. "I would have ducked," I said.

Looking at my bandage, he said, "Should have ducked better, Round-Eye," and smiled back.

"This?" I asked holding up my wounded arm. "I didn't get shot. Captain Bob bit me."

Todd backed up so fast he would have fallen out of the back of the truck if Ship hadn't grabbed him.

"You saw him?" asked Alvarez. He had just climbed down from his perch and was now standing with us next to the truck.

"Yeah. Up close." I held my arm up again. "I took care of him." He nodded.

Remo smoked a straggler pus-bag with his knife near the back of the truck. "Stay frosty," was all he told us.

"Hello down there?" someone yelled down the ladder. "Anybody home? I would like to come down and speak with you about our current situations if that's okay? I'm armed, because I would be nuts not to me, but I will keep my weapon holstered."

We conferred for a moment. Kinga was dead-set against it, citing that the bad guys would know our numbers, but the rest of us wanted to talk with someone. "Come on down," Alvarez yelled, "but just you."

A dude in black BDU-type pants and a black T-shirt slid down the ladder like it was a fire pole. He turned, looked at us, and raised his hands. He did a complete circle with his hands in the air and began walking toward us.

"Well isn't this... behind you." He pointed at Ship. The big guy spun, taking out a shambler with his blade.

"As I was saying," the new guy continued, "isn't this nice. Everybody in one place." He looked around. "You're not getting out of here other than back the way we came," he nodded his head toward the ladder, "so I think we should talk." The guy was wiry. All muscle, but not muscle-bound. He moved with a catlike grace, sure of every step. The arrogance with which he spoke, his athletic build, and the way I just knew he knew about everything in this room with one glance, expressed to me exactly who he was.

"May I put my hands down?"

"No," Kinga, Remo, and Alvarez all said at the same time.

"Wow, tough room. Anyway, let me introduce myself, and tell you exactly what's about to happen. My name is—"

"Lynch," I finished for him, "his name is Lynch."

THE HULK FEELS NO FEAR

No, Dear Reader, it wasn't the same guy who took me away months ago. My Lynch is either stumbling around looking for someone to eat, or more likely, was torn to literal pieces and would never rise. I could just tell that the guy in front of me and the guy that kidnapped me were of the same ilk though. I met a guy named Dallas maybe ten weeks ago who told me he had also met a spook named Lynch who was equally as douchey as my Lynch. I successfully negotiated kindergarten, and can put two and two together. This shit just added up.

"How astute," the guy said with a giant smile as he stood between several recently destroyed infected. "But no. I do know a few Lynches, dicks mostly. The kind of dick who would offer a reward for some guy, but offer up no reason as to why. The kind of dick who has a big mouth, and gets the rest of us dicks sent out on retrieval missions. I will say that if you've met someone named Lynch who was capable, that man takes orders from the same powers-that-be who provide mine. My name is irrelevant, but what is wicked relevant is that no matter what happens, I will not allow this man" (he still had his hands up, but he nodded toward me) "to leave this ship except in my custody."

Wicked relevant? "Shoot him," I said. "Just fuk'n shoot him now."

He raised his left eyebrow, but didn't tense in the least. "White flags were shown, *bruh*. That would be all kinds of wrong. Like, breach of etiquette wrong. If you think for one second—"

The guy's head snapped back at the same time I heard a report from behind me. I jumped as I hadn't been expecting it. Ship's Glock was still raised. The big guy had wasted this asshole in the semi-darkness with a quick draw. Evil government dicknose had never even lowered his hands. Everybody was looking at Ship now, even the zombie who was casually strolling in from the left. Ship holstered his weapon, drawing his machete, but Remo, who was wearing an uncharacteristic grin, got to the thing first and drove his knife into its melon. When the zombie stabbing was complete, Ship's notebook was turned around so I could see it. *It is unlikely he would have kept whatever promise he was about to make. I thought it prudent to be the aggressor in this situation. They will only take you again if I'm dead.*

"If that says that we needed to kill this fuck," Kinga nodded toward the freshly murdered scumbag, "then Ship gets an A+." I was going to say something monumentally witty, when I heard three metallic thumps in front of us. Well, I was turned around looking at Ship, but it was still technically in front of us. Back by the ladder.

Here's a scenario for you: You're on a boat. Boat catches fire. No way to put it out. Shark is in the water. Big one. What do you do? Stay on the boat and you are certainly going to die horribly. Jump in the water and the potential for dying in an equally as horrible fashion exists. Answer to this trivial quandary? You jump in the fuk'n water.

"Grenade!" screamed Alvarez and we all dove for cover. Dove into infection. Except Todd. He was just a second late, but that was enough. Well, Donna didn't hit the deck without help, I dragged her down. The grenades were about forty feet away from us, but there wasn't a lot other than the bodies on the floor to protect us from shrapnel. Unfortunately, those bodies were all mangled, rotten, and most importantly, infected. We were laying in a pile of infection, and pretty much everybody was in some way injured such that there was an open wound.

Ears ringing, NVGs knocked askew, and on my stomach, I felt someone tugging on my right shoulder. I blinked a few times trying to figure shit out and looked at who was yanking on me. When my focus returned, I could see the tugger was a dead kid, and she was chewing on my tactical vest. She didn't like what she was eating, (it was probably a texture thing, you know how some folks just hate coconut?) and she looked me right in the eye as she opened her horrid mouth, leaning toward me. I got my uninjured hand under her chin and pushed. Her grip was like iron, but her body was like mush, and my hand went right through everything, my digits latching onto her spinal column. You know what? You weren't there, so all your *eews* and *yucks* and *grosses* at the thought of what was happening can't compare to what I was going through as it actually transpired. I couldn't really do anything with the kid's spine, so I viciously twisted my hand and the bones and cord snapped like rotten twigs. The little girl thing crumpled instantly.

I heard gunfire through the ringing in my dome, and saw Ship, Alvarez, and Remo shooting at the ladder. They had killed or at least seriously fucked up the two stooges that had come sliding down. I sat up, a colossal task considering the pain, exhaustion, and confusion that were fighting for control of me. Donna helped me the rest of the way up, and I got my NVGs situated. I used my MP5 to give a 9mm facial to a couple of undead stragglers who were closing on us. I was beginning to feel pretty yucky. My insides were roiling, my mouth dry, and my arm was hurting quite badly. My side was a dull pain in comparison.

"Anybody else comes down gets the same fuk'n thing!" Alvarez yelled.

I blinked again and saw Remo on one knee. Kinga was on his face on the deck, and Remo rolled him over on his side. Kinga had thrown himself at Todd when the 'nades came down the hatch, and they had both gone down in a heap but not before my buddy had taken the brunt of some hot jagged steel. Todd climbed out from under Kinga and over a re-killed zombie. He seemed unscathed. Alvarez put down yet another straggler.

Kinga was wheezing this horrible rasp. He sounded like one of the dead. I could see the tip of a hunk of misshapen metal sticking out of his right side about an inch and a half. Blood soaked everything. Kinga's red stuff and that black shit that zombies have in them coated my pal.

"Shit," Donna said, and knelt down to check him out. She stood back up immediately. Kinga coughed a great gout of thick red. "He has a lacerated lung." She said shaking her head, "I... I can't..." My MARSOC buddy nodded as well as anyone can with a hunk of grenade shrapnel in his bronchial tubes. He wiped his mouth with his forearm, looked at me, and whispered one word: *Live*. He was reaching for his sidearm, but couldn't quite get it. I could see the agony all over him. My Sig was empty, and I had no more ammo for it. I lifted my MP5 and he smiled. He smiled at me. *Thank you, Round-Eye* he mouthed. I took aim and shot him between the eyes, then I cried like a baby. Donna was there for me, and Ship put his hand on my shoulder. Remo began removing anything useful from Kinga's body, and yanked his dog tags.

He stood and looked at Todd. "Where's this crew service hatch?"

The engineer pointed. "It's through here," and he began to move forward. Remo put a hand on his shoulder.

"Just tell me, I'll go first."

We began moving, me wiping my eyes. I checked Donna's bullet graze, and no zombie shit had gotten near it, but I would imagine everyone here would have to sit through a two-day quarantine if we made it back to *Atlantis*.

We smoked three more stealthy undead on the way to the hatch, and suddenly, we were in front of it. It was tall and wide and in the side of the bulkhead, not the deck as I had thought. "This leads to the port-side, about fifteen feet below the port rail. There are handholds in the exterior bulkhead," Todd told us looking at the white steel. "I really would rather not go up there." He swallowed and looked at Remo, "It's worse up there than down here."

"Tell that to Kinga." Remo looked the hatch up and down, then at Alvarez. "Cover." Alvarez turned around, the business end of his M4 lazily pointed back the way we had come. A small, hand-held operating thingie with a red button and a green button rested in a holster next to the door. Remo grabbed it and pressed the green button. The hatch immediately began to lower. It was like a mini-gangway where the top moved down.

The sounds of a helicopter were evident with the door open. It was above us, out of sight, but Remo stopped the hatch when it was open about two feet. The pitch of the helo sound changed, and suddenly, the bird rocketed into sight. It was leaving, but I had no idea which direction it was heading. I also realized that I was woozy. I flipped up my NVGs putting my hand on the bulkhead to steady myself. Ship's immense shadow suddenly appeared, blanketing me in just a little bit more darkness, and I looked up at him. His face completely changed when he saw me. He pressed the tactical light button on his M4 and shone it in my face. I was too damn tired and dizzy to lift my hand up in front of my eyes, so I closed them.

"Do you mind, Big Guy? You're already all looming and shit, do you have to blind me too?"

Sasquatch moved his light off slightly, leaned in (way in) to look at me, then did something I had never seen him do before. He took a frightened step back. In all the battles we'd been in, Ship was a rock-solid superhero. He was always the first one into a fight and the last one out, and this includes battling hordes of infected. He wasn't just brave, he was *smart* brave. Never reckless, always prepared, and the size of a pissed off Bruce Banner. This guy simply did not acquiesce to fear. Him, taking that half step back with that look on his face, was one of the scariest things I'd seen since the beginning of all this shit.

Donna furrowed her brow and made to take a look at me, but, in the second scariest moment of today, (and don't forget I had been shot and chewed) Ship put one of his massive mitts out to stop her.

"What the hell are you doing, you big gorilla? He's losing blood and I need to check him!"

Ship nodded no. He didn't move his hand off of her chest, and short of using a chainsaw, or nuclear device, nobody was moving Ship's paw when it was firmly planted. The silent bastard pointed at my quizzical face, and Donna squinted in the semi light. Then it was time for the next bit of fear in a long litany of chilling shit for today. She gasped. She looked in my eyes and gasped.

Now everybody was looking. Did I grow a penis on my forehead? What the fuck was everybody staring at? They were all wide-eyed and stupid looking and I wanted to fucking kill them all! I blinked, the idea of my last thought haunting me. I loved these people, what the hell had I been thinking? I shook my head and my eyes began to water. I wiped them with my knuckles and suddenly it was hard to see. I looked at my hands and they were bloody.

My eyes had started bleeding.

INFECTED. AGAIN

Since this whole Armageddon-apocalypse thingy started, there have been several instances transcribed into these journals where I related that a particular moment in time was the scariest ever. I just wrote it down up above if you remember correctly. Being chased by machine-gun toting rednecks on snowmobiles? Scary. Zombies coming for me in the dark? Scary. Running through a military base overrun by thousands of infected with bullets flying, and tank rounds going off all over the place? Pretty damn scary. Being bitten. Now that was frightening as fuck, because I absolutely *knew* I was dead. Worse, I didn't have the balls back then to swallow a bullet, so my shambling corpse would have been forever trapped in a shitty 1960's Airstream trailer. When I got better after the first couple of bites, I realized that I couldn't contract whatever it is that both kills someone, and then brings them back to life. Maybe *contract* isn't the right word, because I do get sick, but then I get better. I don't know, I'm not a friggin' doctor.

The point is, for a split second, I had wished violence on the people I care about. I don't mean I wanted to shout *I hate you* at them. Everybody's done that and felt bad about it afterward. I had wanted to eviscerate them. Play with their innards and squish their eyes and stuff like that. It popped into my head so fast I couldn't help it. The feeling was gone just as quickly as it had come, but still, that isn't me. I will kill someone to save me and mine. I will most certainly smoke an infected. I will even murder living people as a preventative measure for the protection of the folks I love. They would have to be assholes, but there it is.

This time, I had really wanted to kill my friends, and that scared me on a level I hadn't known I possessed. I had seen this type of wanton behavior before. Each and every Runner must exist in a state like I just had. It's my theory that they don't just *want* to rend, gnash, and kill, but it is a primal *need* of theirs. They have to do it, just like you and I have to eat, or drink, or watch football.

I had fought off this infection thing a few times now, but this was the first bite that was actually damaging. I had to reevaluate my situation. What if because this bite was so deep, it did infect me? Turn me into a Runner, so I could scream that horrible scream and tear into people. Kill my friends and anyone else that got close.

I couldn't live with that.

Todd was all kinds of shocked, "Your... your eyes are bleeding."

"Figured that one out all by myself there, Chief."

"He's bitten!" he shouted. "And now his eyes are bleeding! He's going to turn!"

"If anyone was not going to turn, it would be him," Alvarez told him.

"What? Nobody lives through a bite. I've seen dozens. Before the news stopped broadcasting, they said anyone bitten or scratched had to be isolated." He pointed at me. "He doesn't look isolated! Nobody lives through a bite," he repeated.

"He does," both Alvarez and Remo said at the same time.

I felt my ire rising again. They were talking about me like I wasn't here. I quelled my pent-up pissy, closed my bloody (not British bloody, actually bleeding) eyes, and counted to ten. "Todd," I began, "I've been bitten before. The reason those assholes that were just shooting at us were here is undoubtedly because they are aware that I have survived a bite. I was in a secret government lab for a few months where they experimented on me.

"And you escaped?"

"Kind of. Much like on this stupid boat, the very same assholes decided it was a grand notion to stock a secure facility with shit-tons of dead cannibals for study. In a shocking turn of events, the infected broke out and killed everybody. I made my hasty exit during the ensuing carnage."

Todd looked at me funny. "What?"

"I broke the fuck out."

"Oh."

Remo dropped the crew door all the way down, tested it with his boot, and stepped out onto it. He peeked (do badass military guys peek? No, they assess) around the corner and up, then ducked back in.

"Can't see shit."

Todd looked longingly out the door at the ocean. "I haven't seen the sun in two months."

Ship scribbled for a minute, then passed his notebook to Remo. Remo looked at it, said, "Huh," and passed it to me. *We've most likely killed the leader of the men attacking us, or at least their mission commander. The departing helicopter may be indicative of a failed mission for them. Rather than go up and across the deck, I suggest we double back and use the stairwell they just cleared to obtain access to the wheelhouse.*

"Ever the smarty-pants," I said with a grin, handing the book back to him.

He began writing immediately, and passed the book back to me when he was finished. *That doesn't mean we shouldn't watch you. You've explained to me in great detail of your previous encounters with the infected, but never mentioned bleeding eyes. Has this happened before? If not, I would hypothesize that this bite is somehow different. For that matter, maybe something you ate, or a hormone imbalance or any number of bodily or environmental factors prevented infection from taking hold prior to now. Perhaps those factors are no longer present. Then there's a hypothesis that this plague could be nothing more than an allergen, and after repeat bites, you have finally reached your allergic threshold and can no longer fight off whatever this is. You could very well be infected.*

I wiped away another crimson tear. "Dude, for someone who can't talk, you sure don't know how to shut up."

Remo stepped away from the hatch. "He's right though. Their ride just left. They also threw grenades at a target that they were supposed to acquire." He looked at my blank expression. "You. They tried to kill you, or at least didn't give a shit if you died. That guy," he thumbed at the guy Ship had drilled, "was probably the driving factor in their mission, and once he was dead, compounded with the fact that they had sustained losses, they just took off. Besides," he said looking at his watch, "we should be having company soon, and that would have scared off any chopper."

He moved back the way we had come, and we followed him. I looked at Kinga's body on the way by. It was fucked up that we were going to leave him here, but that's how it was now. Remo stood over his body for a second, then glanced at the ladder. He slung his rifle, and picked Kinga up by his armpits. He began to move him back toward the crew hatch, and it dawned on me what he was about to do. I slung my rifle as well, and made to pick up Kinga's feet, but Donna was suddenly there.

"Don't even fucking think about it. You're not picking up anything heavier than that rifle for a week."

I stared her down. "This is different."

Her eyebrows raised and she stared right back. "Do you think he would want you to open up your already-bleeding wound to help carry him?"

Ship, who I have no doubt could have carried Kinga's body while it was in a horse-drawn carriage, horses and all, bent to pick up my dead buddy's feet. "I got it," Remo said, and effortlessly threw the lifeless man into a fireman's carry. Remo brought the body to the crew door, opened it with his free hand, and gently placed Kinga on it. He knelt down, said something under his breath, and pushed Kinga over the edge.

Remo strode past us and climbed up the ladder without a word, using his collapsible stick-mirror to check around while at the same time keeping his head out of the way of bullets or teeth from above. We followed, and I noticed that the heavy guy that we had lost to the dead was moving. There wasn't much left, but he was still attempting to crawl toward us. I stopped Todd, and tried to borrow his broom handle.

"Oh," he said, looking at the pathetic thing that had been a human being less than a half hour ago. "You're hurt." He strode past me, putting a hand on my chest. He tried to thrust the sharp end of the spear through the dead man's head, but it wouldn't go. It kept sliding off. Ship appeared, and gave the dead man a kick that nearly decapitated him. That did it, and whatever damage my pal's huge hoof did was enough. The thing ceased moving.

Remo did this cool slide thing back down the ladder and approached us, getting down on his haunches. "There's nobody up there that I can see, living or dead. I can't believe they didn't breach the galley, as well as coming around like we did." He brushed the deck with his hand and began to draw with his Sharpie marker. He drew the galley, the corridors, the stairs, and pointed to where we were. It was amazing. Ship looked impressed at Remo's recall powers, and it was not easy to impress Sasquatch. "I'm going to go first. You and you next." He pointed to Todd and Donna. "Then you. Ship can help." Guess who he had pointed at that last time? "Alvarez, you're up last. Check your six when you're the only one down here. When we're all up there, I'm still moving first. Nobody goes past me for any reason. I will clear the way. If I go down, Alvarez is on point and Ship covers the rear. If they die, the rest of you are on your own. We're heading for the wheelhouse by way of that stairwell. Whoever hit us must have cleared it or they wouldn't have made it down to us. Absolute, utter silence as well. Don't say anything unless you believe not speaking will get someone killed. Questions?"

Other than when he had been training me in hand-to-hand combat, I had never heard Remo say so much at once. Todd meekly raised his hand. "Can I have a gun?"

"No."

"Why not?"

Remo looked at him, and Todd lowered his hand. "If you need a weapon, there will be plenty on the deck." He pulled something from his pocket and passed it to me. I thought it was his magic marker, but it was Kinga's mirror. "You said you wanted one." With that, he looked at each of us in turn, stood, spun, and was up the ladder looking into his mirror again before we could reply.

I wiped my eyes. They were really irritated, and come to think of it, so was I. I was beginning to rage about these assholes who had killed my friend. And who was Remo to tell me what to do? This whole fucking op had been my idea. Did he think just because he could kill me, that he was the boss of me?

Holy shit, it had happened again. I looked around at the folks with me, Donna now climbing the ladder after Remo. I was pissed and wanted to smash something. The nearest things were my friends. I took a couple of deep breaths and it passed, but it was beginning to really frighten me.

Todd was up and it was my turn. I climbed for what seemed like a half hour, looked down, and saw Ship's chest. I looked up and he was eye to eye with me. I had made two rungs. He nodded in an upward direction, indicating that I should continue climbing. When I had made five rungs, the big guy grabbed me by the back of my legs. I looked down at him and he nodded, lifting me up to Todd and Donna, who grabbed me and helped me up. I was getting weak.

Ship came up, followed by Alvarez, and we were all there. Todd began walking toward the open hatch which would lead to the galley doors, looking in all directions with his spear in front of him. He got about fifteen feet before Remo said *Stop*. He hadn't said it forcefully, or loud, but there was definitely an air of *do what I tell you or you're fucking dead*. Todd turned, swallowing, and Remo told him not to move. *Not even a step.* Todd nodded and stared at Remo.

My MARSOC buddy moved toward the frightened guy slowly, reiterating the *don't move* command. Remo had his hands up in supplication, like he was on the end of a mugging, with his rifle dangling as he moved toward Todd. He got on one knee in front of the crewman. "Really, don't move. At all," he said, and fished out a pair of clippers from his pack. Remo was bent over looking at something. He looked back at me. "I'll need that toothpick back."

I limped forward carefully, removing the cellophane wrapped, pointy piece of wood from my tactical pants. The end of the dental helper had broken off in my pocket and I saw Remo's eyebrows raise as I handed it to him. He shook his head as he returned to what he was doing. I looked over his shoulder, and even with my bloody, irritated eyes, I could see the words FRONT TOWARD ENEMY raised in the green plastic. A claymore. A fucking *mine,* the trip wire of which was resting on the top of Todd's boot, most assuredly with the aforementioned raised words pointed toward all of us. I had seen what these things could do to people in an outside environment and it was devastating. *Devastating.* Inside a metal corridor, there would have been nothing left of us except something all over the walls resembling a demented Jackson Pollock painting.

Apparently, my pal could not only kill people with a toothpick, he could totally assassinate a mine with one as well, because his shoulders relaxed noticeably, and he snipped the pretty much invisible wire with his cutters.

"I told you," he said calmly, "that I would go first." Todd could do nothing but nod, no doubt his shorts in full code brown. Remo stood and looked back at us. "I will go first." We all nodded. Then I noticed something I wish I hadn't. Remo stuck the mine in his pack. He had taken it. You can't make this shit up. He had taken the claymore. I realize I just wrote the same thing three times, but this guy had just put a fucking device made to shred human beings in his pack like it was a box of tissues.

I looked at everybody and they did the only thing they could, they looked back at me. Remo was already through the hatch when we began following him. We made it all the way past the spot where Jarek had smoked all the infected and into the galley proper without incident. Remo was standing in the center of the room. "Don't touch anything."

He moved about, inspecting things, picking things up and returning them to their resting spots. "Clear," he told us and he moved through the hatch that the bad guys had blown open. This led to the corridor between the galley and the stairwell, the one we couldn't go through because it had been jam-packed full of infected before. They were all dead. Or re-dead, I guess. They had been surgically destroyed with ammo that had been in superior supply to ours. This corridor looked just like the one that suffered from Jarek's handy work, and they were ankle deep all the way to the far door. We could see the open hatch to the stairs.

Remo studied the corridor for about ten seconds. "Nope." He turned around and moved past us back the way we had come. The plan was now to backtrack through the original route we had used to get to the galley. We got through two open hatches before we found a closed one. Only one of the handles was in the locked position, but that was enough to set off the MARSOC alarms.

"Everybody back. Get on the other side of that hatch," he pointed to the one behind us, "and close it." We did as we were told, and he fiddled with his hatch. Soon, he knocked on ours, told us it was clear, and we came through. Nothing looked amiss when we all moved through the third corridor. Remo shone his light into an open door as he moved past it, and kept going. We had closed all the doors on the way here. Why was this one open? It was my turn for an alarm to go off, but it didn't happen until I was in front of the open doorway. I made to tell Remo and the beam of my tac light cut the darkness of the empty room. Except it wasn't empty. A figure moved into view from out of sight to the right. It looked at me and I looked at it, recognition flooding me. It was Jarek. I saw his face, and the twitchy, feverish look on it only took a half second to process. He processed faster than I did, and was on me in a second, screaming.

He hit me at chest level like a linebacker, and we both slammed into the bulkhead. Before I knew what was happening, I was atop him, pounding and slashing with my bare hands. He tried to get up and I stuck my thumb in his eye. I felt it go with a liquid squish, and I kept hitting and hitting him, smashing his face with my fists and clawing at him with my nails. He stopped moving in short order, but his screaming didn't. Realization that it was me who was screaming hit me, so I stopped. I looked at what I had done after what seemed an eternity. There was nothing left of his face and neck. I had ruined it, and could see bone in several places. We were both covered in him. As I heaved, I looked at my hands. They were curled into claws. I wiped my mouth with the back of my bandaged forearm, and noticed a smear of blood on the bandage. I felt stuff in my mouth and spit something out. It was a piece of Jarek. Horrified, I started to rise, and heard a sharp intake of breath behind me. I whipped my head in that direction and saw every gun other than mine pointing at me.

"He's turned," Alvarez said, and instead of pointing his weapon in my direction, he aimed at my head.

DEPARTURE

Well, obviously he didn't put one through my melon, or how would I have finished that last journal entry? He did say, "Sorry, buddy," and tense like he was going to squeeze the trigger. Hey, I had been shot in the head a couple times already. Smacked in the dome by a wrench-toting gorilla as well. Bitten, burned, beaten, shot, tortured, experimented on. Why not Alvarez? Pop me.

Ship was there, and he gently pushed the barrel of the kid's rifle to the side, nodding his head. Nobody said a word, (especially Ship) and I felt compelled to express gratitude for not being shot.

"I'm me," I said. "Mostly, anyway." Nobody rushed to give me hand. Or a hug. I stood, and everybody still looked wary. I sighed. "Do infected talk? Do they not attack? I mean other than with Jarek." Pain began to slowly ebb its way back into my side and arm. Then it came back with a vengeance and I had to lean against the bulkhead. During my leaning, I glanced at what was left of Jarek. It was horrible, and I had to look away fast. I began to furiously wipe at my face with my hands, and Donna made to come to me.

I put my hand up. "Stop!"

She did, blinking, and looking a bit hurt.

"At the very least," I began, "I have his infected shit all over me. At worst, I'm contagious as well now. I need a change of clothes and a bath before anybody touches me."

"But you're immune!" she yelled at me.

"At this point, we don't know. When I was at Baldy Mountain, they took every fluid I had, and did months' worth of tests. They never found anything different in me than in any other human test subject. They also couldn't find anything in the infected fluids of the dead. Basically, they had no fucking idea what this thing is."

I was tired. Damn tired, and I needed to rest, but there was no time. Remo read my mind. "We need to keep moving." Two more hatches and we were at the base of the stairs to the wheelhouse. The doors off of each landing had been secured with chains, so nothing was getting in, at least not quickly. Infected were stacked on the sides of the stairs like cord wood, with a path all the way to the top. We were staring out at the sun through the wheelhouse windows when Remo said, "Clear."

I moved to the broken front window and stuck my head in the hole. I felt the warmth of the sun and the sea breeze on my face and it was fantastic. Then I got a waft of what was on deck and looked down on a couple hundred rotting corpses. They were in zombie dormant mode, and were just meandering around slowly. They would do this until they received some stimuli, then they would go ape-shit and try to eat whatever they saw. They hadn't seen me yet. I looked to the left, (port side) and noticed a large, gray vessel steaming toward us. It was the destroyer, *Stockdale*. No wonder the bad guys had left in a hurry. There aren't a lot of helicopters that would be able to survive a battle with a ship designed to kill everything. The modern day destroyers are like World War II battleships. Badass.

I felt a tap on my left shoulder and turned to face it. My girl was there and she took a surprised step back when she looked at me. I smiled, "I still look like one of them?"

"No," she replied a little too hastily. "I just..."

"Don't sweat it, kid. Maybe I can scare off the infected instead of shoot them now?" She moved in to hug me and I stopped her by stepping away. She didn't look hurt this time. I pointed at myself. "I still have this shit on me. When we get back, you will receive some significant *hugging*." I fluttered my eyebrows and gave her a leer.

"You wish! I'm not touching your infected ass!"

I had missed this woman. I had missed them all, and now I would never get to hang out with some of them. Captain Bob, Zero, and Kinga had been my friends. I had just met Jarek, but he was also a hero. They were all dead. So many had died, and so many had been killed by assholes and infected. My ire started to rise and I willfully suppressed it. It was a monumental task, but I got it done.

Alvarez and Todd were talking. Todd was pointing toward the incoming *Stockdale*, and Remo was looking at the closed hatch to the roof. Ship was in Heaven, studying the myriad wheelhouse controls. We were almost done on this ship of death, and although we had suffered key losses, we had succeeded in our mission. I looked up. Shit. Donna saw the look on my face. "What?"

"The key. We left it on the roof of the monkey island in case we didn't make it, but we never considered a second group coming here."

She looked at me in confusion. Confusion was way better than the revulsion from a moment ago, but I guess I'm significantly more terrifying with these broken blood vessels in my eyes. "What the fuck is a monkey island?"

"It's the nautical term for the roof of a wheelhouse," Remo answered. He had gone all ninja again and was standing next to us looking at the incoming vessel.

I looked back up. "Do you think they took it?"

"Gotta go up there and see. That's our exfil point anyway." He took his rifle and began knocking out the glass shards in the window. Everybody was looking.

"Uhhh, what's happening, Chief? You're not going to use the hatch?" I pointed to the closed hatch above us behind the control consoles. Everybody looked at where I was pointing.

"No," he said and everybody looked back at us. It was starting to feel like a fucking tennis match. "I can't see what's on the other side. They could have booby-trapped it. Be a shame to be so close and get killed for not being thorough, don't you think?"

He had me on that one. I would probably already look like badly mangled Swiss cheese covered in raspberry sauce without this friggin guy. There was a problem though. There was no way in hell he could climb out this window and get to the roof (monkey island). The windows slanted outward, but the top of the superstructure jutted a good ten feet out above us. He would never be able to reach. The jarhead had already dangled over the top of the windows when he scouted the room, and the dead hadn't gotten him, so no way. He turned around. "Ship, could you hold my belt please?" Huh. Didn't want me to do it. Probably because I was missing a piece of my arm, had caught a bullet, and had recently partaken in the evisceration of a Runner with naught but my own teeth and hands.

Ship came over and held him while he went as far out the broken window as he could. He came back in shortly, shaking his head. "Not going that way. Can't reach."

It was almost like I had just thought that.

"So what's the plan?"

He looked at the port side hatch to the outside. "I'm going to need what ammo you have." He turned around and put his MP5 on the console. Pulling two magazines, he inspected them. He pointed at Donna's Beretta. "Any ammo?"

She shook her head, "You cannot possibly go outside. You can't."

He raised his eyebrows and flashed a very uncommon smile. "Do you want to go? Somebody has to go out, climb the access ladder, and check the other side of the hatch."

"But the deck is crawling with them!"

He stopped smiling. "And the only way off this boat is through that hatch." As if to punctuate his statement, we heard the sound of a helicopter. "That's our ride." He moved to the wooden closet where Kinga had stashed the communications gear. He ran his fingers all along the outside of the closet, then opened the door just enough to fit his mirror inside, shone his light in, then opened it wide. He pulled out the briefcase thingie and set up the umbrella, sticking an earbud in his head. "Pluto, this is Hammer One, how copy? Roger that, Pluto. Hostiles, over." It was really annoying only hearing half of the conversation. "Achieved primary mission objective, waiting on transport, over." Let's just understand that after every damn thing Remo said on the phone, he said the word over, it's a pain in the ass to keep writing it. "Have transport hover one hundred feet to starboard side of *Majestik Maersk* until comms are made again. Hammer One copies all, out. Is there any ammo in that M9?" He pointed at Donna's sidearm again.

"No."

"Does anybody else have any 9mm?" No hands raised. Alvarez pulled his .410 gauge pump shotgun off of his back and inspected the load. "For those close encounters," he said passing it to Remo, and winking at me. Refer to the movie I mentioned at the beginning of this journal for the wink reference. "Four shells left."

Remo took the weapon, strode to the port side hatch, looked through, and glanced at Alvarez. "It's clear. Cover me to the ladder. Close and lock the hatch the second I'm clear. I won't be coming back this way. At least not while I'm alive." He opened the hatch and disappeared through it. Alvarez aimed down the sights of his M4, but didn't fire before he stepped back into the wheelhouse and locked the hatch.

Alvarez nodded. "He made it. It was only ten feet across the landing, but they saw him and started up the catwalk." He locked all six handles and made sure the tamper-proof lock was engaged. A knock came from the hatch, and Ship moved to the ladder. Two rungs up and he was able to unlock the handle. How had the bad guys locked this from the inside and then escaped via the hatch? All our weapons were pointed at the hatch, but it was just Remo's face. He seemed to approve that we were aiming at him.

"Come on, it's clear."

Ship came back down and helped Todd up. Todd wouldn't let go of his spear, and almost took out Ship's eye with it. The rest of us made it up, and Remo passed me a little chain. The fuckers hadn't found the key! Alvarez passed Remo the sat-com equipment, and he called for pickup.

We were going home. I felt woozy just thinking about it. Or it was from blood loss? The bird was above us when I passed out.

I awoke in the helicopter, with my hands zip tied, and a bandana gag in my mouth. I get it, it was prudent. I looked up at my friends and smiled through my gag. They didn't see me, but I was able to pass out again knowing I would be either very safe, or die in a fiery crash. At this point, I would take either one.

RELAXATION?

I've taken a break from my journals for a bit, but everybody says I should keep them current. The writing is supposed to help me heal.

We got to the *Stockdale* in under a minute after leaving the *Majestik*, and were exiting the bird in under ten. They carted my mostly unconscious body to medical. The doctors on board the destroyer opened me up like a tin can and dissected me. They actually found two bullet fragments, so it was good they cut me open. There wasn't a lot they could do for the bite, and as it happens, Captain Bob missed everything vital when he chomped me. I will have a wicked scar when I'm able to keep the bandages off. Now that I've been up for a while I gotta tell you, the arm hurts way worse than the bullet wound.

I learned that Schumitz (captain of the *Stockdale*) blew several holes in that fucking ship of death, and the *Majestik Maersk* and all its infected now reside at the bottom of six thousand feet of Gulf. I was exceptionally pissy when Alvarez told me of the sinking. I really would have liked to have seen that.

We steamed back to the floating asylum called *Atlantis* that I call home as soon as Schumitz got the key and the hard drives, then sunk his target. Donna, Ship, and Alvarez were with me the entire time. During one of my lucid moments, I called to Donna. "By the way," I began, and she raised her eyebrows, "you look good for just having kids." I passed out immediately after, and she thought I was hallucinating, until Remo told her about the two kids Remo, Tim, Kinga, and I had brought to *Atlantis*.

They brought me via stretcher to medical on the rig, but honestly, the sick bay on the *Stockdale* was infinitely more comfortable. I was in recovery for two days. That was a week and a half ago.

While I was in there, I had a plethora of visitors, including the twins, Richy and Chloe. They had come up with a dog someplace, a border collie by the name of Dusty. The thing is one hundred percent ape-shit, and super smart. Apparently, he made a home with Tim and the twins in my shack in the two days I've been away. Actually, I was only back from my months' long incarceration for a few hours before setting out again. I sound like an idiot. I have a buzz. The doc has found a piece of skin on the back of my shoulder that looks wrong. He wants to do a biopsy, but doesn't have all the shit he needs should it turn up malignant. Wouldn't that be ironic? I'm immune to the worst plague in the history of earth, but I die of cancer two years in?

So I'm in recovery, stoned on some good pain meds, when Remo comes in with Austin. Austin is the leader of *Atlantis*, and he's holding my first journal. After a brief moment of embarrassment when Remo said my ramblings were funny, Austin said he would like me to read them aloud to people each night in the TV room. Apparently, regaling my rig-mates with my comical tales of the apocalypse would boost their spirits. Good for morale or some shit. On day three, when I was finally able to get up and take a piss in an actual toilet, all my close friends except Remo came in at the same time to see how I was doing.

"Great!" I told them. The twins, Ship, Alvarez, Tim, Greg, Austin, and of course, Donna were there with Dusty running around everybody's feet. *Ape-shit* really is the best term for this mutt. I asked where Remo was, and Austin told me he was on the *Stockdale*. We all had a one-sided conversation where I told them what had happened to me since I had been stolen in great detail. Tim piped in a few times to confirm, especially when the crazy, unbelievable shit was revealed.

When I was done, Austin and Greg told us what had happened on *Atlantis* while I was away. The *Stockdale* had shown up. One of the roughnecks that had been living on the rig had died of a heart attack, but the system they had in place to warn everyone and dispatch the undead had worked, and no one had been bitten. One of the ships that I had done some engine work on, the *Spirit*, had been overrun from within. Austin and Schumitz had been able to rescue nine folks off of the boat, then they cleared it. It was anchored a quarter mile off of *Atlantis* with a skeleton crew. Plans were underway to secure one of the abandoned rigs, cover it in soil, and farm it. There were several other ideas and some of them sounded pretty good.

I spent today watching the kids play with the dog. (There are sixteen kids here, and school starts in three weeks. You should have heard the groans.) Richy, Chloe, Donna, and I are living together. In my shack. It's basically a ten-by-ten room with three bunks, a door and a dirty window. The only stuff we have are things that will help us survive. I don't have any trinkets in here other than my journals. Donna has her medical stuff.

There is a Frisbee and a football for the kids. Chloe does not throw like a girl. Donna does.

Richy was not allowed to play video games when he was growing up. His parents were against it. There are several video gaming systems on board *Atlantis*, and this kid has been going HAM on them. Put an adult diaper on him, and he would starve to death playing those damn games. Video games are like heroin, I guess. Donna and I have spoken about limiting his time being a vidiot. Chloe has been helping out in the kitchen, and Richy is showing aptitude with our weather system's analyst.

We are in the midst of a plague which turns your friends and family into murderous cannibals. Until a year ago, I had no such friends or family. Now I have multitudes of both, and the world, which had gotten huge for a while, has shrunk to infinitesimal. How can I protect all these people?

The dead can't get to us, but eventually, we're going to have to go to them. There are abundant supplies here, but abundant is also finite. Our stockpile will get low, and we will have to send teams out to procure more stuff. Although wounded, I'm up and around, and I'm going to suggest to Austin that we don't wait. We should go out now so we don't deplete our reserves. *Now* being in about a week. Donna will go bananas, and the kids will be upset, but I'm probably the third best qualified to go. I would say Ship would go nuts too, but I have no doubt he will say it's a good idea, then accompany me. I think a team of about six is optimal, not big enough to draw attention, but not small enough to be outnumbered. I'm going to ask Remo if he will come. He spends most of his time on the *Stockdale* now, but he still comes up to check on us and listen to my journals when I read them out loud. He's going to start a combat training class. Personal defense tactics (my idea).

Kat has taken to the kids as well as Donna. Kat lives with Alvarez across the deck from me. They share a shack with another two people who hot-bunk. One of those people is Tim. Tim is a bona-fide hero to these roughnecks, and not because of the stories I've told. Screw zombie hordes. Screw crazy bikers and super spies. Tim can *fix* shit. The various computer systems on this rig are Tim's to command. This guy blows away anybody for probably a thousand miles when it comes to computers and networks and communications. He's corrected a hundred problems already, and has only been here ten days.

The only issues I had were that my arm hurt, this piece of skin on my shoulder itched now and then, and I was bored. They wouldn't let me work yet. Because my arm hurts. Did I mention my arm hurts? Because it hurts.

I would love to tell you that we all lived happily ever after. That we spent our days on the rig, making forays, and were finally able to live in peace once all the infected rotted away. Alas, this was not to be. It didn't take long for everything to go to shit either.

I had finally been cleared to go back to work. Much like Tim, I fix stuff. Not computer stuff. F that noise. I fix mechanical things. Cuz I'm a mechanic. There was never a shortage of shit to fix on an oil rig either, and this one was huge. Not only that, but as I've mentioned in a previous journal, I get pimped out to other rigs and ships in the Gulf as well to fix their broken shit. That, as it happens, was where the proverbial feces struck the fan.

The *Ocean Diamond*, a semisubmersible drilling rig, had a failure in one of her air compressor motors. Yours truly was asked to come aboard and take a look. It was my first time being back on the job since I had been kidnapped. I jumped at the chance. What a fucking idiot. They sent a boat to pick me up. They offloaded two hundred gallons of fuel for us. Fuel was generally the mode of currency in the Gulf, although there were several others. You might think it odd that gasoline and diesel were currency when every ship and rig in the Gulf was mining oil, but oil was a resource everybody had and everybody knew that refined fuel was worth more than gold. Absolutely everything out here ran on fuel. Even the electricity was generated by fuel. Sure, there were wind and solar rigs, but they still needed gas. *Atlantis* had her own refinery, and there was a refinery ship aligned with us anchored not a thousand feet away, but we took the fuel anyway.

So I get on the boat, and Remo and Ship both decide that today is the day that they are going to come with me. I think they were both worried that I would get hurt my first day back because of my preexisting injuries. The three of us zip six miles across the waves, and are soon standing on the deck of the *Diamond*, Ship carrying my tools. A smallish woman, whom I had never met, maybe in her early fifties, greets us and introduces herself as June. Hands are shaken, pleasantries exchanged, and soon we are sitting in June's office with six of her guys pointing at maps of the rig and where the compressor in question is located. She asks me about my bandaged arm, and I tell her it was a rig injury. She nods and gets us three cups of coffee, me thinking it would be rude to say *No thank you, coffee tastes like dirt, but I could really use a Mountain Dew.* I have never had a cup of coffee in my life, and I wasn't about to start another habit now. I accept the coffee, as do Ship and Remo, and suddenly we are staring cross-eyed at the business ends of every weapon in the room.

June opens a drawer, pulls out a very familiar, laminated but weathered photo and slides it across the desk. It's a picture of me, my dome adorned with gauze.

"Sorry," she said, and looked the part.

It started with a tomato. A little grape tomato in a salad. June and the guys from the *Diamond*, the guys with guns, escorted us to the galley. The brought us in lunch, which consisted of: you guessed it, a salad. They had that oil and vinegar dressing with those friggin herbs that I absolutely love. Anyway, they were sitting around us, sort of paying attention to us eat while talking. They were talking to us, questioning me as to who I was. I would not answer. They didn't seem to get frustrated or angry at my refusals. I got the impression that these weren't bad people.

These were not professionals either. I know this because had they been, they would have separated and bound us somehow. They had disarmed us, but just looking at Remo and Ship should frighten most people. I believe that these people were not used to the shitheads that seem to flourish during an apocalypse. Other than point weapons at us, the worst thing the folks from the *Diamond* had done to us was serve us lunch.

So the tomato. There had been several in the salad, and I was going to eat every damn bit of this salad because number one: it was delicious, and number two: I was thinking I was going on a long trip that would end with me strapped to a hospital bed in another government facility, and the food there couldn't compare. I got to the last tomato, and it was covered in that fantastic dressing. I stabbed at it with my plastic fork and missed. I tried again, and was able to puncture the tomato, but it fell off the tines. The third, fourth, and fifth times the little round devil rolled off the tines un-punctured. I got mad. Pissed at that fucking piece of fruit, then at the assholes who were prepared to turn me over to another, worse group of assholes, and for what? Payment? More fucking tomatoes? I began to shake, and my eyes began to water. Of course, by this time, you know it wasn't water.

I was a bit hunched over, looking at that damned tomato in the bowl, and shaking when one of the gun-toters asked to the general public: "What's wrong with him?" They had taken me prisoner and were going to sell me and they wanted to know what was wrong? REALLY?

As my hands turned into claws, I said, "Remo, try not to kill anyone." Before anybody except my buddies could process that, I launched myself at the nearest asshole, hitting him under the jaw. He went sprawling and this shit was on. I punched the guy to his right in the temple, then kicked the guy on the ground in the balls. I heard a shot fire and had to hope none of us was hit. I looked the standing guy in the face as he held his head and he saw my blood red eyes and screamed, dropping his weapon. I grabbed his head and smashed my forehead into his nose before he could move. I turned to June, and she screamed as well, fumbling for her sidearm. Remo had already incapacitated the two idiots near him, and Ship had taken out both of his captors with one backhand swipe. Remo was pointing the gun at June, and she just lifted her hands in the air and begged *Please!* I shot across the table, taking her to the ground and straddling her. I snarled the most terrifying sound, and her bladder let go. I screamed and slapped her with an open palm. She began to cry frantically, and I removed her .357 magnum, standing and cocking the hammer. "Get up." She was beyond hysterical, so I nudged her with my boot. Okay, so it was more of a kick, but I hadn't hurt her. "GET UP!" I pointed the cocked weapon between her eyes and she just closed them, crying.

Five or six people burst in, but we had all of our former captors including the leader of the *Diamond* on the ground and covered. "Drop your weapons or we kill you all," Remo said calmly. I think his tranquil demeanor was more terrifying to these people than if he had fired his weapon. Every one of them acquiesced immediately. I heard weapons hit the floor. Remo was telling everybody what to do, but I wasn't listening. I was heaving, and thinking about Donna, the kids, and that damn dog.

Without altering my gaze, I pointed at the guy I had kicked in the balls, "You, help her up." He limped to her and did just that. She had calmed, but the place was still as tense as the OK Corral just before high noon. I looked around, and all the douches were on their knees, hands behind their heads, ankles crossed. Ship was behind them and Remo in front.

"What now?" MARSOC asked.

"How about we tie them up in this room and I fucking bite her?" I pointed at June, and everyone in the place went dead silent. "Why?" I demanded. "Why would you do this? Do you have any idea what the assholes you were going to give me to are going to do now?"

"They have my husband and brother," she shouted, beginning to cry anew. "They'll kill them if we don't deliver you!"

I uncocked the hammer on the .357 and sighed. "Well, shit."

EXCHANGE

Hostages. What's left of the American government had procured hostages in order to procure me. That was a crazy time. I pointed at one of the guys that had just shown up. "Get me a radio." He stood, obviously terrified. "If you bring anybody else back here, I will tear them and you to pieces, and my buddies will execute every last one of these assholes." *Tear him to pieces.* Epic. These people thought I was some kind of sentient infected, and I wasn't going to let them off the hook so easily.

Scaredy-cat returned in a few minutes, and handed me a radio. It was big, and it had a huge collapsible antenna. Looked like something left over from Khe Sanh. We had all our captives facing the wall, on their knees, ankles crossed, hands on their heads, just like before. I made a call to the *Stockdale*, and Schumitz was on the line pretty quickly. We hadn't thought to initiate call signs. *Everything alright?*

"Decidedly not. They pulled guns on us, tried to subdue us, and had plans on shipping me off to what I'm guessing are the same assholes who had me before."

Any casualties?

"One guy will have sore nuts for a while, and the boss over here," I looked at June, "is going to need a change of panties, but other than that no, everybody is okay."

I meant were any of our team injured?

"Oh, no, we're good."

Dispatching a team now. Glad you boys are okay.

"Yeah, about that. I'm having a hard time believing that whoever wants me decided to come to these idiots first. Why didn't they contact you and demand you roll me and hand me over?"

He paused for the slightest of moments. *They did. I told them to fuck off. We are now rogue elements of the US Navy. They told me they were dispatching a carrier group to Atlantis to relieve me of command.*

"And you didn't think to tell me this?"

I don't work for you. You're not even Navy. Like I'm going to inform you of classified communiques. This having been said, I was

*going to discuss it with the group tonight. I just found out you weren't on
Atlantis right now.*

I looked at Remo, who looked back at me. "I didn't know any of
that," he said.

Fair enough.

"Captain, would you mind sending two teams? I have a plan."

Another slight pause. *They're on the way. ETA one hour.*

"Thanks, I'll talk to you when we get back." We ended the call, and
I sat at one of the tables. "Everybody up. Sit over here." Both Remo and
Ship tensed, not knowing what I was up to, but the crew of the *Diamond*
did as I asked.

I looked at June, "Look, I'm sorry for any part I caused in the
capture and holding of your family. At the end of the day, it's not really
my fault. I get what you did to us and why, but that doesn't excuse it."

"They're going to kill them." She looked down and started to cry
again. "They're going to kill my husband and my brother."

"No," I said, "they're not."

The plan was simple. June was going to call the dickweeds who
were threatening her family. We would agree to meet at a neutral
location, and June would pretend to exchange me for her men. The
twelve men Schumitz had sent, Remo, and Ship would jump out, yell
Surprise, the bad guys would surrender, and we would send them
packing with a simple but efficient message: Fuck off.

Remo was torn. Everything in him said to kill whoever showed up,
but as they were probably guys he served in the same armed services
with, he was unsure if the murder was necessary. The guys that were on
the *Majestik* had killed some of us, so it was self-defense on our part.
This was different. We would be holding all the cards; at least we hoped
so.

We had discussed the plan in front of June and her second, the rest
of the douches were being watched by six of Schumitz's heavy hitters.
Max, June's lead roughneck, raised his hand, "So does this mean we're
cool? Can we have our guns back?"

"No, and most fucking definitely no. You cannot have your guns
back. If you reach for them, we will shoot you. If you ask again, we will
shoot you. In fact, if I hear you fart loud, we will fucking shoot you."
The guy swallowed hard. "Once we get your people back, we're done.

We're going to leave and you assholes will never do business with us again. At least if I have any say about it anyway. If something breaks on this POS, you can read a fucking manual."

Both of them looked down and nodded. I was shooting for shame and had hit a bullseye. I reaffirmed my notion that these were not bad people, just desperate. I felt a twinge of guilt for shaming them until I realized what would have happened to me if their evil plot had succeeded.

"Why do you look like one of them?" June asked me, horror and revulsion evident on her teary face.

She was sitting and I was standing, so I got down on my haunches and looked deep into her white eyes with my red ones. "I am one of them."

Her eyes widened, and I stood. "If word should make it off this piece of shit rig that there is an infected monster with a toolbox roaming around the Gulf, it will become my personal mission to make you all dead and turn this tub into singed scrap metal. Spread the word not to spread the word."

They both nodded again.

"June, you look," I glanced down at her urine-soaked jeans, "*pissed.* You need to change. Two of my guys will go with you, then you'll all come right back." I did the red-eye stare again. "Don't dawdle, June."

She was back in twenty minutes. All fourteen of my team were talking over the plan when one of the stooges from the *Diamond* showed up with his hands raised. We let him in the cafeteria-galley, and he passed her a much younger and smaller radio. "It's them."

Remo was suddenly standing next to us. He put a hand lightly on the terrified woman's shoulder, "Like we planned, June."

She took in a deep breath and depressed the send button, "This is the *Diamond*, over."

Diamond, this is Ares. Have you secured the package?

The package? I'm the *package*? If I hadn't been so enraged by this situation, I would have burst out laughing at his colloquial indiscretion.

"Yes, Ares, do you have our men?"

Affirmative. We will be landing on your helipad in thirty minutes. We don't want to see any weapons. Repeat: No weapons. Understood?

Yes, Ares, we understand."

See you in thirty, out.

Why did they want to meet here? Why not on their home turf, or at least someplace neutral. I looked at the commander of Schumitz's two teams, "Can you be ready in thirty?"

"We'll be ready in three." He spun on his heel and began to address his men.

True to their word, the douches were landing on the helipad in exactly thirty-one minutes. I'm not good with helicopter models, but this one was big and black and military looking. Six guys, also in black, with those balaclavas on their faces, fanned out with their M4s panning in all directions. I was on my knees, hands behind my back, with June and Max on either side of me. I was also wearing sunglasses. One of the guys strode forward, extremely confident looking. Apparently, he and I had come to the same conclusion; that the folks on the *Diamond* were completely useless, and destined to die. He lowered his M4, which had been pointing at Max's face, and snorted the snort of the complacent. He looked over his shoulder at one of his stooges, "Bring 'em out." Two guys were dragged out and placed in front of the douche in charge. They both had hoods on their heads with their hands bound behind their backs.

The rest of the operators seemed to relax, and while they didn't lower their weapons, the barrels drooped some. Douche number one let his rifle dangle on its sling, and pulled the hoods off of the two men. June sobbed and made to move forward, but the guy in charge said, "Uh-uh." Although the arrogant prick didn't raise his weapon.

He snipped the zip ties on June's family and they walked to her. Guy in black stepped up and looked down on me. "Lot of people are looking for you."

I looked up at him through the ancient, mirrored aviator glasses. "Do you know why?"

"Didn't ask. Don't care." Snide asshole. "Let's go."

He made to reach for me to help me up, but I whipped out the Sig Sauer I had behind my back and poked him in the stones. All my guys sprang up from absolutely fucking nowhere. Each of his boys had two of mine covering them. The guy on the helo that was manning the machine gun got a rifle butt quickly to stun him. Both sides started yelling *stand down* or *drop your weapon*, or *freeze*. It was comical and terrifying at the same time.

He kept his hands out as I stood. The yelling stopped and we seemed to be at a Mexican standoff. "You are all going to fucking die," he told me in that same superior voice.

Very slowly. Every so slowly, I reached up and removed my sunglasses. "I'm already dead, fucktard." He did what everybody does when confronted with my red eyes; he took an involuntary step back while at the same time having his eyes go wide. "Guns down or we fire in five seconds, then I'm going to eat you."

"How do I know you won't just kill us?"

"You fucking don't. But I guarantee we'll kill you if you don't lower your weapons."

The rotor wash was blowing my hair back, even though it was fifty feet away. It felt good with the sea air. I thought for a moment there was going to be a bloodbath, then this asshole confirmed it. "Kill them," he said.

None of them fired. None of us fired. "Lower your weapons and we will let you live," I shouted over the rotor. "And kill the engine on the bird." Remo and Ship were with me by that time. Everybody looks at Ship funny, and this guy was no exception. Ship had his M4 pointed at this dumbass while Remo spoke, "This is over. I don't want to kill you, but your five seconds are up." Remo drew his sidearm and pointed it at the guy who finally looked scared. To the dude's credit, he still didn't say shit.

"Wait!" one of his guys yelled. "Okay! Okay! We're dropping our weapons." That was all it took, and they all followed suit, removing slings and allowing themselves to be disarmed.

"Idiots," the first guy said. "Now they're going to kill us all."

"No, we're not. Not if you play nice." I tried to look as overly pensive as I could when I said, "Although you did threaten to kill us all. Actually, what you said was *you're all going to fucking die.* Then you told your guys to kill us. We're still not going to kill you, but I do have some questions."

Ten minutes later, the helo's (a Blackhawk, the military guys told me) engine was off, and we were once again in the galley with a bunch of shitheads on their knees. They were all trussed though, ankles and wrists. Our guys had searched their guys up and down and removed all of their weapons and anything else that looked dangerous.

The leader, who would not give up even his name, was sitting on the bench across the table from me. He wouldn't say anything, and it was pissing me off. I pointed at him. "Clip his tie." The three sailors that were guarding him looked at me like I had three heads. I made a scissoring motion with my index and middle finger. "His zip tie, handcuff thingie. Cut it." That got through, and one of them produced a pair of cutters and snipped his bonds. "All I want to know is how you keep finding me?" Nothing. "You're not gonna tell me anything, huh?" Nothing. I sighed. "Ship, tear his arm off."

The guy snorted. He didn't move when Ship came over and stood next to him. Ship indicated that he should stand, but in an epic move of insolence, the guy did nothing. Ship grabbed him by the scruff of the neck and lifted him up like a kitten. Sasquatch shifted his grip and held the helpless guy by the throat. His feet weren't dangling off the ground, but if you for one second think Ship was incapable of one-handing this guy into the air after all the shit I've written about him, put this book down and kill yourself right now. The dude started to hit my buddy, and Ship gave him a buffet to the side of the head, stunning him. Then he gripped the guy's wrist. Holy fuck, was he really going to rip this poor bastard's arm off? I was just kidding!

"Ship, stop. This douche can't answer anything with you crushing his windpipe to the thickness of the ace of spades." Ship gave the guy a forward slap and let go of his throat. "Do you have any doubts he's willing to do what I ask?"

The guy was obviously grateful to be able to breathe. He was so grateful that he took a deep breath, coughed a little, and flipped me off. I was really starting to like him.

I sighed again. "I was hoping it wouldn't come to this." I sauntered over to the guy and grabbed his arm. He didn't resist at all. I lifted it a bit and glared at him.

"You think if I wouldn't say shit when Gargantua had me I'm gonna talk to you?"

"Nope," I said, pulled his arm to my mouth, and bit him. Hard. Motherfucker did not expect that. He yanked his arm away, cradling it. That semi-circle bite mark that signified death was just starting to bleed. It was just a bit, but I had broken the skin. I hope the guy doesn't have hepatitis or some shit.

"You... you killed me."

I hadn't infected him, two hundred plus doctors had confirmed I can't transfer whatever the fuck this plague is. He was painfully unaware of this fact though.

"Cuff him to that guy." I pointed to one of his men. "When he turns, he'll tear into him, and then we'll feed the rest of you to him one at a time until somebody tells us what we want to know."

"You bastard!" one of them said. "You swore you wouldn't kill us!"

"I'm not going to." I thumbed at the guy I had bitten, "He is."

"You've got a tracker on you," the leader said. He looked sad. "Now just kill me and please let them go."

Fuck! Fuckity-fucksickles! A tracker! I began to check my clothes before it dawned on me. I pulled my shirt over my head and drew my SOG. "Remo, it's in my shoulder." I handed him the knife, handle first, and he looked at my shoulder. He nodded, and before I could tell him to count to three or some shit, the point of the blade was in me. "Ow! Fuck! You couldn't have told—"

"Stop moving, pussy." I stopped, scrunched up my red-eyed face in pain for a couple of seconds while he dug around in there, and a moment later, he was showing me a bloody chip with a little tail on it. A transmitter. I had been fuk'n bugged like Douglas Quaid. Cancer my ass. I was pissed about the bug, but happy that I wasn't going to die of melanoma.

I looked at the guy I had bitten, my rage beginning to escalate. He was staring at the floor, resigned to death. This was a guy who would never let himself turn. He or one of his buddies would have his brains on the wall the second they were able. Poor bastard was probably just doing his job. I mean, he was a prick and working for what I consider the bad guys, but still. This false power I had over people, them thinking I would or could infect them, was helpful, as it unnerved everyone. I could see it coming back to haunt me if it got out though. Nobody would want a carrier of the plague on their ships or rigs to help fix stuff. You and I know I'm not a carrier, but nobody else would buy it.

"Look at me asshole." Ever the nonconformist, his face was still pointed down, so I grabbed his chin and made him look at me. I took a deep breath before I began, "I can't infect you. Whatever this is, I can't pass it on. I've been studied extensively by scientists and doctors and they can't find anything different inside me." He blinked, so I continued. "You're not infected. You're not going to die. You're not going to turn."

It came to him quicker than it does to most. Not the fact that he wasn't going to die, I'm sure that was a good feeling, the other thing.

"Jesus Christ... you're immune." He had looked at me a lot of different ways since he had landed in his helicopter. Superiority, shock, fear, and most assuredly hatred. Now it was awe, proving once again that I am, in fact, awesome. "That's why they want you."

I touched my nose. "*Werrp!* Give that man a cigar." I heard a couple of *holy craps*, another *Jesus*, and at least one *bullshit*. From the crowd, but honestly, I didn't give a rat's ass. "That's why they want me. The thing is, the top surviving minds from the government have already studied my ever-so-sexy ass, and they came up with bupkis. They can't figure out why I'm immune, but there's more than that. They can't even figure out why this is happening or even what it is. There's nothing different between me and everybody else that they could find. In fact, they can't see any type of new virus or bacteria in any of the infected either. Basically, they don't know anything. I mean, they asked me if I was abducted by aliens."

"Were you?" one of the guys from the *Diamond* asked. Fucker was serious.

"No. But that doesn't change the fact that the powers that be want to study me to see if they can come up with a cure. Cut me up, stick me with needles, probe my brain. Fuck that. I'm done with their bullshit. And before you start citing duty, I already did it all. For months they worked on me and came up empty."

Remo stepped up. "Fabulous. This mission is over. Let's get back."

He was right, this shit was done. Team Ares was already standing up, and Ship clipped the zip ties on their feet. The leader, already unzipped, stopped when I put my hand on his shoulder. "You can take this back to the assholes you take orders from." I dropped the bloody tracking chip into his open palm. "I swear to God if we see you guys again, there will be a lot of dead people." He looked at the chip, put it in his left hand, then did something I totally didn't expect. He stuck his hand out for me to shake.

"Good luck."

I warily shook his hand. "You too. Stay alive."

"It's you that needs to stay alive. I hope I don't see you soon."

"Me too," I told him. We escorted them to their helicopter, which I thought would be an excellent addition to our air force, but honestly, I didn't know where to put it, or if we commandeered it, where to put the guys who came in on it. Then there was the issue of a pilot. Remo was playing with the mount for the machine gun, and within seconds, he had the weapon off of the bird and in his capable hands. "For our trouble." The bad guys didn't object as they boarded the helicopter.

The fast boat that had dropped off Schumitz's teams showed up as the bad guys were leaving. Max, June's second, came up to me as I was stepping into the boat. "Look, we never would have tried this if—"

"Forget it."

"I thought if—"

I cut him off again. I just wanted to go home. "I said forget it. It's done. Good luck and goodbye." With that, I got in the boat and we cast off. I looked back over my shoulder at the *Diamond* as we sped across the waves. I felt bad for them; they were in way worse condition experience-wise than we were. They were still alive though, and that was something.

WHAT A DIVE

The past few weeks have been exceptional. I haven't been writing because I've been so busy. Usually, I'll grab the pen and hammer out some words right before I go to sleep, or if something particularly interesting happens, I might jot down a few notes and scribble it in later. Now is the later, as I've been so exhausted from the work around here that I pass out each night as soon as I hit the pillow.

When we returned from the *Diamond*, I spoke to Captain Schumitz about events. Past, present, and future. He and I are never going to be drinking buddies, but we've come to a mutual understanding that we sort of need each other. We did actually have a drink together in his office when I got back. He apologized for not speaking to me about the call he had received demanding he hand me over. I apologized for being a douche and challenging his authority. We're cool now, and we have more than just a grudging respect for each other. I think it borders on actual respect.

I've been out to two other rigs this past week, both times with armed escort. We're hoping nobody else knows that I'm a fugitive with a price on my head, but we aren't taking any chances.

Some things of note have happened since the fiasco on the *Diamond*. Another boat, this one a huge ferry from Florida, the *Constance*, called in a distress call. She was in the process of being overrun. Schumitz sent a team and they rescued three people, the rest were shamblers. One of the rescuees tried to hide a bite, but she was discovered during quarantine. She had that slim hope that the bitten have: *maybe I'm not infected*. She was, and she died. She didn't spread any infection, and that was good.

One of the helicopters from one of the rigs out here discovered a half-sunk military vessel in the shallows on the coast of Louisiana. A team from the *Stockdale* went in for a closer look and they told us that the wreck is the *USS Cole*. Another Arleigh-Burke-class destroyer. The *Stockdale* has a shit-ton of spare parts and a machine shop way better than the one on *Atlantis*, but plans are underway to hit the *Cole* on a scavenging mission.

A small pleasure boat drifted by yesterday. It was covered in blood, and didn't respond to multiple hails by either *Atlantis* or the *Stockdale*. Schumitz sent a skiff out to check it, and we all saw the lone zombie on board. The stupid thing tried to attack the skiff, which was about two hundred feet away, and fell overboard, slipping beneath the swells, hopefully forever. The skiff sunk the boat with a couple of blasts from its machine gun.

I've been working on sign language with Sasquatch so he can use his book less. Remo has been teaching self-defense classes, and there has been a shitload of cross training on everything for obvious reasons.

My foray idea was put on hold for a month until we can rule out this carrier group coming to take the *Stockdale* and enforce a court martial on its captain. It hasn't shown up on radar, and scouts haven't seen anything. Schumitz said he will not fire upon the US Navy, so if they come, he's surrendering peacefully. In two more weeks, he will call bullshit on the whole thing, and we can return to business as usual. He had a big meeting with his entire crew telling them that he had plans on a mutiny from the Navy, and that they would all be considered rogue. He and Austin offered sanctuary on *Atlantis* for any sailor that wished to stick with the Navy instead of the *Stockdale*. Not one crew member decided to leave.

If the carrier group shows up on radar, or any other way, I am taking off and heading to the *Drifter*, one of our buddy rigs. I'll stay there until they leave, and if the Navy is still there in three weeks, I will take my chances on the mainland. Ship, Donna, and Remo will come with me, but Tim and the kids are staying behind. Tim is needed here, and I'm not bringing the kids to the mainland.

Other than the undead on the little boat yesterday, I haven't seen a zombie since the *Majestik* a month ago. Hopefully, good times lay ahead.

I had to open my mouth, or my pen rather. After all the shit I've seen and done and been through, I just couldn't shut up. Full circle to shit magnet. Evil finds its way to me no matter what I do. God hates me, that's got to be what it is. I said that last sentence out loud the other day, and Ship flashed his notebook in my face. *If God hated you, you wouldn't be immune. Maybe, dumbass, he likes you more than anybody else.*

He had signed it to me first, but all I got was *immune, more,* and *anybody.* That was also the first time I have ever read a swear word in his book I think…

Schumitz called Ship, Alvarez, and me to the *Stockdale* for a meeting. Austin and Remo were already there, as was the leader of the team that had come save my ass on the *Diamond.* His name is Ensign Everly. One other guy, introduced as Smithers, was also there. Yeah, all I could think of was the Simpsons too.

"We've discovered a half-sunken vessel a day's sail away," began Schumitz.

"Yes, sir," I said, "the *Cole.*"

I had added the *sir* on purpose; it was the first time I had used this particular term of respect with the captain, and it didn't go unnoticed. I think it took him off guard for a moment. Or maybe it had been my interruption.

"Negative, not the *Cole,* the *Kanawha.* She's a USNS Auxiliary Force ship. She's an oiler actually."

I screwed up my face in confusion. "You mean there're two half-sunken Navy ships nearby?"

"Yes." He looked at me, waiting for me to intrude upon his brief again. As I was trying to get a better rapport with this guy, I shut up. "She has something aboard that we're going to need." He stared at me again. "You're a mechanic and a machinist, correct?"

"Yeah."

"So is Smithers. He's the best I have, and I want you two to work together on how to get what I need off of the *Kanawha.*" Little pause before he asked: "If you're okay with that?" Seems I wasn't the only one out to mend fences.

"Of course, Captain. Dare I ask what we're after, or is that need to know?"

He smiled. "Need to know, and I'm sorry, but you don't."

"So a smash and grab? What do you need from me?"

"You mentioned you were an underwater welder?"

"Yeah, two years."

"I want all of you to accompany a team of my men to the *Kanawha.* They will board the ship and retrieve the item. It is entirely possible that the location of the item is submerged, so divers will be ready." I didn't like where this was going, and my expression said it. "You won't have to board the ship or dive," he added quickly, "I just want you there as a consultant. We may have to cut through some bulkheads, and the item is most likely in a safe."

"Why Captain, are you robbing the US Navy?"

"No." It was his turn to smile a smug smile. "*We're* robbing the US government. The item in question could provide us additional security. It would definitely be worth almost anything to the executive branch, if there are any left." He looked me right in the eyes. "It's probably worth them leaving you alone for a trade."

I looked at Ship. He had one thumb up. I looked at Remo, and he looked bored.

"We're in."

I worked for a day with Smithers on how to best get at Schumitz's mystery item. "The safe is located in the captain's quarters," he told me and pointed at an electronic set of blueprints on his tablet (finally, like *Aliens*!), "here."

It was sort of in the forward-center of the ship, one deck down from the galley. Depending on how the ship looked when we got there, it would be an easy walk to the captain's quarters, then cut the safe open with a torch, grab whatever it is that was needed, and bug out.

Easy. I need to stop thinking that.

Dawn of the following day saw me looking at the beached *Kanawha*. We were surveying the wreck from the rear deck of the *Mary's Joy*, a forty-four-foot pleasure craft that had been used to get some desperate people from the mainland to *Atlantis*. This boat had been some rich guy's pre-apocalypse toy. There were pictures of small children inside, and it made me sad.

The fact that the *Kanawha* was 4/5ths sunk and at a twenty or so degree port angle also made me sad. These guys would have to dive, no two ways around it. The fact that there were a couple of dead crew members meandering around the foredeck gave me cause for concern as well. I just got back from a damn zombie-infested ship. Now I was ten feet from the rails of what could be another one. This one was mostly underwater, even if it was a mere eighth of a mile from what was once probably a beautiful Texas beach. Six or seven dead things had been on the shore, but when they heard our boat motor, they splashed into the surf toward us and disappeared.

Fuck this.

The *Kanawha* was a weird-looking boat. She had a bunch of big, gray cranes on her front and mid decks. Most of the mid-deck was sunk, but the front of the vessel was sticking out of the water. Waves slapped against the foredeck, and I saw an infected crawl up and out of the water. It came toward us, but slipped on the angled steel and slid back beneath the black surface.

"How many crew were on this thing before it sunk?" I asked Ensign Everly.

"One hundred and eight crew, but there were probably refugees as well. I know there were high-level US government officials on board too."

Smithers was suiting up and he had company. Five other guys were also getting ready to dive. They were kids. Young Navy boys about to dive into a hell most people couldn't possibly understand. I grabbed one of the suits and began putting it on. It was a dry suit with an auger mask and a rebreather. Shit. So, for those of you who don't know what that is; a wet suit is made of neoprene and lets a thin layer of water in to be warmed by your body and keep you warm when you dive. It's very buoyant and you need weights and a buoyancy compensator to get you up and down in the water. A dry suit keeps you encapsulated in dry air and the water never touches you. The auger mask keeps your whole head inside an air-filled helmet so you can install a radio to communicate with your buddy. The re-breather acts like a scuba tank, but scrubs your exhalations so you can breathe underwater for a lot longer than with a conventional tank. Rudimentary explanation, but there it is.

I felt a massive mitt on my shoulder. I didn't stop picking up the suit, so using his Sasquatch powers, Ship spun me gently around like a child. He was nodding his head in the negative.

"I have to, buddy."

He nodded no again, and mouthed, *No!*

"I have more experience with this equipment than all these guys combined." Everly and Smithers both looked at me. "They might need some help down there." He scribbled furiously and turned the book to me, *Which is why there is a communications system. You cannot go down there!*

"Have to, pal. I might have to see what they're looking at, or think on the fly. What if Smithers buys it down there, they'll need a backup."

"Thanks," Smithers said with a wry smile.

Everly moved over to us. "You really don't need to go, they've got this covered. They're all rated with this equipment."

"Sure. Rated. I was using it for two years solid in New England, some of the coldest, darkest water in the continental US, before they were even in the damn Navy." I leaned in to whisper to him, "They're babies for Christ's sake."

He looked at them, then back at me. "They'll be fine. They're trained."

"Nobody's trained for that," I said, and pointed at the undead who had struggled up the deck again and was reaching for us over the gunwale. Its head snapped back and there was a report from nearby. Remo holstered his M9 and I looked at him.

"I am."

"You're trained to kill everything else, not something that's already dead."

"What's the difference? Whether I get shot or eaten, I still have to kill the enemy before he kills me. Every operator would say the same."

Ship began searching for another set of gear, but Everly stopped him. "There are only eight rebreathers. Besides, on what planet would there be a dry suit big enough for you?" He turned his gaze to me. "I still say you don't have to go, but Schumitz said not to stop you if you wanted in."

I smiled. That prick had me figured out. I wish I could figure me out. "Whatever is down there," I thumbed at the sunken vessel, "could keep these government douches off of me and all of us. It's a no-brainer, we have to get it."

Ship, obviously pissed, showed me his newest missive. *How you have the ability to simultaneously exist as a smartass and a dumbass is beyond me. YOU MUST NOT GO!*

Twice he'd swore now. Granted *ass* was the worst thing he'd written. Another message: *I can't protect you if you pursue this folly!*

I smiled. "Touching, big boy, but I can't be protected forever. Besides, who's better qualified to go down there? I have the experience, and if I get bitten, it's no big deal."

Your blood is key to this plague. I disagree with the methods employed by the government, to obtain it, and the fact that they kept you against your will, but if you die for someone else's agenda, this planet may never recover. In addition, you are the only human being with my complete trust.

I read that and smiled even harder. "I get that last part, buddy, I do. Those fuckers took every fluid I have and did every test they could and came up empty though. I've done my duty, and I don't think I can help." He began to write, but I put my hand on his book. He looked up in surprise. "Donna has eight vials of my blood preserved with EDTA on *Atlantis*. Doc H. has another twenty. Nobody's getting any of my other fluids. Well, almost nobody." – Lecherous smile there.

I was attaching my ankle weights when Everly brought me the re-breather and helped me get it on. "Plan is to go in through the starboard window just there," he pointed to a partially submerged window in the superstructure, "then follow the map to the safe, cut it open, grab the loot, and get back."

We had all seen the map in detail last night. It was fairly straightforward, and everybody had a laminated drawing with a red line for our course on a card zip-tied to their gear.

I stared at the inky water surrounding the half-sunken ship. Jesus, I was doing it again. Hadn't I just thought *Fuck this*? I got my helmet on and everybody checked in. *Orca One, check. Orca Two, check.* There were seven of us and when it got to me I said, "I want to be Red Five."

Quit screwing around. Check in and speak only when necessary.

That had come from one of the kids. Oh shit, I had been chastised by somebody that had been in high school three years ago. "This is Orca Seven then." Everly was chuckling as he passed me a cattle-prod-looking thing. It was a bang-stick. A twelve gauge shotgun shell on the end of a pole. When you shoved the pole against something, the shell went off. Basically, a single-shot underwater rifle. It had been developed for shark defense. We each received ten special shells, and we all knew how to load them. That and my knife (not my SOG) were my only weapons.

I heard two more shots through my helmet. Remo and Everly had dispatched the remaining undead on deck, and it was time to go. Most of the time when you see TV or movies with someone going into the water with dive gear, you see them fall in backwards over the side of the boat. We used a giant stride method, and scissored our legs as we hit the water. It felt fantastic to be under water again.

Secondary comms check came through the headset. All six Orcas sounded off, and then so did I. I kept my mouth shut about being Red Five, even though that would have been way cooler. We adjusted our buoyancies, checked each other's gear, and swam to the starboard window. We actually went a deck below, maybe ten feet underwater, and decided to go through that window, as it would be one less floor to negotiate. Our dive lights penetrated the inky darkness through the glass before Orca One, our dive leader pulled out a little device that looked like a pen. He pressed it against the window and the thing exploded into glass shards that looked like mirrors as they sunk. Cool tool, and I wanted one.

One used his bang stick to clear away errant glass debris, and he swam in. The rest of us followed. As I was the odd man out, I had two buddies, Five and Six. Smithers was Six. We both had cutters consisting of two oxygen cylinders, a line, the cutting tool, and six cutting rods. The small gas tanks were so heavy that they had their own buoyancy compensators.

Everything looked wrong, as the ship was partially leaning on its side. Our light beams were thin columns of visibility in the blackness of the sunken vessel, and they cast eerie shadows against the gray steel. It was weird to see seven shafts of light cutting in so many directions. Orca Two was passing an open door when he freaked, swimming back against the bulkhead quickly. It was short-lived because the fish-belly white dead man floating in the doorway was truly dead. When I swam past, I saw a wicked wound on his neck, and a bullet hole in his forehead. He was floating with his arms out like a zombie trying to attack. The sound Orca Two had made when he saw the thing was undignified, and everybody laughed at him. Everybody but me. I was starting to wonder if what little sense I possessed had fled the building.

The first stairwell loomed in front of us, a black cavity that descended at a sideways angle off to the right. Orcas One and Two were in the hole after a quick check with their lights. The rest of the team moved into the darkness. God help me, I followed.

Stuff was suspended in the water a deck down. Paper mostly, but some other crap too, most of it unidentifiable. What I mean is, our lamps showed us only that there was shit in the water, not what it was. This is also where we found our first signs of trouble. One of the Orcas panned his light down, and he told us to look. The beam showed us dozens of expended bullet casings, the light glinting off the brass in stark contrast to the gray of the bulkhead. The nylon sling of an MP5 undulated above the discarded weapon it was attached to as we moved past. There were bullet dents in the steel ahead of us as well as another unmoving corpse. The *Kanawha* must have had her own outbreak, and there had been a stand here. There was only one weapon left behind, but there were several calibers of brass. The fish that were nibbling on the severed arm a bit further down the stairs swam off when our lights hit them. This shit was getting real. *I'm not liking this,* one of the Orcas said as he swam past the appendage.

The ship decided to make an awful sound right then. It was like bending metal, and it was scary enough that everybody grabbed something to hold on to. The horrible noise echoed through the black water for a moment and subsided. The boat hadn't moved though.

Moving down another two decks via the stairwell, we discovered our first moving corpse. It was horribly mauled, and handcuffed to a railing. It had its back to us, and was trying to get at the beams that were shooting past, putting spots of light on the bulkhead in front of it. The thing was pawing at the lights like some demented cat chasing a laser pointer. It was stretched out, using its legs to pull against the handcuff so hard that bits of its wrist were flaying off and drifting briefly through the water before they slowly sunk.

It was gross.

I'll take this one, one of the Orcas said, and moved forward. He pulled his knife, swimming in just behind the dead man. He grabbed its hair to drag its head back so he could stab it, but the scalp came off in his fist. The thing, now exhibiting extreme male pattern baldness, spun around as fast as a dead thing can spin, and latched onto the kid. It leaned in for a bite, but the kid was faster and jabbed his blade into the side of its melon. When the kid jerked his knife back out, my light showed some foul fluid dispersing through the water in a nasty cloud.

The boss kid's voice came over the radio, *Everybody stay on their toes, there's bound to be more of them.* We swam-walked down the corridor until we got to a big room. It had higher ceilings (decks) than the previous steel tubes we had traversed. Two of the kids moved into the room, panning their lights back and forth. *Clear,* One said before a white hand snaked from above and latched onto his auger mask. The thing pulled up, but in doing so came down on the kid, latched its other hand onto him, and bit his mask. By this time, the boy was struggling with the creature, but the dead man wouldn't let go. It couldn't get purchase, and just as I could hear panic coming through the radio, I saw a stick dart forward and impact the thing's head. The creature's noggin came apart like an over-ripe cantaloupe, all kinds of nasty shit literally exploding into the water. The boom of the stick was muffled, but wicked loud too, and it scared the shit out of me. The shot shell must have been heard over the comms by the crew of the *Mary's Joy*, because Everly demanded a report.

I flashed my light up, and looked into Hell. Hell looked back as a dozen or so dead folks fought physics to reach us. They had bloated with gases though and weren't getting to us anytime soon. They were only about ten feet above us, but couldn't figure out how to swim, so they just reached for us, wiggling around like nasty worms on the ceiling of the room we were in. The one that had grabbed the Orca must have been less gassy, or maybe the gas had leaked out of the multiple bullet holes in its chest and abdomen.

We were all looking up. Orca One had been very wrong when he said the room was clear. *Nothing, sir,* the kid told Everly, *just a few dead people trying to eat us. Tangos are down... er... up. Orcas are clear, over.*

We moved as a unit through the big room, which looked to be some type of storage from the shit all tied down with ratcheting straps. It was unsettling swim-walking underneath the dead things. They really wanted us, and we really wanted not to be there. It was terrifying. They were totally silent, their lungs no doubt filled with seawater.

We made it to the second stairwell and started down into more foreboding darkness. We got to the second landing before we saw our next zombie. It had been burned so badly some of its skeleton was visible, the bones a sickly yellow instead of white. This particular zombie was one of the nastiest I'd seen. It looked broken in addition to burned, and part of its shoulder blade stuck up out of its back. This one was not gassy. It started toward us immediately, its scorched boots making scary, echoing noises as it thudded up the slanted steps. It was using the railing as a... well... a railing, and pulling itself toward us. One of the kids waited patiently until it was almost on him, then he stabbed it through the left eye.

Two more decks down, and we figured out why the ship was under water. There was a giant, blackened hole in the side of the hull. Had to be ten feet across and eight feet tall. *Torpedo?* one of the Orcas asked. *No, couldn't be. Torpedo would have cut her in half, or at least shown more damage than this. Looks like a mine, or a shape charge did this.*

"It came from in here too," I said. "Look at the way the steel is bent outward." I panned my light across the charred breach, pointing.

Smithers agreed. *He's right, you can see the scorch marks and the way the metal is going. Somebody sunk her from on board. Why would they do that?*

Our mission is to retrieve the package, Orca One communicated, *I don't give a shit about how this tub sank.*

"Well you fucking should," I answered, ire in my voice. This kid was starting to piss me off. "Whatever reason someone had for sinking this ship could very well mean our deaths if we aren't careful."

You're a consultant, he shot back. *When I need consulting, you consult. Until then be quiet and—* the *Kanawha* made another one of those rending metal sounds, and this time, she did move. Only a bit, but it was there. The good news was if something happened right now, we could just swim out the breach in the hull that was right next to us.

Unless, of course, the entire angled stairway we were standing on and part of the deck near it gave way, crashing into the ship below us. The clamor of stretching metal reached its crescendo, something snapped incredibly loudly under us, spewing bubbles skyward, and we were all sucked down through a huge chasm that had appeared in the deck. The metal must have fatigued enough from the blast that our weight on the steps was the camel's straw.

I twisted as I fell, the cutter handle being torn from my grasp and my light beam going in all directions as it spun away from me. The total darkness was made absolute when something heavy struck me in the back of the head as I tumbled to the depths.

DEEP SHIT

Noise. There had been a loud noise. I blinked my eyes but couldn't see anything. I brought my hand to my face to check what was wrong, but my hand hit some type of barrier. Panic began to well up, and I heard *Sound off! This is Orca One!* come through my head. I remembered I was underwater in the pitch black, with a helmet on my head. That was why I couldn't see or touch my face.

Then the pain hit me. My fuk'n dome was splitting again. I couldn't rub or cradle my noggin either. I don't care who you are, from the President to the Pope, if you can rub your head after you bump it, it feels better. Screw you if you disagree, I'm not in the mood.

Orca Three here.

"Orca Seven is alive. Mostly," I added.

Orca Four is... what... AHHH! Four began yelling, then screaming. We could hear the terror over the radio, then a crunch and some gurgling. There was momentary static, then nothing.

Orca Four, what is your status? Four, come in! Where are you, Four? Come in!

Four didn't come in. It was an absolute certainty in my damaged head that Orca Four had, in fact, gone out. I searched in the darkness for my light, but it was gone. My hand did come across the hose for my cutter, and I pulled it to me. I tried to move, but my right foot was pinned. It didn't hurt, and I could feel it, so it wasn't crushed either. I put my hands up, and impacted something hard and heavy above me at almost full arm's length.

We need to assemble. Orcas, sound off. This is Orca One.

Three is okay.

"Seven here, but I'm stuck."

Don't panic, Seven, we'll get to you. Three, do you have a light?

Negative, Three is blind, lost chem-lights as well.

Chem-lights! I had forgotten I had them! What a dick! I reached my paw up to my shoulder and pulled one of the lights out of the Velcro pouch there. I snapped it, shook it, and held it in front of my face. Not three feet away were the dead, red eyes of a zombie looking right at me.

It lunged and got about six inches. I shuffled two or three inches back, my stuck foot not allowing me to get any further. The thing kept trying unsuccessfully to lunge. It was also stuck on something. The something was the collapsed stairway that must weigh three thousand pounds. I had been fortunate enough that the ton and a half of steel that we were on when it collapsed had missed me. I was pinned by a railing, and it had hit me at an angle. Had it been another inch down, I would be walking lopsided for the rest of my short life. I wasn't freeing my boot anytime soon, but thankfully, I would keep my foot.

The dead guy wouldn't. Just when I was thinking that this dead bastard would stay three feet away forever, his right leg tore free from his trapped knee. I heard it rip away through the water and almost puked in my mask. The fucker still couldn't reach my face, which is what all zombies want to bite first, but he could sure as shit now reach my trapped appendage. The thing was stretched out so all it could do was grab my boot, but you try being trapped and having a dead monster paw at your foot. Now try it while underwater and using a glowing, green chem-stick as your only source of light.

The whole time I had been going through what you just read, Orca One was still trying to get in contact with his other men. "Seven has a problem," I said into my helmet.

What kind of problem? Is your rebreather damaged?

"The dead kind, and no, but my sanity is a bit damaged."

Hang on. We'll get to you as soon as we can. Three, you still with us?

One, this is Three. Affirma... ing for a... ght source... My ceiling is only about five feet high here and I... ell whi... is up with this buoyancy.

Three, One, you're breaking up.

I heard a crack, another tear, and whipped my head over to check on the status of my new dead buddy. Black shit was floating out of his legs, and I knew he had ripped free of both of his lower extremities. His left pant leg was still trapped under the crushing weight of the collapsed stairs. That and the fact that his belt was firmly attached to his waist were what was keeping him off of my important parts for now.

My bang stick was nowhere to be seen, but I still had my knife and a pry bar. I moved the chem-light around some, and noticed the cutter hose. I grabbed it and pulled the cutter and tanks to me. I had heard about these cutters before. They were the high-speed plasma-type used by the military. The thing grabbed at the cylinders, but was woefully short. I turned on the oxygen and pressed the electronic start (yes, it has an underwater electronic starting mechanism, don't get your panties in a bunch) on the cutter. It fired up immediately, and I honed the flow. I couldn't sit all the way up, so I scrunched myself into a fetal position and started to cut at the railing.

This is One, I see a glow!

"One, Seven, the glow is my cutter! Can you make it to me?" I added hastily.

I can't tell yet, there's a ton of debris in the way. Three, can you see the glow? Three, come in. Shit, his comms must be down.

Everly was also bellowing for a report, and I could feel Ship in the background mutely demanding answers.

I got most of the way through the first cut on the tube steel when hands grabbed me from behind. The hands pulled me back and the thing that leaned over me and bit my helmet was a black-garbed horror. It was horribly burned, like the thing that had been on the stairs. So were the three behind it that were slowly making their way toward me through the wreckage. My knife slid easily into the creature's temple, but it took a few seconds for it to cease trying to bite my face through the glass. It had smashed its face into my mask, and the view plate was now covered in gooey smears. I wiped the goo away, but the thing twisted as it collapsed and my knife was torn from my grasp.

Legless had gotten free and was now crawling through the railing to get at the rest of me. It grabbed my free leg and I kicked it off, then kicked it in the nose. The blood and goo that was now in the water was friggin' nasty, but I had more pressing issues. The thing latched onto my kicker again, but this time had me firmly in its grasp. It used my leg to pull itself all the way through the railing, and was trying to bite every part of me it could. I used my leg to keep it from succeeding, but eventually, it would get a bite in. I got in one more swat with my boot, and it fell to the side. It was up again in a second, and now it was on me. It was all I could do to keep its teeth from ripping into my dry suit. It continued to drag itself up me until it was trying to bite through my helmet just like its brother had, except now I was knifeless. I grabbed the forgotten cutter with my right hand and put the nozzle against the dead man's forehead while I held his neck. It took less than two seconds to burn through and then the single most disgusting thing that had happened to me since the start of this plague occurred. The overpressure from the heat inside the zombie's head shot the rotting contents of its skull out the hole, past the cutter beam, and all over me.

I pitched the thing to the side, and glanced over my shoulder at his pals. They were on top of me as well. The anger that I had just been experiencing turned to stark terror. I was going to go out like this? Underwater with three dead guys all dressed in black camo eating through my dry suit.

Fuck.

I lay back and began to fight over my head with the first of them. It latched onto my hand, trying to relieve me of a few fingers, but I was too fast and yanked my hand away. Light flooded the area from behind the dead, but all that did was blind me for a crucial couple of moments. In that time, the thing I had been battling with was able to grab my wrist and bite down. On my dive watch. It hurt like hell, but my suit hadn't been breached. I had to pull the thing closer to deal with it, and the oxygen cylinders were snagged on something, so the cutter was not an option. I began to smash my hurting head up in a steel-covered head-butt into the thing's face. The light was everywhere now, and I saw one of the black-clad things get jerked back into the brightness. My head was about to explode, but the thing on me was stunned, and I jabbed my fingers into its eyes. I felt both of them go, but this wasn't my first rodeo with that. This fucker was blind now, but had fully functional teeth, so was still deadly. I smashed my head upward again, and destroyed a couple of those teeth. Green circles began to dance in front of my eyes as I fought to stay conscious with my head in such pain. Literally, the last thing you want to do when you get smacked in the dome is use your melon as a battering ram. Write that shit down, because it's a life lesson.

I heard grunting and gasping, and I realized it was coming through my headset. I heard and felt the explosive whoosh of air and water that accompanies one of the bang sticks going off. The blind thing was yanked off of me in a fear-filled moment. I blinked, thinking if I passed out I was lunch, and Orca One was staring at me through two panes of glass. He smiled. *So you're not dead.*

"Day ain't over."

He glanced at the three things he had killed, and the two done by me. *Damn. You're lucky.*

"Don't feel lucky."

Can you say more than three words at a time?

"Only need two," I extended my middle finger, "Fuck you."

He smiled again, and helped move the dead guy off of me. *C'mon, Seven. We have to find the others, get the package, and get out of here.* He panned his light around, and we found one of the Orcas. It wasn't possible to tell which one as all we could see was his glove sticking out from under the collapsed stairs. I hope it had been painless.

That was at least two dead. Orca Four had been eaten, and this one crushed, so we were down to five with only two accounted for. One pulled my knife from the black-clad creature's temple, passing it back to me. He also passed me the cutter, which was still on. In less than a minute and a half, I was free, and it felt great.

Orca One, this is Rampart. Report.

Rampart, Orca One. At least one dead and four missing. I am with Seven, and we will make our way to the target searching for survivors along the way. Had contact with Three, but his comms are down.

Along the way? Was he nuts? I took stock of my surroundings and realized everybody was dead. They had all been squished by a ton and a half of broken boat. We might find that other guy, I couldn't remember which number, but that was it. I stepped on something turning my ankle, but not badly. It was my light, broken and useless.

When we could stand, we stepped over the bodies, and I had to wonder what was up with the black camo and why they were burned. Moving down the corridor, we saw more bullet brass, and another dead black camo guy with a head wound. It almost looked like there was a two directional firefight here.

Orca One looked at his map and then at our surroundings. We moved at a fairly brisk pace and to the door of the captain's quarters quickly. It was then I realized I was done calling my only friend down here Orca One. "What's your name?" He looked through the glass at me like I had three heads. *Call me Orca—*

"Fuck that, what's your *name*?" I put emphasis on the word *name* so he would get it.

Uhh... Frank.

"Well, Frank, look at that." I pointed to the door. Scrawled on the steel in Day-Glo orange marker was a note. Probably left for us.

DEAD INSIDE.

Where did everybody get all this orange marker? I'd seen it in three different places since the apocalypse came to dinner. Was it a common item in everybody's survival bag? I ask because I don't have an orange marker. Do you, Dear Reader, have an orange marker? Don't get one. Every time I've seen it used, a bunch of people were dead.

I was looking at the door when I noticed Frank look past me down the corridor behind us. He shined his light down that way and we were pleased to find that Orca Three was making his way toward us. We breathed a sigh of relief until we noticed that he was coming a bit faster than the casual swim-walk we were used to. When he got closer, we could see there was an air of panic to his movements. Frank's light showed movement behind Orca Three, and the panic was not unwarranted. Ten or twelve of the dead crewmembers followed Three at a speed and distance that told me they would be on us in a couple of minutes. At least one of them was wearing a shredded dry suit. Three made it to us with something wrapped around his right leg, and pointed to his head, mouthing shit inside his helmet. He also pointed back behind him. "Can you hear me?" I asked into the comms.

He shook his head in the negative, so I pointed to the door. Any idiot could see what he said through the glass of his helmet when he read the words. One syllable. Rhymes with *Fuck*.

Three had his bang-stick, as did Frank, but my only weapons were my knife, the cutter, and my incredibly sharp wit. I was one-quarter out of oxygen for the cutter, but my wit was at full capacity. "The Devil you know?" I asked thumbing to the growing crowd of underwater pus bags on the way toward us, "Or the one you don't?" I nodded toward the door.

We need what's in there.

I tightened my balls, "Okay then," and tried the knob. Shockingly, it was locked. This was a cabin door, and as such was like any other wooden door, so I used my pry bar to Jimmy the lock. As soon as the lock broke, the door was pulled from my grasp from the inside and I looked into the face of a dead guy in a suit. He looked great other than he was dead and had a bullet hole where his heart was. He reached for us, but Frank was faster and shoved his stick into the thing's face. His head did what anything would do when confronted with a twelve-gauge persuader: it ceased to exist. The remnants of his noggin exploded backwards into the face of another suited dead man, who got Three's bang stick and the cranial-popping occurred again. The third guy in a suit was a bit further back, and a fourth dead man was experiencing the extreme bloating that the floaters from before had and was floating up near the ceiling. This time, we were well within reach though.

Frank passed me the light, and I flashed it around as we stepped into the room, both of them reloading as we did so. I moved forward with my knife, careful to stay out of reach of the floater. I stabbed the mobile one in the eye, the comedy of him sinking to the deck in slow motion not lost on me. Three's stick made short work of the guy on the ceiling. A better search of the room with the light told us that was the end of the dead in here.

There was fuck-all in the room to brace the now broken door with, so we would have to improvise. An old whaling harpoon was attached to the wall over a desk, and I broke it off passing it to Three. He wedged it diagonally into a groove next to the door. It would slow down the infected, but they would get through it. I know what you're thinking too: *Use the harpoon as a weapon, dumbass!* But it was one of the old types with that big ass barb on the end. It might be possible to get it into the skull of a dead man, but you were never getting it out again.

A fifth body was behind the desk, but it was mostly a skeleton. The things in here must have gnawed on it. It was nasty and unmoving, as the faceless skull had a big hole above the right eye socket.

A dozen or so pictures and photographs adorned the wall, and I began to rip them down. The safe was under the third painting; a portrait of Abraham Lincoln sitting in a chair with his chin in his hand. I fired up the cutter and got to work.

The safe wasn't a Chubb Sovereign, but it wasn't cheap either. It was a newer model Sentry Hideaway, with a standard three number combination. Two rods on the top, two on the bottom, and three on the left. No tar layer to create smoke, and more importantly, no copper plate for heat dissipation. The weak part was the combination wheel, and that's where I started. The cutter was through the wheel in four minutes. I popped the wheel with my pry bar and inspected the tumblers. One had to be cut before the others would disengage, so I turned the cutter on that. Another two minutes and I was through. I used the bar to pry the second and third tumblers into position, turned the handle, and looked at my prize.

It was a briefcase. I had been hoping for gold or jewels or a map to a porn palace, but I had gotten a fat, leather briefcase, the size of a backpack. I reached for it, but Frank stopped me. *Let me,* came through the headset.

I shrugged and stepped away. Frank grabbed the case and the door that three was guarding received its first thud. It was followed by several more, and the door opened as far as the harpoon would let it, maybe four inches. Dead hands reached through, pushing, pulling, and hoping for flesh to grab.

Rampart, we have the package, but there are hostiles on us. Report again when we've dispatched or evaded.

The only access to this room was the door we had come through. Of course, that meant that it was also the only egress. I looked around, searching for magic, but there was no joy. I tried to imagine what was above and below us. Above was most certainly another stateroom, but I had no idea what was below. It would take me about fifteen minutes to cut a hole in the ceiling of this steel box we were in. I had, maybe twenty minutes of oxygen in my cutting tanks. I went to work on the bolts for the leather couch first.

So you're on a ship. You can't have furniture sliding around willy-nilly in six-foot swells, so you bolt all your shit to the deck right? Those were the bolts I was after. I was through the fourth bolt in two minutes. Eighteen left to cut into the deck above us. Frank knew what I was about, and pushed the couch over to Three, who was doing a shitty job bracing the door against a concentrated undead attack. The couch moved against the door just as the harpoon was giving way.

I stood on the wooden desk and began to cut into the ceiling. The initial cut took moments, and I began to move the cutter flame in a wide circle. We would have to fit ourselves and our rebreathers through the hole.

I heard a small muffled explosion, and dared a glance at the door. Three had used another shotgun shell, and Frank was poking his stick through the partly open door. The couch moved just a bit back into the room. Three moved back to push the couch, but it wouldn't budge and actually moved a tiny bit more toward him. Frank chose another target and shoved his bang-stick through the gap again. Something on the other side got wise and grabbed it. Frank yanked it back, but the dead bastard held firm. We had been talked out of spear guns, and I couldn't help but think that at this juncture they would have helped.

Let GO! he yelled, and the thing complied, the living man stumbling back into the room. He reloaded and did it again, the whoosh of the explosion louder this time.

Quarter through my cut, but it was hard to see as the cutter was the only light source, our one light being focused solely on the door between us and a couple dozen voracious monsters. I snapped another chem-stick, but it didn't add tons of visibility.

Halfway through my circle, the first thing got its head and shoulders through the door. Orca Three was pushing for his life (and ours), but it was a losing battle. Frank popped the nearest creature, re-killing it, but it was halfway through the portal. That door would never close again with the body in the way. Not only that, but with the door as open as it was, it was much easier for the dead things to push. Another thing got partly in, Frank destroying it with a jab. A third gained access as Frank was reloading. I could see Three sliding back on the end of the couch.

I hooked the orange glow stick onto the end of my webbing, trying to pry the piece of steel with my bar as I cut, but it was a no-go. I kept cutting as two more dead men got through the door. Three tried to use his stick, but he was too far away. The first thing grabbed Frank and tried to bite him through the helmet. The Orca dropped his stick in favor of his knife, dispatching the beast with a sideways stab to the dome.

I was two-thirds of the way through my cut before I realized we were fucked. It dawned on Frank too, because he started screaming *Come on!* to the dead as they entered the room and moved toward the nearest target: him.

The couch made a screeching sound as it slid a bit, then some more, and the door was suddenly open wide enough for the dead to pour in. Being underwater screwed with their already poor coordination, but in this 15x20 room, it would be over for all of us shortly. Frank's bang-stick was lost under the feet of the dead, but he used his knife like a ninja, taking out two more of the rotting things.

Three reloaded quickly and took out another creature. There were six of them in the room now with more coming. I was most of the way through, and tried to pry the circle, but that shit still wouldn't budge. Frank was still yelling when I finished the cut, and the piece of metal fell into the room. It missed my foot by inches, digging a furrow into the wooden desk and clanging away to the deck. It had to have weighed two hundred pounds. The sides of the hole were going to be too hot to even casually touch, and sharp as fuck, but that was still better than staying in this room

"I'm through!"

So am I, Frank said and began to yell. *Get out! Getoutgetoutgetout!* The dead had him and now he began to scream as he fought them with his gloved hands and a knife. Three seized the briefcase and made his way to me. He pointed at the hole I had made and started to climb up on the desk. I thrust off of the wood and shot through the opening perfectly. Spinning around, I grabbed the package that Three passed to me. He pushed off of the desk, but dead hands latched on to him. I reached down and began to pull, but there were many dead yanking the other way. I couldn't hear him as his comms were down, but I could tell what was happening. He closed his eyes, scrunched up his face, and opened his mouth wide in a silent scream. Bloody water flooded his helmet and his mouth as they pulled him from my grasp. There were a dozen or so on him, tearing.

Frank had stopped screaming as well, and I realized I was alone.

HAPPY AS A PIG IN POO

So it was pretty dark and quiet in my new room. I extended my hand using the chem-light to survey my surroundings, and was rewarded with about an extra foot and a half of vision. My light revealed stuff I was familiar with. Tools, parts, barrels of liquids. I had cut into some type of storage area, and the stored stuff looked to be mechanical in nature. This would be a good room to loot if the ship hadn't been crawling with the living dead.

Thinking about the dead, I looked back into the hole. By the light of my dropped plasma-cutter, I could see the things feeding on Three. I could also see one of the things standing on the desk reaching for me. It was able to get the tips of its nasty fingers on the edge of the newly melted steel and was rewarded with burned fingers which would have incapacitated any human from the pain. I hadn't been able to hear Three scream, but I heard those fingers crisp up like forgotten hot dogs on a grill. It made me suddenly hungry.

"Rampart, this is Orca Seven, come in. Rampart, Orca Seven with status report, over?"

Nothing. I tried a few more times, but either I wasn't sending, or I wasn't receiving. I couldn't tell. I moved past a few shelves and found a bulkhead, then ran my hand down that until I found a door. This one was locked with those six handles, and I turned them all. Pushing the door open, I was reluctant to step outside the room, but I also had no intentions on making this my new home, so a Man-Up was necessary.

My right boot hit the deck soundlessly, and the rest of me followed. I looked to the right, then back to the left. Right angled down, further into Hell. Left was the opposite, and I really didn't want to go play in the rest of this sunken, infested boat, so my options were limited. I began trekking slowly upwards, using a handrail to help me forward. This briefcase was friggin' heavy, but I would be damned if I would leave it behind. My whole crew had gotten killed for it.

A dozen steps more, and there was a man in front of me. He had his back to me, and was holding onto the railing as I was. He was motionless, and dressed in that same black camo that I had been seeing all over this tub. I took a step toward him, and his head moved. He looked like he was listening for something, but I hadn't made a sound. The thing took another step forward, which was away from me, and stopped, sort of staring into the darkness ahead of it. At this rate, he would reach the end of the corridor in about six days, so he had to go. I reached for my knife. It was still stuck in the head of one of the dead a deck below me. I didn't have my bang-stick, my cutter, or even the luxury of using harsh language against this creature as it probably couldn't hear me.

I pushed the orange light down toward the floor, but the only thing there was more spent casings. They had all rolled to one side of the deck because of the list of the ship. There was fuck-all here to deal with this creature. How was I going to get past this asshole?

I decided a search of the briefcase might yield me a weapon. There were two belt-buckle pockets up front, and a small pouch in the back. The pouch held a book in a plastic Zip-Lock style bag. The left-side pocket contained a hockey puck with a signature I couldn't quite make out. The right side offered me a silver Cross-type pen and pencil. There were matching seals on the writing implements, and the graphic looked to have gold in an exterior ring with a blue center. There was an eagle in the center as well. I couldn't make out the writing by chemical light, but what was important was that I now had something to kill the zombie in front of me with.

Re-death by pen, bitches.

What if I couldn't get the thing through his head? It was difficult enough to stab a dude through the noggin with a knife, but with a pen? It would have to be the temple. Or better yet, through the eye. I would have to go all ninja on his ass with five and a half inches of ink-filled metal.

As sneaky as possible, I slunk up behind him. Making a fist, I put the pen between my middle and ring fingers so it stuck out. The gloves would only get slightly in the way. I nodded to myself. Yeah, this shit was doable. I tapped him on the shoulder, and he looked in every direction but at me. Rolling my eyes, I pulled back on his right shoulder a little. He fought me and pulled away, actually taking a step further down the corridor. Was this a joke? A fucking undead prank? *Tee hee, I'ma fuck with my food before I nibble.* I pulled harder, and this time, he did turn enough to see me. Of course, he lunged immediately, and of course, I punched him in the eye. The point of the pen scraped the outside of his nose and plunged into the thing's orbit. It went between the eye and the socket, and that shit went deep. The creature's hand, which had been grabbing for me, went limp-ish and sort of hung suspended in the water. His eyes glazed, and I gave him my smirk through the mask. You know, that awesome half-smile that melts a woman's will and makes their panties hit the floor? That smirk. Oh? You can't do that? I'm available for lessons.

So, mid-smirk, the thing's eyes snap back to me, completely focused. I had half a breath to think *Oh shit!* and cease smirking before his hand was on me and he was all teeth. He let go of the railing, spun, and had both hands on me as fast as a cobra. Snapping, he pulled me toward him as he leaned in, and he smashed into the glass of my helmet, losing a tooth. Undeterred, he kept up with the snapping, and actually bit off a chunk of his tongue. That shit was nasty, as it was attached to him by a string of tongue-meat and flapped in the water.

Stupidly, I was still holding onto the briefcase, so in a moment of genius, I let it go to fight off the undead menace. I grabbed his neck with my left and began punching him with my right. He looked at me with those dead, red eyes, and I could tell this fucker had been a bad guy, even in life. All these black camo motherfuckers had most certainly boarded this vessel and caused her to sink. They had killed the people on board, or had died trying, but they had undoubtedly put a large hole in the side of the *Kanawha*, causing untold destruction and death.

Assholes. I think per capita, our planetary asshole ratio had gone through the fucking roof with the onset of this damned apocalypse. Why can't we all just get along?

I was not getting along with this fuk'n dead guy, that was for sure. He wanted my entrails to be my extrails, and that shit was bothersome. I gave a monumental shove with my left hand under his chin, and for a split second took him by surprise. I was able to push his head back just enough to give him a palm-heel strike, and drive that pen into his head up to the hilt. Well, pens don't have hilts, but if they did...

He instantly stopped moving, other than his eyes, which blinked a few times before they rolled back (past the pen) into his head. I was taking no chances, and when he hit the deck, I stomped on his dome until I heard a crack. That stomping shit is way harder underwater.

I put my hand against the bulkhead for a sec to catch my breath, and looked for my briefcase. It hadn't wandered off, so I grabbed it, then decided I wanted my pen back. Try as I might, I couldn't dig it out. The end of it was flush with where his tear-duct was, and it was stuck fast. I tried like hell, even squishing the fucker's eye (second time in an hour), but it was a no-go. This prick would have a beautiful pen in his skull along with some fish and maybe a hermit crab in the coming months.

I had to think about that. Can you imagine the jealousy and hate from all the other hermit crabs, when you have one walking around with a human skull as his house? I started laughing in my helmet. Great big guffaws. I even danced a little jig. I gave the dead guy another kick for good measure and began to laugh again.

Damn, I was in a good mood! I took two deep breaths to calm down. I was a bit tired from the fighting/stabbing/stomping/thinking session.

But I shouldn't be. I was in the best shape of my life. Granted, everything overexerted a person when underwater. But the happy and the tired? Those were dead giveaways, and I was immediately concerned. Happy, but scared. Tired but pissed. I laughed again. How stupid is it to be happy and frightened at the same time. I mean, aren't they mutually exclusive?

I felt something move behind me. I didn't hear it, but I just knew something was there from the pressure differential through the water. I spun in a wide arc, and, well, you already know what it was. I mean this is a damn zombie story.

It was a zombie. This one was not clad in black, it was a seaman. Really, that was the first thought that popped into my head. Seaman. So obviously, in a display of natural immaturity, I began to laugh about homonyms. I was still chortling when the bastard grabbed me. I laughed even harder when I noticed the knife sticking out of the creature's neck, and the slung MP5 around his shoulder. He looked ridiculous! I giggled as we grappled, pulling the edged weapon out of him and stabbing him in the head with it over and over. He went limp, and of course, that word got me going again. How many penis related jokes could there be in one minute?

My smile evaporated, and I began to feel anxiety. Not scared, per-se, but just *off*. Something was up. I had figured it out after I destroyed zombie number one, and I almost had it again a moment ago before this asshole decided to dine on me, but the thought had fled.

I stood there on the angled deck, staring at two re-killed dead men, wondering WTF I had been thinking about just a minute before. I was diving. There were zombies. I was alone. I was happy. I was angry. I could barely see… Whoa. Just whoa. Back up. Diving and happy? Full of anxiety?

Fuck.

I'm narc'd. If you're not a diver, you might not know what nitrogen narcosis is. It's a condition that divers suffer from, usually at depths over a hundred feet, where breathing air at pressure increases the solubility of gases in body tissues. It basically gets you high because the gas in the blood passing through the brain is pressurized differently than the pressure around you.

It could be deadly.

All I would have to do is get to a shallower depth and I should be fine. But I was only about forty feet down. The only way I could be suffering from narcosis is if… oh shit… if there was something wrong with the scrubbers in my re-breather. I might not be getting all the carbon dioxide out of my breathable air. Holy shitballs, I'm in trouble. Must have happened when the stairs collapsed.

I snapped another chemical light and hung it on my vest. This one was green, and it was the most illuminating. Gave me about three feet of visibility. I started walking quickly up the companionway. I was tired, and I shouldn't be, which led me to a bit of fear. The knife was in my left hand, which was the hand I needed to use to pull myself forward. The briefcase was getting heavy in my right hand, but what could I do?

I detected movement in front of me. Initially, I thought it was me seeing things, but no, it was there. I moved steadily toward it because back the way I had come was not an option. I leaned forward, straining my eyes to see what was there. Four dead men materialized out of the gloom. They were headed toward me at a ridiculously slow speed even for the living dead. They were way further away than the three feet I thought the chem-lights would allow. I squinted, and realized there was light behind them. Faint, but there. I had come, maybe, sixty feet since I had cut the hole in the deck, so I should be coming up out of the water in just a minute or so. Well, after I dispatched these dead douches.

The pus bags had definitely seen me. One fell as it moved forward on the deck, but its three pals seemed to be having little trouble.

One knife, one briefcase, and four undead. Oh yeah, and time. I needed out of this monkey suit soon, or I would slip into a coma. I switched my weapon and briefcase hands, I wanted the knife in my strong hand. I was dizzy when the first one and I met. He was nasty, all burned and black. I stabbed him in the right eye as he lunged. One down.

Uneventful. Events transpired when I tried to take out number two, however. I slipped as I brought the blade around in a sideways arc trying to get into the temple, and ended up getting him, you guessed it, in the neck. He was on me before I could pull the knife out, and this time, he had friends. The first one closed his teeth around the dry suit on my left shoulder. It didn't get me, but he was yanking on my suit with his mouth. Fucker was chewing through the rubber. Another grabbed me around the waist, and we went down in a heap. This heap happened to be in front of the third one's face, and he tried to bite me through the helmet like all his buddies had. I fought for all I was worth, but there were three of them and I was in a dry suit. Shoulder-guy decided he didn't like the taste of rubber, so he switched to my arm. Still rubber, but he seemed to enjoy this more. I couldn't see him, as he had the arm with the briefcase, and I was frantically stabbing with the other hand, his buddy straddling me. It felt wet where the bastard was chewing on my forearm, but the dumb thing had still only gotten my suit. If he pulled out a chunk, I was in deep shit as my suit would flood.

I managed to get a fatal jab on the one who was trying to eat my face. He collapsed, but on my stabbing arm. His pal was chewing on my chest and I decided enough was enough. I bucked and kicked and fought to get them off me. I freed my right arm, but not before a searing pain came from my left. The fucker had bitten me. I didn't feel water gushing in, just a wetness, but it was cold so it wasn't blood. He had just pinched me through the neoprene. The one on my chest had also gotten purchase, and I felt a brief pinch there too before the bastard was yanked off of me. I rolled to my left and grappled with the one gnawing on my arm. We both rolled around for a sec, me stabbing him but not penetrating his skull. Shreds of his face and scalp came away as I repeatedly thrust the blade at him. He batted my hand away and I lost the knife. I put both mitts on his throat, pushing and squeezing. A living person would have been choked out in moments, but this dead thing actually increased its assault if anything.

I was tiring, and he wasn't. My arms were losing strength and the thing leaned ever closer until suddenly two inches of steel were sticking out of its forehead and its un-life fled. I looked up into the face of Smithers, who put his boot on the back of the zombie's skull, yanked his blade out of the thing's dome, and extended a hand down to me. His face turned from smiling to concern, and he grabbed my arm. Bubbles were leaking from the spot where the dead thing had bitten me. My suit was ruptured. He inspected it as I lay there, then helped me up. He was talking a mile a minute into his mic, I could see it, but I couldn't hear him, so I let him know. He nodded and we moved uphill toward the light.

Fifty or so labored steps and our heads broke water. All kinds of shit was floating in the room we entered, plastic bottles, paper, oil, and a dead guy with a hole in his head. I was dizzy as hell, and began to pull my suit off. Smithers stopped me, shaking his head inside his helmet. He grabbed my hand and began pulling me toward the far hatch. I could see waves breaking over the side of the *Kanawha* through the broken porthole. I smiled in spite of my anxiety.

The hatch stuck but for a moment, and then we were outside under the cranes. Smithers closed the steel door, then helped me get my helmet off. I took a deep breath and instantly felt better. Three breaths later found me perfectly fine. Fine is better than in a coma.

I glanced at the *Mary's Joy*. I saw Remo and Everly pointing at us from the rear deck. Ship stood there with his tree-trunk arms folded, giving me the stinkeye. When I got my helmet off, I saw the glimmer of Bigfoot teeth, and knew it was possible for a Sasquatch to smile. Two of the crew were on the *Kanawha* in a couple of ticks, and they helped Smithers and I make it the rest of the way. One of them asked if I needed him to carry the briefcase, but fuck that. I had procured it. I had carried it. I had wielded it as a club to fend off undead attackers. I was going to see it to Everly.

Everly looked past us at the empty deck of the half-sunken *Kanawha*. "Nobody else?"

I looked back at the ship as well. "I don't think so, but I thought Smithers bought it in there too."

I felt a tap on my shoulder as I was shrugging out of my suit. It was my giant smarty-pants friend. He passed me a glass with ice, a clear liquid, and fuk'n pink umbrella. His closed-mouth smile said it all: he was happy to see me.

"Roger that, sir," I heard Everly say into the radio, "package is secure. Yes, sir. We lost five. Yes, sir... five." I heard expletives come through the receiver. That was unlike Schumitz.

Ship had also given a glass to Smithers, and I could see four more glasses, all with umbrellas, on the back table. The fuckers had been drinking without us? I took a slug of whatever it was in the glass. It was water and it was delicious.

"Thanks, Big Guy." He signed that I was welcome, but more importantly, I understood it. He put both hands on both shoulders of mine, leaned down about thirteen feet, and looked into my eyes. *Never again,* he mouthed. I shrugged out of his grip. "Underwater zombies, sunken ships, and important briefcases, and you have to go and make it weird." I finished my water and put the glass with the others.

We pulled a couple hundred feet off of the *Kanawha*, and discussed the possibility of surviving Orcas. I knew of four for certain that were dead. Frank, Orca Three, whoever belonged to the glove that was under the stairway, and whoever was stumbling with dead buddies inside a dry suit in the companionway. That left one unaccounted for. Probably Orca Four, who had begun screaming and then was cut off. Likely dead, but I hadn't seen it. Smithers told us he'd actually been sucked through the hole in the side of the ship when the stairs collapsed, but had swum back in immediately after. He hadn't seen anyone other than the crushed Orca under the stairs, and a bunch of dead crew.

Everly decided to put on a suit and go looking for the last man, but I talked him out of it. Both suits were damaged, and my rebreather was screwed for sure. It would be dark soon as well. We waited two hours, then left. I felt bad, but we were extremely lucky to get off the *Kanawha* alive. Everly sat in sullen silence the entire ride back to *Atlantis*, no doubt thinking about his lost men.

HA HA! HERE'S THE FUNNY THING

It's two days since the events of the *Kanawha*, and I'm sitting at dinner with my family; Ship, Donna, Kat, Tim, Alvarez, and the kids. Grilled mahi-mahi with potatoes and asparagus. How the hell did *Atlantis* have asparagus? It was steamed and delicious too, and we all know asparagus is the food that keeps on giving. You're reminded of eating it every time you take a piss for the next two days because your pee *reeks*.

I'm relating the story of how we got what we went to that sunken boat for, when suddenly Remo is standing sort of behind and next to me.

"Need a word."

Everybody stops talking and looks at him. Tim and Chloe slide down a little on the cafeteria bench we're on, and Remo plants his ass next to mine. He looks around for a second, reaches into his vest, and pulls out a skinny book. It takes me a second, but using my superior intellect, I am able to figure out that the book, which is some type of ledger, looks suspiciously like the one that was in the briefcase that I pilfered from the *Kanawha*.

The jarhead puts the book on the table but doesn't open it. He looks at me and takes a deep breath. "I had my misgivings on what that briefcase was when you brought it on board." He points to a piece of asparagus on my plate, raises his eyebrows, and I tell him to go ahead. He hoarks it down and continues, "Damn, that's good. Those dead guys in the suits that attacked you in the captain's quarters were secret service. They were guarding the briefcase in the safe. Usually, that particular bag is handcuffed to a very important person, or his designee. It is never out of his sight when he travels with it. During an attack on the *Kanawha* by a very well-trained paramilitary group, the dignitary was quickly evacuated, but he had to leave the briefcase behind. A mine was deployed, and the ship sunk, killing everyone on board that wasn't already dead from sustained firefights between the crew and the assholes who attacked them."

"I figured those black-clad dickweeds were straight-up bad guys." Richy sniggered at my use of profanity, and I smiled until I saw Donna's look of reproach. I didn't look at Ship because I could feel his stinkeye burning through the back of my head.

"They were not friendlies," Remo continued, "but a hostile group after two things: The dignitary, and that satchel. Can you guess who the important guy was?"

I was coming up empty, and I was eating. "How about you just tell us, buddy?" Ship passed me his notebook with two words: The President.

"President?" I asked. "President of what?" Ship rolled his eyes, but Remo just stared at me waiting for me to get it. There were several gasps from around the table, including both kids. I looked around and Chloe said, "The *President*!"

I blinked. "Like, of the United States?"

Now Chloe rolled her eyes, "Yes!"

"But he's dead!" I pleaded, hoping to dissuade everyone from thinking I was a dolt. "Everybody knows he's dead."

Remo looked very serious. "There's a new President of the United States then."

"I don't recall an election!" I objected, perhaps a bit loudly. The other few folks that were at different tables all looked at us. Like I gave a shit at that moment.

"They don't need an election," Tim offered. "In times of crisis, those in power can appoint a President if the hierarchy is dead or missing. It's called the Designated Survivor rule."

"You mean they picked some waitress or a garbage man to be our Commander-In-Chief?"

Tim smiled. "Unlikely. It was someone in the Presidential succession." He saw blank looks and clarified. "A cabinet member or somebody in Congress. Someone who didn't get eaten or killed some other way." Tim's smile evaporated. "But that means that the briefcase is..." He let that hang and I wanted to kill him for it. Was I the only one who couldn't figure this out?

Remo nodded very slowly. "Yes. It's the football."

Tim and Ship both leaned forward, Alvarez leaned back and put his hands on his head in shock. WTF was happening?

"What the hell are you talking about?" I demanded.

Ship began to write furiously, but Tim beat him to the punch. "That satchel that all those men and you almost died for? It contains information, including tactical sites and launch codes for a nuclear retaliatory strike. The President's nuclear football." I looked at him with my eyes very wide. "Dumbass," he added.

I felt sick. My delicious mahi-mahi threatened to spew forth onto the table. I swallowed. I had used that briefcase to bash a zombie. I had thumped an undead with the end of the world. What would have happened if I had set off a hundred nuclear missiles and ended everything that wasn't already ended?

Tim assured me that couldn't happen. I would have to input codes, and the folks manning the silos and the subs were the ones who nuked a couple billion zombies and living people. Now Schumitz had those codes. What was his plan?

Remo read my mind. "He's going to barter the codes."

I couldn't believe it. Schumitz was going to sell nuclear launch codes capable of vaporizing the planet. What could he possibly get for those codes? Anything I guess. "For what? What is the captain getting for the briefcase?"

"Us," Remo said, and opened the book. He flipped to the last two pages and began reading:

POTUS is safe. Just received radio confirmation of proof of life from Cooper. He and the rest of the team were able to get POTUS on board the escape craft and they have exfiltrated to the rendezvous point. Carter, Manzetti, Mayberry, and I came back for the football, but were cut off by elements of the force who have attacked us. Most of the Kanawha crew is dead, murdered by the same operatives who are firing at us from down the hall. Manzetti is going to detonate the limpets in two minutes if we can't repel the boarders.

Too many. Mayberry is down, and that's given me an idea. He told me to let him turn so he could attack anyone who came to get the football. Carter and I are going to shoot each other in the heart to do the same. Hopefully, the ship will sink before the hostiles can get in here. Manzetti just caught one in the throat.

I set off the limpets. The whole ship is listing. Our depth should put this room underwater, and the hostiles should assume the football went with POTUS. Manzetti is getting up. He's dead. Carter says there's water coming down the companionway. I will store this notebook in the safe with the football. Carter is fighting Manzetti, and the hostiles are coming. Special Agent Durnin out. God Bless America.

"Holy shit," I breathed through suddenly dry lips, "they killed themselves to protect that damn briefcase?"

Remo looked surprised. "Wouldn't you? Who knows who those hostiles were? What if they decide to target Barro or *Atlantis* with a nuke?"

"Why would they do that?" Chloe asked, frightened.

Remo looked at her. "Because they can, honey. Crazy doesn't need a reason." He looked back at me. "This football, if traded to the proper folks, could guarantee safety for us. Especially you." He pointed at me.

Ship passed his note to me and I read it aloud: *While I agree with Remo to a certain extent, there are no guarantees. They could take the package then wipe us out to get you as well. In my mind, you are more valuable to them than nuclear launch codes, but I am not the President. The codes could destroy the world, but when you think about it, the world is mostly gone already. If they get their hands on you, they could manufacture an anti-viral vaccine. They could distribute that vaccine as they see fit, which is a much more effective bartering tool and weapon than a nuclear arsenal. However, manufacturing a vaccine for a virus is next to impossible. They would have to run tests for years, possibly decades to perfect it, all the while they would need you on hand, running tests and drawing fluids. This all assumes that whatever has happened is because of a virus. It could come from a bacterium or a fungus or countless other sources.*

Alvarez shook his head. "But we don't know if *they* know he's here."

Ship pointed to his notebook. I handed it to him and he wrote quickly while Remo slid my plate in front of him and started shoving my fish in his face.

Exactly. We don't know. Prudence dictates that we assume they know. Someone knew, when they tried to blackmail the Ocean Diamond. Those men were government.

Remo looked thoughtful. "He's right about that. Those hitters that came for you on the *Diamond* were well trained. And shit, we..." Dusty the Border Collie, who was strictly forbidden to be in the galley, was of course at the feet of the kids, gnawing on some type of bone. He stood up, very alert. He looked in a few directions, then started barking like crazy.

"Shut up you mangy, leg-humpin' mongrel," Donna pleaded. "You're not supposed to be in here!" That damn dog would not cease with the barking no matter what was said, and we were drawing attention. Ship stood up, immediately yanking his sidearm from his shoulder holster. He looked into the air like he was thinking.

Remo and Alvarez both stood as well, drawing their own weapons.

Tim looked right at me. "What's happening?"

"Why is everybody always asking me that? I don't know. I never know! Why are you guys all up in arms n' shit?"

Remo had his rifle with him, but nobody else did. He pulled the charging handle back just a bit so he could check his load, even though there was no way in hell he hadn't checked it seventy-five times today already. "Dogs get fussy when there's something wrong."

Ship snapped his fingers and that damn dog shut up instantly. Fucker could talk to animals now. Ship pointed up, and we all heard it. A helicopter.

There was no chance any aircraft would be able to come within miles of *Atlantis* without the Stockdale turning it into smoking bits of ruined metal, so I had to wonder WTF was going on.

We were all outside in a moment, watching a Blackhawk helicopter land on the pad. It was surrounded by a plethora of armed men from *Atlantis*, and covered by the very M60 machine gun we had liberated from it before. Yes, Dear Reader, I knew it was a Blackhawk because Remo had told me the last time I had seen it. It was the same bird that had come to spirit me away off of the *Ocean Diamond*.

The engines shut down and the rotor began to slow. Austin was there, and he moved to the side door, keeping his head low. The door slid open, three unarmed men stepping out onto the landing pad. I had seen two of them before, and had bitten one. The third guy was in a suit, and he looked important. He shook Austin's hand, and the four of them came down the ramp from the helipad together. Austin looked around until he saw me, then motioned for me to follow them with that *c'mere* hand gesture he was always using.

We all had our weapons out now. He made the gesture again as I looked to Remo, who shrugged. "Let's go."

"Where?"

"To see what they want."

"Fine," I acquiesced. "Everybody comes. All of us."

Remo smiled and we moved off after the group of them. It took a couple of minutes to convince Ship that we were going with or without him, and he was *pissed*. The notebook flew back and forth a few times, and let me tell you, Ship had found his swear button. I ended the conversation telling him that these were unarmed people who already knew I was here.

Captain Schumitz was waiting in Austin's office with two of his officers. He was speaking with the suited dude. There was barely room enough for all of us to stand in there. The satchel containing the football was on the map table.

Schumitz tried to introduce us, "This is SECNAV."

"What the fuck is a secknav?" Richy smiled and Chloe outright giggled.

Schumitz and Austin glared at me like I was the embarrassing kid. "Secretary of the Navy. SECNAV?"

"Oh."

The guy in the suit came around the desk with a big smile and stuck his hand out to shake mine. I stared at it for a second before I put my Sig in his face. His smile evaporated, and he looked nervous for a moment before he quietly spoke, "We're unarmed."

"Then you're an idiot. Did you miss the apocalypse? Being unarmed is the stupidest thing you can be nowadays." I pointed to the kids. "They carry weapons at all times. We demand it."

"I felt it prudent considering the circumstances."

"Oh, you mean kidnapping me, taking me from my home and my family, incarcerating me in a medical prison for months while they probed me and stuck me with needles..."

He lowered his hand, "About that, I'm sorry—"

"I wasn't finished," I snapped. "Then I get back and you send a team to get me on the *Majestik*. A team that killed some of my friends. We kill most of your assholes and chase the rest off. Then you kidnap the family of one of our sister ships, trying to blackmail them into giving me up. Am I missing anything?"

"No. That's about right. I'm sorry for what happened before, but we're desperate." He looked genuinely sorry. "Maybe we could speak in a more private setting?"

I lowered my weapon. "No. Anything you say to me I'm just going to tell all of them," I spread my hand wide, "the moment we're done here. What about the hundreds of people that were killed because of your stupidity?"

He looked confused, so I rolled my eyes. Is this what Ship felt like all the time? Because it was great. "You filled both the *Majestik* and

Baldy Mountain with hundreds of infected. That's the work of shitheads."

Schumitz began to speak, "I don't think this is the best way to—"

I held my hand up, forestalling his comments. I never took my eyes off of SECNAV's though.

Mr. Secretary of the Navy said something then that I really didn't expect. I truly thought this was going to be a shit-show, but he disarmed me with two words: "You're right."

I sighed and shook my head. "What do you want?"

"That, for starters," he told me, pointing at the football, "and you, if you'll come with us." Ship flipped the safety off of his weapon with an audible *click*. You could have heard a pin drop after this douche asked me to come with him, so the safety was crazy loud.

I looked at Schumitz. "Don't give it to them. No matter what they say, they'll never stop coming. Use it as leverage to keep them away."

Schumitz began to speak, but suit-dick cut him off with a wave. "I've put up with your shit long enough," he confessed, his demeanor completely changed. "You want to stay? Fine, we'll leave you alone, but if I leave here without that package, or worse, if I don't leave at all, this place will be a pile of ash by nightfall."

I looked past him, shaking my head once again in disbelief. "How long before they order you to house a hundred infected on *Atlantis* for study, Captain? They'll probably just sink the *Stockdale* anyway, just like the *Kanawha*."

SECNAV looked taken aback. "We didn't sink the *Kanawha*. We asked for help in getting the football. We have intel on who we think sunk her, but that's classified."

I believed him. Both about the *Kanawha*, and killing all of us if we didn't give him the satchel. I did not believe him about letting me stay here, although I would play it up like I did.

I had never heard Austin's menacing voice before, and it was kind of scary. "We're giving them the satchel. Nobody is going to stop you," he told SECNAV.

Suit-dick spun on his heel, picked up the briefcase, and turned back to face me. "Are you sure you won't come with us?"

"I'm sure."

"Fair enough." He looked at Schumitz. "Captain, you have thirty-six hours to meet at the rendezvous point. See you when you arrive."

"Yes, sir."

When they were filing out, the team leader who had tried to kidnap me on the *Diamond* slowed down as he passed me. He made sure his boss wasn't looking, and he looked me in the eye, leaning in. *"Run,"* he whispered, and strode from the office.

GONE

The Stockdale left that evening at 2000 hours. That's twenty hundred hours, and it means eight o'clock in the evening. Twenty hundred sounds way better.

Earlier, I had spoken to Captain Schumitz about how he had originally said he was going rogue, and that he would be here, with his boat, to protect *Atlantis*. The captain told me that he had made that decision because he hadn't heard from any type of naval command in months. Now, with a fleet of naval ships down in Panama, Schumitz felt compelled to follow orders, especially when those orders came directly from the highest power in the Navy. He did offer any absolutely non-essential crew members the opportunity to stay on *Atlantis* if Austin was okay with it. Schumitz would convey to the Navy that those crew members had been killed. He would lie. In a true testament of loyalty to either his command, or the power of the United States Navy, every crewmember left with the *Stockdale*.

Remo is not a crew member. He is retired Navy if you remember from my incoherent babblings earlier in this journal.

Austin was in the room when I spoke to Schumitz. He blinked several times and managed a shocked, "What?" when I told him I was leaving.

"Eventually, that Navy suit-dick is going to come for me. Either he will send people to snag me, or someone will order him to do it. They know where I am, and that makes me a danger to everyone here." I actually hung my head in sadness.

"Where will you go?" He sounded bewildered. "There's nowhere safe."

"You're right, there isn't, but I can't be responsible for the deaths of everyone here. What if they aren't interested in me saying 'no'?"

Schumitz chucked in his two cents. "He's right. Eventually, they will swing back around to thinking he's got the cure for all of this inside him. What they simply can't understand is that it's too late. Everything's already gone." The captain stuck his paw out to me. "Good luck."

I shook it. "You too."

We exchanged more pleasantries, including a glass of some type of really expensive whiskey that Austin had hidden in his office. It tasted like lighter fluid. I would have preferred a Bud Light, but the sentiment was great. I left and went to pack my shit at just before 1700.

Donna and Ship were in my shack waiting for me.

"Of course I'm coming," Donna said. Ship nodded his giant dome as well.

"I know, but have you considered you're the best medic on this tub?"

"Damn right! We have two doctors here now, they don't need me. You do."

"Damn right," I whispered and touched her face. "But the kids—"

"Are coming too," she finished. I started to say something, but she gave me that look. If, Dear Reader, you're a guy, then you know that nut-shriveling look your woman gives you. The one that both tells you to shut up and not to fuck with her at the same time. If you're a woman, Dear Reader, then that look is inherent, and needs no explanation.

A noise from the doorway made me glance to my right. Remo was leaning against the doorframe, Josey Wales-style with a toothpick angled out of the corner of his mouth instead of a cigar. "The kids should stay here. When was the last time you were on land? It's bad."

"Doesn't matter," Donna told him. "If they stay here, they deal with bullets and grenades from the people who will come for the cure, or someone wanting *Atlantis*. If they leave with us, they deal with the dead. The dead are easier."

It was true that the dead didn't shoot guns, or use advanced tactics, but there were way, way more of them. People just don't get what *everywhere* means when you tell them that the dead are everywhere. Ship put his gorilla mitt on my shoulder. "Yeah, I know you're coming. I wouldn't be stupid enough to leave this place without you. Or him," I added, pointing at the jarhead.

His raised a thin eyebrow. "And what makes you think I want to keep saving your ass over and over again?"

I shot back with an epic eye roll. "Because you're already dying of boredom here. You didn't become… whatever the fuck it is you are, for the money. Besides," I pulled up my shirt exposing the bullet and surgery scars, "save my ass? Of all the people on this asylum, you're the only one who's shot me."

Ship snapped his fingers. I looked at him and he was nodding *No*. Seeing my dumbfounded look, he pointed to the poster on the wall of a kitten with its claws in a tree branch. *Hang In There* was the caption.

I might not be Ship-caliber smart, but I could pick up what he was putting down. "Oh yeah. Kat shot me first. Sorry, Remo, you lost that game. Besides, you love me. You're coming, we all know it."

He didn't smile, but I've known him long enough that I could tell he wanted to. "Any extras coming?"

I counted on my fingers. "I've got eight. Tim, Remo, Ship, the wife n' kids, Kat, and Alvarez."

Ship was holding up one finger, then pointed his thumb up like he was hitchhiking. I looked at Remo, who did that little *huh* thing he does while looking elsewhere briefly. "He means there will be nine of us. You forgot yourself, dumbass."

I raised an eyebrow. "Fine. Whatever. We can leave tomorrow. Right now, let's pack and figure out how we get where we're going."

Donna looked at me, "And where is that?"

Tim walked in right then, excusing himself past Remo, and dropped his stuff on my bed. "Where's what?"

"We're leaving," I told him, my head hung a bit low.

"About damn time. I think I got more sleep running for my life. I hate it here. We going to San Francisco or what?"

Ship was making this ridiculous *huff-huff* noise and I turned to look at him. He was laughing. "You sound like an idiot," I told him, smiling. He pointed to me, to his eyes, then held up one finger, and started laughing harder. Meant I look like one. An idiot, I mean. Everybody started to laugh, and soon we were crying-laughing. A couple of people walking by looked at my shack, shaking their heads and moving on.

Ship came up with a map, and we looked at North and Central America. "Here," I pointed at a spot south of Brownsville, Texas, "we should land here, cross all the way to here, El Colorado, Mexico, get a boat, and go north."

Remo sauntered over to the map. "A few hundred miles north of one of the most populated cities on earth. Ten miles south of a city with a population of about a hundred and eighty thousand. From here to here," he drew his finger across the map, "is nothing. Not United States nothing, where there's a gas station or convenience store every twenty miles. Mexico nothing, where there's *nothing*."

"Nothing is good though, right?"

He looked up at me. "Maybe. There shouldn't be any infected, but there won't be any water, and that's all scrubland and desert until you hit the mountains here." He pointed at a green swath on the map and raised his eyebrows. "And look," he put his finger on the map again, "Monterrey. Right between us and where we need to go. Monterrey is a big city. More than a million, I think."

We talked about what to do until 2200, and decided we would land between Brownsville and Corpus Christi, Texas. We would head west and see what happened when we hit the coast. Then north to Frisco. Yeah, I know nobody from San Francisco says *Frisco*, but this is my journal, and you can screw. I'm not from there and I can say or write what I damn well please.

Chloe got off her shift at the kitchen just as we were finishing up. Richy showed up an hour later, and we told them what was happening. They were apprehensive to leave, but didn't want to stay without us. "Can we take the PlayStation?" Richy asked hopefully.

"Yeah Rich, you can plug it into your butt!" his sister chided him.

We snickered, Richy too, and began to pack our stuff.

Tim moved off to his shack to get his shit together and to tell Alvarez and Kat what was happening. Alvarez showed up half an hour later, telling me Kat's stuff had been packed for weeks. Alvarez didn't have a lot of things. None of us did, really, but Alvarez was bringing bullets and underwear.

Alvarez, Ship, Tim, and I showed up at the galley, and there were a bunch of sundries already packed for us. Austin had apparently told the cooks, who were also the keepers of the food stores, to give us what we wanted. They had pre-packed and labeled the food and water. "I didn't give you any of the asparagus," Gabriella, my favorite cook told me, and burst into tears. She threw herself at me in a hug, sobbing, "I didn't think you would be able to cook it on the road. I'll miss your stories."

I kissed her on the top of her head. "I'll miss telling them." Gabriella was in her late forties, short, and made the best damn apple cobbler on earth. All four foot five of her looked up at me. "Austin said there was some more stuff on the *Mary's Joy*." She passed me a key.

We grabbed the stuff, including two five-gallon water bladders that were damn heavy, hugged Gabriella and Shawn, the other cook, and brought the stuff to the boat. The key Gabby had given me was for a footlocker. Inside were two MP5SD3 submachine guns with a thousand rounds of subsonic 9mm, and another thousand rounds of .556. Two tactical Beretta M9A1 handguns were also in the locker, with eight suppressors, three that would fit our M4s, three for the HK416s, and one each for the M9s. A short note accompanied the weapons and ammo cache:

Sorry, this was all I could spare. Just had the suppressors for the rifles milled on board. I would have given you a set of NVGs, but I never did get one back after the Majestik mission... Best of luck, and I hope I never see you again.

Schumitz, you old softie. The note wasn't signed, but I knew who had left the stuff. I hoped I did see him again. I would buy him a drink as long as he wasn't trying to capture me for experimentation.

I locked the locker and put it in one of the storage bins under the seat cushions. To be fair, Tim helped me because it was damn heavy, and I was still a bit sore. I rubbed the scar on my arm where Captain Bob had bitten me. It was always sore.

Donna and the kids hauled the rest of our essentials down to the boat. There wasn't much besides what we needed. We would never have enough weapons and ammo, but I had my dead friend Ray's EBR; a .308 battle rifle with a sexy scope. Alvarez had his M4, and Ship had acquired a beautiful Benelli tactical shotgun with a pistol grip.

It was just before 2300. We would leave our stuff here, post a guard, and split in the morning. We were all on the boat, Kat walking down the gangway with her stuff, when Remo and Ship did that staring at the sky thing that I have learned means deep shit. The two goons looked at each other, then Remo looked at me, "Trouble." He had his HK416, and he nodded to Alvarez. They both took off back up to *Atlantis*.

"Shit!" I huffed and started to run after them.

"Where the hell do you think you're going?" Donna demanded.

"Richy went for the fucking PlayStation! You shoot anybody who comes down here that isn't us!"

Donna spun and looked around for the kid, but he had slipped away. Kat jumped out of the boat with a rifle. "No!" I yelled a bit loudly. "You stay and protect the boat! I'll be right back." I could tell she wanted to come, and honestly, I would be happy for her aim, but she nodded and hopped right back in. Ship, however, would not be deterred. Not that I even tried, I wanted him with me.

Ship and I were on the main deck in just under a minute. It looked totally fine, but I had seen Ship's and Remo's Spidey-Sense in action before and I didn't doubt it. What I didn't see right now were Alvarez and Remo. They had melted into the darkness.

I could melt. I could melt into the darkness too. Ship was used to melting; he was seven feet tall, three hundred pounds, and never made any type of sound if he didn't want to. I could do that.

He followed me as I ran to the rec center looking for Richy. The kid wasn't there, but the PlayStation was. The place was empty, which was weird for ten PM. I looked at Ship and whispered in anger, "Fuck! He didn't come for the stupid video game, he went for that damn dog!"

Ship spun on his heel and sprinted for my shack. The guy might be big, but he's *fast*. One of his strides is like three of a non-sasquatch's. Still, he made not one sound. I caught him when he stopped near one of the shacks. He held his hand out for me to stop, and I did. His hand is the size of a dinner plate, so I really had no choice. He pointed toward his own, recently vacated, shack. A furtive figure was just exiting. Clad in black, it carried a suppressed weapon which looked just like an MP5. It moved into the next shack. I moved to go after it, but Ship's mitt hit me in the chest. He pointed to another figure, similarly garbed, covering the first. It was dark, but I had seen that black camo before. The dead dickweeds that had been on the *Kanawha* had been wearing it.

I tapped Ship on the shoulder, indicating I would slip in behind the guy and cover him. Ship nodded, pointing his shotgun at the crouching douche, covering me. I snuck right, moved through the superstructure, up three stairs, hooked left, and came up behind the lookout between the shacks.

"Harvester Two copies all," the guy whispered. "Harvester One, eliminate all hostiles until you find primary target, then we exfil, how copy?" He put his finger to his ear, and I began to shake in anger. I willfully sent that shit away quickly. Don't get me wrong, I was fucking pissed, but I wasn't going to go all red-eye on him. There were probably plenty of these assholes to question, so I grabbed his forehead with the palm of my left hand, pulled it back into my shoulder, and drove my SOG downward into his throat up to the hilt. For good measure, I sawed back toward me and his red stuff literally exploded from his neck, coating the shack next to us. I had seen someone do this exact maneuver, and I have to tell you, it works. I yanked my knife out of him, lowered him to the ground, then stabbed him in the left eye, turning the knife when it was in. It was a bitch to pull back out, but I needed it, so I got it. I dragged his body back between the shacks, and crouch-ran to the door his pal had gone through. Ship had moved up, switched positions, and was covering me with his shotgun, across from the door.

The bad guy exited the apartment in front of me, but I was a damn ninja and hid behind a vertical pipe. He made it to my door, but it opened from inside and out strolled Richy with the dog on a rope-leash. He looked right at the guy in uniform, asking, "Who are you?"

The guy began to raise his SMG toward the kid, and I was too far away to do anything. I didn't have to. Ship blew the dude out of his shoes. The boom of the weapon made every shack lamp on *Atlantis* light up, and this shit was on.

Gunfire erupted from all over and the fire alarm, which had become the *anything at all that is wrong* alarm, began to sound. I hadn't heard so many alarm klaxons, or even known what the word "klaxon" meant until this fucking plague.

Both Ship and I sprinted to the wide-eyed kid, who was doing his best to control the now absolutely ape-shit dog. Ship did something then that I didn't even consider. He didn't pick up the kid, but scooped up the pooch and clamped a gigantic mitt over the thing's jaws effectively silencing it. Sasquatch then used his massive boot to turn the dead, black-garbed asshole's head into oatmeal, with a side order of *yuck*. He nodded his head toward the boat and Richy followed. I trailed them for a few steps to let Ship think I was with him, then veered off and headed for Austin's office.

Atlantis was suddenly lit up like a Christmas tree, with every work light on board flashing to life. This would make it harder for the bad guys to be as stealthy, but it would work against us as well. I heard suppressed gunfire in front of me, so I skidded to a stop. Some female screaming came from my left, but it was cut off almost immediately. Austin stumbled from his office up above me on the catwalk. I climbed the steel steps three at a time until I reached the walkway. "Austin! Do you know how many of them there are?" I whisper-yelled. He was looking the other way, sort of glancing around. Guy was probably terrified. I dashed to him, put my hand on his shoulder, and spun him around. He lunged at me, grabbed my shirt, and did his best to get a nibble. He was ghastly white, except for his shirt, which was a deep crimson down the front. A wide gash ran across his throat, deep enough I could see the tube of his trachea. Although surprised, I was able to use one of the moves Remo had taught me, and I punched upward under his arms, then brought my arm around and over, slamming my forearm over both of his. One hand let go, but the other was on me like iron. I thumped him in the face with the butt of the battle rifle, stunning him. He let go, staggering back a step, and I took that moment to give him a kick, aim the rifle at his face, and shoot without using the long-range optics.

I hadn't fired this weapon before. This was not like a .556 weapon, and I was unprepared for the kick. It was substantial, and it hurt my shoulder a little bit. Usually, when I fired my HK416, or one of the M4s, the head of an infected would snap back, or a small bit might fly off. It was a bit disgusting, but I was used to it. This thing was more of a sniper rifle, and most of Austin's head, from the upper lip on up the right side, simply ceased to be attached. It flew off to my left and he flew backward, landing on the steel mesh of the deck. In a moment of grand stupidity, I looked at the rifle and then back at my dead friend.

A fairly large explosion from a deck lower and behind me brought me to my senses. I climbed up the side of the ladder on the office, situating myself on the flat roof. I was in a small rain puddle, but I would deal. Looking through the scope on the weapon was tough, because even though *Atlantis* was covered in light, it was still dark outside. I panned the weapon to my left and saw a guy in black camo raising his rifle. There were two bodies next to him, both in civilian clothes. I put the crosshairs on him, pulled the stock of the rifle close to my shoulder, and squeezed the trigger.

The outcome of my second shot was much better on me, and I remained at a 100% kill rate. I had struck the douche high, between his neck and his shoulder on the left side. I was maybe a hundred and fifty feet away and much higher than he was. He flew to his right, undoubtedly dead. I fired again at another prick in black and missed my target. The guy figured out where I was, aimed his rifle at me, and I took him square in the chest. Several rounds pinged off of the steel of Austin's office, and I ducked back behind the edge. One of the hostiles had seen me.

Another explosion ripped through the night, and I could see flames. I didn't know if the dick that had shot at me could see me, but I was hoping he had other things on his mind, so I rolled to the edge of the roof, scuttled over, and climbed down the ladder. It was tricky, as I didn't have the rifle sling around me, but I made it down without being shot.

My home was burning. There were fires all over, people running every which-way, and guns going off. Greg, one of my friends, stopped in front of me, aiming his hunting rifle right at me. He lowered it immediately, his eyes wide. "We're leaving, come with us!" I shouted.

He began to say something, but three holes stitched across his side and he collapsed. I threw myself down and Army-crawled to him. He was wheezing, and I could see he was done. He looked at the blood on his hand, then coughed, obviously in agony. He gurgled, spit out some blood, and looked at me.

"Don't... don't let me t... t..."

I held his hand. "I won't, pal."

He closed his eyes, nodding. I stood, aimed at his head, and shot him. My eyes watering from grief and rage, I looked around for another target to kill.

Atlantis was lost. Shambling figures roamed freely, and the smoke was so thick I couldn't tell friend from foe. I could barely hear the throaty diesel engines from two of our boats that were heading out into the Gulf. Some folks had gotten away. That thought got me going, and I decided that it was time for me to get away too. I ran.

I heard something behind me as I was racing over the mesh, turned to look, and smashed into someone in front of me. We went down in a heap, and I could see he was dressed in black camo. My rifle was pinned between us, and this guy was doing everything he could to get away from me. I grabbed him around the right arm and began punching. I was able to get an elbow into his nose and it exploded, showering both of us with blood. He brought both hands to his broken schnoz, so I dropped the same elbow in his nuts. Now he leaned forward, and I gave him a straight punch to the nose again. He was stunned, so I jammed my knife into his belly, and he made this *hoooaahh* sound. He looked at the knife through watery eyes and began to cry.

The fucker had come to destroy my home and kill my friends, and he was crying.

"Who are you assholes?"

He managed something audible, but I couldn't understand it. He tried again and I got it. "I'm not Triumvirate," he squeaked. "They made me come. I didn't want to hurt anybody."

"Well, you did," I told him and yanked my blade.

I could see some shuffling figures on the way, and the fires must have reached the oil, because there was a great flame funnel shooting skyward. Atlantis wasn't just lost, she was doomed. This was no time to be generous and mercy-kill this asshole, so I left him to his fate and ran.

I saw a few of the former Atlanteans, all dead and walking. A group of them had taken down one of the shitheads, and was dining on him. I hope he tasted good. Two dead bad guys were splayed out on the stairs to the lower dock, I hopped over them, ran to the next landing, and there was a gun in my face.

"C'mon," Remo said, "we're waiting on you."

We both hustled down the last three flights of stairs, my whole crew covering our retreat, with the exception of Ship at the helm, and the kids safely below deck.

I untied the bow line, Remo got the stern. Both spring lines were already cast. I hopped in and fell on my ass on the damp deck. A huge explosion from way up above rocked the whole rig, and flaming shit fell through the bottom of the superstructure about sixty feet away from us, making a huge splash. That rending metal sound was getting loud up there, and I wanted out from underneath untold tons of collapsing steel.

"Punch it!" Remo bellowed, and the boat lurched forward.

We all looked back at our home as we shot across the waves. What had once been beautiful sight at night from the water looked like a scenic photo from Hell. Fires raged, and even as I thought that, a gigantic, flaming mushroom cloud shot into the air, spewing burning oil all over the Gulf. The ocean was burning. The lights flickered and went out, leaving only the flames for illumination. I can't see how any of the assholes that had attacked us made it out alive, but they had killed I don't know how many good people.

It might have taken a lot longer this time, but death found me yet again and unleashed his limitless anger on those that had sheltered my ass.

GET AWAY

When I was a boy, I had a dog named Harley. I had never had a dog before, so when my mom came home with him (without telling my dad), I fell in love immediately. If you're a kid and there's a puppy, you love it or you have mental issues. Harley had this issue with his leg where he couldn't bend his knee. My dad paid a ridiculous amount of money to get the pooch's leg fixed, but it didn't take and Harley ended up getting mean. He never snapped at me, or anyone else in my immediate family, but he would outright attack certain other folks without provocation. We had a backyard party in the summertime, and one of the neighbor's little girls wandered away from the group and found the dog. She came back screaming, and had the tiniest scratch on her face, but that was enough. Even I, a boy of nine, knew the dog had to go. My dad called the dog officer, and the cop took Harley to a shelter. That night, my dad had the bright idea of giving the dog to my grandparents, whom the mutt loved. Pops called up the shelter, and they told him they had put Harley down because they did some safety exercise with him and he failed. I cried like a baby, even though I knew the dog was dangerous.

I was a kid, and kids don't really understand death until it hits them in the face. I remember feeling both completely helpless and a profound sense of loss. I hadn't felt a loss like that until now. I had lost friends to both living and dead assholes, but in each case, I knew someone was going to die. I was usually being shot at or chewed on myself, so my grief was tempered. It's one thing to lose a place, it's another to lose both your home, and the dozens of good people you shared it with, in one fell swoop.

Sitting on the back deck of the *Mary's Joy*, with the sun coming up behind us, I had to wonder if all of this death was because of me. It isn't my fault I'm immune to this shit. To the best of my knowledge, I'm no different than anyone else. Of course, I know that isn't true, I can't catch this thing, and absolutely everyone else dies from it. Everyone has suffered so much loss from this fucking plague, but it seemed that everywhere I went, I survived when others didn't. Was this a legitimate curse? Did God or the Devil or some other supreme being hate me? Did these powers think I was worth something, or worse, want to torture me, and so had cursed me with living in a dying world?

I was contemplating all this crap when Dusty came over, jumped up on the bench seat, and put his head in my lap. I had just been thinking about both my twenty-year-dead pooch, and the loss of a lot that was dear to me, and this mutt decides to put his cute fucking dome across my legs and look up at me with those goddamned dog-eyes.

Big, fat tears spilled out of me and onto the dog's face and he didn't budge. The dumbass just blinked when a tear would hit it in the eye. I sniffed and stopped the crying, and the little prick licked my face. Just once, then put his head back down.

Clairvoyant bastard.

Richy and Chloe, who seemed to fire on all the same cylinders at all times, both came out on deck stretching. Everybody else was asleep except Ship, who was piloting the boat, and Remo, who had no idea what sleep was, and was up next to Ship on the high deck, with a pair of binoculars affixed to his face.

"Wassamatta?" Richy asked, blinking and digging grit from his eyes. The kids had the power to sleep no matter the conditions, for whatever time they were given, wake up, and be instant superheroes.

"Something in my eye. I'm just sad we lost *Atlantis*."

They plopped down on either side of me, Chloe petting the dog. "We were leaving anyway," she reminded me.

"Yeah, but we were supposed to leave everybody alive. Those assholes killed them." I was done talking to these kids like they were kids. All coddling would do was get them killed. They had figured that out, but none of the rest of us had until right now.

"This might sound harsh," Richy said, "but better them than us."

"Rich!" his sister chided.

"No, he's right," I agreed. "There wasn't one of them I would trade for any one of us. It's a miracle we all got out alive."

Chloe shook her head. "It wasn't a miracle. It was you. If you hadn't decided to leave, and take all of us with you, we'd be dead."

"Huh. I was just thinking that all this death was because of me."

The girl stopped petting Dusty, furrowed her brow, and punched me in the arm. "Ship is right, you *are* a dummy. Did you kill everybody else on the planet too? None of this is your fault."

"Everywhere I go, death follows."

She punched me again. This shit would have to stop because it hurt. "Death is a jerk!" she shot. "Maybe he needs a vacation."

"Maybe he's *been* on vacation," Richy added, "and that's why people won't stay dead."

I rubbed my arm and had to agree. "As good an idea as any about all of this." I heard someone coming down the stairs from the upper deck. It was Remo.

"Ship asked me nicely to pass this to you." He handed me a piece of notebook paper torn from Ship's universal communicator. It read simply: *Land ho.*

I looked up and there was indeed land. It was in front of us, and it was as far as the eye could see in both directions.

I sighed. Then I sighed again. "And so departs our safety."

The four of them (dog too) looked at me. I shrugged.

"You two," Remo looked at the kids, "come with me. We have magazines to load." Dusty's head popped up on high alert and his tail started smacking the seat cushions at light speed, while he stared at Remo expectantly. "Fine, c'mon." The pooch hopped (can a dog hop?) off of the bench, the kids stood, and they all left. I was alone again with my thoughts. My thoughts sucked right then.

Everybody was up by 0830. We were drifting about a mile from shore when we began planning our departure from the boat. There wasn't a soul, living or dead, on the beach. Turns out, when we looked more closely at an actual boat chart, what we were seeing was a barrier beach called Padre Island. Yeah, the chart says it's the longest barrier island in the fuk'n world and there was a giant lagoon on the other side of it, between it and mainland Texas. Between *us* and mainland Texas.

Remo had his chin between his thumb and forefinger. "Shit. I didn't see that. Shit."

"You said shit twice," Richy told him.

"This is worth two shits." Remo drew his finger down the chart to the south, and Ship put his finger on something to the north.

"Yeah," nodded Remo, "yeah, that's it, Ship."

"What's what?" Tim demanded.

"There's a bridge there, which means there's a canal or break in the land or whatever. We can get through it or under it and sail on to the mainland."

It took two hours to get to what was left of the bridge. We had seen evidence of destruction as Padre Island passed by on our port side. Several abandoned vehicles on the road, the burned hull of a boat, and our first infected. It was a man in shorts, and he had either been burned or his skin had turned black from rot. He staggered into the water, but stopped when knee deep. I hadn't seen that before. Were these things afraid of water? I had fought the creatures under water, and other than buoyancy issues, they were just as deadly. Why wouldn't the dead bastard just wade into the water until he disappeared to get to us? The dumb thing followed from the beach at a pathetic pace, and was soon out of sight.

The bridge had been destroyed. Remo said explosive charges had been used, probably to slow the infected down or stop them from travelling in one direction. Twisted steel and bits of concrete stuck out of the water in front of us, and both Remo and Alvarez stood on the bow of the boat as we came up to the wreckage.

Alvarez got on his belly and poked into the water with a long boat hook. "Take us in slow, Ship."

The *Mary's Joy* moved at a snail's pace, with Remo surveying and Alvarez poking into the waves, looking for debris. There was one small scrape against the starboard hull, and we were through. Ship opened up on the throttle a little, and we shot across the waves toward Texas proper. I have to say, plague thoughts aside, the scenery was absolutely beautiful. The water was a blue you just don't see in New England, and the beach both behind and in front of us was pristine. Tim said we were due east of a town called Port Mansfield, but there were no statistics on the municipality. Looking at the town from the water, I doubted if it could support five hundred people, but I had thought that before, and half the state of Utah had shown up for dinner. I had lost two buddies that day, but we had gained the kids.

We sailed down a wide channel, with buildings on both sides. Some really pretty houses greeted us, with a few businesses. It looked really cozy.

"Should we check this place out?" Kat asked as we pulled up to a fishing dock. I could see the back of Harbor Bait and Tackle, and Y Knot Rentals off to the left in a sort of big hangar-type structure with a bunch of garage doors. It was eerily silent, no bird or bug sounds. I waited for the scream of a gull, but it seemed they had better places to be.

Donna had come up wearing a T-shirt with a fish on it from below decks. I was staring at the fish (I swear!) and wondering where she had found the shirt.

She managed a wry smile. "Focus. Eyes off the girls."

I whipped my gaze upward, but not before Kat shook her head in mock disgust.

Remo looked thoughtful. "If we can find a vehicle and some fuel, it would save a lot of walking. There are nine of us though, so we'll need a truck."

A dead guy came strolling out from between a couple of buildings, followed by a couple of his pals. They made their way to the dock and slogged toward us. Alvarez and Remo tied us up to a piling, and moved to challenge the infected. Alvarez had his boathook, and Remo had borrowed Ship's machete.

Alvarez jammed the end of the pole into the middle of the first guy, and Remo cleaved the thing's head in half from dome to nose. He struggled briefly to yank out the blade, and had to put his foot on the truly dead thing's chest to pull it out. The next two were closer together, so one got the boathook in the belly, while Remo decapitated the other, then took the top off the hooked one's head.

It went like clockwork... or boathook work, I guess.

We piled off the boat and stood on the dock, stretching. The *Mary's Joy* was beautiful, but we were happy to be off of it if only for a moment. Our safety just went out the window insofar as being outside the reach of the infected, but at this point, were we truly safe anywhere?

Remo, Alvarez, and Tim would search the surrounding area for a viable vehicle while the rest of us watched the boat. Kat put up a stink because she wanted to go with Alvarez, but once again, she saw the logic in setting up as a sniper on the bow. She lay on the front of the boat with Chloe and Donna, talking and scouting. Kat wore a Texas Rangers baseball cap. No accounting for taste, but it kept the very bright sun out of her eyes. She would pay for this horrible transgression of attire later. When you're from New England, you wear a damn Red Sox cap, apocalypse or not.

The boys were already gone, so that left Ship, Richy, and I to sit up on the top deck and talk. Well, Ship can't talk, but you know what I mean. Ship signed a few things to me, and I tried my best to sign back. He corrected me by showing me exactly how to position my hands and fingers. I had a couple of motions wrong too, and we fixed that up. Can't be signing *fuck off* when I mean *come here* and shit.

Richy was watching us, and when we had finished our sign-versation, he said, "That's pretty cool."

I signed *thank you* to him, and then told him what it meant. We began to talk in a three-way, part-speaking, part-signing conversation, when Kat barked from the bow.

"Incoming!"

I didn't know whether to look for undead or jump into my foxhole. I chose the former, and noticed we had a small crowd heading across the parking lot toward us.

"Richy, let's untie the boat. Ship, you think we might want to move off a hundred feet or so?" The big guy nodded, and started the boat. Richy was down the stairs fast, and we untied long before the things reached the dock. We pushed off as best we could, and Ship had us backing away in short order. We were back up with Sasquatch to see the infected make the pier.

My radio spoke to me. Remo was on the other end. *Mary, this is Trio. SITREP. We heard the boat start, over.*

"Trio, Mary. Everything's okay. A small crowd of about eight pus bags showed up looking hungry, so we put a bit of distance between us. How's shit on your end?"

I didn't hear any reply, realizing just a half second late that I hadn't ended my radio chatter with *over.* Remo let me know about this lapse, and I felt small. I pointed at the radio and made like Remo was a dick. Richy smiled.

This is Texas, Remo chided, *if you don't own a truck, they shoot you. We've tried four vehicles, got one started, but it wouldn't stay running. Tim thinks it's bad gas.*

Made sense. We were more than a year into this end of the world thing, and any gasoline not in an airtight container would be shit by now.

"Check the bait and tackle store for some octane additive," I told him. "That will help. If you can find a hardware store with some xylene-based paint thinner, you might be able to add a small bit of that to the gas in a tank and the truck will run. Don't add more than a couple or three ounces to about ten gallons though, or it will explode when you start it."

How do we know how much gas is in a tank to add the paint thinner?

"I didn't say it wasn't a gamble," I told him as I watched the pus bag stumble down the pier. "If we hear a big fuk'n boom, we'll take the *Mary's Joy* down to Cabo for Margaritas. Mary out."

Ship was staring at me, incredulous.

"What? I know some shit."

We did hear a boom about a half hour later. It was a series of booms actually, the backfiring of a vehicle. Either there was a Sanford and Son class jalopy about, or the boys had gotten one of the trucks started. It really is a pity that if you've survived this long in the plague you're most likely young and strong, resulting in the fact that you have absolutely no idea who Fred Sanford was. I only know Mr. Sanford's exploits because there was one television in prison and you watch what the big guys watch. They liked Sanford and Son, so I did too.

The first dipshit undead had walked right off the dock, splashed into the water, and sank like a ton of bricks. The other two, not particularly giving a rat's ass about their buddy, milled about at the end of the wooden structure, occasionally reaching for us. When the backfires sounded, they looked a bit torn. Stay and reach for us or follow the noise. The noise won, and they began moving back down the dock toward the town.

The inevitable gunshots began to sound, and although I knew they were coming, it still put me in an even more heightened sense of awareness.

Mary, this is Trio, Tim's voice came through the radio. *We've engaged hostiles of the room-temperature variety. There are significant numbers, but we did get a truck running. Great idea with the paint thinner. We'll meet you across the channel by the Get-A-Way Adventures Lodge. You reading me?"*

"Copy that, Trio. Moving across the channel now. See you soon." I can't even begin to tell you how cool it is to say *copy that* like I just had. This was going to be a good day.

The Get-A-Way Adventures Lodge is a small, light-yellow, picturesque building with its own private dock. There's a set of slips, covered by an aluminum carport-type structure off to the left. We pulled the *Mary's Joy* up to the dock, but didn't tie up. I needed to check the place out, but I was a bit apprehensive to go alone, so I decided that now would be the time for Kat to come with me. We all met in the living area of the boat. Of course, Donna had to chime in, "I'm coming too."

I sighed. "Look, I realize who wears the penis in our relationship, but not this time." She got that look, but I forestalled her with a hand. "I need you to watch the kids and take care of the boat. Ship will steer, but I need someone down here with them."

She looked at the kids, who were standing next to each other, then back at me. The look went from *I see your incredibly valid points and support them unconditionally*, to *this is how it's going to go, and I will brook no insolence or questions of any kind from the likes of you.*

"Richy," she began, "you're going to stay here and back Ship up. If anyone or anything tries to get on the boat, you shoot them. You need to stay near the radio too." She opened the lid of the now unlocked box of goodies, and passed him an M9. He immediately ejected the mag and checked the load. Several of the sailors and soldiers had been training the civvies on the use of firearms for a while on *Atlantis*, so the kids were prepared.

She continued, distributing weapons as she spoke. "The four of us are going to check this place out. Ship, you take the boat back out a bit and honk if you need us." She passed Chloe an M9, and doled out MP5s with three spare magazines each to herself and I. Kat would keep her .30-30.

"You," she pointed at the dog, "Sit." He complied.

I was smiling. Although I didn't like the idea of Chloe with us as we went into the unknown, she had to get her proverbial feet wet sometime. She was a cool kid, and I knew she would be able to handle herself. Turns out, I was right on both counts.

We hopped off the boat and Ship backed her up into the middle of the channel. Now it was on. We had no escape route other than into the unfamiliar, or swimming, which was out of the fucking question as I didn't know if the entire channel was crawling with submerged zombies.

The near end of the dock met a gorgeous yard which sloped to the back of the lodge, complete with palm trees and a pool hidden behind a wall of green shrubbery. The grass was lush, green, and overgrown. The rest of the foliage was quite pretty, with two huge, unpruned rose bushes as the focal points. The pool was nasty with thick and horrible standing water. I had seen undead in pools before, and told everyone to stay away for that reason. Anybody going for a dip in that shit-pond was never setting foot near me again on general principles anyway.

The back of the main structure had a propped open door with dried palm leaves just inside. It was too dark to see more than a few feet inside. Donna started toward the door and I stopped her, nodding in the negative.

"We circle the structure first, then bang on the door back here. Wait a couple minutes for pus bags, then we go in." As an afterthought, I added, "Okay?" to reassure her she was in charge of all things non-tactical. She gave a curt nod, and I could see she was a bit nervous, with her eyes darting everywhere and bit of lip chewing going on. Kat and Chloe looked a bit nervous too, and I had to wonder how I looked to them. I certainly didn't enjoy what we were about to do, but I had done it a lot more than they had.

"Should we split up and—?" Donna began before I cut her off.

"No. Not a fucking chance do we split up, possibly ever again. Four guns and eight eyes are better and there's safety in numbers." I got the nod again, and knew I would keep my nuts, if at least for a while.

We moved left, and saw our first infected. It was a dead five year old, and she was plodding toward us in pink pajamas. The feet on the feetsy-Barbie-jammies had long since worn away, and this kid looked pretty rough. I heard all three girls take a sharp intake of breath and knew this was one I would have to take care of. The thing was closing at a pathetic shuffle, growling like no child could.

"Turn away," I told the girls. "Cover behind us."

I didn't wait to see if they had followed instructions. This kid would make me cry if I kept thinking about her. Then I got mad, both at the situation and myself. This poor child didn't deserve this, but more importantly, this was no longer a child, but an abomination that had murdered her and stolen her body. I started to shake with anger, and realized it would not do. I drew my SOG and calmed myself.

When the thing reached for me, I side-stepped and she moved past me slightly. I drove the knife into the base of her skull, just where the spine and head meet. She collapsed instantly, but was still snapping even with a severed spinal column. One kick and her little melon cracked, killing her.

I was disgusted. So much so that I failed to see the dead old man with overalls that had come around the corner to the side of me. Apparently, the girls had indeed followed instructions, because nobody said shit until he had me and I squealed. This fucker hadn't made a goddamned sound until he had his mitts on me, and by then, he was making that hissing hacking sound that they do. I tried to push him away, but this guy was big, and he really wanted a taste. He kept leaning in and

I kept jerking him away, but the bastard simply would not let go. I used two different moves that Remo had shown me, and one broke the thing's wrist, but it didn't give a shit and continued its assault.

"Stop friggin' moving! I can't get a shot!" Kat whisper-yelled.

Yeah, so if I stopped moving, he was going to bite me. I heard *No! Don't!* and I thought for sure I was going to have a lead headache in a moment. What I didn't expect was to see a five-foot-four streak of black and red hit my attacker's right knee. Both the dead thing and I looked to see what had hit him. It was Chloe in her Harley Quinn shirt. She kicked again with lightning speed in the same place and there was an audible snap as the infected's leg broke under the knee. The knee pretty much tore lose as well, and as the guy was heavy, and was not letting go, we both went down. Chloe wasted no time, and shot the dead guy in the face with a suppressed 9mm round as we hit the grass. I got his goo on me, and although it stunk, it didn't get in my eyes or mouth. It couldn't infect me, I know, but c'mon? Would you want that shit in your mouth?

I stood and looked at the living kid, my mouth so wide open in shock, an American Bald Eagle could have nested in there.

"Don't get mad," she said a little nervously. "You looked like you could use some help."

I closed my mouth with a distinct and noticeable pop. The rest of my expression didn't change.

Chloe looked back at the girls then at me. "What? I took American Kenpo for six years before everybody started to eat everybody. Remo has been training Richy and me for two months with his stuff too."

I did a quick scan of the area as I managed a stunned "Thanks." We were clear, for the moment, but my shirt had to go. I removed my tactical vest, then my shirt, balled it up and threw it into the grass. I put my vest back on, which did not feel good in the heat. Fucking things stick and chafe on bare skin.

Donna raised her eyebrow. "I knew you'd get your shirt off somehow."

"Wonk-wonk," I told her. "You sound like Charlie Brown's teacher." I nodded in the direction we needed to go, and we all moved that way. We made a complete circuit of the building, scanning around it too, and soon found ourselves at the open but foreboding back door again. I shined my light into the opening, seeing nothing but bird droppings and some dried palm leaves. I gave five good whacks to the doorframe, all of us backing off to see what happened next. We gave it three minutes, then entered the Get-A-Way Adventures Lodge.

Some brown leather furniture greeted us under a vaulted pine-board ceiling complete with motionless ceiling fans. An errant palm leaf sounded like a gunshot when I crushed it between my foot and the stone-tiled floor. I could only imagine what Remo and Ship would have done if they had been here and heard me do that. A short, four-step set of stairs led to an elevated, railed corridor which ran all the way around the room for standing patrons. At the back of the open room was a bar. Straight ahead was a stairway down to a sunken floor with a bunch of chairs and a pool table. More steps brought you back out of the sunken area and up to the bar at the back. There were framed pictures of fish and people holding fish all along the railed corridors and behind and over the bar.

The place was beautiful. The best part of it was that it didn't have any signs of the plague at all other than the open back door. No overturned furniture or signs of struggle. No blood or bodies, and no zombies that we could see.

I moved behind us, shutting and locking the door. "Kat, you stand guard here. If we come back, we might need to get out fast. Make sure we don't gather a crowd out back either."

She nodded, and sat down in one of the leather chairs. She shifted, and of course the leather made a fart noise. It was my turn to look at her in mock disgust.

"I didn't—"

"Uh-huh." I turned away not giving her time to explain, and tipping a wink to a silently giggling Chloe.

Donna, who had volunteered to go to possibly the worst place on earth, the *Majestic Maersk*, in the hope of saving some folks, actually looked nervous now that she might face the undead again. Her eyes whipped about, scanning everywhere at once. "The plan?"

I pulled my radio. "We clear this place, call the boys, and wait for them to show. In the meantime, I kick your ass in pool." I pointed to the pool table.

We began our clearing session, and found a truly dead woman in one of the rooms. She had taken her own life with her handgun. She had probably lost everyone, or just couldn't wrap her head around what was happening. I felt sad for her, and closed the door on her final resting place. Chloe reached for one of the doorknobs and I hissed for her to stop, nodding no. I opened the door, and this room, like all the others was devoid of any living or living dead people. There was a big bird's nest of some kind in the pine rafters of one of the rooms with an open window. The room completed its ensemble of pine-board walls and more fishing pictures, with bird shit and broken eggshells. The birds had seen fit to vamoose a while ago by the look of the place though. Too bad, as this was probably prime real estate for a flock of whatever.

We made it to the front lobby, and noticed two dead people milling about out front who hadn't been there when we had circled the building. They had most likely heard the sound of the *Mary's Joy* pulling up to the dock, but had lost the sound when Ship pulled her back into the channel. We backed off and they hadn't seen us. The front doors were glass, and there were floor-to-ceiling windows as well, but if they didn't know we were in here, then fuck 'em.

"We can't leave them there," Donna thought out loud. "Let's take care of them."

I considered smoking the two out front for a moment, but then nodded no. "Believe me, they'll come to us as soon as Ship comes back with the boat."

I realized I had broken my own rule if only for a few minutes. The thing was, a minute was more than long enough to make a deadly mistake nowadays. Hell, a bad second would get you dead. We had left Kat alone guarding the back door. Stupid, just stupid. Nothing had happened, but that is exactly how people got killed. When we got back, I motioned for her to come over, and I racked the balls on the table. "Me and her," I said, pointing at Chloe, "against you two slackers."

I called Remo, and Tim answered. "Trio, Mary. We have two out front, but the structure is clear. Waiting on you, over." (I'm gonna skip the "over's," Dear Reader, you get it by now).

The truck is running rough, but it runs. We'll be there in about twenty minutes. We keep drawing a crowd, and you guys are on a peninsula. We don't want to trap ourselves and have to abandon the truck for the boat.

"Copy that. We'll clear the ones we find in the vicinity, and get our gear off the boat." I looked at the pool table. One game wouldn't hurt, would it? We could do teams and finish in five minutes. Easy peasy.

Yeah, nope. How To Get Folks Killed 101. Might be my new major. We had the time now to do all the shit I just said. I don't know what will happen in five minutes, maybe another apocalypse. Aliens this time? I looked back at the pool table and sighed, "We can play later, let's get the food and weapons off of the boat and get Ship in here with us."

I called the big guy, and we went out the back door and onto the dock. I hadn't forgotten about the infected out front, but Ship and Richy might need a hand tying up the *Mary's Joy* to the dock. Richy was waiting with a box, a duffle full of stuff, and a dog. He passed it (except the pooch) to me over the gunwale. We tied up, and had just begun to unload when the two pus bags from out front made their debut. Kat raised her rifle, but I told her no. I raised my suppressed MP5, but Chloe said no.

"I need the practice." She took up a firing stance, lined up her M9A1 on the dead girl's noggin, and squeezed the trigger. The thing's head snapped back and it collapsed. Kid had gotten a headshot on her first try. I was impressed. She missed the second shot, but got the dead guy with no lower jaw on the third.

We had everything including the Sasquatch off of the boat and up by the back of the lodge when we heard the truck out front. It didn't take long for gunshots to sound. My radio came to life, but the voice wasn't directed at me. It was a conversation.

"*...see what you boys got in there.*"

"*We don't have much, just this truck,*" Alvarez said loudly. I looked at Ship and he nodded. I motioned for everybody to put the stuff down, and we snuck around the side of the lodge. Right out front, exactly where the two zombies had been, were six guys with rifles, two were aiming at our recently acquired blue Ford F250 quad cab, but the rest were nodding or smiling.

Fucking people. Plague of the living dead, and there are more assholes than good folks left. I shut my radio off, and motioned for Ship to take Kat to the far side of the building to flank them and possibly catch these douches in a crossfire. They made it to the other side just as one of the dickweeds punched Alvarez in the stomach. They were jeering and shouting racial epithets. I could see where this was going. Tim saw us, and nodded helplessly and not a little sadly, as he knew what I was about to do.

I got down on my haunches and looked at the kids. "Listen, you cover the rear. Face that way. If things go south, Donna will take you back to the boat. Then you run. Rich, hold Dusty, and keep him quiet."

Donna's brows furrowed in anger, "I'm not—"

"Yes, you are," I snapped. "If we can't save them," I pointed at the kids, "then what the hell are we doing any of this for?" I would not have the kids murdering humans until it was absolutely necessary, and if Ship, Kat, and I couldn't take these assholes by surprise when we were already behind them, then we should hang our shit up now and quit. I turned and looked around the corner of the lodge. Ship had his massive melon poking through a shrub, and he nodded.

I sighed, sighted the nearest asshole who had his rifle aimed in the general direction of my disarmed friends, then began walking toward him. I could see Ship in my peripheral copying me. We got to within thirty paces before one of the douches spit out a cigarette and leaned forward to crush it out with his filthy sneaker. He saw me and I saw him see me. I gave a three-round burst to his pal, then he got one, and I moved the barrel of my sub-machine gun to the right selecting targets. Ship did the same, shifting his weapon until we met in the middle.

The guy who had hit Alvarez got a .30-30 round through his back. He didn't fall forward, he just collapsed straight down, dead.

The two shitheads who used the often employed but rarely successful tactic of getting too close to Remo, turned their gaze toward the commotion and, well, you know what's coming next. I saw the jarhead grab the closest guy and literally tear his head off. Okay, so it didn't come off, but he wouldn't be using it again. Remo stepped up, reached around the guy to grab his face, and administered a stiff push into the dick's back, while giving a vicious upward jerk to his chin. I heard the snap from twenty feet away. I missed what happened to guy number two as I was focused on killing everyone else. Tim would tell me later that Remo reached up to his own face, grabbed his toothpick, and jammed it into douche number two's eye. The guy got a chance to let out a quick scream before he had his Adam's apple crushed by his own rifle butt. I was busy checking my bad guys to see if any were still kicking.

Death by toothpick. Told you.

Two were alive, but one wouldn't be for long. The guy I shot in the back was trying to breathe, but his lungs were on the pavement in front of him. I gave him a quick tap to the dome for a finish. Alvarez had the surviving captive. Ship was about to crush some heads with his boot, but I stopped him. "Fuck 'em. Let 'em turn."

The last survivor was on his knees with a bunch of guns trained on him. "You gonna kill me now?"

"Yup," I answered and pointed my weapon at his face. He pissed himself and I lowered my weapon. I shook my head and called him a pussy. He was both seething and glad that I hadn't shot him. He would also need a change of pants.

A small crowd of undead had heard the commotion and was making its way toward us, but they were far off.

"You got him?" Remo was speaking to Alvarez about covering the remaining asshole.

Alvarez smiled a wicked smile. "Yeah. If he moves, or if any more of his buddies show up, I'll shoot him in the lower spine. Won't kill him, but he won't walk again. Should be fun in today's world."

The rest of us ran to get our stuff. There was quite a bit, but we made it in two trips. The infected were closer by the time we finished loading, but we had plenty of time. Alvarez had wasted another stray that had come from the surrounding neighborhood, and had destroyed all the shitheads who I wanted to turn. I asked him why and he said they had started to move.

The truck was a Texas truck, and had all kinds of accoutrements: Rifle rack, huge tires, roll-cage with lights, dual exhaust, and a shit-ton of bumper stickers. *Texas Big!, I Brake For Big Hair, They Can Take My Gun When They Pry It From My Cold Dead Hands.* I'm sure there is some type of governmental regulation in Texas clearly stating mandatory four-wheel drive, so we got that too. The only issue was that the truck was a short-bed.

Remo would drive. The kids, the girls, and Tim would ride up front, while Ship, Alvarez, and I, would ride in the bed with our shit, although I didn't see any spare gas cans in the bed. We climbed in, and I began to reload my MP5 magazine. It was cramped back there, but on his best day, Ship would take up three spaces in the cab. He had to be back with us.

"What about me?" the surviving asshole asked.

"You can fuck off and die for all I care. I would shoot you now, but I think watching you run is better." I pointed exaggeratedly to the fifteen or so infected a hundred feet away. He hadn't seen them until now, so the douche's eyes bugged.

He held his hands out. "You gotta cut this!" He was referring to the zip-tie that Alvarez had cuffed him with.

"Did you not hear the *die* part of fuck off and die?" I banged on the back of the cab, and Remo threw the truck in drive. The guy began running back toward the lodge, his hands still tied in front of him.

"His name is Dave," Alvarez told me.

I cupped my palms, bullhorn-style, in front of my mouth, to get a good echoing yell. "Bye, Dave!"

Remo thumped into one undead as we zoomed down the street. He avoided the others, some of whom had abandoned the chase for the truck as they noticed Dave running away.

I harrumphed. "At least Davey-boy will have a nice new boat to keep him safe." Ship smiled and dug in his pocket.

He held up and jingled a set of keys attached to a small float.

MOMENTARY RESPITES AND MISTER ED

Turns out, we weren't on a peninsula. Tim had misread the map, thinking the Port Mansfield Chamber of Commerce was where we were, when in fact, it was the Get-A-Way Adventures Lodge. Shit happens. It was definitely a good thing that we weren't on a piece of land surrounded by water on three sides while driving a truck, because there were a lot of infected to contend with.

I don't know how we kept finding legions of zombies in very small towns, but there it is. They got thick fast, and with the abandoned vehicles, (this is Texas, so they were all giant fucking trucks), fuck-tons of infected, and coastal roads that hadn't been maintained, we only had a top speed of about ten miles per hour.

Remo pulled up behind a jackknifed eighteen-wheeler in front of Sweet Gregory P's Smokehouse Grill. I wanted some ribs. The jarhead skirted the big rig to the left, and ran smack-dab into a hidden horde of about fifty shamblers. I had hardly ever… no, wait, I had *never* seen Remo lose his cool, but when he ploughed into the first ranks of pus bags, and they all turned to look at us, I heard him yell, "Fuck!" before he threw the truck into reverse. The vehicle sputtered and died, and we all collectively shit our pants. The things were slapping on the hood and all four windows went up quickly while Remo fought to bring the truck back to life.

It was that typical horror-movie scenario where you groan when the vehicle won't start and you think *cliché man, cliché*. Well fuck you, you weren't there. Try it. When the first of them reached over my side of the truck bed and brushed my naked bicep with its rotten fingers, I thought for sure we were screwed. They were three deep and getting deeper around the sides of the truck before we even had a chance to fire on them. Ship used his machete, trying to save on ammo, but F that noise, I selectively fired into the group with my MP5, dropping them one at a time. Alvarez was firing too, and his M4 was damn loud. One of his expelled brass casings hit me in the cheek, which caused me to miss my target. There were too many of them. Fifty might not sound like a lot to you, but when they're so dense they begin using their destroyed brothers as steps to climb into the truck, fifty is more than enough.

Dusty, who was usually as quiet as a mouse, and had learned to keep his dog-yap shut, went ape-shit, and began barking like he and rabies were well acquainted.

Alvarez and I both yelled "Loading!" together, but there was no time. The MP5 isn't really a rifle, it's a big pistol. It's not made for thumping victims, melee style, but I smashed it into one of the things that had almost made its way into the truck bed, then another. Remo finally got the truck started and he backed up quickly, dragging a few of the infected with us, and almost throwing Alvarez and me onto the street. The three of us in the back shook off the hitchhikers with our weapons, the infected rag-dolling to the pavement at fifteen (yeah, I know that's more than the top-speed I just mentioned, but this was a special event) miles per hour or so. We were finally clear a few moments after Remo got us turned around. There were a dozen and a half bodies in the street behind us. The entire ordeal had taken maybe forty seconds, but that's how fast your world can go to hell.

We made it to Route 186 and stopped to catch our breath for a few minutes when there was nothing on either side of us but scrub land. Tower Road was off to our left, but I didn't see any towers, just a couple big radio antennas. The truck was not running well, but it was all we had. We piled out of the vehicle and I realized I was getting a sunburn on my back and shoulders.

Remo spread a big map across the asphalt road while Tim and Alvarez kept watch. Ship pointed out the Charles Johnson Airport to the northeast on the map, but we didn't know what it would look like. Who knew if there were any planes that would carry nine plus our gear? Not to mention the condition of the runway might be for shit, and there was the question of fuel stability. Then there was the landing part. I had done the whole plane thing twice already, and I wasn't in the mood to crash again. Tim had called it a *water landing*, but fuck that, we had crashed into the damn Gulf of Mexico. Screw planes. Screw 'em.

The plan was to head south along Route 186, then hook east. We would look for more supplies in a small town called San Perlita if it wasn't too overrun.

We made San Perlita in no time. The little town was empty. Devoid of anything, living or dead. I didn't so much as see a mosquito. Are you getting it was empty? Because it was empty. It was also hot. Over the one-hundred mark on the thermometer on a random brick-walled house.

We were able to get a couple of gas cans, and I added a bit of the paint thinner to the fuel we scrounged. Tim, Richy, and I put another eight or nine gallons of treated gas in the tank.

Raymondville was a few more miles down the road. It would be dark in a few hours, and we figured we would loot what we could and move on. This was a bigger town, so we decided to stick together as a group. We pulled into a CVS parking lot, looking to loot anything we could. The front door to the drug store was gone. The whole thing. Someone must have pulled the door off with their vehicle, but they also must have taken it with them because it was nowhere to be seen.

WTF? Where was the door?

We entered as a group, Dusty, Chloe, and Alvarez standing guard at the front entrance. (I almost wrote front doors). One side of the place had been cleared out, and there were bloodstains and drag marks at the top of one of the aisles. The place was gloomy, but not dark, with the windows letting in the end of the daylight. We cleared it in under two minutes and began to shove shit in bags. We got as many drinks as we could out of the dark refrigerators, and made six trips full of water, soda, and snacks. There wasn't any real food, but we were able to procure a whole bunch of nuts and dried fruits. We left feeling pretty good. Hadn't seen an infected and got some good stuff.

Is it some latent sense of camaraderie that makes these fucking things group up? There are lone zombies all over the place, I know, but if there is a large swarm, any infected nearby will join it. Maybe it's a flock mentality where there's both safety in numbers, and a better chance of success in hunting is achieved. Maybe it's just because a swarm of the rotten bastards makes so much noise that the others follow the sound. I don't know.

What I *do* know is that, at the risk of repeating the sentiment in the last sentence, a large group of infected is *fucking loud.* This is what I'm staring at now, inside the cupola on the peak of the red-tiled roof of the Sleepy Times Motel, just off of Route 186 in Raymondville, Texas.

The truck sputtered when we were passing Sleepy Times, and Remo pulled in. The motel was a two-story with eight rooms on each floor and an attached office kitty-corner to the main structure. Both ends of the small building had wooden stairs and both floors had an ice machine and vending machines equidistant from the stairs.

The truck engine quit when we were in a parking spot outside the main office. This also had a thermometer, and yeah, it was still on the north side of one-hundred. Remo tried to start the truck a few times to no avail. "Pop the hood," I told him, and we piled out.

I inspected a few things on the truck while Remo and Ship looked the motel over. I did what I do best, but couldn't find anything wrong with the exterior engine components or lines. Whoever had owned this truck before must have been a bit of a gear-head. The engine was pristine, with a chrome fan and valve covers, and pretty red and blue bushings and bolt caps.

I came to the conclusion that it was our fuel, but draining and refilling was going to be a bitch. We would need another vehicle, and some more fuel. Maybe I hadn't added enough xylene, or maybe the gas was too far-gone. Neither of those ideas changed the fact that when Alvarez nudged me and I looked across the parking lot, I saw something weird.

A black cloud was coming our way, maybe a mile off across the scrub. No, Dear Reader, not a funnel cloud, that's a different book. This was just... I don't know how to describe it; weird. It was really low, and it moved like no cloud I've seen. I radioed to the guys, and when they returned, Ship's eyes got really big. He pointed to the motel and began to scribble. He passed me the note when he was done and I shared it with everyone as he began to grab shit out of the back of the truck. The dog was uttering a low growl.

That is a cloud of insects. The only reason there would be a cloud that big is if there were an equally large group of undead.

The entire band of us, other than Ship and our furry friend, squinted into the distance. I couldn't make out any infected, but Ship was rarely wrong, and what he had just said made sense. There was no time to get another vehicle, pack our shit in it, and hope it worked. There was no place to hide or run to either. I was about to start barking commands, but Remo beat me to it.

"Everybody get as much stuff as you can, and get it to the top floor. Alvarez, you and I will clear the rooms now."

No zombies jumped at them from the rooms upstairs, which I consider a boon. Ship took off down the upstairs hallway after he had brought a bunch of stuff into one of the rooms. He disappeared around the corner to the far set of stairs. I packed the shit in one room, checked my MP5 magazines, then went to see what Ship was doing. He had begun making a bit of a racket at a time when we should be extremely quiet. I turned the corner and had to marvel, yet again, at Ship's ability to be a smarty-pants and the Hulk at the same time. He didn't have any tools, so he used brute strength to straight-up rip the treads off of the stairs. He got to the fourth one before he saw me. I nodded to him and he nodded back.

I called to Kat, and she came running. "Cover Ship. I'm going to start on the other set of stairs." She nodded and began scanning without a word. I booked it down to the truck, checked behind the rear bench seats, and lo and behold, there was a toolbox. I love Texans. I came back with the box, which not only held a plethora of useful tools, but contained a .38 special revolver and a half a carton of shells. I feel compelled to reiterate my affection for all things Texas. You put an already-fired piece of brass in a vehicle by mistake, and it's a felony in Massachusetts. Here they have guns in toolboxes. I grabbed Alvarez, and the two of us began ripping off the treads of the east-side stairs. There were no risers, but the center stringer had to go as well. Never know if a zombie gymnast will be able to negotiate the balance-beam of stringer-steps.

Oh, sorry. Treads are the part of the stairs you step on. Risers are the vertical part of the stairs, but this was an open stairway (you could look through them), so there were no risers. The stringers are what the treads and risers are nailed to. Now you can look at steps and know what the fuck each piece is. Yay.

It took fifteen minutes for Alvarez and me to destroy our set of stairs. When I looked up, dripping with sweat, Ship was leaning against the second-floor wall, drinking a 20-ounce Pepsi. He passed one to Alvarez, who uncapped and drank quite a bit before letting out a billion decibel belch. I looked longingly at the soda, and Ship passed me my very own cola. Yup, you read me right; cola. I looked at it, then at him. He blinked, smiled, reached behind him, and passed me a Mountain Dew. He winked and I smiled as I took a huge pull. I let out a burp too, but it was nothing compared to my friend's. Alvarez shook his head, "Pussy."

The toolbox held a small (very small) hand saw, and we used that and Ship's giant foot to rid us of both center stringers. There was no way any infected was getting up here now.

"Let's get inside," Remo said, looking at the cloud. It had gotten significantly closer, and we could barely make out figures moving beneath it. Lots of figures. I followed Kat into the second room, and holy shit. Just holy shit. Two twin beds on the right, with a chair, a small table, a beat-up TV, and a dime-store picture of a horse on the wall. It looked like a bad paint-by-numbers jobbie, and that was the good part. Hideous black and white wallpaper adorned the walls with hunting pictorials from the 1700s. Muskets and deer and did I mention holy shit? I'm no interior decorator, but, damn. Shouldn't there be good-old-boys toting lever action rifles and wearing cowboy hats? Dusty was sitting on the floor in the heat, his tongue lolling, staring at that horrible wallpaper. I've heard that dogs only see in black and white. This poor fucker probably loved the scenes.

Each room had two doors that opened into the other rooms as well. Soon, we had the entire top floor for ourselves. Every room had identical RCA TVs and that horrible wallpaper.

It was perfect. We were off the ground and the pus bags couldn't get to us, so we ate, cleaned our weapons, and waited.

The sound hit us first. You know it, that awful hacking rasp. Moans, cries, you've heard it. The bugs hit us next. All kinds, but mostly flies. They swarmed the motel, but weren't interested in us when they had a mobile smorgasbord. There were fuck-tons of them on the screens, and soon, the rooms had a few buzzing around as well.

We had the curtains drawn, but we kept peeking. The first of them stumbled into the parking lot a half hour before dark. It was about then that I got a look at my first, honest-to-God swarm since Keesler Air Force Base was overrun in Mississippi. There were thousands. They must have come from one of the cities nearby, and it was just my luck that they picked this direction to travel. The kids sat back down and actually hugged each other. They had never seen anything like this. It was new for Tim too, but he took it differently. He had seen mega-swarms on satellite cameras, but not up close.

He was fascinated. "Look at the way they move. They're like a flock of birds, or a school of fish. There doesn't seem to be any alpha, they just go whichever way they go. I wonder if a noise or something they saw in any direction would make them go in that direction until they received some other stimuli?" Ship passed him a note, and Tim nodded vehemently. "Yes! I agree!"

He had said that way too loud, and everybody hissed at him to *Shhh*! Tim looked properly chastised, and he and Ship moved down a couple of rooms to speak nerd.

The kids looked scared, so I tried to comfort them. "Don't worry, as long as we're quiet, they'll move off while we sleep tonight."

"Sleep?" Chloe asked. "Are you friggin' crazy? You think anybody can sleep knowing those things are out there?"

"Then there's the noise," Richy added. "They're hella-loud."

He had me on that one.

We hunkered down, and tried to sleep, but both kids were absolutely correct. If the noise wasn't enough, the fact that there were a couple thousand zombies twenty feet away kept us up. The things broke into the lower rooms and the office in the middle of the night. We could hear them below us smashing shit and shuffling about on broken glass. They couldn't know we were here, or get to us if they did, but the whole episode was still unnerving.

I woke up at first light, one kid on each side of me on the shitty motel room bed. I guess I *could* sleep. The first thing I noticed upon waking up was that I was uncomfortable. I was drenched in sweat from the coastal Texas heat and humidity. I was sticky and it was hard to breathe in that horrible room with the heat and the smell of unwashed humans. Two other people on a bed with you in hundred degree temperatures is not conducive to keeping cool either. The second thing I noticed was that the sounds of the dead, while significantly diminished, were certainly not gone.

Remo sat in a chair, leaning it back on its hind legs with his back to me. He surveyed the parking lot through the white curtains. I hadn't made a sound, not a stretch or a shift on the bed. I truly believe this fucker had heard my eyes open. He didn't look at me or acknowledge that he was speaking to me at all, but there was nobody else in the room other than the sleeping kids.

"There are quite a few stragglers."

Now I did stretch. "How many?" I asked through a yawn.

"Too many."

Both kids had woken up when I had spoken, but they stayed in bed as I sat up. I rubbed my eyes, digging out the accumulated crap from the eight seconds of sleep it felt like I got. I shimmied down the bed and tossed my feet off the end so as to disturb the kids as little as possible. Difficult, given three people in a twin bed. Donna looked at me, smiling, from her bed next to ours. Everyone else had picked different rooms, but I doubted they got too much sleep either.

I slunk up next to Remo and he glanced at me and stated, "This could be problematic."

I had to agree. There were a couple hundred dead shuffling around the tarmac. They looked hungry. They also seemed to be searching for something. Three guesses as to what it was. I have no idea how they knew there was food about, but they did. From my vantage, I could see that they were rummaging through the office, and not a few of them had decided they wanted to take a peek in our truck. Our non-functional truck.

Tim strode into our room, gnawing on some beef jerky. He peered at Dusty, who was on his back with his paws in the air and his lengthy, pink tongue flopping out. Tim tore a piece off a piece of jerky and tossed it to the dog, who wasted no time in hoarking it down. "Ship estimates that there are just over two hundred of them left from the two thousand or so that were out there last night. He thinks that the others, if they were moving at one point five miles per hour, and have been gone for eight hours, are twelve miles away given level terrain and no distractions."

I huffed, "Does Ship happen to have a phased plasma rifle in a forty-watt range?"

Tim stared at me for a moment before he asked, "What?"

I flaunted an absolutely epic eye-roll. "Never mind. We need to think about what to do here."

Tim brightened. He sure was chipper considering the circumstances. "Ship says we need a diversion."

"Full circle to the plasma rifle. My meager math skills tell me that without a diversion, we're looking at about twenty head shots a piece."

"That's no good," Remo piped. "Too much ammo."

"Well," I began, "I'll—"

Remo interrupted, "I'll do it." Obviously, he meant he would jump down from our safe place to create the diversion we needed.

A car alarm began to sound from an indeterminate distance off.

I looked at Remo, my eyebrows raised in disbelief, "What, are you a fucking Jedi, now?"

The effect of the alarm on the swarm was immediate. The pus bags looked in the direction of the sound and began to slog off. Three forms, whom I hadn't identified until then, shot off after the noise at full sprint as well. Two from the crowd, and one from out of a room underneath us.

Hopefully, it was just me being tired, because mistaking a Runner for a pus bag was a deadly mistake. The rest of our group congregated in my room, everyone staring at the departing dead or trying for a glimpse of the source of the sound.

We began to pack what little stuff we had, and when the last infected had been gone from sight for a few minutes, I moved out on to the elevated walkway to assess the situation. I got on my belly and leaned over the closest stairway that we had demolished. I couldn't see anything, but I heard a clippity-clop and directed my gaze toward this new and unusual sound. A man and a woman, each on horseback trotted across the asphalt, stopped short of the truck, and looked at me.

"Got maybe, five, ten minutes before that alarm stops," the man said up to me.

"Morning to you too," I replied, my eyes giving away my wariness.

"Y'all got kids with you," the woman said. "Says to me you ain't lookin' for trouble."

"We're not." The rest of my group, dog included, came out onto the walkway. Everyone was armed.

The man looked at the woman, and she nodded. "Y'all can come with us," he told us. "We got a place that's as safe as any."

"Not giving up our weapons," Remo stated matter-of-factly.

Both of the newcomers smiled huge Texas smiles. "Son, I would think less of you if you did, but I wouldn't ask in the first place. Name's Matt, and this here's Stacy. We been watchin' you since you got into town. Sorry about your truck, but she's prolly like the rest of the world: dead."

"Y'all are welcome to come back with us," Stacy offered, "but we should leave soon."

Matt looked to where the pus bags and their speedier cousins had moved on down the road, "Don't want them followin' us. Besides, if the bigger herd comes back and follows them to our place, we're in some trouble. Gonna have to fight off some stragglers in the scrub as it is."

That didn't sound fun, but trapped in a shitty motel, with wallpaper that was just *itching* to drag us all into an abyss full of fire and torture, sounded even less fun.

The group looked to me for a decision. Me. They wanted me to choose life or death. What had come to pass to make these people think I had any idea what the hell I was doing? This kind of resolution should be handled by Remo, or Ship. Both of them were looking at me expectantly.

I gave a nervous sigh, "We'll come with you... If you're sure..." I let the sentiment hang.

Stacy tore her eyes away from staring after the dead and squinted through the sun at me. "Wouldn't have asked you if we weren't."

We moved as a group back into the motel rooms, grabbed our stuff, and brought it out to the walkway. Matt was off his horse, Stacy holding the reins. There was a brained pus-bag on the ground not far away. "Drop me your stuff and I'll pile it up for ya," he said.

I dropped him my duffel, hung from the hole where the stairs used to be, and dropped the few feet to the ground. Alvarez dropped me a bag, and followed suit. My group passed the rest of our shit to the three of us on the ground, and we piled it up. The humans were next, and they came down one at a time, Ship doing a final walk-through to make sure we hadn't left anything behind.

When he was down, we divvied up our considerable supplies and doled them out to people by strength. Matt offered to take some of our stuff, but Remo wouldn't part with the ammo or the weapons, and Ship said he would carry the food. The food bags alone had to weigh a hundred pounds.

"It's three miles from here," Stacy said to Ship. The big guy just nodded, shouldering the duffels.

"Don't say much, does he?" she asked no one in particular.

The nine of us plus two horses and their riders moved off to the northwest at a moderate pace for summer Texas weather. It was faster than I would have liked, but slower than we could move. I may have mentioned it was hot. I tried to think of snow to cool my ass down. That shit didn't work.

Matt leaned over his horse to ask me a question. "What did you think of the wallpaper in there?" He thumbed back over his horse's ass to the Sleepy Times Motel.

I gave a mock shudder. "Damned evil. Who thinks that kind of shit up? And who would put it in a motel?"

Matt smiled another huge, toothy smile and nodded. "We're gonna get along just fine."

TWO MILES OF DEATH

It was still hot and I hadn't had a shower in a while so you can imagine what I smelled like. I was taking a selfie-sniff when I noticed Matt pull a small radio from his belt. We were about a half mile into our trek. "Darcy, this is Matt. We got some strays we're bringin' back."

How many? I heard from the other end.

"Nine, plus a dog." He looked us over for a sec. "They look competent."

Really? What kind of dog?

"Focus, Darcy"

Oh, right. We'll be ready for ya. Got some chicken grillin' up now.

"Alrighty. I'll check in again when we see the gate."

Gotcha.

They didn't use any overs or outs and *they* knew what each other was saying. Screw that military shit. I glared at Remo, but he didn't care and was focused on his toothpick chewing. No idea where he had gotten another fang-splinter, but this was Remo. He had probably fashioned it out of a telephone pole when I had my head turned.

My mind began to wander as we traipsed across our second mile of scrub. To keep my thoughts occupied, I began to talk to Tim about Baldy Mountain, his family, and the *Majestik Maersk*. We slogged on, conversing in the oppressive Texas heat, until the first squish.

Horse shit. Really, when you think of it, you think *shit from a horse*. I guess that's what it is, but I've gotta tell you: horses have it *made*. Horses can poop on the fly. What other domesticated animal in North America can do that? Can you imagine just battling some undead, and they literally scare the shit out of you, but you don't hesitate and just drop a deuce during the battle? No squatting or wiping or stink? Epic.

Until you step in it. Even the dog had the foresight to step around the poop.

There I was, talking to Tim while we trudged across our second mile of scrub toward Matt and Stacy's place, and I looked forward to see a horse's ass. The beast was swishing its tail, and I could see poop just dropping from his butt. What I didn't realize was that this was the end of his movement, the rest of it being on the ground in front of me. Horse excrement isn't as bad as any other type of feces I can think of, but who wants to put their boot in it?

The short answer is: not me.

Know what other super-power horses have besides the poop thing? They can smell zombies. I'm standing there, leaning over with one arm on a chuckling Tim for support, using a small stick to dig the shit out of the grooves in my boot sole, when the stallion in front of me makes a weird noise. I pause in my cleaning to look up, and notice the creature is looking in all directions with his ears straight up. He's giving nervous snorts and begins pawing at the ground with his hoof.

"Where is it, Beast?" Matt asks him. "Which way?"

This beautiful animal began to furiously nod its nose toward the west. The damn horse was talking to Matt! The horses had beaten Dusty to the punch on the scent thing too, but now he was alert.

Tim and I looked in the direction indicated, and I could see a solitary figure making its way toward us on an intercept path. I was having a hard time believing it was luck.

Matt saw it too, and he decided it needed to go. "I got this one."

He rode off toward it, and came back in a few minutes. "There's a few more in a washout over there. Might need some help with 'em."

I furrowed my brow. "How many?"

"Bout a hunnert." (He meant a hundred, but that's how he had pronounced it.) The pus bags crested the walls of the gulley they were in and started toward us, spread out both in front and to the right in a long line.

"Should we just leave them and go?" asked Tim.

Stacy shook her head in the negative. "Naw. They'll just follow us home. Once they see you, or get your scent, they don't give up. We used to pour bleach on the ground to kill our trail, but we ran out some time ago. 'Sides, y'all won't get through them on foot." She pointed and I could see she was right. Somehow, the bastards had cut us off from the north and east.

"Get ready," Remo said while he checked his rifle. The sounds of magazines ejecting and weapon actions were now commonplace. We all did as instructed and triple checked our gear. Beast, the big, black stallion with white socks, currently walking under Matt's balls, began to do that pawing thing, and started nodding his gorgeous head really fast again.

"We know, Beasty," Stacy said from atop her brown and white Pinto. The Pinto also began to wag its head and make those cool sounds horses make.

Matt stood up in the saddle and looked back the way we had come, "Oh."

I put my hand up to shade my eyes as I squinted east. I couldn't see anything. "What is it?"

"More," was all he said. He looked at Stacy and she nodded. He was on the radio lickety-split.

"Darcy, we might need some assistance on this one. Got a good crowd of 'em headin' our way. Dunno how we can lose 'em. Prolly end up bringin' 'em all the way home. We're gonna need two trucks I think, and a couple more guns."

Where you at?

"'Bout halfway between you and Ray-ville. Mile and a half southeast of The Double Hoof in the scrub."

A man's voice came over the radio. *How many, Matt?*

"Plenty. Couple hunnert maybe? They're headin' at us from the east and southwest too, so hurry. These folks ain't got a ride."

We're comin'. If it gets bad, you get as many as you can on each mount and high-tail it out of there.

Matt looked right at me.

"Kids first," I told him, "including the big one. The rest of us will be fine."

He swallowed hard and nodded, knowing if it got bad enough for him to run on his horse, the rest of us were all dead. I'm ashamed to write that it occurred to me, for the briefest of moments, that we could just take their horses and probably save six of the nine of us. The thought came and went as fast as a slap, and that's just what it felt like. There was a little time to feel like shit, so I did.

The group in front was two hundred yards away. They kept coming up over the rise and right at us. There were a shit load of them, and they were in all manner of disarray. They looked dry and rotten, which would make sense considering the temperature. There were too many to go hand to hand. Oh, and there was a clown in the bunch. This was my first zombie clown.

"Firing line," Remo barked. "Spread out ten feet apart. Pick your targets and fire. Richy and Chloe, pick a horse and climb on now."

Richy looked affronted. "But we can—"

166

"*Now*," said the jarhead in his not-to-be-fucked-with voice. Dusty began to growl.

Matt and Stacy helped the kids up, and Stacy noticed something behind us. "Got a fast one comin'."

Matt stood in his saddle again and considered. He drew a partially brass lever-action rifle from a long holster attached to his saddle, sighted, and fired. "Done and done." He was a good shot. He was using iron sights, and the Runner was far off.

Kat's rifle was scoped, and she fired when the things were four hundred feet out. She bolted in another round and fired again. Two targets down. Alvarez began firing his M4 and the infected began to fall. I heard the lever action rifle fire again, and again. I passed the EBR to Remo. I'm a decent shot, but I know he could shoot the wings off of a fly from here even if that fly were on the international space station.

"Quarter-mile behind," Stacy said calmly over the gunfire.

Ship joined the fray and began selectively firing his HK417. Donna and I were useless with MP5s until the infected were much closer. Tim fired his pistol twice before he realized he wasn't going to hit anything from three hundred feet. The sexy sound of rifle fire kept up, but there were still plenty of dead. It was then that fear began to creep its way into me.

Kat began to reload from her bandoleer, both Remo and Alvarez shouted *Loading* at the same time. At eighty feet or so, Donna began to fire, but she didn't hit anything. "Not yet," I told her.

"When?" she demanded in a tiny, scared voice that was unlike her.

"When they're thirty feet or so away, I'll fire first."

She nodded a bit too quickly, and I realized it wasn't just me that was frightened. I heard engines, but they were far off. The seventy or so dead would reach us before the trucks did.

"Matt," I yelled over the din, "get the kids out of here. Kat, get on the horse with Stacy and Chloe."

Kat threw me that sideways glance as she reloaded again. "Fuck that!" She fired into the crowd twice more and was out. She slung her rifle and drew her .357 revolver.

"Kat, now!"

"We'll be right behind you," Alvarez told her and forced her over to Stacy. The three of them were tight on the Pinto as Kat climbed up, crying.

"Hold on! Hyah!" Stacy grunted, and the horse looked relieved to be moving. They would be able to plow through the skinny line of infected ahead of them with ease on the horses. If someone fell off, they were in trouble though. Chloe was between the two bigger women, and Richy was holding on tight to Matt.

Matt fired once more. "Good luck!" Beast took him and Richy off pretty fast.

"Now is good, I think," I told Donna, and began firing. She did too, and so did Tim. Between the six of us, we did pretty well. We began to back up, but I could hear the swarm behind us now, so eventually we were going to get pinched. The dead in front had reached the gear that we had dropped, but they didn't give a shit about it. They wanted us and just stepped over or around it.

"Last mag," Alvarez said and slammed it home. The bass boom of Ship's .308 stopped and I saw him draw his Sig.

Remo dropped his pack. He had kept it when we had put our shit down a couple of minutes ago. "Alright, it's time to run!"

We fled to the north, the way the horses had gone. They were well past the line now, having broken through, and Matt was shooting back into the crowd. A couple of stragglers had reversed direction and hunted the horses and their riders, but most were still coming at us. When we were ten feet from the first of them, I gave a full auto blast to try to make a hole to run through. Everybody else followed suit, firing whatever weapon they had loaded, and soon, there was a passage through the infected that was closing as I saw it. Dusty weaved through reaching hands, one of which closed around his fur. He reached back and bit the hand, tearing free and was through quickly.

The trucks were in sight in front of us when we hit the wall. Ship used his machete to hack off the arm of a dead good-old-boy who reached for him. Remo let out a vicious kick which destroyed the knee of another rotting Texan. Tim fired point blank into the face of an emaciated young woman who was missing half of her throat. Alvarez used his rifle butt to push two attackers away. Remo and Donna got through with no problem, he telling her to run. One of them grabbed me, but I shook it off, firing into the faces of a couple more. Tim yelled and used his empty M9 to crush the eye socket of a dead young man. He raised his arm to slam it into the thing's face again, but something grabbed his arm and pulled him off balance.

They swarmed him before I could do a damn thing. He looked at me helplessly for the briefest of moments before they took him down. Ship decapitated one more creature before he grabbed me and lifted me like a child, pulling me away from Tim. The Sasquatch dragged me along through the hole we had created, Remo and Donna firing so close to us I swear I felt the rounds go past.

The trucks reached us and they began firing into the crowd.

"I can get him!" I screamed, trying to shake Ship off, but he was too strong for me by a longshot. He kept dragging me while I fought to get loose until I saw Donna. She was crying, and begging me to come with her.

"Get in," one of the men shouted. The other truck slammed on its brakes, skidding across the dust into the crowd, knocking five or six of the things back before the driver threw it in reverse. We piled into the back of both trucks, Ship helping me just to be sure I wouldn't run back to help our friend. There was a huge pig-pile of infected in the place where Tim had fallen. They were fighting each other, the ones in the back trying to yank their brothers off the pile. I looked away and put my head down.

"Save your ammo!" I heard one of the newcomers yell. "There's too many!" I was sitting in the bed of a black F350 and I tumbled backwards when the driver threw it in gear. Ship righted me, keeping his hand on my shoulder and giving it a quick squeeze. I put my hand on his and looked at him, nodding and wiping my eyes. I was appreciative of the consolation. If you think, Dear Reader, that this was unmanly, then you can kiss my ass.

The trucks caught up to the horses in no time, and we transferred the kids over. "Where's Tim?" Kat demanded instantly. She was in the other truck, but I heard her plain as day. "Where's Tim!" she shouted when nobody answered her. Donna hugged her and half our group was soon in tears.

"Matt, you and Stacy head back toward Ray-ville," one of the newcomers advised. "Circle around, hit the creek, and follow it for half a mile before you turn northwest. Check in every fifteen minutes."

Both riders nodded, turned their mounts back the way we had come, and galloped off. The trucks turned around, and we headed over the scrub to the west. The line of dead was to our south, and we were on a parallel course back to Raymondville.

Donna looked frightened. "Where are we going?"

"We're heading back toward town before we circle around, ma'am," one of the gunmen said through the rear window of the vehicle. "We'll throw off their scent 'fore we head home."

We were almost to the town limits, just before the first buildings jutted out of the dirt, when the trucks stopped. The man that had told Matt and Stacy to ride off got out of our truck. He was tall, maybe six three, in his late forties, with short-cropped, salt-and-pepper hair. He was wearing a beat-up, blue baseball cap, jeans, and a Harley Davidson T-shirt. He put his arms on the sides of the vehicle and addressed us.

"My name's Deek Meeks. Deek is short for Deacon, and any jokes about the rhyming names I've heard before. Ship stood and stuck his hand, way, way down for Deek to shake. Mr. Meeks did what every single person in the universe does when they see Ship. He looked the corresponding way, way up, raised his eyebrows, opening his mouth a little in surprise. Considering Ship was standing in the back of a truck, he was now about nine feet tall, so he had to come down on his haunches to actually get a grip on Deek's hand.

"This is Ship," I told him, "and this is how he says thank you."

"Y'all are welcome. Both for the ride and the accommodations you're about to spend time in. I own a ranch called the Double Hoof a few miles from here. We'd love to have you, and if y'all agree to helpin' out while you stay, you can stay for a while. It ain't much, but it's home."

I stuck my paw out for him to shake when he was done with Ship. "Thank you, Mr. Meeks."

"HAW! Ain't nobody called me Mr. Meeks in more'n a year! Deek'll do fine."

I nodded. "Deek then. Forgive us, we just lost a friend."

He looked down and then back at where the swarm was. They were heading in our direction as fast as their rotting legs would carry them. "I'm real sorry about your friend. Happens too much now; losing people. We can talk more when we get back to the Hoof. We're gonna give the dead ones something to chase, then head on home. Hit it, Hank!"

The horn on the F350 blared to life. Hank leaned on it for a solid minute, the driver of the Dodge Ram 2500 following suit. After twenty seconds, that shit was annoying, so most of us covered our ears. A couple of shamblers came from the town side, but the horn had been for the swarm. One of the guys from inside our truck passed Deek something, and he began to fiddle with it. He was winding up an old, double-bell alarm clock.

"I set her for fifteen minutes from now. She'll go off until something shuts her down, and them things is pretty dumb, so it might ring for an hour. That oughta do it. Saddle up!"

He put the clock right in the center of the steaming hot road. The tick tock sound it made was crazy loud, and for the briefest of moments, I considered it would be impossible to sleep with that stupid antique next to me. Then my thoughts returned to Tim. Tim had worked for the NSA. He had brought communities together, travelled across an infected country with me, battled countless undead, and he had saved my life. He died in the Texas scrubland because some assholes had blown-up our house. I stared at the bed liner of the truck, thinking about how I would miss him, and how wrong it was that a man like that was dead when there were so many assholes still vertical. Anger set in, and I seethed until we reached our destination.

ME TOO

It never ceases to amaze me what people are capable of when there are no rules and supplies have become difficult to obtain. From the good to the evil to the necessary, man will do what he must to survive. A copier repair man can become a zombie-slaying hero, while a police detective can turn into a serial killer unchecked. The propensity to build a safe haven for your family and then defend it, is paramount for those who can't or refuse to run. The creations that I have seen people construct with scavenged materials is astonishing.

The Double Hoof Ranch is 847 acres of beautiful green grass, Acacia, and Ash trees hidden in a shallow valley in the coastal Texas scrubland. The entire acreage is surrounded by a four-foot, barbed- wire fence that stretches as far as the eye can see in both directions. As you come up on the small gate that crosses the packed earth road, you can't see any structures or even realize that there is anything other than more scrub on the other side of the gate. One of our saviors exited our vehicle, opened the flimsy, wooden, barbed-wire gate, and closed it when we were through. I didn't think that this gate or fence would stop a jackrabbit, let alone a swarm of infected dead former-humans.

A half mile past the gate, there was a better wall. A ten-foot wide, five-foot deep trench had been dug as a dry moat of sorts. The earth that had been removed had been placed on the far side of the trench and sloped sharply backward. This was a fantastic barrier against the dead. A guard tower made of welded steel and stained planks stood behind and to the right of an interesting gate. The gate was one piece of steel, maybe ten feet across, which was attached to a payloader by chains. The machine lowered the steel into place as we approached the gate. It was a drawbridge, reminiscent of a castle, circa 1500 AD, and it was solid as fuck.

The guys from the truck waved to the two gate guards as we passed, and we travelled along the dirt road for another mile or so. The path then began to slope downward sharply. At the crest of the long ramp, before we started into the valley proper, I could see there was a distinct geographic difference from the land surrounding this area. Where everything behind us was dry scrub, with small bushes and the occasional cactus (or dead guy), the land in front of us was lush and green. I could see a large pond to the right of several smaller structures and a massive barn. Forty foot trees on either side of the now-paved main road gave ample shade from the oppressive sun as we drove beneath them.

We pulled into the cobbled driveway of a moderately sized stone and wood house with a non-functional, Mexican-style, round fountain out front, and began to file out of the trucks. The place was beautiful, with a red-tiled roof and big windows. All of the ground floor windows had rebar welded over them into metal frames, and I was thinking Ship would have trouble kicking in the front door when it opened and a small woman in an apron strolled out wiping her hands with a cloth.

She looked to be about fifty, with silvery, shoulder-length hair, and she was just a tad on the portly side. She smiled and said, "Welcome."

The last cooked meal I had eaten, other than with an MRE heater, was linguine with freshly caught mahi-mahi when we were back on *Atlantis*. It had been delicious, and we had eaten it a few days ago, so I shouldn't have been as hungry as I was. When the smell of cooking food wafted out that door and hit me on that cobbled driveway in east Texas, it almost brought me to my knees. Then I thought that Tim would have enjoyed the smell of the food we were about to eat, and I grew somber.

The woman in the apron, who introduced herself as Kelly, shook each of our hands as we followed Deek and filed past her into the house. The smell intensified a zillionfold (relax, I know that isn't a real word) when we entered into a big mud-room of sorts. My mouth began to water. Deek told us we could leave our stuff in the mud-room, and we left everything but our weapons.

A girl of about twenty-five named Darcy, two guys in jeans, boots, and cowboy hats, Dix and Javier, and a medium-sized, rust-colored dog with the awesome name of Rusty, were in the great room of the house. Rusty and Dusty were instant best friends, and they trotted off to explore each other's butts.

We were invited to lunch, and to trade stories. You know ours, so I'll skip it. Theirs was interesting enough.

The Double Hoof had been a horse ranch, but had fallen on tough times in the past decade. Most of the staff had been laid off or had moved on, until only family and a couple of hands remained. Plague hits, a few of them die, they build the fortifications, gain a few more people, and live under constant threat like everyone else. There had been a couple of serious undead attacks, but the nature of Hidden Valley (yeah, like the old salad dressing) was that it was just that: Hidden. Nobody outside of a few people in the neighboring towns knew it was there, so no bad guys had shown up.

The Double Hoof was home to thirteen people now, but thirteen was a damn small amount to constantly check the perimeter fencing.

Another reason these folks were still alive was a natural, underground spring that fed the pond. They had abundant fresh water, and this was the reason the valley existed in the middle of nowhere, and also the reason Deek's grandfather had built the ranch in this spot. They farmed and hunted inside and outside the barbed wire, but the moat and earth wall only surrounded a hundred or so acres of the ranch.

"A hundred acres?" Donna asked Deek. "You dug a trench around a hundred acres?"

Deek smiled a half smile. "Took two months. We got six machines, three of which we liberated from some road construction south of Rayville."

We heard a woman's yell from the left, "Lunch is ready!"

"Follow me," Deek told us.

We filed into a huge kitchen, with an equally huge wooden table in the center of it. The table was fifteen feet long, at least, and there were fourteen mismatched chairs surrounding it.

A short, heavy girl with thin, auburn hair worked at the sink, her back to us. When she heard us all file in, she turned and made a funny run to Deek. "Daddy!"

Deek smiled and caught the girl, "Hi, Kate! Didja miss me?"

She nodded vigorously, and I noticed she had a wicked scar that split her hair above her left ear. She turned around and went back to work quickly. She looked to be in her early twenties, and she had Downs Syndrome. Deek pointed to the table and said, "Please," indicating that we should sit down.

We picked chairs and sat. It felt good. Kelly, Darcy, and Kate brought the food, while Dix set glasses filled with water from the sink about the table. I was amazed that their plumbing worked, but then I remembered the pond. Something equally amazing happened next: Dix opened a fully functional refrigerator, pulled the top door, and grabbed two trays of ice.

"Solar and two wind turbines," Deek commented, noticing our shock.

We got to talking again as we ate the delicious chicken and rice. The water was so cold it would crack your teeth, and Dix added ice to it anyway. Deek sat at the head of the table with Kelly on one side, and Kate on the other. Kate's eyes locked onto mine, and she would not look away. Her mouth opened in an O, and she openly stared.

"Him too..." she said quietly. She looked at her father. "Him too!"

He looked at her questioningly. "What's that, Kate?"

"Him too," was all she would say.

We finished the meal, everyone pitching in to clean up, then retired to the great room. A fire smoldered in the fireplace, and I thought that was odd considering it was a billion degrees outside.

Kelly took Kate back into the kitchen, and Deek looked right at me, leaning forward and putting his elbows on his knees. "She's not my daughter," he said under his breath. "We were out at the road construction back about three months after the first dead started to walk." Dix and Javier both nodded in agreement. "We were trying to start one of the backhoes and a small herd snuck up on us. Dix started shootin' 'em, and me, Mike, and Javi joined. There was, maybe, thirty of them, and we just shot 'em all. I aimed at one of the last few, popped off a shot, and missed." He sighed. "Mostly. The thing grabbed its head, fell down, and started to cry. The four of us couldn't believe it. We were so shocked I almost got bit by one of 'em that came up behind. She was standing in a group of them, moaning just like they were. That's how I met Kate. She's been here ever since."

I was thoughtful. "The dead don't attack her?"

"Nosir." (Deek said it like it was one word, I swear.)

I nodded. "Seen it before. The fast ones will go after her though, that I can tell you."

Deek raised his eyebrows and looked at his buddies. "Now that there? That's pretty critical information. Thank you, son."

We chatted some more, and soon, it was time for bed. There were vacant rooms in one of the houses, formerly for ranch hands, and we stayed in there as a group. Alvarez stood watch until the wee hours, then Remo took over. First light came, and I woke up, looking over a sleeping Donna and out the window. I stretched, turned the other way, and looked right into the pointing index finger of Kate.

"You too," she said.

I jumped a little, and it woke Donna, who jumped as well.

Donna looked at me, then at Kate, "What's this?"

I stared at the girl as I answered, "I dunno."

There was no malicious intent in this kid, I could tell, but I have no idea what she wanted. She put her finger down, but still stood there. I got out of bed, put on my jeans, and took her hand. I opened the door and she followed me out. Remo was in a chair at the top of the stairs. He noticed us and shot to his feet.

"How did she get in here?"

"Damn fine lookout you are." I shook my head in reproach and strode past him with her in tow. I smiled hugely, knowing that I could chuck this transgression in Remo's face forever. Deek was on the other side of the front door when I opened it. His eyes went wide at the surprise, but he sighed in relief when he saw Kate.

"Sorry, son. She does that." He took her hand. "Katie, why don't you come back to the house now?"

It went like that for the next four days. Remo was on watch for three of them, and in each case, Kate was staring at me when I woke up. The first two days it was creepy, and on day three, I just smiled at her. On day four, I was on watch until sunup, then I went to bed to catch up on a little sleep. Donna came back from the bathroom down the hall a few minutes later and woke me. Kate was standing there. I had been asleep for five minutes.

During those four days I mentioned above, we helped out around the ranch, repairing some fences, helping feed the twenty-eight horses in the massive barn, and working on some of the vehicles and the generators. We also went back to pick up the shit that we had left behind in the scrub. There were signs of the horde, trudge marks in the dirt and bits of nasty shit they leave behind, but the actual walkers were absent for now. Three of us took horses to get the ammo and supplies. Not having been on horseback in years, it was actually kind of fun for me. I got to talking with Remo and this guy Javier, who everyone called Javi. (Pronounced Have E for you dumbasses.) Remo and Javi had gotten into a conversation about guns. Remo had his Sig, and Javi had a .45 semi with an extended mag which he kept in a shoulder holster. On his hip, he had a beautiful, blued Colt .45 with a pearl-white handle. A single-action jobbie, which meant you had to pull the hammer back with your thumb to cock the weapon before you could pull the trigger.

Remo looked the weapon over and shook his head. "Too slow."

"Is that what you think?" Javi had said with a smile, and we began talking about other shit.

I got the feeling from the many conversations I had with these folks that these were good people, and they thought the same of us.

At noon on day five, Matt and Deek came strolling up to Ship and I as we were working on a stuck water pump. He stood there, hesitant for a second as I wiped my face. Ship folded his tree-trunk arms expectantly.

"Why don't you folks stay on here?" Deek asked quickly. "We could use you, and you're safer here than on the road."

Ship and I looked at each other, then back at our host.

"Deek, I'm a shit-magnet. Wherever I go, bad things happen."

He reached into his vest and brought out a beat-up, many times folded, laminated piece of paper, which he handed to me. "Shit like this?"

I knew what it was before he passed it over. I glanced at the paper, which had a picture of guess who on it with the word REWARD at the bottom. Ship put his hand on his sidearm, an act which didn't go unnoticed by Deek. I smiled and so did both Matt and Deek.

Deek looked at me, then up at Ship. "I wouldn't have asked you to stay if I thought you were dangerous." His expression changed for a moment. "You aren't, are you? Dangerous I mean?"

I handed my wanted poster back to him. "That's the point, my horse-riding friend: I am. I won't hurt anybody here, and I would probably die to protect you all, but at some point, either the infected or the assholes will come knocking."

"We have guns too," Matt said, "and we can deal with whatever comes directly if we need to. Way I see it, we're all on borrowed time. Eventually, that herd, which has been wandering the scrub, is gonna find us, then we'll have to fight 'em off. No different than coyotes comin' for the chickens."

"It's a little different," I told him. "We'll think about it."

"Offer's good forever, so take your time," Deek said. He tipped his hat (no shit!) and they strode off.

Later in the day, our crew got together. As a group, we were discussing whether or not to stay, when Dix showed up with Darcy and Javi. The men were both in their late thirties, but where Dix was a big guy, with eternally tanned and weathered skin, graying brown hair and a bit of a belly, Javi was wiry and quick, with the olive complexion of Mexican descent. They worked well together in everything they did, and I could see they were best friends. Darcy was young and pretty, with short auburn hair and she liked to talk. Her boyfriend, Mike, was on gate duty with Clint and Jake. I hadn't really talked to those other three guys; they were usually on gate duty, or night duty and sleeping during the day.

Javi spoke to Remo, "You wanna see who's faster now?"

Remo, leaning against a doorframe, just nodded. We talked as we moved to their little shooting range. Richy and Chloe had popped off some rounds down here to practice, but none of the rest of us had yet. Dix set up six paint cans on six posts, and the two boys got ready.

"Feel free," Javi said to Remo with a smile. Remo drew his Sig and fired off six quick shots, hitting every can. As with all things Remo, it was perfect.

Dix ran out and set the paint cans up again.

"Feel free," Remo echoed with a hint of a smile.

In one motion, Javi thrust his hips forward into this weird position, drew his weapon, and fired. I heard two shots before he fanned his hand over the hammer firing four more shots. All six cans were down and the weapon was back in the holster in less than two seconds. Keep in mind, this was a single action revolver.

Remo's smile vanished. "Holy shit," was all he said and he stuck his hand out to Javi, who shook it.

The gunfire is probably what drew it. It must have slipped past the barbed wire and somehow climbed over the dirt wall. Nobody saw it and it didn't make a sound until it was three feet away from us. For a group of people living with the undead for a year and change, we were pretty complacent sometimes. This could have been disastrous, but the stupid thing let out one of those rasps as it shuffled toward us. About ten billion guns pointed at the thing, but Kat was the quickest, and she had a bolt-action rifle.

Dix was on the radio in an instant. "Mike! Mike, come in!"

Keep your hair on, I'm here. What's on fire?

Dix furrowed his brow in worry. "You have trouble near the gate? We got one in here, it was all the way up to the range."

Naw, nothin'. Jake n' Clint are out on a perimeter run. Been gone a half hour.

Dix, this is Clint, said a new voice. *We see where it came over. We were just about to call it in. It was more than one by the looks of it too. A couple or three at least. We're on the wire side of the moat, and I'm not liking it out here right now. Gonna need some repair on this part of the wall too, the embankment has caved into the trench.*

"Want to ride up to the bob-wire and check to see if the herd is in sight? I got a bad feelin'."

Will do, Dix. We'll check in in fifteen.

"Okay, folks, we should get back to the house. We'll make sure everybody is safe, then we'll go lookin' for the strays."

We moved as a large group back to the main house. Clint called in as we were arriving, *Herd is a mile off outside the fence and moving west. Anybody talk to James and Daniel?*

James and Daniel? Who the fuck are James and Daniel?

"Who are James and Daniel?" I asked.

"They're more free spirited than us. They don't sleep in the house much and they've been out checking Doolittle for parts at the Tractor Supply for a couple days."

Dix told Clint that he hadn't spoken to them, and he slung his radio. The front door opened and Matt stepped out with a shotgun, locking the door behind him. "House is buttoned up, everybody's accounted for and Kelly and Stacy are watching Kate. Deek is gonna coordinate from here and we call back in. C'mon, let's figure out what to do."

"Richy and Chloe," Remo began, "you two—"

"—are coming," I finished. "Make sure your weapons are loaded up and on safe."

Yeah, like anybody in this world didn't have a loaded weapon these days. Remo was looking at me funny. "Don't mean to step on the toes of a jarhead," I told him, "but they need as much real life practice as possible. If there are only a few inside the wall, we'll take care of them as a group."

Both kids looked at me and nodded. God help me, they looked ready.

"Darcy," Matt started, "I want you on the top deck with a pair of binocs and a radio. You'll have height and range. Call 'em out if you see 'em." Darcy used a key to unlock the door and entered into the house. "Your people with you and mine with me, okay?"

Matt had been speaking to me.

I counted heads. "There are eleven of us. Five and six sounds better than eight and three, plus you three know this place way better than we do. We'll take Dix, and you take Alvarez, Remo, and Ship." Both Remo and Ship looked at me funny, so I looked back funny. "What? You pissy because I get all the girls? Nut up, we'll be fine." I nodded to Dix. "You lead the way, my friend."

Like in every horror movie in the history of mankind, we split up, and like in every horror movie, there was a scare. I had thought we would be safe in groups of five or more. I was wrong.

The first place our group checked was the barn. The horses made a bit of noise, and Dix told me the horses were the lifeblood of this place. I could see why. When we were a hundred feet away, a couple of the beasts started going ballistic, so we hurried. Sure enough, two of the dead fuckers were reaching through the stall bars at one of the horses. This particular horse had a strong disdain for the undead, and was kicking the stall door. Dix raised his rifle (It was a Henry rifle I had learned, but that didn't mean shit to me), but I put my hand on the barrel. He looked at me and I nodded *No*.

"Richy," I said loudly, "you get the one on the right, Chloe the left." Both pus bags looked at us when I spoke. Chloe aimed her pistol, but Richy holstered his and drew the combat dagger that he had appropriated from one of the corpses of the douches who had attacked us when we got off of the Mary's Joy. I was impressed at his intestinal fortitude.

That hacking rasp that they do still gives me the willies, and as both rotters were making that sound, there was no shortage of shivers down my spine. The sound of the shot from Chloe's M9 echoed in the barn, and the horses, who were already going nuts, got louder. The infected on the left crumpled. The one on the right came on strong, walking all fucked up with this weird hip thrust. It had no lower jaw, with strings of flesh and who knows what hanging from it, but it could still infect this boy I had come to love if something bad happened. We all had our weapons on it as Richy stepped forward, no fear on his face at all.

The thing lunged at the same distance they always lunge from. When they're fifteen feet away, they're slow as fuck, but when they're within grabbing distance, they turn into lightning fast predators, if only for one burst. The creature used this burst to clutch at Richy, but he deftly sidestepped, and the pus bag fell forward. The kid kicked out with his boot, the toe catching the thing under its already smashed face and sinking into the soft palate slightly. It was stunned for a second, and the boy jammed the knife into the socket of its missing right eye. Richy turned the knife a couple of times, going for the scramble, and the thing, which stunk to high heaven by the way, collapsed.

Richy looked back at us, smiling, then yanked his weapon and leaned back down to use the dead thing's pants to wipe his blade.

In truly spectacular fashion, the re-killed thing sat up, grabbed the kid, and bit him on the forearm. Initially scared, like you would be if you saw a spider on your arm, Richy gave a little panicked yelp. He recovered quickly, and laughed as he shoved the stinking thing away and gave a stab to its good eye, again going for the scramble.

I made it to the boy and the dead thing first, yanking the kid up and checking his arm. There was no bite. How could it bite him with no lower jaw, Dear Reader? That feeling of both relief and stupidity you have right now? Yeah, mine was worse because I was there. Plus, I will neither confirm nor deny the code brown that may or may not have happened in my skivvies. I turned his arm over a few times in my hand, wiping it and looking for broken skin. There were no fluids or marks of any kind.

Last fucking time I send my kids to kill a zombie when I can do it. If I lived that was. I glanced at Donna and she was about to blow her top when the infected sat up again and Dix blew its head off. The damn Rasputin of zombies.

"He's fine!" I pleaded to everyone. "He's not bitten."

Chloe walked up to the one she had shot and shot it again. "Just in case."

Dix's radio squawked at us, *Dix! Dix, we heard shots! Everybody okay?* It was Matt.

"Yeah, we're good. The *kids*," he both looked at me and emphasized kids, "took care of two dead ones. You find any yet?"

Nothing yet. Some tracks but we lost them in the grass. Daniel would have them already if he was here.

"We'll keep looking," Dix said and slung his radio.

We searched for the rest of the day, but came up with nothing but a filthy, bloody piece of cloth on one of the tractor fenders. That meant at least one of the damn things was still inside the perimeter. Matt tried to use Rusty, Dusty, and a couple horses to sniff the bastard out, but they came up empty.

Sitting around the dinner table, with our chicken enchiladas finished, Remo was turning Richy's arm over in his hand just as I had done. The marine was *livid*.

"You're some special kind of stupid, aren't you?" Remo said with menace.

Nobody said anything, so I had to ask, "Me?"

"He could have been killed. Did you think about that? He's a kid."

I put my fork down and took a breath. "If he's a kid, he's dead. If you're weak, you're dead. If you hesitate, you're dead. I asked him to kill that fucking thing *because* he could have been killed." I could see Remo was still seething, and it pissed me off even more so I continued. "They've been trained by us. By *you*." I pointed at the jarhead. "What happens if we're all dead tomorrow except Richy and Chloe? Then who's going to kill the bad guys or the infected for them? I'll tell you something else too," now I thumbed at the kids, "they did better than six billion other people on the fucking planet. Those six billion are dead and these two are alive." I didn't want to go all red-eye in front of these new people, but my ire was rising.

Donna put her hand on my shoulder and I gently removed it, smiling at her. I glared at Remo. "If there's somebody out there that can give better training than what you, Alvarez, and Ship have provided, I need you to point that fucker out, because I want him on the team." With that I stood, pushed my chair back, and grabbed my plate for the sink.

"Him too," Kate said and took my plate.

I smiled at her. "Thank you, Kate."

"You're very welcome." She turned to put the dish in the sink and I turned to storm out. I about faced and put my hand on her shoulder.

"Kate, why do you keep saying 'Him too' in regards to me?"

She smiled even wider and reached for me. It shocked me a little so I took a half step back and she stopped reaching, her hand extended part way between us. She laughed a little and said, "It's okay," then continued to reach. I let her touch me, and she pulled the collar of my T-shirt down. She nodded, then tapped on the wicked scar of the healing bite wound on my arm. I didn't get it until she pulled up her shirt, exposing her left side all the way up to her bra.

A circular pattern, which could be nothing else but a bite mark, adorned the skin over her left side ribs. It was clearly healed.

She took a deep breath and stepped in for a hug. "Me too."

TO THE RESCUE

"Yes, Deek, they experimented on me. They stuck needles in every place you can think of. And yeah, I mean *every* place." Every guy in the room made the same face, and Dix crossed his legs. "This is why they want me, and this is why you can never tell anybody, *anybody*, about Kate. Ever."

Deek and Kelly, who were the official masters of this place, looked at each other. "But couldn't your blood save the world or something?" Kelly asked.

I shook my head. "I was in that underground hell-hole, being jabbed and studied for a long time, by all kinds of doctors. Not only did they not get my blood to do anything special, but they couldn't discern any differences between my blood and the blood of a normal person. Actually, at the time I was in Baldy Mountain, the doctors had no idea what the hell was causing all of this." I spread my arms wide. "They couldn't find any type of virus or weird bacteria in any of the infected." I got blank stares. *"They didn't know shit."*

We talked for another couple of hours about surviving bites, what that meant, and who was after me. It wasn't until Darcy came in to tell Deek there was a radio call for him that we stopped. He came back into the great room quickly, looking nervous. We all stared at him expectantly.

He took a deep breath. "James and Daniel are trapped by a herd of them things in the Hidalgo County Courthouse in Edinburgh. Daniel says they got enough water for one more day, but they're out of ammo."

Dix, Javi, Alvarez, and I all stood.

"Let's go get them," I said.

Deek sighed. "Son, I can't ask you—"

I cut him off with a play from Matt's book. "You didn't. We're volunteering."

The light from the window was eclipsed by Ship's seven-0foot stature as he stood. He signed one word to me: *No*.

"We have to, buddy." I shrugged.

He scribbled in his book and passed it to me. *We have to, you don't. You must live, and you are constantly throwing yourself into dangerous situations. It has to stop. I'm putting my foot down.* He signed again, *No.*

I signed back with one finger. This was not the sign language equivalent of yes, but it got my point across.

I smiled. "You're putting your foot down? Like you're my mom? Were you not listening for the past hour? They couldn't figure it out, Ship. They had the best equipment and doctors from USAMRIID and the CDC. I'm the same as you. I'm not throwing my life away. I'm going to go help some folks. I'm fucking good at it. I'm good at saving people, you should know." He held his hand out for his book and I tucked it under my arm. "Shut up. You and Remo are coming with me, Dix, and Javi. Matt and Deek will watch over everybody else, and Alvarez and Kat will help Mike and Clint find the stray fucker that's inside the fence someplace." I hadn't raised my voice one little bit. I didn't need to get angry again, but I'm not going to be put on a pedestal, never to help people in need because somebody thinks I have the cure to all this shit inside me. I don't give a shit if it's selfish.

"I have to go apologize to the toughest marine alive. Uhhh… come with me?" I returned his book to him. Ship nodded slowly. We went to find Remo.

"Really? I mean, fucking really?" I passed the binoculars back to Dix, who passed them back to Remo. The jarhead shook his head and sighed. Ship made no sound at all. Shocker there.

We were stretched out on our bellies under the collapsed awning of the completely looted Stripes Convenience Store, and it was still fucking hot in the shade. What we looked at was nothing short of spectacular. The two guys we had come to save had drawn a crowd of several thousand undead. This particular swarm rivaled the one that had attacked Keesler AFB when I was a resident there. I was doing the math in my head, and several thousand would be better described as tens of thousands. It looked like Fenway Park on Memorial Day. All the damn zombies were the fans, and the courthouse was the field. The infected were two hundred deep in a circle around the building. All of the first-floor windows in the courthouse were destroyed, and we could see infected on the second and third floors through those windows. The structure was five stories high, and completely infested. A small annex was to the left of our vantage, and that was where the boys were.

Oh, I may have forgotten to mention, because I certainly wasn't told and had to figure it out for myself, that we were now smack-dab in the middle of a fucking *city*. Five miles outside Edinburgh was scrubland that our horses had had no trouble with. Here, there was nothing but paved roads and a pretty park next to the college. Yeah, there was a University of Texas here. The census on the map, dated 2014, listed a population of approximately 774,000 for Edinburgh. I feel we had been denied critical information on this one. Javi and Jake were holed up with the horses in a firehouse about a half mile behind us; we made sure it was locked up tight. "Holy shit, they're dead," Dix breathed. "How do we get them?"

I looked at the emaciated, dry corpse that was next to me under the awning. "What do you think, buddy? Think we should ride in there and kill 'em all? No?" I looked at Dix and thumbed at the thing, which was long dead with a bullet hole in its skull. "Ed says we need a diversion. A big one."

Dix gave a quizzical look. "Ed?"

"Does he look like a Steve, or a Joe to you?" I turned back to the corpse. "Some people." Focusing my gaze back to Dix, I asked, "Why don't you give the boys a call and ask them to come out on the roof if they can? Oh, and Ed is a little pissed that you and your crew forgot to mention that we would be entering a city of more than three-quarters of a million people."

"Tell them not to come near the edge," Remo said out loud.

I rolled on my back. "Got any ideas on what we blow up to get their attention?"

"Arkansas?" Remo answered. Remo had made a joke. That was good. He was seeing this as a challenge that we could complete. I was skeptical. Remo continued, "Explosives would get their attention, but we need to keep it."

"Keep what?" Dix demanded.

"They're attention." The jarhead shot his hand out, desiring the binoculars for another peek.

"We'll need a diversion that keeps emitting sound, like music or an alarm."

This was not my first rodeo with that. Huh. I'm in Texas and I keep thinking about rodeos. Freudian, or is it the heat?

"Yeah, so during my valiant and daring escape from torture at the hands of evil doctors in Montana, I stopped at a small town to help a guy out. During the stop, I was sort of conscripted to help some other guys, one of which turned out to be a douche. My long-winded point is that we broke into a record store, stole a radio, and used that as a diversion. That shit worked too."

"I have this." Dix produced an ancient alarm clock that looked oddly familiar.

Remo looked at it. "Good idea, but it won't sound off for long enough. We need something that will draw them at least half a mile off, and keep them there."

Ship passed Remo his book. Remo read it and passed it to me. I read it aloud for Dix.

A diversion is not going to succeed. There are a minimum of thirty-thousand infected surrounding that courthouse. If we draw away ninety percent of them, that still leaves three thousand to deal with. This does not include the ones inside the building already.

"So what do we do?" I asked, passing Ship's book back to him. I looked back through the binoculars that Remo had passed to me. Stragglers were both leaving and entering the area, dragging others with them. It was very loud, even from our vantage, and the clouds of insects were extreme. There was absolutely no breeze in this horrible city, so the stink of the dead was blissfully absent.

Remo looked to our right. "Hang on." A dead man shuffled into view from around the corner of the store, and began walking toward the crowd. For reasons unknown, it spun its head in our direction and began coming toward us. Remo got up and took care of it. I didn't even watch.

I began ticking off options. "Set them on fire? Electrocute them? Blow them up?" I looked expectantly at Ship, and he was scribbling away. I really needed to get better with my sign language. Or the mute Sasquatch needed to grow some functional vocal cords. I looked through the binocs again for a moment, and felt a tap on my shoulder. It was Ship's book.

We have several options. The safest option, which keeps the maximum amount of people alive, is simple: We leave. As I realize you will never allow this, another option is that we find an operational helicopter with sufficient fuel to extract the men from the roof. This option is unlikely as airfields are likely damaged or overrun, and fuel is probably spoiled by now. I have been working on an idea which may actually work in the future, but we would need a few garbage trucks, decent fuel, and some steel mesh. That sounded intriguing. *Ultimately, the possibility that we extract these men with no casualties is extremely low. As previously stated, the diversion will not work. However, I believe that short of abandoning these men, or the aforementioned helicopter, a diversion, however insufficient, is the best option. We must also bear in mind that the thirty-thousand undead we see are approximately 740,000 less than a full city's worth. The others could be gone, or they could be just out of sight. Also, if 0.001 percent of the infected are of the fast variety, this means that there are 740 sprinters lying in wait.*

How the F did he write so fast? "You know, my silent pal, I didn't have a buzz, but if I had, you would have straight up murdered it right there." I sighed. "Dix. Dix, we can't get them."

Dix said something right then that will haunt me until I die. "I know. We should get back to the Double Hoof." He radioed the guys in the Courthouse, "Daniel, come in."

We're here. Are you guys close?

"Yeah, we're down the road a piece."

Then you've seen the trouble we're in?

"Yeah."

I heard both air and hope expel from the guy's lungs in a long-winded sigh on the other side of the radio, *Then go home.*

"I'm sorry, Daniel. I'm sorry, James."

I stuck my hand out for the radio and Dix passed it over to me. "Daniel, James, you don't know me, but I'm going to do what I can to get you out of there." Everybody was looking at me. Stinkeye from Ship. "We're going to create a big diversion. That should draw away most of the dead, but there will still be a lot to deal with. We'll meet you..." I pointed to the map and Dix nodded, "at the Tractor Supply outside of Doolittle. We'll wait a day."

Look forward to meeting you.

The mic went silent, and I gave the radio back to Dix.

"So what's the plan?"

Hanson's Ford was probably a nice Ford dealership before the plague. Now filthy and partly damaged vehicles sat forgotten on the lot, probably forever. Ship had eluded to a plan and had us backtrack the half mile to the lot.

Ship is a genius. You've probably gathered that from me writing that Ship is a genius so many times throughout these journals. What you really need to understand though, is that Ship is a genius. After we hopped the fence to the dealership, Ship finalized his plan, and we all read it. It was perfect. Some might say *genius*.

Sasquatch got a battery tester from the garage and tested the batteries on sixteen vehicles, all of which were viable. My POS Ford Explorer Sport Trac, possibly the worst vehicle designed, and certainly partly responsible for my untimely incarceration prior to the plague, couldn't go two weeks without needing a jump. These cars and trucks all had good batteries after more than a year of non-use. Ford can suck it for installing my shitty battery, and *Yay!* to Ford for putting good ones on these. Toss up, really.

Anyway, I digress. It's the heat.

Ship found all the keys to the cars, and a black CD case full of shitty CDs. The four of us lowered the windows to four of the vehicles, and you guessed it, shoved CDs in the slots and cranked the stereos. It was really loud in the extreme quiet of our section of town, but I didn't think the pus bags would be able to hear it over the sounds of themselves. Yes, Dear Reader, quiet may be extreme.

We drew a crowd fast on the other side of the fence, and Remo stabbed them through the chain link as they arrived. Ship literally ripped one of the little poles adorned with multicolored plastic flags out of the ground, swung it over his head and onto an unpurchased Blue Mustang, triggering the alarm. *That* was loud enough to get the horde over here.

I was immediately terrified, and I could envision every single pus bag at the courthouse turning toward us in unison, then beginning that slow plod. F waiting to make sure, we headed for the back of the lot, climbed the fence, and ran like a bunch of pussies.

We met up with Javi and Jake, who were shitting themselves because of the noise, and we all got the fuck out of Dodge, or in this case Edinburgh.

Heading at a brisk trot northward toward Doolittle, we could hear the echo of the swarm as it reverberated between some of the buildings and homes. Someone shot at us as we passed the college, and we booked it out of there as fast as we could. We came upon an overpass of I69C which had been under construction when the shit hit. It was then we figured out that the swarm behind us wasn't the only swarm. Hundreds of pus bags filtered in and out of the horrendous traffic jam that bogged the newly constructed highway. They were on the way toward the diversion we had just created.

I had seen this before. The construction forced two lanes down to one on the overpass, and this created a jam. People had become trapped in their vehicles when nobody could move, the tide of the dead from the city washing over them and destroying everything living in its path, converting them into the enemy, or outright consuming them. I can't imagine the horror of being trapped with your family in your car on an overpass, while a wave of rot caught up to you. The things would beat on the windows until they gave way, then they would crawl in and feed.

They were about to do the same to us. One of the horses gave a whinny at the smell of the dead, and it was on. They all looked at us, then decided we would be a decent brunch. Dix turned his horse around, and we all followed suit.

"Hyah!" he yelled and his mount bolted. Ours followed, but keep in mind I hadn't been galloping on a horse in many years. I could trot, I could fucking canter, I could not gallop. Suddenly, I remembered that all I had to do was sort of stand up a little in the stirrups, hold on for dear life, and the horse would do the rest. This particular horse, a chestnut Arabian by the name of Shaitan, was a bit smaller than the others, but wicked fast and dumb as a stump. I had been one of the lighter guys, so they had given me this horse. The beast took off like a rocket and it was all I could do to stay in the saddle. I should also mention that the girlfriend who had owned horses when I was younger used English saddles, and I was now astride a western.

When I realized I had outdistanced everybody by a full block, I yanked back on the reins, but Shaitan was having none of that. He told me to fuck off, and if anything, sped up. This was about the time the dead stumbled out from between the houses and vehicles, ambling into the street with hungry eyes. The nauseating smell of the dead, which had held off because of the lack of wind, was full bore now, so I had that going for me too.

The dead in the street were reaching for me as we thundered past, and several were knocked aside by my mount. I felt a hand grip my jeans for a split second, but the force of us galloping freed me before I was caught. Another slapped my leg, and then another. I felt a sting and knew that I had been scratched by one of their filthy nails. Probably death for anybody else but me.

Everything since the overpass had taken about a minute. I dared glance back over my right shoulder to see how close my friends were, and it was my undoing. My left foot slipped from the stirrup, and as I fought to shove it back in, I felt myself sliding off to the right. Not being able to hold on with my hands and one foot, I fell off that asshole horse in slow motion. I was fortunate enough to have a piece of shit, rusty-silver, Honda Civic break my fall with its back window. I went right through it, ass first, pushing the entire window in, and the car was not empty. Another corpse, this one really gooey, reached for me as I struggled to free myself of the spider-webbed, green safety glass. Thank all that is holy that the poor bastard was eternally seat belted into his vehicle. He could still reach me though, Civics aren't huge, and he grabbed my T-shirt. I panicked a little, but freed myself, tearing my shirt in the process. If I had thought the smell in the street was bad, the smell in the car was nothing short of debilitating. I puked that morning's flapjacks (I would have called them pancakes, but we were in Texas) down the front of my newly ripped shirt.

I put my hands on the window frame of the shit-box to extricate myself, and a lance of agony shot up my left arm from my elbow. I got out anyway, and saw what was headed for me. Hundreds of them, all slogging through the hundred degree Texas heat, and all coming for yours truly. A huge crowd of them shuffled from the right, and I could see where this was going. Putting my feet on the concrete sidewalk, I dodged a lunging set of hands and shot the lunger in the face. There were only about five hundred more to deal with.

No sign of the other horses, so I decided that discretion was the better part of valor, and fucking ran for it. I dodged outstretched hands of the street dwellers, any one of which would slow me to the point of capture if they locked on to me. One did catch me, but my already-ruined shirt tore away, and the thing would get nothing more than my sweat to dine on.

They were coming from all sides, and I was getting a bit fearful. Just a bit, I'm a badass now. My boots slapped against the pavement as I sprinted to a nearby office building, cradling my left arm the entire way. I ran up the steps, but the door was locked. One of them started up the stairs after me, but I hopped the railing and landed in a bark chip mulch bed, overgrown with weeds and grass. I made it to an open window with tattered curtains, but my arm was throbbing and fucked up, so I was having trouble climbing. I kicked over a blue recycling bin and used it as a step stool. The things were on me, and I had to kick one off before I pulled myself through the window. No rest for the wicked, and the rotting kid that was in this room came at me with a faltering gait. My SOG thrust forward, and I put the poor boy to sleep.

I was in an office. The sweltering room contained a blood-stained, blue sleeping bag, and two empty and two full two-liter bottles of orange soda. A bunch of food wrappers were scattered about. The kid had obviously been hiding out here. I checked the three doors in the office I was in. One was a closet with office shit in it, one led to another office, and the front door led to an open cubicle area. There were at least two dead people shuffling about the cubes. They hadn't seen me, or heard the commotion, so I closed the door and tried to think. I could see hands from about the mid-forearm to the wrist just outside the window I had just crawled through. The fuckers were loud too, so I grabbed both bottles of soda, my boo-boo arm screaming in protest, moved into the connecting office, and sat in a wheeled desk chair.

I looked at my elbow, which was already starting to swell. It hurt like holy blue hell too. I could move it, so I didn't think anything was broken, but it hurt. I know, I wrote that twice but tough shit, it hurt. It *still* hurts.

I didn't have a radio, so I was on my own. I'm sure my friends made it, but I hope that fucking Arabian horse is in the gullets of a bunch of zombies. Douche. If he had done what he was trained to do, we would both probably be okay.

By the way, Shaitan means devil.

ALONE

The cube-critters heard the shitheads outside banging and just being fucking loud, and forced their way into the office I had vacated to investigate. The ones inside thought the ones outside were dinner, and vice versa, until each saw the other through the open window. I had heard the cubicle ones break into the office as I drank some hot orange soda. It wasn't overly refreshing, but it was liquid, and my water bottle was only half full now. That damned nag had run off with my water bladder attached to the saddle. Dick of a horse.

The shitheads outside left after a few hours. They must have found some other stimulus and slogged off to eat it. I had only seen two infected in the cubicles, but that didn't mean there wasn't a back-up team hiding in wait for me.

I could stay here until I ran out of supplies, or I could go now, and use what supplies I have on the twenty-five-mile hike back to the Double Hoof. My elbow was killing me, but I knew to remain here was death. I packed the soda in my bag, quietly checked my weapons, and made for the door to the cubes. Maybe I could catch the dead fuckers in the office next to me and quietly shut the door, locking them in behind me as I made my hasty but silent exit.

The knob was very quiet as I turned it. The hinges made no sound as I opened the door. Ninjas had nothing on my stealth. I didn't see anything in the cube farm, so I took a quick peek into the office with the sleeping bag, and lo and behold there were two pus bags in there. One stared out the open window in parody of a twisted art piece. The other sat in an office chair with its head cocked to one side, staring at its buddy. The door frame was splintered around the catch, so closing the door was useless, but as I still didn't need these assholes following me and catching me with my pants down, (hey, everybody poops) they had to go.

I crept up behind the one sitting down, yanked its head back by the hair, and came away with a handful of rotten scalp. It turned to face me, white skull covered in black goo. With my elbow screaming, I stabbed it in the eye. It slumped back in the chair, re-killed. I glanced at the one standing, but it hadn't moved. Stepping past the seated one, I snuck up on the other and tapped it on the shoulder. It didn't move, so I gave it a little shove. Nothing. Fucking stupid zombies. I mean, really.

"Hey," I whispered, and that did the trick. I would like to tell you that the thing turned slowly and I smoked it, but in actuality, it whipped its head around and came at me instantly. Guess where it grabbed me? Yeah, by the boo-boo arm. That shit hurt, so I responded by bringing an overhead stab down on the forehead of the thing. This thing had a wicked receding hairline, so it was more like a sevenhead instead of a forehead, but the knife went right through his skull and into his brain on the first try.

It couldn't have cared less. He jerked his head, and I was so unready for that, my knife went with him. He brought my fucked-up arm to his mouth, and I yanked back so as not to be bitten. Tendrils of agony shot up into my shoulder, but it would be worse if this thing got its way. We played tug of war for my flesh for ten seconds or so before the thing abandoned the game and lunged. The bastard hit me and we both went down over the one in the chair. He landed on me, pinning my already screaming arm between us. He looked into my eyes, and I put my free hand on his throat, wrenching my left arm free from the sandwich. Fuck that hurt, but I was able to get my left forearm under his chin, tear the knife from his skull (took a sec), and stab him in the eye. I scrambled shit about for a second, and the rotten fucker fell on me.

I shimmied out from under him, gritting my teeth from the pain. Hey, he hadn't bitten me, so I should count my blessings. I stood, looking out the window, then back into the cube farm.

Nothing. My undead battle hadn't been soundless, but it wasn't loud either. I still needed to be sure I wasn't going to be inundated with infected. I crept into the cube farm, observing as best I could. I was done playing, so I wiped my knife on a stuffed pig on the corner of one of the cubes and sheathed it. My MP5 would be a bit difficult to use with my injured elbow, but it would be better than what had just happened. I considered staying with the knife to conserve ammo, but conservation wouldn't help if there were several pus bags at once, and I needed to be prepared.

The cubes were this sanitary-white material about as high as my lowest rib. They spanned about a seventy-foot length and were three deep with spaces for tables between each grouping. A slim hallway on the right led past the farm, with office doors dotting the wall at mismatched intervals. I had just stepped out of one such office. I checked the cubes as I snuck past them, but other than computer monitors, some dead plants, and a really cool R2D2 bobblehead, there was nothing of value. I would have taken the R2D2, but I didn't have the space for it. Each cube had a small locker-type closet integrated into the desk, and I decided not to search them until I remembered where I was. This was Texas. There would be guns.

Except there weren't. I checked all the lockers and file cabinets, none of which were locked. There were some Chili-cheese Fritos in one locker, but they had been opened, and the prick hadn't used a chip clip. I shut the doors to the offices as I moved past them.

There were seven sets of cubes. The third cube held the mostly consumed remains of something in a brown pile of stuff. From the broken-open skull I could see that it had been human. It was gross. None of the other cubes had anything, but the last office held an occupant. He was just standing there. Maybe he had been motionless for months, I don't know. I do know that I was the impetus for him to move. He was six-two with a huge beard which had once been white, but was now off-white and held morsels of something vile in it. He was also pushing three bills with an enormous belly.

"Fuck off, dead Santa," I told him, and gave him a subsonic round to the dome. His head snapped back and his cranial contents sprayed the drop ceiling and paneled wall behind him. Big guys produce big thuds when they fall and this guy was no exception. I waited, ready, but nothing came for me after his landing. Zombie Santa, bringing infection to all the good little boys and girls. Isn't that just craptastic?

I got to the exterior doors I had tried to enter a few hours earlier. They were steel fire doors with a key code entry from the street side. Weird to have doors like this on the front of a building, I would have had a glass entry, but whatever. There were no windows in the doors, but one of the offices facing the street had plenty of glass. I peeked. I could see two of the dead bastards milling about out there and figured I could take them easily. I was moving to leave, when a figure streaked past the window in the street. It stopped and looked around, twitching and flexing its hands into claws. It had been a woman, (is it still a woman? Is it human anymore?) and it sprinted at one of the two dead men, stopping short, changing its mind, and running at the other one. It started beating on the dead guy, and then it bit him, tearing a chunk out of the thing's rotting face.

The dead thing tried to go about its business, its teeth now clearly visible through the tear in its cheek, but Speedy kept clawing and hammering at it. The dead one didn't really care about the injuries it was receiving. When it would fall over, it would just stand, and eventually, the Olympic sprinter chick got bored. She ambled off (Texas!) at a slow pace toward the diversion, limbs jerking and looking feverish. I did notice that she didn't spit out the dead guy's face. I had seen this before and now it was confirmed that the live infected ate the dead ones. Pity it didn't go both ways.

It was beginning to get dark when the noise from the vehicles stopped. The car lot was a good distance from me, but where the only other sounds were from the dead, when the last stereo stopped, it got pretty quiet. I hoped the two dudes trapped in the courthouse got to safety. I also hoped that the stereos drew most of the infected that way because it was time for me to vacate. Twenty-five miles back to my friends. Less than a half-hour ride on the highway in another time. Unless there was traffic.

Only one of the dead things was swaying near the exit to my sanctuary when I opened the door and stole a quick glance about. It had its back to me, so I just hustled off to the right. I was travelling southwest, and needed to go northeast, so I hooked two rights and furtively avoided any infected I saw. Most were plodding toward the now silent sounds of the diversion, but some just stood there, or meandered around. By the time I got to the community pool house at a rec center, it was pretty dark. There were no more street lights, but I could see a little by way of the stars. I could see a dozen or so through the chain-link fence to my right shuffling around on the concrete by the pool. There was no way the disgusting water was devoid of undead, and the thought of them all bloated and nasty nauseated me. I shook my head in disgust, and almost shit myself when one of them threw itself at the fence between it and me, making an enormous clatter. It began to growl and hiss and shake the fence and shit, which was even louder. All his buddies began to stumble our way, and I looked left. Sure enough, there were a couple on this side of the fence, and they were coming.

Cradling my arm, which was beginning to tingle, I moved northeast at a brisk pace. I left the pool and associated buildings behind, moving down a road into a more rural suburb. I saw the sign for Doolittle road, but I didn't know if that meant I was in Doolittle. I sure as fuck didn't know where the Tractor Supply was.

I realized I was tired. Damn tired. I did one of those little tests you do when you've injured yourself and extended my left arm. It was a mistake, and the dude in charge of pain turned on the juice. I hissed an intake of breath, and was amazed at how loud it was on the empty street.

Fuck this. I needed some sleep. I picked a little ranch house with a brick front and slunk cautiously into the backyard to case the joint. The rear of the house was surrounded by a six-foot board fence, the neighbor's houses maybe forty feet away on either side of the house I had chosen. I tapped on the rear slider, waiting for something to come, but it looked as if the house was empty. The slider wasn't locked, but when I pulled it to try to open it, it jammed on a stick set in the track by the floor. I smiled. This was every thief's favorite anti-theft device. Setting my pack down for a moment, I stuck my SOG between the two sliders through the weather stripping, gripped the end of the sawed-off broomstick with the tip of my blade, flipped it up, and the house was mine. I locked the fully functional but previously unused lock on the door.

The zombie apocalypse sucks for so many reasons. Being *alone* in the zombie apocalypse amps up the suckage a billion fold. Not having someone covering your back, or keeping watch while you sleep, can be deadly, especially when you're breaking into a place to sleep. Fucking *horse*!

I could see starlight glinting off chrome, so I assumed I was in the kitchen. The entire house was shrouded in darkness, but I was nervous about using my tactical light. So, do I bump headlong into an undead monster in the pitch black, or turn the light on and attract a horde of a hundred thousand? Either one was a potential death sentence, so I might as well not collide with a zombie in the house. I flicked the light on my MP5 and panned it around low. The house was dusty, but well kept. All the windows in the kitchen and living room looked intact. I turned left and flashed the light down a short hall. Two doors on the left, one on the right, and one at the end.

I crept into the front room. Two chairs and a couch in front of a big picture window facing a silent TV. Pictures adorned the wall, and there were some in frames on a couple of small end tables, and a big one depicting a young soldier displayed on an easel with a folded US flag in a triangular glass case. Sorry for your loss, house.

I hooked a left, going down the short hall of this small dwelling. First door on the left was a bathroom. Standard stuff except for the small carpet and matching toilet seat cover. Horrible dark green and completely out of place. Yuk.

Right side door led to a small bedroom. The room was devoid of monsters and everything else, except a bed. All the shit in this room had been moved out.

Same gig for the second door on the left, but this one had been lived in. Teenage boy by the look of the shit in there. Poster of a band I never heard of on the wall, a Yoda poster with *Do Or Do Not, There Is No Try* on the bottom, a poster of some hot chick I didn't recognize in a bikini. Shit tons of video games and a computer on a desk. I closed the door and moved to the last room.

Fuck me. A mom, a dad, and a teenage boy, all with holes in their heads, were lying on the bed. The small revolver on the floor next to the dad. So the family loses a son and brother probably in some country halfway around the world, then the plague hits, and the idea of being eaten is strong enough to make the family check out as a group. I can't figure out if I respect that or not.

There was no smell, the three of them having been dead for more than a year, but I knew that the undead could smell the living and I couldn't, so maybe they could smell the dead too. If so, the family would mask my stench a little, so I opted for the teenager's room. It was homier than the older son's empty box.

The lock on the kid's door was as completely useless as the door itself, but I locked it anyway. I kept my clothes and boots on, and my pack next to the bed just in case I had to make a hasty exit. I put my MP5 on safe, and put my Sig under the pillow, which I shook out to rid it of dust. There wasn't much. My SOG was sleeping next to me.

Exhausted, I sat on the bed and swung my feet up. I crossed my fingers behind my head and thought about where I had been since this whole thing started. I'd been all over the country and travelled more than I had before travel was deadly. I'd met great people, who I now considered family, and I had committed murder. Living in a survivalist's house, a gated community, a military base, an oil rig, an underground government facility, and now on a horse ranch had added to my skillset as well.

I had also learned not only how to survive, but how to kill from the toughest, most well-trained soldiers and sailors on earth.

My apology to Remo for lighting him up at dinner had gone over with few words. We both understood each other. He had also said he was sorry for calling me out the way he did. We left it at that.

I drifted off thinking about Shaitan. That bastard was going to get an earful if he wasn't already zombie chow.

THE DEVIL AND THOSE TRAPPED

T'was the night I was alone, no friends to be had,
In the next room a dead mom, son, and dad.
My Sig and my SOG placed next to me for fun.
And on the bed leaning, a submachine gun.

I lay in the youngest boy's twin-size bed,
Weapons close, to fend off the dead.
I had searched the house over, bedrooms and halls,
To make sure no zombies would bite off my balls.

Visions of pus bags shot through my head,
Remember: the family were all fuk'n dead.
The father had shot them so they wouldn't rise,
Yet I heard sounds resembling undead cries.

I sat up quickly, I don't fuk'n spring,
Realizing my refuge held an undead thing.
Sounds from inside, real close, hereabout,
Made me gather my weapons to check that shit out.

Sure as shit I could hear them, I don't know how many,
It didn't matter, the frightening number was any.
How had they found me? I questioned myself,
I had snuck in here like a deranged elf.

I checked my guns, my knife, and my stuff,
Thanking God I hadn't slept in the buff.
The things were anxious, and looking for me,
They scared me so much that I had to pee.

A scream from the kitchen, a guttural growl,
Made piss an afterthought, I emptied my bowels.
I hadn't really shit myself, I wrote that in jest,

But my heart thundered loudly, trying to escape from my chest.

You may not have figured it, here's a shocker, a stunner:
The scream from the house meant that there was a Runner.
They're brutal and nasty and wicked fucking fast,
In a sprint for my life, I wouldn't outlast.

I had to kill it before I could leave,
Death would slow it, my only reprieve.
Outside the door to the teenager's room,
I heard tentative scratches indicating my doom.

A loud fucking thump was all that I needed,
Training from Remo and Alvarez heeded,
I fired through the door with my MP5,
Opened the window and out it did dive.

I landed with grace, and seeing nothing in sight,
Vaulted the fence and ran into the night.
My lonely predicament having just one source,
I vowed sick-ass vengeance on that fucking horse.

I'm not a poet, I'm not, but I'm pretty proud of that. I was thinking up verses as I fled the area. There may or may not have been some manly giggling. One verse had some shit about demons and death, but I can't remember it. That pisses me off. It was zombie Santa that got me thinking about Christmas.

Christ, I'm having trouble focusing. I have no idea how much sleep I got earlier, but it couldn't have been much. My thoughts are all over the place right now and I want a cheeseburger.

Right, so, I rounded a corner, thinking about something that rhymes with "many" when I ran headlong into a pus bag. Fuck those doctors at Baldy who said these things couldn't be surprised, because the outright look of astonishment, complete with raised eyebrows (in this case brow) and mouth shaped like an O, was all over this thing's face as we hit the pavement.

Fucking ouch. Like ouch and shit. No, Dear Reader, I didn't land on my messed-up elbow, I thundered into the zombie, we both fell, and I skidded on my other elbow across the concrete sidewalk. Who thought up elbows anyway? Jackass.

So I left my skin on the sidewalk. I could see it. I looked at my skinned elbow and it wasn't bleeding. Then it was. A lot. The infected I had just knocked over also saw my skin, but realized there was more of it on me, and stood, looking famished.

This one was gross, I could see he was missing half of its face, the bone catching the starlight in the darkness. His face looked like my peeled elbow. He also had an arrow sticking out of his back, and a couple nubs of bone where his left hand should be. He reached for me with one hand and one nub, so I shot him with the MP5.

It was a one-tap, but it couldn't have gone unnoticed, even with the suppressor. They aren't silent like in the movies. I may have mentioned that before.

I made myself scarce, and booked it down the sidewalk, dodging a knocked-over baby carriage and skipping past the bony carcasses of several permanently dead people. I reached a crossroads, with nothing in front of me but road and scrub, and lo and behold there was a Tractor Supply. Smiling, I jogged over to it, expecting a warm welcome from my friends. Nope. It wasn't the correct Tractor Supply.

There was more than one. There was more than one Tractor Supply in Doo-fucking-little Texas. I mean, how many tractors could these people have? Not only was there a surplus of tractor businesses I could care less about, I had chosen the wrong damn one.

I sighed, expelling tired air, and when I did, something that had been sitting on its haunches behind a dusty, but still pretty, red backhoe, stood up. It had its back to me, but it knew I was around. It was the speedy infected chick from outside the building with the cubicles. I ducked behind the backhoe as she turned. She hadn't seen me. I could see a couple dead folks coming down the street. They saw me, but their proximity wasn't alarming. The fast one was five feet away on the other side of this machine. I could hear her sniffing the air, and I looked down at my bleeding arm. Could they smell blood? Could she smell me even if I weren't bleeding? Did she prefer curtains or drapes?

I snuck around the corner of the backhoe, leading with the MP5 and hoping to catch her unaware. Unaware? Unawares? Shit I dunno, I'm still tired. I leapt out, prepared to fire at her, but she wasn't there. My moment of confusion almost cost me my life. I heard footsteps behind me, and spun to see her rounding the same end of the red contraption I just had. We sort of saw each other at the same time, and were equally as surprised. A low growl emanated from her and she narrowed her eyes. She began to intake a breath, and the ball-tightening scream that would follow would bring every infected within earshot. I gave her a quick burst before she could let loose with the howl. She stumbled backwards and fell on her ass. She sat up and gurgled, but I think it's physically impossible to scream when your lungs are filling with blood. She tried to stand, not giving a shit about the agony she must be in, and I tapped her in the dome with a subsonic 9mm round.

I looked around, trying to gauge how many infected were inbound, but could only see the two that had seen me. They were about a hundred feet away, so I felt it prudent to switch mags in the MP5, and then felt it even more prudent to save ammo. I looked around for something to use as a club, but came up empty. When they got close, I did both of the things with my SOG, one up under the chin and one through the left eye.

The street was empty when I moved into the Tractor Supply building (the wrong one) to get some rest. The structure was the only two-story building in the area. With a fantastically giant and extremely un-zombie proof front window, I thought twice, but the second floor would be higher than anything else around except for the water tower two streets over. I would use the water tower tomorrow to look for my pals, but I really didn't want to get trapped up there.

Deciding not to smash the enormous window or break the glass front door, I moved around back to check for rear access. There were two. One roll-up jobbie on a short loading dock, and a metal door. It was locked, but then I remembered the crowbar that Deek had given me. It was in my pack. I had a crowbar. I blinked twice. I had a crowbar. The perfect zombie-killing device that I had searched the ground for not five minutes ago.

Idiot.

I jimmied the door, and stepped inside. No smell of death; that was a good sign. I couldn't see shit and that wasn't a good sign. I gave a quick whistle, wishing for the NVGs I had left on Atlantis. Nothing came stumbling or sprinting out of the darkness. I pressed the grip button for my tac-light and a thin beam sliced the darkness. I panned it around and saw I was in a large storeroom. Empty of anything that wanted to eat me, and no blood or signs of struggle. This was a big place, and I would have to clear it, but I needed to see to the door I had just come in first. I had broken the lock on the journey through, but whoever had locked this door before hadn't engaged the two deadbolts, so I obliged. I stayed out of the front display room, which contained a few pretty tractors, backhoes, and some ATVs. I was able to skirt the entire room and lock the door into it.

Stairs behind another door led up and I followed them cautiously. Three offices greeted me, with a water cooler, a coffee maker, and a big copy machine in the hall. I cleared the offices and the little bathroom. No couches to sleep on, but at this point, the floor called. I looked at the picture of a fat woman and two equally fat kids. They were probably part of the horde that was in this general vicinity.

This place was as safe as any, so I shut the office door and sacked out. I looked out the rear window and noticed that the sun was just coming up.

I woke up in a sweat. Not because I heard something or because I was terrified, because it was hot. Like, damn hot. I was extremely uncomfortable and dripping with sweat. I looked out through the curtains again and could see that that sun was really high. I guessed it was probably noon. Or I could just look at my watch. It was 11:51.

I drank the last of the orange soda out of one of the bottles and filled it back up with water from the cooler. I put my weapons on the office desk, sat down, and took an ammo count. 54 rounds for the SIG, two suppressors left. Three full mags of subsonic for the MP5 after I unloaded two of the half mags and consolidated. Two loose rounds as well.

Shit was getting tight. Three more MREs, my full canteen, two liters of water and two liters of piss-warm orange soda. I used a small whetstone that Javi had given me to make the edge of my SOG gleam, packed up my shit, and I was ready to go. As an afterthought, I drank as much out of the water cooler as I could without getting too full to move.

I parted the curtains and took a peek outside. Nothing moving, but I couldn't see in the direction I wanted, so I checked the other office windows. A few stragglers, but they seemed to be moving off back toward the city.

I was back downstairs and looking into the display room in a few moments. It was really hot in there too and I gave another short whistle to see if the place was empty. It was. I stepped into the room and looked at the shiny red Kubota backhoes or yellow and green John Deere tractors. It was funny, because Tractor Supply stores in my neck of the woods (back in MA) didn't actually sell tractors, just all kinds of other shit. This place had all kinds of other shit too, like gun safes and bags of seeds, but what was most appealing to me at that moment, was the gigantic map of this tiny town. On it, noted with two big, green stars, were two other Tractor Supply stores. Two others. Doolittle is a town of, maybe, three fucking people, so they each got their own store? WTF? Didn't make sense. I guess Edinburgh had a serious need for tractors.

Regardless, I knew how to get to the other two stores. Murphy's Law says I pick the wrong one and get eaten, but F Murphy. I never met him.

The first store was a mile away, and about the same distance to Edinburgh that I was now. The second store was a mile and a half away, and much closer to the city, back the way I had come. The city meant more pus bags, so the logical decision was to head to the one that was away from the vast hordes of undead.

Weapons with full load, and my belly full of water, it was time to go. A quick scan and I could only see a few of the things, all shuffling away from me. One street up, one over, and take Cesar Chavez Road all the way to the other store. Cake.

I unlocked the glass doors, slipped out, and made my way left. A quick right and I cut across a lawn to Cesar Chavez. I was attempting stealth and was doing pretty well. Two more lawns and I saw something remarkable. Three houses down, munching on some kind of green bush, stood an extremely familiar horse. The big bastard was quite unafraid now that there were no undead about, and just casually having a fucking snack.

I made my way to him and he looked at me then quickly looked away.

"Really? You won't even look at me now?" He lowered his nose a bit. "What kind of horse are you anyway? Running off at the first sign of danger?" Nose further down, this was effing great. I grabbed the loose reins, pulling his face to mine so he would have to look at me. "We'll deal with the horse in the room later. Right now, I would really like to not get dead. Our buddies are at a different store and I know where it is," I gripped the reins tighter and touched his nose with my nose, "but if you try to run off, I will absolutely fucking shoot you." I held up my index finger. "You get one of those. One. That shit is used up, you feel me, dog?"

I checked to see if my water bladder was still on him and it was. I took it off, unscrewed the fill cork thing and he perked right up, his ears standing straight into the air. "Thirsty from all that cowardice? Uh-huh." I held it to his lips and let him take a big drink. We spilled some, but I knew we would get back to the Double Hoof much faster with me on him, and he needed water. Boy did he drink too. I tried to pull the bladder away when it was half empty, but he put his teeth on the neck of the fill piece and held on. I gave him some more, and pulled it back. "That's enough. There's plenty back home." I reattached the bladder to him and he gave one of those horse alerts. Ears and head up, looking in all directions, he started nodding his head. Sure enough, a small crowd of the bastards had found us.

"It's okay, they're a quarter mile out. We have time." I used a stirrup to launch myself onto his back. I had a little friction burn high on my ass from the saddle rubbing and it stung immediately when it touched the saddle. My elbow still hurt like hell too. "Let's go." I pulled the reins to the right, and we trotted off toward the other store.

We didn't get a half mile when we came upon two other guys on horseback. I shifted my MP5 on its tactical sling and put my finger on the trigger. The two guys looked to be of Native American descent, and they were armed to the teeth, both with Henry Rifles and pistols on each hip. One had a compound bow and the other looked to have some kind of axe in a holster. I was nervous, they looked capable.

"Mornin'," one said in a Texas drawl. "Been' trackin' you since that house you slept in. Left two of the dead ones behind in there. Sloppy."

The other one reached back to grab something. "Don't," I said, raising my weapon. "Please don't."

Both of them did something then that I thought was weird. They both put their hands up and smiled.

"Now why would we want to kill the guy who saved our asses?'

I was confused. My expression must have shown it because they both laughed.

"I'm Daniel," the one who had already spoken told me, "and this is James. You created a diversion so we could escape the courthouse."

James nodded to me. "Thank you."

"I'm going to reach back and get something to give to you, okay? Don't shoot me."

I raised the MP5 and pointed it at him. "Slow. Real slow."

Daniel produced an extremely familiar book and held it towards me. He gave his horse a slight spur to the sides and the creature moved forward.

In a moment, I held the book in my hand and smiled.

This is James and Daniel, they are friends, and have volunteered to find you. Go with them and they will take you to us. We are waiting outside of town as our previous rendezvous point became a focal point for undead. Don't dawdle.

Guess who signed the note?

My puzzler was tired, so I wasn't going to try to figure out why Ship or Remo weren't with these guys. I straight-up asked them.

Daniel answered me with a question, "Ship is the giant and Remo is the badass, right?"

"Yeah."

"The dead got our horses when we got trapped. Your friends gave us these to track you." Something smelled funny, because Remo was a damn fine tracker, and should have been with them. "And your soldier buddy might have a broken ankle."

"What are the horse's names that you're on?"

"This is Smiley, and that's Bil," began James. "You're on Shaitan. We work at the Double Hoof for Deek Meeks. Been there ten years, stayed on when the dead started to walk. The ranch is about twenty-five miles northeast, and I would really like to get back, so can we go?"

I was relieved. If these weren't the guys we came for, then they already knew everything they needed to attack the ranch, so fuck it, I would go with them.

"Yeah."

Daniel smiled. "You talk about as much as your giant partner."

I raised an eyebrow. "Wait a half hour. You won't be able to shut me up."

They both turned their horses around, and we all walked together toward the new rendezvous spot.

Christ, I was tired.

DECISIONS AND THE DEAD

"He's not a doctor." I pointed at Remo. "You're not a doctor. How do you know it isn't broken?"

He shrugged, moving his booted foot in a slow, and obviously painful circle "I can walk on it, it just hurts."

"Ship has some medical training, let him look at it."

"I did," Remo replied. "He doesn't have X-ray eyes, so he can't tell for sure. You want to look too? Turn my head and cough?"

"How about I remain the funny one and tell the jokes, and you just keep killing shit?" I smirked. "How'd you do it?"

"Stepped wrong."

"Stepped wrong? Stepped wrong! You don't step wrong. You're... Remo."

He shrugged. "Shit happens."

That was good enough for me.

Eight people, six horses. We got Remo on the back of Daniel's horse. He had to switch off with a couple other horses on the way back to the ranch so we wouldn't exhaust our mounts. Shaitan was a smaller horse, so I got to keep on him by myself. Ship was bigger than the horse he was riding, so by rights, the animal should be on Ship's back. Javi rode with James.

Deek offered to send out a truck with a couple of the fellas to give Remo and Ship's horse a break, but Dix talked him out of it and told him to save the fuel.

We had the horses walk or jog, and it took the remainder of the day to get to the Double Hoof. When we arrived, the heat was starting to get tolerable. Nothing tremendous had happened on the return trip other than my saddle sore increased in size.

Deek and Kate were waiting for us with a couple guys in the tower. Kate waved immediately upon seeing us.

After a shower, and a wicked bitch session on how I need to stop trying to get myself killed from Donna, she and I met everybody not on watch for dinner in the main house. Chicken wrapped in bacon with mashed potatoes and green beans. I'm pretty sure everything we ate had been alive the week before. If you're reading this and starving, I'm so sorry, but the food at the Double Hoof was ridiculous. Every meal was fantastic.

As we were eating and talking, I took a long look at the folks around the table. Just as the food had been two weeks ago, these people were all living on borrowed time. Eventually, some douche rednecks, military assholes, government pricks, or the dead would find them. It's amazing they had made it this long. I looked at my mostly eaten chicken (I ate the bacon first, I'm like that), and gave a heavy sigh.

All of the bad guys in the last paragraph were drawn to me like a hunk of iron to a billion-volt electromagnet. I looked at Donna, who was talking and laughing with the twins. I looked at Kat and Alvarez; she had playfully stolen a green bean off of his plate and he was glaring at her in mock rage. Dix was telling a story of how we saved James and Daniel, with Kelly and the Double Hoof folks captivated by the tale. I looked for Tim and felt a moment of sadness. Then I thought of *Atlantis* and all the people who had died there, and stared again at my plate.

I had to leave. Not the table, these people. Donna would hate me. Ship would never forgive me. Kat would fucking kill me. My choices were simple: Stay or go. The plan had been to take everybody with me, but wouldn't that be selfish?

I loved these people, and their only outcome was death if they stayed with me, or more to the point, if I stayed with them. This ranch was as good a place as any to set up shop. They had a farm for Christ's sake, and unlimited fresh water. They were off the beaten track, had a wall and power, and a shit-load of guns.

My only problem was Remo. He would track me down, of that I had no doubts. Whether or not he would drag me back here trussed up like a turkey was unknown, but find me he would. 'Course he had a busted wheel right now, so maybe my time was nigh.

I looked at the folks who were still doing what they had been doing, and then looked at Remo. He was looking right at me, chewing. He stared for a second, then Deek asked him something and he looked away from me.

I would go to Alcatraz, where hopefully the plane that Dallas was on had made it. I would let them know that there was a force of US Navy at the Panama Canal, then I would call Schumitz somehow and turn myself in for testing. I needed to think about that last part, but just because the shithead scientists at Baldy hadn't found anything didn't mean there was nothing to find.

I hoarded supplies for the next few days, storing them near the solar panel array. I had to be careful not to get noticed because everybody would think I was stealing if I got caught. I mean, I *was* stealing, but not for me. I was doing it to protect these good folks. I thought about walking to Alcatraz, but I would be too slow and easy to track, so I needed to procure a mount. I know what you're thinking, but it had to be Shaitan. That fucker was the horse that knew me best, and he owed me anyway. He was smaller than the others, which meant he needed less food and water, plus he was an Arabian, so he must have this hot Texas climate genetically imbued into every cell. It would get hotter and dryer as I got inland too.

It was the supplies for my ride that got me caught. I had two sacks of oats, one on each shoulder, and I ran into Kate. She started to cry and threw her arms around me.

"You be safe," she said and trotted off sobbing.

She must not have said anything to anyone, because midnight the following night, I made my escape. I got out of bed, got dressed, grabbed my guns, kissed my lady, looked in on the twins, then crept down the stairs. I thought I would have to tell Remo something interesting, and I had a whole spiel on how I couldn't sleep and was just going to talk to Matt and Deek about something, but Remo wasn't there.

I didn't see a soul as I made my way to the barn. I grabbed Shaitan's saddle and moseyed (this is Texas) past the other stalls looking at the mostly sleeping horses until I got to his. He was awake and standing, considering me. If he whinnied, neighed, or came out with any other horse noises, there would be a fuck-ton more glue in east Texas tonight.

I glared at him, "Keep quiet, dumb nag." He glared back and didn't make a sound.

I pulled him out and saddled him, leading him by the reins. I sighed. "You ready?" He turned his head a bit and let me climb up on him. We ambled (Texas!) out into the excruciatingly humid night.

Light exploded everywhere when I reached the barn doors and I was looking at more or less the entire population of the Double Hoof. Everybody was dressed. Ship had his tree trunk arms folded, cords rippling like a professional wrestler. Remo was leaning against a fence post, chewing his toothpick. Where this guy found so many fence posts I have no idea. Alvarez stood stock still, over the twins, with his hands behind his back at parade rest. Kate beamed. The ranchers had my supplies in front of them, and that scared me a little. That fear was nothing compared to what came next. I noticed Donna and Kat standing together, hands on hips with full-on female scowls. Fuck. I swung my leg over the saddle and dismounted the hay-gobbling dickhead. I remained silent, thinking of what I was going to say.

Chloe was the first to do anything. She strode to me and stopped a half a foot away. WAY inside my territorial bubble. She shot her hands forward and grabbed my wrists. It actually made me shuffle back a quarter step.

"We are never going to be better off without you," she said, and all my fears and trepidations of what was about to happen fell away.

"Y'all can leave in the morning if you want," Deek called over through a smile, "after breakfast."

I felt like a total douche. I *was* a total douche. Someone had seen through my master plan, or Kate had ratted me out, but that was unlikely. I lowered my head as Donna and Kat came over.

Kat shook her head, smiling. "Dumbass."

Donna, also smiling hugged me. "Need you," was all she said, and she grabbed my mitt in hers.

We didn't leave in the morning. We decided to stay.

I have repeatedly told you, Dear Reader, in several paragraphs of this and the other two texts I call journals, that I am a good person. I've killed people, and I have no doubt I would do it again if I have to, but they all deserved it. If there is a God, he has to understand that people need to protect themselves, no matter the cost.

Do zombies count as murder? I mean, when I smoke a living dead thing, it can't be murder. You can't kill something that's already dead, right? If I'm wrong, then I'm fucked. When I stand at the Pearly Gates, and St. Peter is checking out my stats, is he going to tell me to take the elevator down because of all the zombies I've killed? Cuz fuck him. I'll kick him in the nuts and walk right into that cloudy paradise. No guilt.

It was two days after my failed attempt at freeing these wonderful folks of me, two nights actually, at maybe nine thirty, and I was talking to Matt over by the solar array, near the water pumping station. We were talking about McDonald's vs. home-grilled burgers. I was saying that there's nothing better than a home grilled cheeseburger... until you craved a McD's and got one. Eating that horrible, greasy thing out of that yellow wrapper was nothing short of orgasmic. No, it didn't have the fresh cut lettuce or tomato, or your choice of cheese, but it was still fantastic.

Matt had begun to speak about the differences between all the fast-food burger joints when a dark streak hit him from the right and brought him down. They immediately began to battle, and the thing on top of him began to throw haymakers. A handy piece of pipe called to me, and I used it to nearly decapitate the creature now astride my friend. I felt like Ship must feel every time he punches something and the head flies off of it like a golf ball off a tee. The thing's neck broke with an audible snap, and there was a wicked dent in the side of its bald head, the ear now hanging by gristle. Fucker wasn't getting back up.

Matt got up quickly, brushing himself off and checking himself over. He had two scratches on his face, but I couldn't tell if it was from the Runner or the tackle. A feral scream rent the air behind us, and of course, we both turned to stare into the darkness for a split second of indecision. Dozens of the slow variety infected were bearing down on us. The quiet bastards knew the jig was up, or they just straight-up saw us, and that fucking moaning started. We didn't wait around to see what they wanted, and without a word, we simultaneously sprinted back in the direction of the main house.

Matt yanked his radio as we ran, "Deek! Mike! Clint! Come in! We have infected inside, a whole bunch of 'em! We're gonna have to engage!"

Immediately, light assassinated shadows in every corner of the ranch. Either Matt's message had been received, or the person in control of the lighting had issues of their own. Darcy's calm voice came over the radio, "Fall back to the main house. We'll fight them off from here."

I thought about the lower windows of the two-story farmhouse, covered in rebar, and tried to do ammo and food calculations in my head as we ran. The ammo was stored in the basement and second floor of the main house, with scattered caches in several other locations. The only ways into the basement were a steel bulkhead set into concrete, and an interior kitchen door.

I heard someone running behind us as I thought about our fortifications, and knew those footsteps weren't friendly. I skidded to a stop, had a brief moment to aim my Sig, and put two into the chest of the bloody-eyed, six-foot woman who was chasing us. Bitch was big, and she looked strong. She clutched at her chest and fell to the side heaving. I didn't wait to see if she got back up, I spun and sprinted after Matt, who was turning around with his own weapon, pointing it back in my direction. I caught up to him, and gave him a brief, "Come on!" before we continued our run back to the house.

We didn't encounter any infected on the way, and hadn't heard any other shots. The door opened as we ran up to it, Deek, Kelly, and Stacy all pointing weapons at us.

"Human," Matt managed between catching his breath and holding his side. I could hear Rusty and Dusty going absolutely nuts inside someplace.

"Do we have everybody?" I asked as the door slammed and Kelly slammed home or turned the deadbolts of about a billion locks.

Stacy shook her head, "No. James and Daniel are out on the back forty someplace. Mike and Clint are up in their perches, and I haven't seen your daughter and her army boyfriend. Darcy can't raise any of them."

Remo was checking the sling on his MP5. He didn't look up when he said, "I saw Kat and Alvarez by the barn earlier, I'll go get them." He moved toward the door, but I forestalled him with a hand on his arm.

"No, buddy. We need you here. Alvarez will take care of her." I considered for a moment, then added, "More like she'll protect him."

The jarhead nodded. "How many did you see?"

"A bunch," Matt answered. "It might be that swarm that's been lookin' for us."

Donna, Richy, and Chloe came into the great room, and over to me. Richy punched me in the arm. "Glad you could make it."

I was relieved to see them but also very worried about Kat and Alvarez. Donna grabbed my hand and Chloe the other. I squeezed, feeling safe.

Remo pulled a toothpick from his shirt pocket. "We should get all the food and ammo upstairs. We need to plan on them getting in here, and—" something impacted the front door hard. Scratching and scrabbling came next. We heard it run down the farmer's porch, then an arm punched through the far left window. It pulled its arm back, infected blood streaking the glass shards and rebar.

They could break all the windows they wanted, they weren't getting in that way, and if they could break down that door, they were damn strong. The thing outside screamed, and began hammering its paws on the side of the house.

"Unnerving damn howl, that is," Remo confessed. "As I was saying, we need to get all our supplies upstairs and figure out how to block the stairway so they can't get up. Eventually, they'll get in here, and we need to be ready."

Deek started to take charge. "Stacy, you and Matt go get the ammo." He pointed at Remo. "Do like he says. Richy, Chloe, you go help with the food. Me and Ship are gonna figure out how to block the stairs." He pointed at me. "You and Donna make sure everything is loaded and we have backups to the guns. Kelly, you, Kate, Dix, and Javi make sure all the windows and doors are secure. Block 'em up with whatever you can."

We heard the moans as soon as we started to get to work. The moans preceded a radio call as well.

This is Alvarez. Is everybody safe?

I pulled my radio. "Yeah, buddy, are you?"

Affirmative. Kat and I were in the barn loft when we heard gunshots, we climbed up on the barn roof and can see infected all over the place. They're coming in from the north.

I was confused. "What were you doing in the loft?"

I was... we were... I mean...

"Forget it. Keep each other safe. Do you have any rations?"

Negative, just what I had on me.

Deek motioned for me to give him the mic. "Alvarez, this is Deek. Is there any way you can get to the horses? I can't stomach the thought of them getting killed in their stalls."

Already done. We let them out and they took off out the southwest end of the barn. I haven't seen them since, but I didn't hear any horse screaming.

Deek heaved a sigh of relief as he thanked Alvarez and passed me the mic back to me.

"Sit tight, you two," I told them. "We'll smoke these pus bags and get you down in time for corn flakes."

I heard Kat in the background through the radio, *Cheeseburgers or I stay the fuck up here!*

One of the windows shattered and a bunch of hands poked through. It didn't take them long to rip the curtains down and then we were staring at a bunch of dead faces through the bars. The other windows followed suit, and a couple people gagged at the olfactory assault. The smell these things give off when they get ripe is absolutely another weapon. I am not even fucking kidding. It's *bad*.

Dix and Javi began firing into the crowd, who had amped up their noises when they saw us. One of them got her little head through the bars, leaving an ear behind, when Javi shot it.

"Whoa! Easy killer." I put my hand on his arm. "We should save ammo."

He looked at me incredulously. "What the hell are we supposed to do, be mean to them? Ask them to leave?"

"Nope, you go do what Deek said, I do this." I stepped to the couch, careful not to get into the reach of any of the shitheads trying to eat me, and pulled it away from the window. I stepped to the side closest to the door, out of view of the dead, and unsheathed my knife. Remo moved to the other side of the window and nodded at me. I could see the shift in their filthy paws as they reached for this new target. I stepped to my right and jammed my blade into the eye socket of the former kid who was reaching for my pal. She collapsed and I stepped back quickly.

Javi looked impressed and moved off with Dix to get to work. Remo nodded in the negative and I knew what he meant. This was way too slow. We needed polearms of some kind to jab from a distance.

I moved over to Remo, daring a glance outside. There were so many of them out there. I couldn't see an end to the sea of dead faces. It looked like there were more coming, but I couldn't tell for sure.

Remo moved his toothpick around in his mouth, looked at the zombies, then at me. "Might need the rifles if we can't come up with something long and sharp."

"You mean you can't just fucking glare them to death?"

"Uh-uh."

I nodded. "And here I thought that was your super-hero power; killing shit by looking at it."

"Nope. It's putting up with your bullshit."

We both looked up as we heard something scrabble up onto the roof of the farmer's porch. It moved quickly down the roof and we heard glass breaking.

"Shit," we both said at the same time and raced for the stairs. There were no bars on the upstairs windows.

That scream that comes from a Runner sounded from inside the house, sending shivers down my spine, and chasing my extremely large nuts up into my stomach. Something was tearing around in the second bedroom on the right. Hint: it was not a bunny. It started smashing things and slapping on something, then human screaming started. "Dadda! Dadda! Daddadaddadadda!"

We got to the door and I reached for the knob, but Remo stopped me and gave a hoarse whisper, "You go left!"

We burst into the room to see it a shambles. The thing had destroyed everything it could in the thirty seconds it took us to get upstairs. It used to be a decent-looking young man, but now it would scare horrors from a nightmare away. Shirtless, sunburned, and bloody, it whipped its head sideways and glared its crimson eyes at us. Those red orbs almost bugged out of its noggin when it stared for a moment. A little pee eked its way out of me right then, and I was as used to this kind of sight as I was ever going to get.

The thing had ceased its beating on the door, but the yells from inside the closet only increased. It was Kate, and she was terrified.

Staring moment over, it decided that the meat on this side of the door was easier, and it came, growling and hissing at the same time. More pee...

Remo and I shot it as it scuttled up on the bed. He hit it in the chest and I got the fucker in the abdomen and leg. It fell face first on the sheets, life starting to leave it in gouts of infected blood. It had a bit more in it, and pushed up to see if it could reach us, but I shot it in the face, the back of its head flying back out the window it had come through.

Kate was crying and howling for her dadda, so I skirted the end of the bed and spoke to her through the door, "Kate! Kate, it's me, the bad man can't hurt you. He's gone. I'm going to open the door, okay?"

She answered after a slight pause, "Okay."

I opened the closet door and she peeked around it and into my eyes. She smiled, came running out into my arms, saw the dead thing, pointed at it, and ran right back into the closet. She tried to pull the door closed, but I stopped her. She fought me for a second, but I told her I wouldn't let anything happen to her. She came out slowly, hugging me and not taking her eyes off of the dead Runner.

We heard a thump behind us and all three of us spun to assess this new threat. It was a wide-eyed Deek. He glanced at each of us, then focused on the dead thing. He looked horrified, and then looked at me. "Is... is she...?"

"She's fine. She's really smart and hid in the closet while the thing tried to eat through it." Kate squeezed me, and Deek let out an audible sigh. We heard gunshots outside, and Deek put the radio to his face, but told Kate to come to him before he spoke into it. She ran to him, engulfing his belly in a bear hug. He stroked her hair as he spoke into the mic, "Who's firing? What you got?"

Alvarez came back, *That's us. We're still on the roof of the barn, but we can see some infected roaming under the lights, and we can take out a few here and there.*

"Keep it up," Deek told him. "We could use the help." He clipped the radio back to his belt. "Dang it. Never thought to bar up the second-floor windows. Didn't think they could climb."

"Some of 'em are smarter than others," I told him. "I've seen some shi... stuff. If you've got any boards, we might want to board up the windows up here just in case we get more of the faster variety."

"Give me hand," Remo asked me, and we moved a chest of drawers in front of the broken window, and pushed the bed against it. "Best we can do until we can fix it permanently."

We filed out past Deek, who was still getting compressed by Kate, and Deek put his hand on my shoulder and nodded a thanks. I nodded back, and saw people bustling when I got into the hall. Remembering what I had been looking for earlier, I called back to Deek, "Hey, do you have anything we could use to poke those things in the head and save ammo?"

Our host gave a gigantic, Texas, shit-eating grin, showing tons of teeth. "Yup. Katie, you go see momma now." Kate took off without a word, and started down the stairs. Deek moved off down the hall and motioned for us to follow him. We entered a bedroom and he pointed to the wall. On six plaque-type shelves resided six swords. They looked commemorative, but I thought they would do nicely in a pinch. I reached for a Roman short sword, a Gladius, but then thought better. There was a Rapier below and to the left of it. Basically, a long, skinny blade with a pointy end used for duels and fencing. Perfect. Remo grabbed the other five weapons while I marveled at what this thing was about to do. He moved to the door and I followed him.

We got some looks as we descended the stairs with a bunch of swords. I heard a power tool start, and noticed Ship under the stairs with a circular saw. He cut the support struts of the stairs under the risers one at a time, and put them back so the stairs were just resting on them. Not very safe, but the whole shebang would come down in an instant if too much weight was on it at once, or if it were cut from above as well.

The house was bustling, both inside and out, and it was loud. The things outside were going ballistic, and the dogs inside were just as bad, barking and running every which way. Richy turned the corner from the basement with an armload of something, began climbing, then stopped on his way up the stairs. Ship looked at him funny, and then I remembered the Sasquatch had just cut the stair supports.

The kid had a stern look on his face as he looked around then focused on something on the other side of the couch from me. "Dusty! Shut up and come!" Both dogs hightailed it (literally) up the stairs after the kid. I heard hammers on nails upstairs over the din of the dead, and figured Deek was getting to work on the upstairs windows.

Remo looked at me, and I at him. I felt a wicked smile cut across my face, and threw my left hand up in a half circle over my head as I did this lunge thing with my new dueling weapon, just like I had seen in every movie based on a Dumas book. "HA!" I shouted and skewered a horribly mangled guy, the end of my skinny sword sticking out the back of its dome. I yanked back and the foil came out of the thing's noggin with ease. I smiled. Fuck dueling. Fuck the Olympics. Fuck French aristocrats! I was the MAN with this thing. I continued shoving my new toy into the eyes of the dead for the next hour. Remo did the same, but he had a wider, cutlass-type weapon. Soon, Javi and Matt joined the fray, and we slaughtered those fucking dead pricks. The stack of bodies got so high that the ones behind were reaching down over their re-killed pals and through the bars.

The things had surrounded the main house, and were banging all over the place. We heard glass break. The back kitchen door had been the target.

"I'll go," I told my merry band of swordsmen. Ship followed me with his machete. The wood reinforced door in the kitchen and bars on its upper window were holding. Revolting shit dribbled down from the lacerated dead arms that reached through the bars and were cut on the shards of glass.

"Watch this," I told Ship and continued one of my best zombie-slaying nights. I impaled another dozen or so brains before I ran out of zombies. They seemed to have their focus elsewhere.

Another Runner howl sent chills down my spine, but it was far off. I wiped my sweaty forehead and made a radio call. "Alvarez, you should be fine, but keep an eye out, those fast fuckers can climb."

Copy that. There are two more of the fast ones, at least. They ran past the barn and toward the house a few minutes ago, so be careful.

"Will do. You two okay up there?"

It's fuckin' hot.

"It's fuckin' Texas."

Copy. Alvarez out.

The outside slapping and pounding had lessened considerably, as had the wails and moans. I heard gunshots and concern began to edge its way into my brain. The radio told me it was Deek, Dix, and Kelly, on the roof of the farmer's porch, shooting stragglers.

It was about five in the morning when the shots stopped and I couldn't hear any more of the things outside.

Darcy came into the great room, and Deek saw the look on her face. "Any word from Mike?" he asked her.

She shook her head no. "I haven't been able to reach Clint, Jake, James, or Daniel either, but it isn't time for them to check in yet."

Deek kept talking, but I'm so tired right now I don't remember what he said. I sat down next to Remo on the couch and sighed the sigh of the weary. He had his boot off and his foot up. I had totally forgotten about his messed-up ankle, and he had never uttered a single complaint.

"Still swollen?"

He glanced at me then at his foot. "Yeah, but I can walk fine." He looked at me hard. "I could walk a few thousand miles if I had to. How's that?"

He had pointed at my arm, where Captain Bob had removed a chunk. I could see the tiniest dot of blood through the bandage. It had been a considerable time, and it was still bleeding.

Ship sat down in one of the armchairs, and it creaked, threatening to spill him onto the floor. He leaned back and his joints complained as loudly as the chair had. *I could walk too*, he signed.

Everybody came into the room, and we all looked around at each other. There was no cheer, but we had won. I didn't yet know if we had suffered losses, as not everyone was accounted for, but other than one Runner, nothing had gained entrance to the house.

I heard Deek behind me. "Alvarez, how you situated?"

I don't see any, but we're not climbing down just yet.

"Y'all should get back in the loft. The sun will be up in a few minutes, and it's gonna get hotter than Kelly's chili up on that roof."

Copy that, it's already hot.

James and Daniel had been out on a run for whatever and weren't around when the horde hit us. They checked in at eight in the morning. Mike and Clint, were attacked while they were on guard duty. They had climbed into the tower at the front gate, and got low so the dead couldn't see them. They waited until most of the dead were gone before they eliminated stragglers and made a radio call. Jake had been on a roving patrol on his horse and we still hadn't heard from him. Deek was furious, as nobody was supposed to go anywhere alone. We never saw Jake again.

We found and killed eighteen more infected roaming the Double Hoof the morning following the siege. One of them, a Runner, got close to Matt before he killed it. The bastard made no sounds at all, it just leapt at Matt from atop one of the backhoes. Fucker. Matt drew his six gun and drilled the infected asshole before it could get to him. He fired twice more very quickly, all three shots center mass, before Javi ventilated its cranium. There were one hundred and eight infected corpses that we piled onto a flatbed trailer and towed out to the back of the ranch. Deek thought it would be a good use of resources to use five gallons of diesel and burn the things. The resulting smoke plume was greasy and gross, and I wondered if anything a few miles away would see it and come looking.

The zombies had gained entrance the same way they always did. A portion of the earth wall had collapsed and filled a five-foot section of the dry moat. Lucky pus bags had found that section and come sniffing. Didn't make a lot of sense, but there it is.

All horses were accounted for as well, other than the one Jake had been riding. One mare had a bite on her leg, and she got sick that night. She died early the third morning. There was nothing we could do. It was the first time I had seen a horse with a bite. She didn't reanimate, thank God.

The night after the battle, my original group, minus Kat, Alvarez, and Dusty the dog, sat in the living room of the guest house. We had called a meeting. When everyone was situated, I leaned forward on my chair, putting my elbows on my knees.

"Should we stay or should we go? The Clash reference notwithstanding, I don't know if we're safer here than anywhere else. This place has its merits, but also its problems. We're less than fifty miles from a combined population of probably a million people or more. I would think we'd be safe here from the infected, but who knows? Besides, eventually the living will find us, and that usually doesn't go well."

"If we leave," Remo began, "these people will have less fighters to protect them, but their consumption of food and supplies goes way down. We've already had a fight with the dead, so we know they can get in, but we won, so we know our fortifications are good."

Ship passed a note to me. *I vote we stay. We shore up our defenses, apply some advanced engineering to the wall and gates, continue to grow food, go on supply runs, and live here.* He reached for his notebook, added something, and passed it back to me. *At least for now.*

"This place is good," Chloe said, surprising us all. "The people are good and there's food and water. I think we should stay."

"Me too," Richy said quickly. "What she said."

Donna nodded. "I'm comfortable here." She put her hand in mine. "But whatever you decide."

I yawned. Hey, I was friggin' tired, shut it. "Vote then. Anybody who wants to stay, raise their hand." Everybody but Remo and I raised their hands immediately. Remo thought for a moment more, then raised his hand too.

"Then we stay," I said.

We should have left.

SIXTY FEET

Four months passed before the next epic shit storm. In four months, Ship designed such wonders for the defense of this ranch, the likes of which were, as previously mentioned, wondrous. I felt a billion times safer.

We averaged about sixteen telephone or power poles a day. Cut them down, cut them into three pieces, then dragged them back to the ranch with the backhoes and some flatbed trailers, or in the appropriated Edinburgh school bus. We drove the poles into the ground on the inward side of the dry moat about ten feet apart using posthole diggers and the backhoes (Deek calls them *machines*), then put up several two-by-twelves between each one. We pushed the dirt from the trench up against the barrier, and now there was a five-foot-deep channel with another five feet of board and dirt on the near side. A ten-foot barrier. Ship even had us dig out ramps so if the dead got in the moat, they could get back out and into the scrub.

Deek owned about 850 acres of land, but we would only put the barrier around forty or so acres of it, encircling the farmland, water sources, power plant (wind and solar), and the structures. It was our main task during the day, and everybody who wasn't doing something else worked on it. In four months, we had gotten the wall around twenty-nine acres of the forty.

Ship had also rigged the batteries connected to the solar and wind arrays to output about twenty percent more power, and with his (and I'm spitballing here, I'm not Ship) rotating (not alternating!) current, he said that the batteries would last about thirty years.

When the temperature reached Fuck-it, we worked on spike walls that formed yet another barrier on the interior of the compound. When we were done, this place would be a fortress. Actually, it was already a fortress, but would become a *better* fortress.

Ship had to go and ruin it by passing me a note saying: *Won't deter armed human enemies enough. I'll work on that.*

I have mentioned a few times in these journals how I have seen marvels to keep out the dead, and this time I was helping make one. It felt damn good. I felt damn good, and I looked good too. I have absolutely no flab on me now, and one night, I was standing bare-ass, looking in the mirror at my awesome new body, puffing my chest and arms out, when my girl told me not to hog all the hotness. That was a good night.

I'm feeling good, looking good, and have a great family that is now well protected. Of course it all has to go to shit.

So the bus. We had removed all of the seats in the back except for the first set, and welded steel mesh over all the windows and both exits. An additional set of steel support rods were put into place to keep the door to my left locked and solid. The bus was sort of an armored transport vehicle for whatever. In this case, we were collecting more poles and we were going to store them in the back. We had a couple of flatbeds, but the rigs needed to pull them were in short supply, and the backhoes were way too slow.

I was driving, with Javi and Remo in the seats behind me. Matt, Alvarez, Kat, and Dix were in the F350 in front of us. We were talking about soup. I used to get this miso soup from this Chinese place before I went to prison. It was great, and I was telling everybody it was my favorite when we reached the bridge over Arch Canyon about two miles south of a shitty town called Encino.

What have I told you, Dear Reader, about bridges? The exact phrasing was: Stay the Fuck Off. In this case, there were only a few dead roaming around. Six to be exact. The stupid town of Encino had a population of nothing, and yet there were six dead fuckers on this bridge in the middle of nowhere. The only thing besides the dead, our vehicles, and us, were the poles we needed to cut down.

The dead came for us and we took care of them. The bridge looked as dead as the infected, but we had to get across. We all got out of our vehicles to inspect the bridge, and it was hot. Like, really hot. I took a sip out of my water bottle and looked at the crack in the concrete. It went all the way across from east to west. There were a few more cracks and some chunks missing from the hundred-foot-long bridge. I took a peek over the side and was amazed to see that there was a skinny canyon, but it was very deep, maybe sixty feet, although I couldn't see the bottom from where I was. We agreed we would take it easy, and got back in the vehicles. Matt drove across slowly and it was okay. I did the same. It looked shitty, but solid, this bridge was.

We cut down eighteen creosote-covered power poles, cutting them into eight-foot sections with our chainsaws. 144 pieces was too much to carry, the sun was starting to go down, and the entire population of Encino was bearing down on us. Maybe fifty or sixty of them. We had loaded twenty-eight of the pole pieces into the back of the bus, and had stacked the others in a few piles along the road. We would come back tomorrow to pick them up. We didn't want to deal with the dead, so we just took off.

It had been a long day. I was hot, tired, and thirsty. It was the apocalypse. All of that together is probably why my mind wasn't functioning properly. That and the fact that some powerful being has it out for me. Remo was now riding with Matt, and Javi was still with me.

Matt was hauling twelve of the cut poles in the F350. He made it most of the way across then I began to follow. I got the bus half way over and the fucking bridge just straight-up broke. I don't know, maybe two years of neglect after Armageddon began, coupled with about a billion years of neglect before the dead rose, and this bridge, which had been constructed while the builders had to be careful of a tyrannosaurus attack, just said, "Nope."

There was the quickest sound of rending metal and the section in front of me and to the right disappeared into the chasm underneath us. The split second decision to either floor it, or jam on the brakes and back up, took about eight years too long. Of course, you have to remember it's me, so whichever decision I made was going to be wrong anyway. It was very wrong. Like epically wrong. I jammed on the brakes, then floored it, yanking the wheel to the left to get around the hole. The hole got bigger, our right rear wheels fell in, and we started moving backwards. Now, moving backwards might not sound like a terrible feeling, but when the back of the bus began to sink into the road, and the nose of the bus went up and up and up, I got a bit scared.

We teetered. We teetered long enough that I was thinking we would be fine if we just didn't move, and said as much to Javi. He nodded, which by definition is movement, the poles shifted and slid back a bit fucking up the balance of our precariously perched vehicle. The added weight in one place on the edge of the broken concrete and asphalt broke off more of the concrete and asphalt, and the back of the bus began to slide further into the hole. The poles began to slip off and into the fissure, and for another split second, I thought we were going to be totally fine as the weight was off our ass end.

Unfortunately, The Powers That Be decided today was FU day, and the whole bus upended backwards and I could now see the bottom of the canyon with crystal clarity.

Javi began to yell, "Holy fuuuuuuuuucccckkkk!" as bits scraped off the bottom of the bus with a screech and we fell into oblivion.

Sixty feet might not sound like a lot to you, but you can suck it. You try looking into a hole that deep with the realization that you are going to impact the bottom of said hole at 120 feet per second while inside a twenty-thousand-pound bus.

The fall was interesting. I was as serene as one could be with the absolute certain knowledge they are about to be dead. I had survived so much shit to now get killed by a fucking hole in the ground.

The one other thing I did notice before the gut-wrenching impact was that the canyon was full of about thirty zombies. Sixty more feet.

Perfect.

STILL NOT DEAD

Growling. A muffled hiss. And was that... was that the clink of chains I heard? Like something was chained up? I opened my eyes to the dancing shadows of a room lit by a candle. The room was made out of barn board, and the best way to describe the place was ramshackle. Twenty by twenty, potbellied stove in the corner, rotten old cot, some supplies, a hunting rifle, and a zombie. One window, but it was dark outside, or the window was covered.

I sat up, noticing my hand was tied to one of the support posts of the shack. Then I noticed that I was really sore. Everything hurt. My weapons were right next to me, including my SOG, which I used to cut my bonds. I reached for the bottle of water that had been placed next to me and noticed a fresh bandage on my arm bite. There was also one on my head, which hurt, but not nearly as bad as in the past. I looked myself over in the mostly dark room, and was covered with bruises, contusions, and scrapes.

I know what you're thinking: *What? But didn't you just tell me there's a zombie in the room?* Yeah, you're probably a bit scared at the proximity, but relax, it was quite well chained up. It also had a leather belt wrapped around its head and through its mouth. It was fresh.

It really wanted a taste of me, and was struggling against the chains. I had to wonder who had put it here and why? Was it to guard me? If I were a threat, why had my weapons been within easy reach? Fear not, Dear Reader, all your answers are coming.

A notebook sat next to the sleeping bag I was resting on. It was open and there was writing right there on the first page for me to see. First thing's first though. I stared at the infected, who was wearing a collar and the collar was chained to another of the support posts. I stood, feeling a bit woozy. My plan had been to stick the SOG in this thing's head, but I opted for a single suppressed shot to the dome. It collapsed, looking pathetic.

I took a swig of the bottled water, noticing another half case of it nearby, then grabbed the notebook. I moved closer to the candle so I could read it.

I had to get you out fast. They were all over the place in that canyon. They must have gotten trapped and couldn't get out. I trap rabbits there. I got bit while getting you out of the bus. There were too many. Looks like you were already bit, but the bite looks old, so it couldn't have been one of them. I bandaged you up. Used my last bandage. I won't need it. I think I set your arm correctly. The dead chased us while I was carrying you, but the bus wreckage and the rocks on the canyon floor slowed them down.

I don't have the balls to shoot myself, so if you live, please do it for me. I looked at the body on the floor with a bit of sadness. *Take whatever you need out of this hunting shack. The other guy didn't make it, sorry.*

He signed the note Travis. This guy had died saving my ass. I looked back at him again, "Thanks, Travis."

I looked at the thing that had been wearing Travis. Some evil fucking entity had taken this guy from me and I never even got to speak to him. We could have been buds. Maybe I would have gotten to save his life. I owe Travis, so I will pay it forward somehow.

Plus, Javi was dead.

The shack was sweltering and gloomy, and I didn't know where I was. I searched the whole place for a map, but it was dark. Leaving now would be a terrible idea. I could stumble into a pack of the dead or fall down another hole in the dark. Travis had left my radio with my stuff, so I tried a call.

My head hurt, and it was the first time I had spoken in a while, so the pain reminded me it was hanging about. "Double Hoof, this is Bus Rider, come in, over. Double Hoof? Darcy? Matt?"

Nothing. No static, just nothing. The radio seemed to be functioning properly, just nobody was answering. I wondered if I was out of range. We had been a few miles shy of Encino, cutting poles down on Route 281. That would put me about twenty or so miles from home. I had been willing to try this little jaunt when I was by myself after The Devil Horse threw me in Edinburgh, but I had known how to get home, and I had known where I was.

I had been checking my surroundings as I thought all of that shit above. The place was as secure as a shack could be. Might stop a stiff breeze, or an undetermined stray dog, but it wouldn't stop an infected for long, and it certainly wouldn't keep out a bunch of them. But this is what I had. The food and water Travis had was complimented by a scoped

Marlin hunting rifle and two almost full boxes of 30/30 ammo. A big red-and-blue backpack that you could probably see from space, sat in the corner of the room. Travis had been prepared, but he didn't *look* like he was prepared. Ha, Grey Man Principle. Too bad you can't Google that. My Google is a seven-foot smarty-pants who I was really beginning to miss. I drew the strings and took a peek inside, pulling out items and setting them apart. A green poncho, some dry clothes, a heavy blanket, a box tent, matches, a giant first aid kit, a big knife, the list went on and on.

Travis knew how to pack a bag. I looked at him again, shaking my head and sighing. I would bury him in the morning.

I covered Travis with the sleeping bag, ate some jerky, drank some water, and sacked out on the cot. Much like the dude who lived in this shack, the cot looked weak but was quite strong.

I had no sheet, and I always have trouble sleeping without a covering. By that, I mean I'm more comfy with a blanket. When it's a billion degrees outside, and there's no AC, it's tough for me to get to sleep because I want at least a sheet on me. I don't know where that stems from, but I was always like that, pre-plague and pre-prison. I had a conversation about this with Ship once, and he told me a bit about why he thinks I need the sheet. He said it is a feeling of vulnerability when I sleep, and that it wasn't uncommon.

I was feeling pretty vulnerable. Travis had set and bandaged my arm while I was sleeping, but it still fucking hurt, as it had recently been broken. It was hot as balls, and I was friendless and far from home. I felt even more vulnerable when I woke up after sleeping for God knows how long, and there were dogs scratching at my shack. Except they weren't dogs, and you can see exactly where this is going.

I don't know if they smelled me, or they had followed Travis as he carried me, or if they had come to investigate the candlelight, but I could only assume that these were the vanguard of a larger force on the way, or these were desert roamers searching for a quick snack. There were three of them, two on the right side and one behind my position. I was hot, tired, and broken, but these fuckers had to go. They weren't making much noise, but as soon as I made any sound, they would follow suit and bring anything in the area to me. Unless there was nothing in the area, I had no idea where I was.

The door to the shack was as rickety as the rest of it. I picked up my MP5, but it would be a tough go, as I was in a sling. I opted for the suppressed Sig, and had to thank Travis again for not leaving my shit behind. I ejected the mag to inspect my rounds by the flickering candle, and when I did, all three of them stopped scratching. They must have heard me eject the magazine. They continued scratching in a moment, not yowling or moaning any louder. I could only see the top two rounds, and tried to load another but the magazine wouldn't take it. I slid it back into the weapon as quietly as possible, but it still made a *snick!* sound, and the things stopped again, listening. It wasn't until I opened the door that they went off with their awful cries.

I plugged number one quickly, moved around the side of the shack, and found two and three. I gave a low whistle, and of course, they both turned around. The second one had no face, and I shot her first. The third was down one second later, and a second after that, the fourth one hit me from the side. Of course, I stumbled, and of course, I fell, and of course, that dead bastard landed on me, squishing my broken fucking arm between us.

I saw stars, both in the quiet night sky, and in my own private agony. The pus bag didn't give a rat's ass about stars, and leaned in to make my Adam's apple his own personal piece of fruit. I thumped him on the side of the dome with the butt of my weapon, and it stunned him. It was awkward to get the long-barreled suppressor up to his head, but I did, and put a bullet through it. He collapsed on me, and I got his melon juice in my mouth. I had been gritting my teeth with a grimace, but his goo still got in there.

You obviously haven't sampled zombie tar-tar, or you'd be dead, but I have to tell you, for posterity: it ain't nice. I pushed the fucker off me, spitting, and proceeded to gag. It was a totality of horrible, as the flavor of death just overwhelmed everything else. The pain in my arm wasn't forgotten, but it took second fiddle, at least for a solid minute, to the disgust of what was happening to me.

It was fucking gross.

It was so debilitating, that it took me a moment to remember I should be afraid. When the fear came back, so did the arm pain, and the trifecta was complete. I pushed him off me, scrambled up, still spitting, and sought out more creatures in every direction at once. I couldn't see shit in the darkness, and didn't want to risk looking with a flashlight.

I got back inside and quickly extinguished the candle. Hopefully, the stench of the dead outside would mask my smell. I lay down on the cot, but sleep didn't come.

My eyes were burning when I realized that the sun was poking through the gaps between the barn board. I got up, got a quick drink of water, and took a peek outside. When I opened the door, the heat of the day hit me hard. It was palpable, and I had to take a step back inside for a moment. I slid quickly through the portal again, doing a circuit of the shack to check just how alone I was.

I was greeted by the scrub. There was nothing else except the bodies of the dead I had smoked last night.

I had to go, and sooner rather than later. I found a shovel, and began to dig a grave for Travis. The other four assholes could rot. That's what I was thinking at least, until I got to about the tenth shovel full of dirt. I only had one arm and it was a hundred degrees in the shade. I simply couldn't do it.

In the end, I put him inside the sleeping bag and covered his face with one of his shirts. I felt bad, but I could literally kill myself trying to bury him, and Travis had actually killed himself in saving me, so I wouldn't fuck that up for either of us. I apologized to him, took a swig of the bottle of whiskey he had on a work bench, and poured the rest on the ground next to him. I still hate whiskey, but drinking to Travis had been a moral imperative.

I packed as much shit as I could in his pack, including what he had in there already, and all the water. There was some food I had to leave behind, but it wasn't much. I attached the hunting rifle to the side of the pack as well. I conducted another search for a map, preferably with a big YOU ARE HERE stamp, but came up empty again. I closed the door on the shack, and put two rocks in front of it after I shut the little wooden latch.

I couldn't put the back pack on with the sling, and it was too bulky to have on one arm, so I had to take the sling off to put the pack on. That sucked, but I was able to do it. I grabbed the pack strap with my left hand, but it hurt too much, so I jury rigged the sling to the pack to make my own sling, and it worked okay.

I glanced at the shack, looked at the compass on the pack flap, and started moving southwest. If I didn't find a road or town, I would eventually hit the Gulf of Mexico or the Mexican border, and I would be able to backtrack and find the Double Hoof from there. Unless I got eaten, or cooked in this oppressive heat. Aren't there a crapload of rattlesnakes and scorpions and shit out here too? Fuck.

I took the first step to the southwest and dared another glance back at the little house I had called home for... I don't know how long. How long had I been there? Something else to contemplate other than my imminent demise.

I took my first rest about five hours after I had started. If I were walking at about three miles per hour, then I was more than halfway home. I hadn't seen so much as a sand flea on the ground, but I did see some kind of big bird flying way up above me. I couldn't tell what kind because it was right in the sun. I stopped for a sip of water another hour or so in, and now I could see three of the fuckers right above me, circling. I took the rifle out of the backpack holster I had fashioned and took aim at one of them to see what it was.

I don't know birds. I mean, I think I can tell the difference between a hawk and a seagull, but that's about it. These were big and they kept flying in and out of my scope, so I couldn't tell. There were five when it started to get dark, then they took off. Fucking vultures are what is flying around up there, waiting for me to die. Assholes. These douches were worse than the zombies. They were going to wait until I was too weak to defend myself, fly their feathered asses down here, and tear into me. I've never been anti-buzzard before, but fuck 'em. Fuck 'em all. All I can think of is that stupid vulture from the Bugs Bunny cartoons saying: *Oh no! Noo, nooooo, noope!* Sanctimonious prick. Hey, I watched a lot of cartoons in prison. I also saw the Arnold version of Conan. Hashtag *tastes like chicken.*

Last night, I had stayed in a shack and not slept. Tonight, I was going to not-sleep on the dirt in east Texas with no shack around me. I thought of every western movie I had ever seen, when they camp out and have that awesome fire with the rocks around it, and they bust out a harmonica and lay down on their bedrolls.

Fuck that.

All I could think about was how a fire would draw the living dead, snakes would bite me, or scorpions would sting my balls. Were there any nasty scorpions or tarantulas out here? They freak me the hell out. I had to lay down on Travis' blanket and hope none of that scary shit came near me.

Sorry, Dear Reader, but nothing did. I actually did fall asleep. If anything nibbled on me, I didn't know about it, and nothing looked swollen or bitten. I stood up and stretched, looking for a place to shake the weasel, and I looked right at the back of a dead guy not fifty feet away. He was walking away from me at such an angle that he must have stumbled by less than twenty feet from me.

Remo, when you read this, realize I have had some traumatic experiences lately and was exhausted.

Spit out toothpick. "That's how you get dead, dumbass," is what he's going to say.

I picked up my Sig, drew on him, and whistled. It was over in a couple of seconds. Any other time and I would have gone with the knife, but I was fucked up. I made a radio call, no joy. Nobody loves me.

A few hours later, and I saw the road and signs for Raymondville. I realized I had gone too far south and headed north.

It only took a half hour to start recognizing stuff. The dusty road from the Double Hoof was under my feet a bit after that, and I smiled a big shit eater. Another hour and I was looking at the gates.

I couldn't see anybody in the tower, so I cupped my hands over my mouth and shouted, "Little pig, little pig, let me the fuck in!"

I was expecting a sweet nursery rhyme come-back, but nope. I called on the radio again and nope. With this gate, and Ship's improved wall design, I wasn't getting in this way, so I circled to the left. In about half a mile, I followed a ramp into the moat and stood in front of a spot where we hadn't shored up the earth wall. I had to leave the backpack behind, but I was able to scale the dirt on the second try, broken arm and all. I was to the east of the compound and couldn't see it, so I began my trek west. I saw the smoke in just a few minutes, and it chilled me to the bone.

Creeping slowly past a stand of Acacia trees, I busted out my little binoculars. I could see there was nothing left of the barn but smoldering embers. Two dead horses lay just outside where the big doors to the barn used to be. I couldn't tell from here how they had died, but there was blood on the grass. The main house had been spared, but the front door was gone. There were no dead here, either living or true, other than the horses that I could see.

I surveyed the area for a while, then cut around to the north to the solar array. The shed was fine, but nobody was around. I couldn't see through the trees on the far side of the array, so I used them as cover to get a little closer.

A Blackhawk helicopter sat behind the trees with two Humvees. Two guys in black pants with their shirts off sat by the chopper playing cards in the shade of the shadow of one of the vehicles. Definitely military, or ex-military.

Two reasons they would be here: To take what Deek had, or they were looking for someone. I nodded to myself, the ire rising. I wondered if my eyes were going red, but I forced myself to calm down, flexing my fingers into fists slowly. I moved back through the solar panels, into the far tree line, and waited for darkness.

RESCUE, SORT OF

The light of the mostly full moon glinted off of the black paint of the helicopter. I watched the same two guys I had seen earlier still playing cards by lantern light. Two Hummers and a helo meant that these guys were just on guard watching the vehicles. I was about twenty feet away, behind one of the big piles of firewood that I had covered with a blue tarp myself, not a week ago.

"Did the L.T. say where they took the prisoners?"

Prisoners? Now I don't know what a fucking doornail is, but my mom used to say *Dead as a doornail* to me all the time. *When your father gets home and sees this, you're dead as a doornail.* Yup, fuck these assholes. Doornails. All of 'em.

"No, but it's gotta be back at the Herc."

"What about the hot one?"

"Same I would think."

The first one sighed. "Shame."

"Time is it?" the first one asked a couple of minutes later.

Guy looked at his watch, flipping his cards so the other guy could see. Second guy was oblivious. "Time to check in." He picked up a radio and made a call. "Command, this is One checking in, over."

One, Command copies, check in confirmed.

They went back to playing their game, and I moved back into the tree line and waited some more.

Ten minutes or so later one of them stood, throwing his hand down and stretching. "Fuckin' cheater. Gotta see a man about a horse." The other guy laughed and leaned back in his camp chair.

Finally, luck was on my side. This asshole was coming straight at me. He moved into the trees, unbuckled his pants, and squatted down. The only sound he or I made was a muffled *MMMFFF!* as I covered his mouth and jerked his head back with my left hand. Pain shot through my broken left arm, but I'm thinking his pain was worse when I drove my SOG hilt deep into his throat and sawed back like I had seen Remo do before. He struggled briefly, more pain shooting through my arm, but he bled out in less than fifteen seconds. I drove the knife into both eyes to make sure he wouldn't surprise me later. I checked him over, but the only thing I took were his radio and six fat zip ties.

"Come on, man, pinch it off, I'm kicking your ass here!"

Oh, I'ma pinch something off, you dirty pouch full of dick tips. Maybe your nuts. I felt a tear come to my eye, but I was pissed, not sad. I wiped it away, but in the darkness couldn't see my hand. Let's face it, Dear Reader, we both know what color it was.

In the movies, either the good guy or the bad guy is always able to sneak up on the guards. I mean, do they have a Stupid Guard Farm where they purchase these dick heads? Why are they always oblivious?

Me? I wouldn't have gone off by myself in unfamiliar territory to drop a deuce anyway, for fear of getting something important chomped off by a wayward zombie. Even if one of my buddies did, I would have watched his ass (literally) while he was so vulnerable. AND, when this guy called out to his pal, and his pal didn't answer, all sorts of red flags would have gone up.

I had my suppressor on the back of his head as he looked down at a weak two pair in his poker hand. Aces and eights. Fucking classic.

"Please start to yell or something so I can blow your fucking mind out."

The guy swallowed, but smartly said nothing.

"On your knees, Fuckknuckles, hands on your head." He complied and I kicked him forward so he was on his belly. "Hands behind your back." I sat on him and used the zip ties to bind his wrists, then his ankles. I used a second one to double up on his wrists. I yanked him up, a bit unkindly, and began my questioning.

He didn't even look at me.

"How many men did you bring? Where are they? Where are my friends? Did you kill any of them? Why are you here?"

Standard questions that you knew I was going to ask him. He didn't say shit.

"Fine." I pulled out my knife and showed it to him, wiggling it in front of his face. His eyes got big, but he didn't say anything. I moved behind him and cut a piece of cloth from his shirt which was draped over the open window of one of the Hummers. I also liberated a black balaclava.

"Open your mouth."

He looked away from me, so I thumped him on the temple with the butt of the SOG. He opened his mouth, and when he did, I shoved the big hunk of shirt in it. Duct tape would have been ideal, but I didn't have the time to go fishing through the vehicles for some. I fastened two of the zip ties together, then threaded it through his mouth securing at the back of his head. He wouldn't be making any sounds.

"Do I really have to do this?"

He looked away, so I stood him up. I sighed, shook my head, and shot him in the left foot. The suppressed shot seemed loud, but I knew nobody would hear it out here. He screamed a muffled scream and collapsed, trying to inch away from me.

"And just so you know I'm not fucking around…" I shot him in the right foot.

I had never tortured anyone before. I didn't know if I was good at it or not, but as previously stated, I didn't have tons of time.

"Listen up, Chief, I put holes in your feet, that's all. They'll heal. Next are your knees, and when that happens, you're dead. At some point, you're going to have to run, everybody does, and you'll never run again with no knees. After your knees, we move up a tad. You with me, Dog?" He nodded quickly.

Okay, so trying to cut off a thick zip tie from around a guy's head is damn difficult with a knife. I was able to do it, but he was bleeding from the scalp before I was done.

"How many are you?" I asked him in my calmest voice.

"Eighteen," he said between teeth that were clamped shut, "but six went back to the plane when we were done."

"Where's the plane?"

"At an airfield near Raymondville. Bell Airfield, I think."

"Did you kill any of my friends?"

He looked at me for the briefest of seconds, hesitated, and said, "No."

"How did you find us?"

"Tracked the group we were hunting by satellite since they left the Gulf. They ended up here."

"Who tracked us?"

"I don't know, all we got was orders handed down and we followed them."

I shook my head. "Douche."

It was time to get this show on the road. I had some other dickweeds to deal with if this one was telling the truth.

I stood and looked around, weighing options.

"You... you can't leave me here like this. If one of them comes along, I'm helpless!"

"Asshole, I care less about you than I do for an individually wrapped plastic spork from KF motherfucking C."

I whacked him in the side of the head with my handgun. He went down hard, but started doing this moaning thing, so I hit him again, and he went silent. This guy also had zip ties, and I put another two around his mouth with the piece of shirt stuck in there.

I would have to be quick. The check in was probably every half hour, and I had inconveniently taken out the checker. I searched the Hummers and the Blackhawk for some night vision, but came up empty, so I skulked up on the main house. The front door was gone, but there was a guard sitting in one of the chairs on the farmer's porch. We had just improved on all the defenses for the main house, so it was decidedly opportune that they were missing the door.

I could hear some people inside talking about the radio and how to fix it. Someone must have either disabled it, or it was hit by stray weapons fire.

I knew the porch boards creaked on the left side, so I had to come in from the right. I snuck up and over the side around the corner from him. Peeking around the corner, I could see that he was cleaning his nails with his knife. He was just a kid. Fuck.

The MP5 was quieter than the Sig Sauer, so I trained the SMG on his head. I got to within about four feet of him before something gave me away. He looked up and right at me, dropped the knife, and put both hands on the hand-made, wooden chair.

"Don't," I whispered.

A sharp intake of breath could have meant a yell, so I put his brains on the side of Deek's house. The boy couldn't have been twenty yet.

"The hell was that?" I heard from inside. "Moore, what was that?"

Thing's went to shit fast when an armed asshole came out on the porch. He looked left and I stitched a quick burst into his side. He smashed into the door frame, and I hurried inside, giving him one in the dome on the way past. The commotion didn't go unnoticed, and three guys came into the great room from Darcy's radio area. I blasted all three of them, but this time, I let go with a big burst. Shit broke as the rounds passed through the men or missed. It was too loud to ignore. Somebody must have heard.

My superior mathematical skills told me that if the dude I shot in the feet wasn't lying, there were five assholes left here, and at least six at the plane.

I searched, but didn't find them on the ground floor. What I did find was the word PRISON scrawled in black on both the ceiling in the kitchen, and the wall in the great room.

I had been doing a little creeping, and some skulking, and now it was time for a bit of slinking. I might even tiptoe. I was standing on the top floor landing in under five seconds. The first room held no one, but the second had a guy sleeping in the top bunk and a guy sitting up and rubbing his eyes on the bottom. He saw me with my weapon and his eyes went wide. He put his hands up and I nodded for him to come to me. I zip tied him, wrists and ankles, then poked his pal in the back.

"Fuck off," he told me.

I looked at his pal quizzically, and he shrugged, so I poked the sleeping guy again.

He rolled over saying, "I told you to…" I put the barrel of the SMG right against his nose and his eyes crossed as he looked at it. I would have smiled if I wasn't so pissed and scared.

I trussed them both up to the bed, using the same trick I had with foot-guy from outside, but I left the mouth of one of them available. I was out of ties anyway.

"I've accounted for two guards by the vehicles, two by the front door, three in the radio room, and the two of you," I told them. "But I seem to be missing three." They looked at each other. "Where are they?"

"Patrol."

"When will they be back?"

He was looking at me weird. "I dunno." Then his eyes went wide as he saw my eyes.

"Holy shit, you're infected!"

His buddy squinted at me, then they both tried to get as far away from me as they could.

I smiled. "Yup. Make a fuk'n sound and I come back here and bite you."

Kill them, I heard in my head. *Don't leave them alive to come for you later.*

It had been Remo's voice, and he was right, but I couldn't do it.

I found some hundred mile per hour tape in a pack on the dresser, and bound the shit out of both of them on top of the zip ties, including their mouths.

After I checked the rest of the rooms, I moved cautiously downstairs. There were some odd noises coming from the porch, so I checked and found a zombie eating one of the dead guys. It appeared to be just one, so I shot it, but my wariness went up tenfold. It had gotten inside our unfinished walls, so maybe there were more. They did tend to travel in packs.

I moved outside the house and waited by the big fountain for the last three guys. I had no illusions that I was Remo. I know who I am, and what my capabilities are, then and now. These guys weren't Remo either. They were soldiers who had survived the plague, which makes them badass in and of itself, but they still weren't all that. I was able to take out most of them, and I'm me.

But why had that one stray zombie been munching on the dead dude? I took a quick peek behind me to make sure there wasn't a swarm of them bearing down on me. All I could see was the barn and dead horses. I hate to say it, but I hope Shaitan made it out. I looked back at the dead assholes thirty feet in front of me with hate.

These fuckers. They were still killing people because of me. Not only that, but what I had predicted for this place had come true. I stayed and they found me. They may or may not have murdered some of my friends, but they sure as shit killed the horses, and they were going to answer for that.

Movement from the right stole my attention from my thoughts. Two of three remaining assholes were in view. They had noticed something was up and were on full alert, crouching and looking in all directions. I lifted the MP5, a smile creasing the corner of my mouth. Something poked me in the back of the head, I almost pissed myself, and somebody said, "Don't. Hands up." I put my hands up and he called to his buddies, "Over here. He was about to kill you two fucking idiots. I told you we had to come in from the front, not the side." This guy looked tougher than the others, and was wearing an olive drab do-rag and a black T-shirt.

They came over, disarmed me, and one of them punched me in the stomach. I doubled over, and the guy who had put the gun to my head a moment ago (that was the poke) said, "Enough. Orders are we bring him in alive."

The one who hit me looked a tad angry. "Fuck him. He was killing our friends and we shot him."

Do-Rag harrumphed. "You want to explain that to the brass?"

"Fine!" the puncher said. "But I can still beat the shit out of him. He can go back *barely* alive."

He grabbed my arm and it was all over. I twisted my hand over his, brought my other elbow down on his elbow, and broke it. My knee came up fast into his face, forcing his head up, and I grabbed his bleeding chin with my right hand. I put my left on the side of his head, and before anybody could do anything, I applied a vicious twist and broke his neck. Thanks, Remo. Pain once again made its presence known and screeched its way up my arm.

"Jesus!" the third guy exclaimed.

They both had their guns on me, and each backed up a step. I folded my arms, a stupid act which resulted in extreme pain, but looked really cool. "Who's next?"

If you're really dumb and aren't getting this, I had just been Remo-level fucking awesome.

Breathing heavily, the guy in front of me said, "We should just—" and his head popped like a balloon full of gooey shit. There was an extremely loud report, and Do-Rag spun to face this new threat.

A figure clad in jeans and a T-shirt levered another round into his rifle and put a grapefruit-sized hole in Do-Rag's chest. The figure stepped into view, and guess who it was?

Nope. Not Remo. It was Daniel.

"C'mon, they'll have heard that."

"I killed the rest of them, except three guys that I—"

"Not them," he pointed behind me and to the right, "them!" I glanced in the indicated direction and saw a few dozen dead people stumbling our way. My ears were still ringing from the gigantic rifle shots from a few seconds ago, but I could just make out the cries and moans of the dead. They were a hundred feet away.

Daniel helped me grab my stuff, and we hustled back behind us. There was no front door on the main residence, so I was thinking we should head to the guest quarters, but Daniel pulled me back toward the pump house by the pond. There were three horses there, one with a guy draped over the saddle, tied down. Initially, I thought it was James, but it was the guy I had left tied up by the helicopter. One of the horses gave me a dirty look. Yeah, you can see where this is going. Shaitan.

I looked for Daniel's brother. "Where's James?"

"Dead. We need to get out of here and find where they took everybody."

"Do you know where Bell Airfield is?"

"Yeah?"

"That's where they are."

We both mounted the horses, Daniel leading the way.

"Southwest, then," was all he said.

We stopped to pick up the stuff I had taken from Travis' shack, and we were on our way toward our friends.

HERCULES

"You got it?"

Our prisoner looked at me, hate overcoming his fear and pain. He crushed his teeth together when he replied, "Yeah, I got it."

He must have been in agony with a bullet hole in each foot, but he didn't bitch about it. He wouldn't be running away from us anytime soon either. In fact, he wasn't going to be doing any running at all.

"You fuck it up, or give us away, and we leave you here and start making a shit ton of noise. You got that too?"

"Yeah."

I glanced at Daniel. He had a pair of binoculars up to his eyes and was surveying a C130J Hercules on the runway of Bell Airfield. It was just parked at one end of the tarmac next to a huge red pickup truck, all buttoned up and waiting. No doubt for the assholes back at the Double Hoof to bring me in. There were two zombies walking on the runway, but other than that, it was clear of infected. We were directly behind it, maybe a hundred yards in the tall grass next to some type of storage shed.

There had been four check-ins via the radio while we traveled from the ranch to the airfield. When the first one came in, Daniel put his gigantic Bowie knife between our prisoner's legs and said, "Do it right." The guy had given a code, but I don't know if it was a panic code or the OK code. We'd find out shortly.

I put my hand on my friend's shoulder and he passed me the binocs. "Sorry about your brother, Daniel."

"He died well," was his reply. Daniel looked at the douche we had trussed up. "It's time." Daniel sat behind him, wrapped his legs around the guy, and put his knife under his chin. I snipped the zip ties, and passed him his own radio.

"Sky High, this is F.O.B. We are under attack by a large contingent of infected. We have sustained losses and need reinforcements, over!" The guy sounded a bit scared.

F.O.B., Sky High. Authentication is required. Over.

"Sky High, F.O.B. Code is zulu-alpha-niner-niner! We need a distraction and emergency evac ASAP!"

Evac confirmed, ETA thirty mics. Sit tight.

The guy had played it off very well. The back of the plane opened a few minutes later, and a Humvee rolled out with a few men in it. It looked like there were five, but that didn't make sense. There were eleven back at the Double Hoof, and one tied up a foot from me, which meant there should be six guys here. Nobody, and I mean nobody, would leave a bunch of people tied up on a plane with one guard. Especially when two of those people were Remo and Ship. I could see two other guys with guns moving around, and a bunch of people sitting on the fold-down seats that lined the side of the cargo bay. They all had their hands behind them, and one of them was fucking huge.

So this guy had been full of shit when he told me there were eighteen bad guys. I rounded on him, putting my suppressor against his balls. "Eighteen of you, huh?"

"Plus the two Airforce guys, yeah."

I was pissed. "What, they don't fuk'n count?"

"I guess you don't know Airforce guys."

Daniel snorted laughter. "Get ready."

One of the armed guards strolled down the walkway and shot the two infected that had come stumbling when the cargo ramp opened. I couldn't even hear the suppressed shots from where we were.

The shooter started to come back to the plane, when Daniel used the scoped hunting rifle I had liberated from Travis to pop one guard in the cargo bay. The shot was LOUD, and the other guard in the plane looked out toward us when his buddy dropped. One of the people on the seats was on the second guard immediately, and had him down before Daniel drilled the last guy.

We left the Holy Footed guy where he was, and sprinted for the plane. I didn't know if there were snipers in the area, or if some douche was inside and would shut the door on us. We made it quickly, and there were several smiles. It looked as if everyone was here, and I did a silent head count.

Daniel used his cutters to free everyone, and there were hugs-a-plenty to go around. I had totally forgotten that these folks all thought I was dead or still missing. Ship gave me the stinkeye, but still lifted me off the ground effortlessly, and squeezed me until I couldn't breathe. He smiled and nodded.

Alvarez folded his arms and shook his head. "Like a bad penny." Ship and Remo made their way up front to the cockpit to check shit out. Everybody else grabbed their formerly confiscated gear from behind the webbing on one of the bulkheads of the plane.

The folks from the Double Hoof were all getting their stuff ready, and I looked at them, incredulous. I put my hand on Deek's shoulder. "Uhh… Deek? What's happening?"

It was his turn for incredulity, and he shrugged. "Gonna go home and evict some assholes."

I shook my head. "Deek, the Double Hoof crawls with dead people."

"Kill them too then." He hugged Kate and stared at me. "These guys are headed for Alcatraz to do I don't know what. They said communications are spotty, but they're going to have some kind of naval carrier group move from Panama up to San Francisco. They said it would take a month." Deek sighed and regarded each of the folks in the plane as they did whatever they were doing. "You better get there quick, son. Come on back this way if you ever have the need, of if you just wanna say hi." He picked up his cowboy hat, and then did something I never would have thought: he hugged me. "Javi didn't make it, did he?"

I shook my head. "No. the guy who pulled me out of the wreckage told me he died."

Deek sighed, "Thought as much."

The Double Hoof folks hugged all of us. When Kate finished hugging me, she passed me a piece of paper. "For you," she said with a gigantic smile. I glanced at the paper, and it was lat/long coordinates for the Double Hoof.

The group got into a red pickup that had been used to bring everybody to the airfield. It started right up and they all waved as they drove away. I wanted to help them, but I also wanted to warn my friend Dallas and Alcatraz about what was coming. Most people would say *tough shit* for Dallas, but I don't do tough shit, and Remo had friends that had travelled to the prison island, and they needed to be warned as well. I knew he wouldn't let that shit go.

Daniel and Matt stayed behind to take the horses back. Daniel hefted Holy Foot over his shoulder, and tossed him unkindly on the ramp of the C130J. "You can have this one. Better lock this thing up, you'll be having company soon."

I shook his hand and he got on his horse. Shaitan gave me a final glance with his huge horse eyes. I smiled and flipped him off. Prick. I would miss him.

Richy and Chloe came up to me with Donna. "Fuel tank is full, and there are thirty-six full fuel cans up on those pallets." She thumbed over her shoulder at the shrink-wrapped cans. "Ship says he can fly this thing, but he wants to keep the pilot alive just in case." There had been no discussion about staying on at the Double Hoof.

"Thanks for not being dead," Chloe told me.

"Yeah," Richy added, "who else can show me how to hot wire a car and shit?"

Donna cuffed him on the back of the head. "Language, Richard." He smiled as he rubbed his head and strode off with his sister.

"Richard?" I asked.

She threw her arms around me again. Her second hug lingered a bit longer than the first one. "I knew you weren't dead."

"How?"

She looked bewildered. "What?"

"How did you know I wasn't dead?"

"Because you would have already pissed off Death, and he would have sent you back."

I kissed her on the forehead. "I think Death is on hiatus. He's gonna be pissed when he gets back and sees all this shit. Somebody's getting fired."

We both looked at the rear ramp as it closed.

Alvarez and Kat came back to us. Everybody had their gear, and I asked about it.

Kat shrugged. "They made us bring it. They said we wouldn't be coming back, and it was safer where they were taking us."

"How are we settled for weapons?"

"There's two racks of M4s, three crates of ammo, and some M9 tacticals," Alvarez offered. "They obviously confiscated our weapons, and they're all back at the ranch."

The engines on the giant plane started with a cough, and it got loud. Remo came back and told everybody to sit down and buckle up, so we did. He did a check on us, and flashed Ship a thumbs up. The jarhead made sure both Holy Feet and the pilot were trussed well, and he buckled them into seats too. The pilot was still out from when Remo had jumped him.

My buddy must have noticed me favoring my left arm, and he pointed at it and raised an eyebrow. I nodded my head at Donna trying to get him to fuck off, and he got the message. He moved forward to sit with Ship in the cockpit and the twins flanked us. Richy pulled his knife and began cleaning his nails while he stared at our two captives. He glanced at me, then back at them.

"They killed the dogs."

The earth was falling away from us two minutes later. I guess a preflight checklist was for pussies.

ALAMEDA

"Wait, what?"

I could barely hear her over the roar of the engines. It was cold in the back of the airplane too, and that was something I wasn't used to recently.

"Yeah, well, I don't have an X-ray machine, but it sure feels broken. That fall was like, sixty feet, and there was a shit-ton of bus around me."

Donna's face said she couldn't believe I was such a dumbass. "And you're telling me this now? Let me see."

She was on my right, so we unbuckled and switched seats. Shaking her head and sighing like I was the biggest moron on earth, she gently lifted my arm and ran her hands over it, pushing here and there. It fucking hurt and I let her know it.

"Pussy. Shut up. I disagree with your diagnosis, Doctor Dumbass, it isn't broken."

"But Travis said…"

"Did Travis go to medical school and then work on an oil rig where roughnecks broke parts of themselves on a daily basis? No? Then I'll pretend to be the medical professional."

Fully scolded, I kept my mouth shut as we moved through the sky. We had been in the air for about five hours. We'd be landing soon, and Ship already had the pilot up front with him and Remo.

Donna had bandaged Holy Feet's, whose name is Ellis, feet with stuff she took from the onboard medic station. He still couldn't really walk, but I don't care. Watching her take his boots off was fun.

"Ten minutes." I heard through the PA system.

I realized I had no idea where we were landing, and my nuts shriveled. "Hang on," I told Donna and hurried up front. "Remo, is this a fucking water landing?"

"No."

"Where are we—?"

He looked back at me. "Alameda. Nice long runways. Go sit down." I looked at the unfamiliar pilot, who was flying this thing next to Ship, and I decided to flee.

I was moving back to sit down, when a hand came down on my shoulder. It hadn't hit me hard, but I was bruised all over, so it hurt. Remo was standing behind me. "Daniel told me about the guy you did with your hands back at the Double Hoof. He was impressed."

I raised an eyebrow. "You realize you just made it sound like I jerked some dude off, right?"

"Ever the smartass. Well done."

"Yeah, your masturbation training has paid off. Come sit next to us."

We planted our asses next to Donna and the kids. Alvarez sat across from us and shouted over, "There are eight M4s loaded and ready. Sixty extra mags as well, divvied up into the packs with rations for each for a few days. As soon as we land, everybody grab a weapon and a pack. Sidearms are in the pack holsters on the right side of each. Suppressors are already on, and there is one spare suppressor for each M9 in a holster also on the right side. Three extra mags each on the left."

We all nodded. I looked at the kids. "You guys arm up too." I looked directly at Richy. "Everybody gets a gun."

Chloe looked at me and asked through a yawn, "Water landing?"

"Nope. Full-on runway. Piece of cake."

"I like cake," she replied, and we began to descend.

The tires made that squeak sound that they always make when they hit the tarmac. We zipped down the runway feeling the plane slow, and soon, we were stopped.

"We're between two major cities," Remo said as the engines wound down. "There's no way every living and dead thing in the area didn't just hear us land. We need to get out of here as quickly and quietly as possible."

Each person, now equipped with a pack and a rifle, nodded in understanding.

Kat was looking at Holy Feet and the pilot. "What about them?"

"Yeah, what about us?" Holy Feet demanded.

"Spork, asshole. You're lucky to be alive. Take this plane and fly off into the wild blue yonder."

"We don't have enough fuel," the pilot said, "or I would."

"All your problems. Good luck."

I heard the back ramp servos whine, turned, and almost bumped into Remo and Richy. Everybody else was at the back of the plane waiting to see what greeted us when the ramp fully opened. Remo looked me in the eyes drew his sidearm and spit out his toothpick. Richy pulled his knife. My blood went cold.

The jarhead moved to make it past me, but I stood in his way, folding my arms, which again resulted in some pain. "No."

His features were deadpan as he asked, "No?"

"No. Not only are you not going to kill these assholes, but we're going to leave them a couple of guns, some ammo, and a couple of days rations. They were just following orders. You remember orders?"

Like a striking Mamba, his hand was on my not-broken arm. He gave it a little squeeze, and I grimaced.

Now he did raise an eyebrow. "Broken?"

"Donna says no."

"K." He turned on his heel and strode to the back of the plane, weapon still drawn.

"They killed the dogs," Richy reiterated.

"I know, Rich, but this would be straight-up murder." He sighed. It sounded like relief, then nodded and followed Remo to the ramp.

I rounded on the two military douches. "There are two M9s in the locker under that seat." I pointed, then looked at Holy Feet. "This is the second time I've saved your miserable life. A third will not occur. Button this heap up as soon as my boots are on the ground or I'll drill both of you."

I moved down to join my friends, watching the guys behind me the whole time. They hadn't moved.

When the ramp was fully deployed, we headed for a set of structures to the southeast. The engines on the Hercules began to spin up right away. I guess the pilot didn't like being on an island surrounded by gigantic cities. I didn't either, and I wondered if I had just killed everyone by bringing them here. Then I remembered that this had been Remo's plan as much as mine.

So basically, if we all get eaten, it's on the leatherneck.

As we moved southeast, I could see there were some cars sporadically parked in several parking lots. I didn't see any moving figures yet, but I knew they were there. They also knew we were here, so they were on the way. We needed to find some shelter and wait out the dead, or better yet, a boat and get to Alcatraz. I couldn't see the prison island from my vantage, but I knew it was somewhere to the north in the bay. Hopefully, it wasn't as dead as the rest of the world.

We were between Oakland and San Francisco, and the only thing I could hear was the plane I had just gotten out of. It shot into the air at a very steep angle and was flying away to the south quickly.

As soon as the Hercules was far enough away, an unnatural quiet came over the area.

None of us realized that we had all stopped for a moment to watch the aircraft, and our safety, leave. The quiet was shattered as Richy took a step forward, crunching his sneaker on the sandy concrete.

"What?" he asked as everyone stared at him. "Are we going to stay here or get moving?"

"Look," Kat said and pointed to a building across and to the left of the massive parking lot. A lone figure had noticed us and begun its arduous trek in our direction.

Richy shrugged. "There's only one."

"There's never only one, Rich," his sister warned.

Two more rounded the corner of the building, then another, then another. Some began coming from to the right, and I could see movement directly in front of us as well.

"That structure," Alvarez told us and pointed to an older brick building, "move!"

The edifice looked as if it were constructed under the supervision of Pharaohs it was so old. Tons of brick-arched windows on the lower level and several doors meant many access points, but our time was limited as the dead had most assuredly found us now. They were coming from even more directions than before.

We all hustled toward what we hoped was a quick refuge from the infected. Remo was still hobbling a bit, I could see it, but he would never say shit about it. Ship got to the door first, and was about to Hulk it open, when Kat put a hand on his arm. He looked at her quizzically, and she shook her head in that *what a dumbass* way that only she could pull off. She put her hand on the door handle, and everybody pointed their weapons at it. Kat turned the handle, pushed the door open and moved out of the way. It was bright inside.

Alvarez shouldered his rifle and cupped his hands in front of his mouth, "Anybody home?"

No noises from the dead or anyone living prompted us to go inside and pan around with our tac lights. They were completely unnecessary, the entire roof of the place having caved in some time ago. The sun streamed through the convertible structure, illuminating the small lobby we were in, and especially the stairwell that climbed up to a partially broken second floor. The entire left side of the second floor had collapsed into the first, leaving wreckage at an angle which was too steep to ascend.

My nuts shriveled when I heard the scream of a Runner which was quite near. I wondered if I were the only guy who suffered from this, and if it would ever go away.

"Up," Remo ordered. "The stairs."

"Stairs?" Donna exclaimed. "Are you fucking kidding? Those are—" Ship fired his M9 into the face of a thing that had tried to get in after us. They had been closer than we thought.

Remo made for the stairs, which didn't look like they would hold Chloe, let alone Ship. He began to climb them immediately. He looked back at us. "Now!"

The marine made it to the top of the steps without issue and we followed. Ship came last, and the whole apparatus creaked and groaned in protest until he reached the top. Remo and Alvarez began to push old desks to the edge of the landing for a barricade.

"Roof access here!" Chloe called out, and I realized that the kids had split off from the group to explore our surroundings. We hadn't cleared it up here yet and I made that known. I went with the kids and Kat to check shit out because my arm wasn't up to snuff, and I wasn't about to make it worse by moving furniture.

I could hear the boys scraping desks and bookcases across the rickety floor behind us. There were six rooms, and one had a huge hole in the floor, but other than that, the search was uneventful. We came back to the stairwell to reconnoiter which was when the door we had just come through started getting a beat down. It lasted about eight seconds before the latch broke and the dead poured in.

There were sixteen of them, and they saw us and started their noises. The more diligent of the group made their way to the steps fast, and Remo started shooting them with his sidearm. The M4s weren't suppressed, so it was up to the pistols to save us. Anybody would could get off a shot fired into the crowd, and they were all down in just a moment.

Richy put the back of his hand over his nose and looked away in disgust. The dead had brought their stink with them, and it was awful. More infected had found us and they filed into the lobby. I moved to the edge of the broken floor to get a better vantage for my aim. Everybody else was by the stairs because that's where the attackers were focused. I fired three rounds more before I went empty. It was like shooting fish in a barrel, but more fish were spawning, and we were already through about fifty rounds of ammo.

I ejected my magazine, stuck it in the mag holster, and slapped in another. I heard this weird sound, and suddenly, I was on my ass sliding because the friggin' edge of the floor had given way. I hit the bottom floor and was on my feet fast, the dust thick in the air.

"No!" I heard Donna scream, and fire suddenly focused on the dead that were coming for a free lunch.

I swear the bastards were smiling in anticipation of a meal. They came slowly, but that's a relative term when you have nowhere to run. My back was to the floor that had just collapsed, and the dead were on three sides of me.

"Switch to the rifles!" Alvarez yelled. A couple of the things looked up, but only momentarily, as their vittles decided to make a run for it. I dashed to the right, heading for one of those pretty, brick-arched windows I mentioned before. The rifled fire started when I plowed through four of the things, not even getting a scratch. One got her nasty fingers on my pack, but they tore off. There was no glass left in the window, so I performed a fantastic dive through, landing on my hurt arm. I was trying to will my agony away for the briefest of moments, and didn't notice the things advancing on me until one of their shoes scraped across the concrete.

Thinking that this was really unfair, I dragged myself up before they could chow on me. I ran for it and they chased me. I hightailed it around a corner, slammed into one of them, and shoved him away. The pack was getting heavy, so I ditched it, figuring I could come back for it later.

A small pack of them filled the street in front of me. I really didn't want to run down the alley to my left, but I had no choice. Of course, it was a horrible decision because the things rounded the far corner, trapping me. I looked for a door and found one, but it wouldn't budge. I kicked and kicked until my kicker was sore, but I was screwed.

A calmness came over me. This was not the first time this had happened. The first six shots from the Beretta were quiet, but this suppressor burned-out quickly from these and all the other rounds I had just put through it. There was no time to change it out, so I slapped in my last mag and dropped as many as I could. I did pretty well. In hindsight, I shouldn't have given Chloe my MP5 in lieu of an M4, but it was easier for her to carry and shoot. My M4 was on the floor of the building I had just run out of.

I glanced behind me. Fifty feet. Thirty feet in front, but there were a good dozen or so of the pus bags, and they were packed in tight.

I smiled. "Come on, then. Come on!"

BUGS' BUDDY

This is a zombie story and I'm the fucking hero. I can't die, right?

"HOWDY, PARTNERS!" a new voice bellowed, and every one of the zombies turned to see who would dare interrupt their midday meal. I actually had to stand on my tip toes to see over the taller infected.

A blond kid, maybe twenty-five, stood in the alley behind the ones in front of me wearing sunglasses. He had a Louisville slugger, and he whacked the shit out of the closest infected to him. The thing dropped, and the kid shouted, "Nine twelve!" He destroyed another and yelled, "Thirteen! Nine thirteen! This is epic!"

He waded in among them, and I swear to God they just turned away from him and started back at me. Now *that* shit was unfair.

"Fourteen! Fifteen! Woo hoo!"

I decided to join the fray and stabbed the one reaching for me with my SOG. I got two more before they got me, but there were only two left and the kid got both of them as they brought me down. Shockingly, the fat one landed on my arm. This was getting tiresome, but the pain kept me straight.

The kid helped me get the nasty thing off of me and stretched his paw down to me. I took it with my good arm, and he hauled me up pointing behind me.

"Oh shit!" I said really fast. The closest was a foot away and did that undead lunge. The kid now had a sawed-off shotgun in his hand and it went BOOM!

He smiled a toothy smile, and I saw a jagged scar on his cheek. "Come on, man. You need to vacate the premises!"

I would like to say we ran for the end of the alley, but when I turned to see where he was, he had the shotgun in a holster on his back and was pointing to the sky with one hand with the bat in the other.

Fucker was calling his shot.

I did a quick survey of the area and there were no infected on this side, so I yelled to him, "Come on!"

He shouted over his shoulder, "Be right there!" Then he spit in his hand and smoked another ten or so of the things. They were walking right past him to get to me.

What the fuck. I repeat: What the fuck.

He pushed through the throng and ran to me. Out of breath, he said, "Takes... takes a toll on you swinging like that. Know what I mean?"

I was fucking flabbergasted.

"What the fuck—?"

"Whoa there, Big Fella. Rated G, ok?"

The ones he hadn't killed were getting closer and I pointed at them.

"Yeah, let's go get your friends." We trotted off back toward the building I had been in before.

He noticed me cradling my arm and pointed at it. "Are you bitten? Because I promise it won't go well for you later."

"No, I'm not. Hurt it earlier in the week."

"Ah, well, then you'll be just dandy."

I could hear rifle fire, and saw Remo and Alvarez turn a corner first followed by the rest of my group. They noticed me with this guy and skidded to a stop.

Remo pointed at him. "Who's he?"

"I didn't catch his—"

"Billy!" the kid interrupted. "Name's Billy. You folks sure did make a ruckus with your GIGANTIC aero-plane, which I saw take off without you, I might add. Half of Oakland is crossing the bridge to say hi, and not the good half. I got a boat, and if you want to get off this island, and let me tell you, you do, then come with me." His jaw dropped and he pointed at Ship. "Put an orange coat on this guy and you got yourself a Gossamer."

Several of my group looked at each other, and Ship looked insulted, but the kid shook his head. "Look, I don't..." he noticed Richy and Chloe and rounded on me, disbelief all over his face. "You brought *children* to Alameda? BANQUET MUCH? Come on, my kids are watching the boat, I can't leave them too long. There are worse things than the dead around too, and they won't be far behind."

I could hear the dead behind us, but couldn't see them yet. There was no doubt they were coming.

"Boat!" Billy said. "Remember the part about the boat?"

He moved off, and I followed him. Nobody else moved, so I told them to.

"We don't know him," Remo said catching up to me.

"Yeah, well, he didn't know me either, and he just saved my ass. Besides, he waltzed through a gang of pus bags and they wouldn't touch him."

We didn't say anything else until we reached the angled stone retaining wall that slipped down steeply into the bay. There was a forty-foot fishing boat off the island maybe a hundred feet. Billy cupped his hands and yelled out to the boat, "Mickey! This is Bugs! Come get us!"

Two kids, one definitely less than ten, the other about twelve, sat up and looked at us. The older one ran forward and the boat started up as the younger one struggled with the anchor. The bigger one came back and helped her, and soon the boat, piloted by a child, was on the way.

"Do *not* put your feet in the water," Billy ordered. "I don't know who's down there."

A hand-made gangway was pushed from the boat to the island. Billy grabbed the end of it and pulled it secure, then made his way across the four-foot gap. Chloe tried to go across first, but Donna grabbed her shoulder. Remo went across and inspected everything in a heartbeat. He motioned for us to come aboard.

When we were all sitting or standing on the open stern, Billy opened a white cooler and passed us all a Coke, noticed we weren't drinking, then grabbed the one he had given Alvarez, popped the top, and took a sip. "Want me to taste them all? I mean, they're sealed for Pete's sake."

I popped the top and guzzled a bit. The soda was piss warm.

He seemed delighted at my trust. "What's the plan, fellow seafarers? Where would you like to go?"

"Alcatraz," I answered. "We have friends there."

Billy brightened further. "Me too!"

Richy gave a huge belch, and the two kids that Billy had on his boat both smiled. I followed Richy's burp with an absolute gaseous explosion from my belly, then Ship put us all to shame. No doubt he could have propelled this boat across the bay with one burp if the tub had a sail. Fucker always has to one-up me. Bastard can burp like a champ, but he can't say shit.

"Do you know a guy named Dallas?"

"Pittsburgh? Yeah, of course I know him. He thinks he's from Texas or something. *He talks like this.*" He added in terrible, thick, southern drawl. "Dallas is a big fella, but not as big is your friend here."

Billy looked at Richy and Chloe and narrowed his eyes a little. "Do you two know who Black Jaques Shellacque is?"

"*Sacrebleu*," Chloe said in a French accent and I thought Billy was going to spontaneously combust. He clapped his hands together and kept them there while he opened his mouth and eyes as wide as possible. He looked exactly like a six-year-old kid who had just gotten what they wanted for Christmas.

Billy planted his ass on the deck, crossed his legs, and put his elbows on his knees. He talked to Richy and Chloe for ten minutes about Bugs Bunny cartoons, pulling the other two kids in on the conversation. Alvarez took over the wheel from the young boy, and piloted us north.

Alvarez, Kat, and Donna all looked sort of crossways at each other as the kids spoke to our new friend. The three adults motioned me to come over to them.

"You think this guy is a little... *off*?" asked Kat under her breath.

"I was in prison, Kat. Absolutely everyone thinks I'm evil when I tell them that." I glanced at the back of Billy's head. "Plus, he saved me when it would have been easier to let me get eviscerated. I'm okay with *off*."

We debated a bit for a moment, but in the end, this was Billy's boat. What were we going to do, throw him and his kids overboard and pilfer it like pirates?

I moved back to Billy and put a hand on his shoulder. "Thanks again for saving me."

"I get that a lot," he answered. He was about to say something else, but I interrupted him.

"Can we call to Alcatraz and let them know we're coming? I don't want to be shot at when we pull up to the beach."

"Dock."

I didn't know what he meant. "Huh?"

"Pull up to the dock and nobody will shoot at you. There will be armed folks there to greet you, you'll have to surrender your weapons and gear and spend a day or two in quarantine, and then you'll be fine. We pull up to any of the beaches, and you won't get out of the boat before a sniper bullet takes the top of your head off. We should wait until we get within sight of the island before we call." He glanced around the bay with his hand shading his eyes from the sun, looking for something. "Never know who's listening, and they have boats too. I don't know how to work the radio, do you?"

He looked like he really wanted to know, so I asked Alvarez to teach him. Billy cleared his throat as The Rock came into view off the port bow. We were crossing under the Bay Bridge, and it looked intact.

"Yoo hoo! Alcatraz folks! Rick? Ali? Are you there?"

The answer was immediate, *This is Alcatraz, to whom are we speaking?*

This is Billy! Remember me?

I don't know you, Billy, do you have the call code?

Uhh... no. I just have some folks who want to hang out with you guys. One of 'em says he knows Dallas."

We see a small vessel coming from the southeast, is that you?

"Is it?" he asked Alvarez, who nodded. "Yeah, that's us."

"Please do not attempt to land on the island. A vessel will come out to meet you a quarter-mile out. You will be disarmed and will have to go through mandatory questioning and quarantine if you want to come in."

"Roger, wilco, over and out!" the kid replied. "That was kinda easy." He looked at the other passengers on our boat, then pulled me aside, next to Alvarez and Donna. He looked at his Nike sneakers for a second, then at me. "My price for the ride is that you take the kids with you. They're better off with the folks on Alcatraz. Things are getting difficult in San Francisco."

I was confused. "You're not coming?

"To Alcatraz? Ha! No way."

"Why not?"

He shrugged. "I'm undesirable. I used to be a psycho serial killer and there are a bunch of cops on the island now. They'd lock me up."

This guy was tough to read. He actually sounded serious.

A big pleasure boat, flanked by a small, black military-looking thing began to move out toward the center of the bay from Alcatraz. They called us and we told them to hang on.

Billy was hugging his kids. "This is what we were out here for. You knew it, guys." They both nodded, and the little girl was sobbing. "They'll take great care of you, but you have to take care of each other too." More nodding and sobbing.

Billy stood, shook everybody's hand, grabbed his pack, and hopped off of the stern into a little aluminum dinghy. We were two hundred feet off of a dock to our port side, with Treasure Island way off to our right and Alcatraz in front of us.

"Ugh. Pier 39. Well," he sighed, "haven't checked out the Hard Rock Café yet. Might have some good stuff in there." He untied the little boat and began to row to the dock. It was filled with infected. So much so that they were falling off one at a time and splashing into the salty water. "Tell Sam I said hi, and give Ali a kiss for me!"

My savior rowed off and was soon fastening his line to a piling on the dock.

"Don't worry," the boy informed us, "they won't touch him."

They didn't. He walked past several of the things, climbed a short, wooden ladder, and moved into the teeming masses of infected as if he were fighting the crowd for the bathroom at a rock concert.

Alvarez moved us off quickly, and we met up with the Sea Ray and its inflatable counterpart in fifteen minutes. The little black boat had a light machine gun on a tripod attached to the front of it, and the business end was pointed at us. There were also all kinds of guns on the pleasure craft, but they were pointed less at us and more toward the air. One other thing of note adorned the pretty boat: an extremely large Texan, with an equally huge grin on his face. His arms were folded and he had one eyebrow raised. I couldn't help but mirror his shit-eater, and he nodded at me.

"Looks like ya found yer friends."

"You too, big guy. Clara and Eleanor okay?"

"Fine 'n dandy." He looked the boat over. "Where's the other fella? Tim?" His face fell. "Oh no…"

"Sorry, Dallas, he didn't make it."

Remo threw a line to a guy and they pulled the boats together. Another military guy hopped aboard our boat and stood in front of the jarhead.

"Look who isn't dead," the guy said aloud.

"Butters," Remo said. "Damn, I was hoping you got eaten." They clasped hands and I felt immensely better. Three other well-armed guys and a well-armed woman came to our boat, checked it over, including our packs, and said we were okay.

"Where's Billy?" the pretty, auburn-haired woman asked.

"After saving us all, he took a small boat and rowed back into Hell. Are you Ali or Sam?"

She looked confused, then stuck her hand out. "Ali."

"I'm supposed to kiss you." Donna raised her eyebrows, and I noticed. "Billy asked!" I added quickly.

Dallas came aboard and enveloped me in a bear hug, crushing my injured appendage.

"Damn good to see you, Hoss."

"You too. We kind of have to talk to the man in charge, Dallas. There are some people on their way here, and they might not be friendly."

"Happens all the time. Most of 'em are dead, but not all. Fightin' the dead is easy. The livin' shoot back."

We unhitched the boats and began to move across the bay to the safety of Alcatraz. I had been on an island refuge before, only mine had been fashioned out of steel.

It had been no safer than anywhere else.

ACKNOWLEDGEMENTS

I haven't written a lot of books. More than most, but significantly less than others. As of the time you're reading this, I've had five novels published, and I'm thankful. On each of the five occasions, I was fortunate enough to have a book hit the shelves, the most difficult part of the process was acknowledging all of the wonderful people who helped make it happen. I'm going to attempt that now, so bear with me. Firstly, I need to express gratitude to my family; Wife, Kids, and Parents. My parents made me; my wife and kids made me better. Thank you for your patience and your love. To the folks at Zombiefiend.com: You people are more than helpful, you push. Without those pushes, all of my stories would still be in my head. My head already hurts, so thank you for helping me get the words out. To the Wardroom (wdrmmta.wordpress.com) and homepageofthedead.com, you helped more than you know with advisements and encouragements. To T-Rex: you made my stuff better. Thank you so much for that. To Shelly Loring, you tried so hard to teach me how a comma is used. Thanks for that, and sorry I'm dumb. To Severed Press: I still don't know why you picked me up, but I appreciate that you did. I will sneak in a quick thank you to James Cameron as well, for writing and directing the movie *Aliens*, which is referenced numerous times in this book. Lastly, I need to thank you, Dear Reader. You have, once again, thumbed through the pages of a book that I worked quite diligently on. You persevered through the good (I hope there was lots) and the bad, (I hope there was none) to get here. Hopefully, you read the acknowledgements too…

CHECK OUT OTHER GREAT ZOMBIE NOVELS

RUN
by Rich Restucci

The dead have risen, and they are hungry.

Slow and plodding, they are Legion. The undead hunt the living. Stop and they will catch you. Hide and they will find you. If you have a heartbeat you do the only thing you can: You run.

Survivors escape to an island stronghold: A cop and his daughter, a computer nerd, a garbage man with a piece of rebar, and an escapee from a mental hospital with a life-saving secret. After reaching Alcatraz, the ever expanding group of survivors realize that the infected are not the only threat.

Caught between the viciousness of the undead, and the heartlessness of the living, what choice is there? Run.

THE DEAD WALK THE EARTH
by Luke Duffy

As the flames of war threaten to engulf the globe, a new threat emerges.

A 'deadly flu', the like of which no one has ever seen or imagined, relentlessly spreads, gripping the world by the throat and slowly squeezing the life from humanity.

Eight soldiers, accustomed to operating below the radar, carrying out the dirty work of a modern democracy, become trapped within the carnage of a new and terrifying world.

Deniable and completely expendable. That is how their government considers them, and as the dead begin to walk, Stan and his men must fight to survive.

CHECK OUT OTHER GREAT ZOMBIE NOVELS

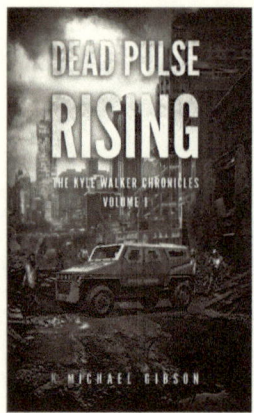

DEAD PULSE RISING
by K. Michael Gibson

Slavering hordes of the walking dead rule the streets of Baltimore, their decaying forms shambling across the ruined city, voracious and unstoppable. The remaining survivors hide desperately, for all hope seems lost... until an armored fortress on wheels plows through the ghouls, crushing bones and decayed flesh. The vehicle stops and two men emerge from its doors, armed to the teeth and ready to cancel the apocalypse.

TOWER OF THE DEAD
by J.V. Roberts

Markus is a hardworking man that just wants a better life for his family. But when a virus sweeps through the halls of his high-rise apartment complex, those plans are put on hold. Trapped on the sixteenth floor with no hope of rescue, Markus must fight his way down to safety with his wife and young daughter in tow.

Floor by bloody floor they must battle through hordes of the hungry dead on a terrifying mission to survive the TOWER OF THE DEAD.

 SEVEREDPRESS

CHECK OUT OTHER GREAT ZOMBIE NOVELS

900 MILES
by S. Johnathan Davis

John is a killer, but that wasn't his day job before the Apocalypse.

In a harrowing 900 mile race against time to get to his wife just as the dead begin to rise, John, a business man trapped in New York, soon learns that the zombies are the least of his worries, as he sees first-hand the horror of what man is capable of with no rules, no consequences and death at every turn.

Teaming up with an ex-army pilot named Kyle, they escape New York only to stumble across a man who says that he has the key to a rumored underground stronghold called Avalon..... Will they find safety? Will they make it to Johns wife before it's too late?

Get ready to follow John and Kyle in this fast paced thriller that mixes zombie horror with gladiator style arena action!

WHITE FLAG OF THE DEAD
by Joseph Talluto

Millions died when the Enillo Virus swept the earth. Millions more were lost when the victims of the plague refused to stay dead, instead rising to slaughter and feed on those left alive. For survivors like John Talon and his son Jake, they are faced with a choice: Do they submit to the dead, raising the white flag of surrender? Or do they find the will to fight, to try and hang on to the last shreds or humanity?

CHECK OUT OTHER GREAT ZOMBIE NOVELS

Z BURBIA
by Jake Bible

Whispering Pines is a classic, quiet, private American subdivision on the edge of Asheville, NC, set in the pristine Blue Ridge Mountains. Which is good since the zombie apocalypse has come to Western North Carolina and really put suburban living to the test!

Surrounded by a sea of the undead, the residents of Whispering Pines have adapted their bucolic life of block parties to scavenging parties, common area groundskeeping to immediate area warfare, neighborhood beautification to neighborhood fortification.

But, even in the best of times, suburban living has its ups and downs what with nosy neighbors, a strict Home Owners' Association, and a property management company that believes the words "strict interpretation" are holy words when applied to the HOA covenants. Now with the zombie apocalypse upon them even those innocuous, daily irritations quickly become dramatic struggles for personal identity, family security, and straight up survival.

ZOMBIE RULES
by David Achord

Zach Gunderson's life sucked and then the zombie apocalypse began.

Rick, an aging Vietnam veteran, alcoholic, and prepper, convinces Zach that the apocalypse is on the horizon. The two of them take refuge at a remote farm. As the zombie plague rages, they face a terrifying fight for survival.

They soon learn however that the walking dead are not the only monsters.

www.ingramcontent.com/pod-product-compliance
Lightning Source LLC
Chambersburg PA
CBHW022033240626
47154CB00007B/2382